From Shadows to Daybreak

Book 2 of Romance in the Rockies Series

Cheryl Fosnot Bingisser

ISBN 979-8-89243-546-8 (paperback)
ISBN 979-8-89243-547-5 (digital)

Copyright © 2024 by Cheryl Fosnot Bingisser

All rights reserved. No part of this publication may be reproduced, distributed, or transmitted in any form or by any means, including photocopying, recording, or other electronic or mechanical methods without the prior written permission of the publisher. For permission requests, solicit the publisher via the address below.

Christian Faith Publishing
832 Park Avenue
Meadville, PA 16335
www.christianfaithpublishing.com

This novel is a work of fiction. Names, characters, places, and incidents are either products of the author's imagination or used fictitiously. All characters are fictional, and any similarity to people living or dead is purely incidental.

Printed in the United States of America

To the doctors, nurses, and all those who answer the call to work long hours and demonstrate compassion and patience in caring for those who are ill, facing procedures, or terminal. I have been on the receiving end of this kind of care more times than I can count, and it truly is a calling. For all of us who have benefited from your kindness, tenderness, treatment, and knowledge, we thank you for answering that call.

He was aware that darkness could take root in pristine gardens, and even good men fall to shadow.

—Ella Rosa Carlos
A Long-Lost Fantasy

Chapter 1

*Small town in the Rocky Mountain foothills
January 1951*

At seven years of age, Lincoln Chase had been on the street for almost two years with only his panda bear, Floyd, and a blanket he had carried with him since the age of two. His father, who had almost beaten him to death when he turned three, had left home and never returned. That left his mother to raise him on her own. She'd been battered since they'd married and been glad to see him go, except she possessed no way to support herself or her son.

She'd inquired at every business in town for employment, but no one had been hiring. Since she had no extraordinary skills, there'd been nothing that separated her from others seeking a livelihood. Without her husband's income, they lost their home. An apartment, in a cement building, with cement floors, and one small bedroom, shared with a family of five, was their new dwelling. The heat didn't operate, and this winter had been bitterly cold and hot water at a premium. Located with others like it, in the slums, she'd become desperate. She seriously considered the world's oldest profession, but just couldn't. She'd rather starve than sell what she prized most.

Most children were ill-dressed for the weather, and a good number of adults weren't much better. Pneumonia became commonplace. Disease ran rampant, and when tuberculosis swept through the slums, adults who were ill were taken away, and most children never saw them again. No explanation was ever given whether they would return. Children were merely left alone. Some had relatives they were sent to live with, but most had no one or no place to call home. They were on their own. Lost, lonely, scared, and freezing, life became more depressing than ever, and survival had been the only thing on their minds.

Stealing became their only channel to food, but the townspeople were beginning to become wise in their devious ways. Some pitied them and didn't mind the stealing—*if* it were merely for food. Absorbing the loss seemed like their civic duty. Others were furious and considered involving the police. No help came from the community to feed and clothe these kids, so who would? The local churches were slow in making decisions about anything, so the problems continued and those people who knew they existed, turned a blind eye.

Elias Butterworth was the new mayor. He had talked about a community meeting to see what could be done with the number of kids who were homeless, and the businesses that were losing money. That's what got him elected. The older and cleverer these kids grew, the braver they became. It wasn't just food they stole anymore. They pinched things that could be sold for profit, then graduated to pilfering wallets, purses, and the like. It was becoming more than just a little annoying, and the townspeople couldn't feign indifference any longer.

But Butterworth was already a disappointment and did little more than talk a good game, strutting his self-importance down the boardwalk like he owned the whole town. He said he was fifty-three, but he appeared sixty-five. Craters covered his face, which for others would have been ordinary wrinkles, and pale blue eyes with bags that were dark and enormous. Sporting a handlebar mustache then performing the comb-over with his sparse hairline, he felt certain he was quite the catch for any discerning female. His three-piece suits were at least two sizes too small, begging the question of why his buttons just didn't revolt and flee. His belly was so robust that people presumed he hadn't seen his shoes in years.

The businesses were already tired of the political rhetoric and wanted action. New businesses were leaving shortly after opening, which did nothing to improve the town already in need of so much relief. Maybe if they just gave him a little more time, he could get it together. After all, he'd been new to this mayorship, and he did deserve a chance. However, nothing changed, and most people just tried to hang on, hoping modifications would evolve with time.

Chapter 2

January 1951

  Ice and snow were still on the ground, and the temperature stayed below freezing. Kathleen Atwood proceeded down the boardwalk when she thought she heard crying coming from around the corner in the alley. She turned the corner and saw a girl, probably around sixteen years of age, sitting on the walkway with a torn dress, sobbing with her head in her hands. The closer she walked the more concerned she became.

  Her dress had been ripped to shreds, and she was shaking violently—uncertain if it came from the temperature or the trauma. Her hair had become disheveled with blood, dirt, and gravel, and her face smeared with dirt and blood. Blotches of blues, greens, and purples appeared where bruises emerged. Seeing she'd been beaten, Kathleen ran to her side.

  "Miss, are you okay?"

  "I'm fine," she said defiantly. She stumbled when she tried to stand and fidgeted to put her dress together, leaving her woefully underdressed for the weather.

  Kathleen helped her up. "What's your name?"

  "Emily."

  "Emily, were you attacked?"

  "No, I'm fine." Denying her predicament seemed like a good idea at the time.

FROM SHADOWS TO DAYBREAK

"You are not fine. You can barely stand. Your eye is swollen, your cheeks are bruised, and there's blood in your hair and on your face. You're about as fine as a trout with a hook in its mouth." Kathleen grabbed her by the arm and helped steady her until she stood on her own, then Emily pushed her arm away.

Still shaking, she screamed, "Leave me alone!"

Kathleen could see the bruises on her arms and legs, but mostly worried about her head wounds and what may have happened internally.

Standing her ground, Kathleen commanded with her usual military-like flair. "I'm not leaving you, young lady, so get that out of your head right now!" She pulled her into a tight hug, and even though Emily fought her for a few seconds, she finally stood motionless and sobbed. Kathleen held her until it subsided. She tried to share the coat she wore, and hoped it might quell some of the shaking.

"Now let's sit down and talk." Removing an embroidered handkerchief from her sleeve, she handed it to Emily. She nodded to the nearby bench while they sat together. "This is what we're going to do. I'm taking you to Doc Anderson to get you checked out. You need to get those cuts and bruises examined and find out if that poor excuse for a human being hurt you on the inside."

Indignantly, she cried, "I don't want a doctor."

"You may not want one, but you need one. Next step. Where are your things, and where do you live?"

"Nowhere, and he took what I had with him."

"Where are your parents?"

"Don't have any. Truth is, they don't want me."

Kathleen winced. "Where are you from?"

"Don't matter. I'm not going back."

"Okay, the way I see it, you're homeless, penniless, and totally without any other resources to care for yourself. Is that about it?"

She nodded, studying her well-worn shoes.

"I have a plan. First, the doctor—and yes, you are going to the doctor. You don't have to tell me anything about the attack or what Doc says if you don't want to, but I would encourage you to do so,

Cheryl Fosnot Bingisser

for your own sake. Are you able to walk? Doc is just down a block or so."

"I think so."

Kathleen helped her up, and Emily, being wobbly at first, steadied herself.

"Okay, let's go." Kathleen offered her arm, and Emily gladly took it. They walked arm-in-arm all the way to Doc's office. Kathleen opened the door.

"Hi, Kathleen. How are you today?" asked Doc warmly.

"I'm doing well, thank you, but my friend, Emily, has a problem she needs to talk to you about, and you will need to examine her."

Doc Anderson had seen many cases like her, so no explanation was needed. "Okay, Emily. The patient room is right in there." He opened the door to the room. "There's a gown you can put on, but you will need to take off all your clothing so I can get a good look at you to make sure you're all right. I'll be back in a moment and give you time to get ready." Then closing the door, he walked over to Kathleen.

"It looks like whoever did this didn't hold back much," he said, shaking his head. "I hate to see this happen to a child. She's so young."

"I know. He beat her terribly and threatened her with a knife if she screamed. She's quite shaken up and scared."

"Yes, she is, and that's normal."

"Doc, while you're taking care of her, I'm going to walk downtown and make some arrangements. Please, under no circumstances, let her out of your office, okay?"

"Got it, Kathleen. I'll hold her here until you get back."

"Thanks, Doc." She walked down the street and turned into the ladies' clothing store. She chose a warm coat, scarf, stocking cap, a few dresses, saddle shoes, socks, boots, handbag, undergarments, pajamas, nightgowns, jeans, shirts, and blouses. She hoped she hadn't overstepped, but the girl had nothing. Then she walked to the General Store to purchase a toothbrush, toothpaste, hair clips and bands, brush and comb, some hand soap, a hand mirror, and even some cologne she believed a teenager might like, in a light floral.

FROM SHADOWS TO DAYBREAK

Kathleen had come into a fortune when her father left her millions from his ownership of a popular car company. She liked having money, but it never changed what she believed about people or considered herself better than others. She simply possessed money and used it for herself and others whenever the need arose. She took great joy in that, and her philanthropy became well known. She owned her father's one-hundred-acre estate, beautifully managed, with gardens that were exquisite and a well-paid staff who tended everything. Once she married Franklin, she moved in with him into his three-room, rustic cabin, but the estate remained meticulously maintained, and she still retained ownership.

Her next stop, The Café where she spoke to Rebecca. A few minutes later, she walked to the furniture store, and when stepping out the door, she directed them to deliver it today. Headed back to Doc's office, she questioned whether she'd done the right thing. There were so many ways this could go sideways. She sat waiting for Doc, who ambled out with glassy eyes and his usual smile faded.

"He beat her up badly, but there's no lasting damage that could hurt her down the road. Emotionally, she's pretty fragile and is hiding it under a tough exterior, which will no doubt crumble at some point. When it does, someone needs to be there for her."

"Okay, Doc, I'll see what I can do."

"Kathleen, I would advise you against bringing this girl into your home right now, being newlyweds and all."

"I know. It wouldn't be fair to Frank or me. No, I've got a better idea."

"Good. Glad to hear it. By the way, congratulations on your marriage. You two are good for each other, and I'm glad God brought you together."

"Not as glad as we are," she remarked, almost glowing with happiness. "Thank you, Doc." She handed him some money. "Will that cover it?"

"Thanks, more than enough. Please let me know how she's doing."

"I will."

"She's changing right now."

"Oh, then I better get back there to give her these. Thanks again. Oh, I think we could use a little soap and water to clean up her face and maybe get some of the blood off."

Doc gave her some water in a pan with soap and a washcloth. "Take your time. She needs all the help you can give her."

She knocked on the door. "Emily."

"Yes."

"It's Kathleen. I've got some soap and water so we can clean you up a little before you leave here. Can I help you with anything?"

"Can you please help me clean up? I can't see everything with the blood and with my eye swelling shut. You can see better than I can."

"Certainly. I'm coming in. Sit down over here, and I'll gently clean up your face and get some of that blood out of your hair. Let's try to get a brush through it. Afterward, you should probably clean those private areas that were violated. Then I have something here you can change into."

She peered into the box in which lay the clothing. "I can't accept this, Kathleen."

"Okay, if you'd rather walk out in the dress you walked in with, that's up to you."

"Well, no."

"Okay, choose one you like and get dressed. Put the coat and boots on too, then I'll take you to The Café for lunch. Does that sound okay to you?"

"I guess so."

"Good. Look, Emily, I only want to help you get on your feet. Ask anyone in town. That's just who I am. I'm a Christian, and the Bible says we are to take care of those who need a helping hand. And you, my friend, like it or not, are in need. Now if you don't like the clothes, I can take them back, and you can pick out what you like. What do you say?"

"They're beautiful. I haven't seen clothes like this since I left home. Why would you do this?"

"I already told you. That's what I do." She walked out of the room so Emily could get dressed. A few minutes later, Kathleen asked, "Are you ready to come out?"

"Yes," she answered, as she opened the door. She wore a light-blue dress that was just a wee bit large. The bodice was double-breasted, with four large black buttons, a wide black belt at the waist, and a full skirt. She had donned her black boots, slung her black leather bag over her shoulder, and pasted a huge smile on her face. Her chestnut-brown wavy hair came down to her shoulders when it wasn't pummeled with dirt and blood. Her deep-set large, espresso eyes shined and danced. Kathleen noticed her cheeks were a little hollow but acknowledged both the dress and her cheeks would look better with a few meals. Obviously, she hadn't been eating proper food. Emily looked pleased, and Kathleen breathed a little easier.

Emily gathered up the boxes and packages, left Doc's office, and walked down to The Café. Kathleen was concerned about this step and prayed fervently that it would go well. She didn't have a plan B.

Chapter 3

January 1951
Atwood Residence

Sitting in his rocker, Franklin questioned what might be keeping Kathleen. She should have been home hours ago, but he'd learned worrying about her quickly became wasted energy since something frequently held her up. It seemed she often found someone who needed her and couldn't help but respond. His marriage to Kathleen filled him with joy. He loved her with such intensity, he couldn't wait for her to walk through that door. They were still newlyweds and had only been married since Christmas Eve.

Hettie, Kathleen's housekeeper and confidante, had moved in with them, and she fit perfectly. He'd come to love her much like Kathleen did. And why not? She was an amazing woman. She had been with Kathleen since a toddler and practically raised her. Her skin tone was a beautiful, light-golden brown, and had warm, brown eyes and curly gray hair. You would never know by the way she moved around that she was in her mid-sixties—at least, she thought so. Since records weren't kept back then, no one knew for certain. Her cooking had become legendary, and her laughter echoed long after it was extinguished. Everyone loved her laugh and her ability to "tell it like it is" without hurting anyone. Kathleen believed her to be *direct*. Never quiet about her faith in God, and it showed in the way she served others—always putting herself last. She rarely did anything for herself; there were always others on her mind who needed help.

After Kathleen and Franklin were married, Franklin built a large bedroom for her off the bathroom. The two bedrooms were separated by that room, and she moved in when it had been completed. Her cheer—infectious. There were times she did go back to Kathleen's estate, just to make sure things were running smoothly, and to give Franklin and Kathleen a little more breathing room. She believed in giving space to the newlyweds.

Franklin's now four-room cabin had undergone some updating and facelift. The countertop had been extended with a new intricate butcher-block pattern. The drawers were installed. The new, white sink installed, and two extra cupboards were added. All the new appliances had arrived and were in working order. Completed and beautiful, Franklin had been satisfied with the results. Even more crucial, Kathleen had been delighted. That's what mattered most. Taking down the Christmas decorations proved difficult. Franklin loved having them, especially since they were set up for the wedding.

Hettie, close to having dinner ready, she and Franklin were stalling, waiting for Kathleen. Hettie sat in the wingback chair and rested. She eyeballed Franklin.

"Frank, now no need to worry none."

"I'm not. It's just that I miss her when she's gone." He lit his pipe and took a couple of puffs. It always made him relax a little, and he still loved the sweet smell that wafted around the room.

Hettie chuckled. "You two lovebirds are somethin' else. I'm glad joy and happiness jes' circles this here cabin like a wreath. Ya both drippin' with it and that's jes' the way it should be."

"Thanks, Hettie. Part of our happiness is *your* cooking." They both laughed.

Kathleen sashayed through the door. She took off her coat, hung it on the new coat tree, took off her boots, walked over to Franklin, and sat on his lap. Placing her arms around him, she looked at him and kissed him enthusiastically for a long time.

Franklin inhaled a deep breath and blew it out. "Well, welcome home, Mrs. Atwood! That's about the best *hello* I've ever received." He declared, chuckling. "Maybe you should try that again."

Hettie and Kathleen laughed.

"I missed you, Frank."

"I missed you too, my dearest." He kissed her again.

"Okay, that's enough smoochin'. Dinner's ready. Git yourselfs to the table so I can feed you two befo'e you both fade away to nothin'." They both laughed.

Franklin snuffed out his pipe. "Not likely," Franklin admitted. "I've got a long way to go before any fading takes place."

Hettie laughed. She had made one of Franklin's new favorites— lasagna. There was a green salad and fresh garlic bread she had made to go with it, as well as lemon meringue pie for dessert.

"Oh, Hettie, you know this is one of my favorites."

"Gotta keep the man of the house happy or he might kick me out." She answered merrily.

"That's never going to happen because then Kathy would try cooking, and we all know what the results of that effort would be." They laughed.

"Okay, enough you two. I'm still in the room, you know."

"I know. It wouldn't be funny if you weren't." Laughter rang throughout the house.

Hettie always made herself scarce after dinner so they could do whatever the newlyweds desired.

"Frank?"

"Yes."

"I have so much to tell you, but I'm kind of tired now. Could we talk later?"

"Sure, darling. What do you want to do now?"

"Well, I'm tired, but not sleepy," she said flirtatiously.

"Oh, I see," Franklin said, nodding. "Well, I don't know. I'm not tired and I have some reading to do." Not able to keep the teasing up, he chuckled. "Are you saying what I think you're saying, my dearest?" He grinned while touching her nose with his fingertip.

She kissed him with fervency. "What do you think, Frankie?" She whispered in his ear.

"I think…I think…" He swooped her up and strode into the bedroom, closed the door, and laid her on the bed. "That's what I think, Mrs. Atwood."

Kathleen giggled. She sat up and unbuttoned Frank's shirt. He pulled it out and threw it at the foot of the bed. Sitting on his lap, she kissed him and ran her fingers through his hair. "I love you, Frankie."

"I love you too…so much." Frank turned out the light. "Mrs. Atwood, I love your ideas."

"Thank you, Mr. Atwood. I do aim to please."

He kissed her with longing again. "Indeed, you do my dearest. Indeed, you do!"

Chapter 4

February 1951

    Raff (twenty-five) and Maddie (twenty-one) had known each other since they were kids and were now planning an April wedding. Raff had given his heart to the Lord just weeks after his father's death. The relationship with his father had been complicated, plagued with misunderstandings and miscommunication that Raff believed meant his father hadn't loved him. Later, Raff found a letter from his father apologizing for his inability to show love, his verbal abuse, and the way he ignored him. His father, George, hoped that Raff would come to forgive him in time. He earnestly wanted the three of them—his wife, son, and him—to spend eternity together in heaven.

    His father had left him some money about which no one knew. Raff had planned to fix up the house and transform a shed into a woodworking place, to make furniture and other wood-related items. Then with what was left, he hoped to invest back into his ten-acre apple orchard and help with the wedding and honeymoon.

    Even though Raff's house needed some remodeling, paint, and repairs, Maddie and Raff decided to move into Raff's home and sell hers instead. She had grown up there, but she understood why Raff's house would be the better choice for them since he had the outbuildings that accommodated his woodworking, a barn for the orchard storage and supplies, and a small shed for lawn gear. They lived right

FROM SHADOWS TO DAYBREAK

next to each other, except the country had spread things out a bit more than a city neighborhood.

It had been a few days since he had seen Maddie, and he missed her. He decided to pay her a visit and maybe have dinner at The Café in town. He drove over and trotted up the steps onto the porch. Still below freezing outside, he knocked on the door, hoping Maddie had a roaring fire going.

Maddie opened the door. Immediately, Raff sensed something was wrong.

"Maddie, what is it?"

"Oh, nothing. I'm just tired."

"Look, you have to tell me the truth, my sweet." He enfolded her in his arms and hugged her tightly. "Now please tell me."

"Oh, it's just that we had a break-in at the store, and they took all the cash we had on hand along with all the antique books we had recently acquired."

Sitting down on the couch, Raff's face registered concern. "Maddie, I'm so sorry. Do you know who it was?" he asked sympathetically.

"The police said there's been a few robberies lately. They have some leads, but they think it's the same guys."

"Okay, that's it. I'm taking you out, but, first…"

He again took her in his arms and kissed her passionately. "Does that help at all?"

She smiled at him. "You know, cowboy, I love it when you kiss me like that. Might I have another?"

He laughed. "Well, I'm not sure. I don't think I'm in the mood for more kissing. One's enough. That's a rule, you know."

"I'm throwing out the rule." She leaned into him and kissed him with all the love she had in her heart and the ache from missing him.

"Wow! You really did miss me, huh?"

She laughed as she grabbed her coat. "C'mon, Mayfield, you're taking me out for dinner, and then maybe…maybe, there might be another one of those I've saved for you."

"I hope you've saved a whole lot of them. That was sweet," he remarked, as he opened the door. He kissed her on the cheek, and they drove into town.

He grabbed Maddie's hand and laced his fingers through hers. "I've missed you. I'm sorry I haven't been around. I'm just trying to get the house fixed up, and it's taking longer than I thought it would. Plus, I'm working for Franklin a few days a week, trying to get his farm implements, his trucks, and tractors in shape for spring."

"I understand, Raff. I do. I just miss our talks and your hugs—kisses too."

"Me too, but time is flying by, and I want to be able to move you in before we go on our honeymoon so that when we come back, it'll be ours—together. Frankly, I can't tell you how much I wish that day were here already."

"Yeah, me too, but you have a job to do and I have a wedding to plan, plus my job too. I was thinking. What do you think of me buying the bookstore with the sale of the house, and then doing whatever we decide to do with the rest of it? It would be a good investment, I think."

"Maddie, I think that's a great idea if that's what you want to do. Why don't we talk to Franklin and Kathleen about it and see what they think?"

"That's a great idea. I like asking them for advice and I don't think they mind. And we've got Mr. Strattford we can ask too."

"True. He's a good resource as well. It's nice to have older and wiser friends we can call on."

"Yes. Since neither of us has parents, it seems like it's a good fit for us," she added thoughtfully. She placed her hands in her lap. "Raff, I'm curious. Where are we going on our honeymoon?"

"Are you sure you want me to tell you, or do you want me to keep it a surprise?"

"I don't know. I guess I'll leave it up to you to decide, but please don't spend a fortune on it. I love you no matter where we go."

"I'll think about it. I promise I'm not spending a fortune, but I do want to whisk you away and just hold you for an entire week. We do need our rest, after all. We might spend a lot of time in our room sleeping." He winked.

"Sounds nice. I love you, Mayfield," she said, dreamily.

Fifteen minutes later, they arrived at The Café. "Okay, we're here."

"I guess I was dreaming about our honeymoon and you just interrupted it." She sighed.

"Alright, dreamer. Let's get something to eat and sit where there's a lot of light to wake you up and keep you alert. No falling asleep with your face plopped in your chili. They frown on that in some circles." He chuckled.

She wistfully placed the thoughts of the honeymoon on hold and concentrated on Raff and their dinner together.

Chapter 5

Yesterday Afternoon
The Café

Opening the door to The Café, Kathleen let Emily walk through first. She prayed that this would work. If not, she wasn't sure what the next step might be. Rebecca, the owner and waitress, scurried about waiting tables while the lunch crowd had begun to disperse. Rebecca motioned to Kathleen to take the table by the window, and she and Emily seated themselves.

"Hi, Kathleen, it's good to see you again. Seems like I haven't seen you for a while. I haven't had a chance to talk to you since before your wedding, and I want to hear all about it," suggested Rebecca expectantly.

Emily looked at Kathleen, surprise written all over her face.

"I can't wait to tell you. But first, I want to introduce Emily to you. She's a new friend of mine. Emily this is Becca. She owns the building here, The Café, and the apartment right above here."

"Emily, it's so good to meet you. Any friend of Kathleen's is a friend of mine. We've known each other for a long time and are best friends."

"Yes, we have, and I treasure our friendship. I wish we had more time to spend together though. I've been so busy. First, you know Frank's and my romance was a whirlwind, and we married within a month of meeting. Neither of us could handle another moment

FROM SHADOWS TO DAYBREAK

apart. But between dating and trying to get a small wedding together, I've hardly had time to breathe. Since then, we've had some work done on the cabin. Frank had a large room built so Hettie could come and live with us, and I had him do some work in the kitchen to update things and make it easier for her, so I've been very busy."

"Sounds like it. Why don't you look at the menu while I see some customers, and we can talk later, okay?"

"Sure. Can't wait. Emily, what do you see that you might like?"

"You just got married?"

"I did. Christmas Eve at our cabin."

"You haven't been married very long."

"No, we haven't, but I've never been happier."

"But you only knew each other a month?"

"That's right, but when God brings two people together, you just know it's the right thing, at the right time, and with the right person."

"You believe in God?"

"I do. Don't you?"

"Nope. God never did anything for me."

"You don't know that. Besides, how do you know that it wasn't God who sent me to you? He does direct people, mostly without them even knowing it at the time. There have been so many times when I've been able to look back and see the hand of God orchestrating my life in powerful and extraordinary ways."

Shaking her head, she declared, "I don't believe that. We're just out here on our own and need to take care of ourselves."

"Oh, like you've been doing, walking around on the street with nowhere to go? How's that been working for you?"

"What happened wasn't my fault, and I'm leaving." She scraped the chair across the floor and stood up.

Kathleen grabbed her arm. "You sit yourself down right this minute, young lady. You aren't going anywhere. Besides, where would you go?"

"I don't know," she pronounced defiantly, as she sat back down.

"Exactly. You have no place to go, and you're in no condition to function on your own. Listen to me. Becca and I have talked, and she wants you to move in with her. You can stay as long as you want and need to. She is excited about the company. Sometimes living on your own can get very lonely."

"True."

"What do you think?"

"Well, she seems nice enough."

"She is, and you're going to love her just like I do."

Rebecca came back to the table. "Well, what's for lunch, ladies? Did you decide?"

Kathleen studied Emily's eyes. She could see the defiance drain from her face.

Emily raised her eyes to Rebecca. "Is it true that you want me to come and live with you?"

Rebecca glanced at Kathleen before answering. "Yes, it is. I've been wanting a roommate for a long time. This will be fun."

Without missing a beat, Emily replied, "I'll have the BLT with fries, a chocolate milkshake, and onion rings."

"Wow! You really are hungry," said Kathleen, quite satisfied with the way Rebecca handled her, and relieved that Emily was eating.

"Okay, and how about you, Kathleen?"

"Well, the BLT sounds pretty good with—"

"Cerispy bacon," both Kathleen and Rebecca said in unison and then laughed. "I guess I am pretty predictable. And instead of fries, I think I would like some of that homemade potato salad you make so well. Love that stuff. Someday you'll have to show me how to make it."

"Oh, it's easy. Just a little of this and a little of that and mayo, mustard, and dill pickles, and just like that, you're done. Easy."

Kathleen laughed. "Yes, easy for you, maybe. Nothing about cooking comes easily to me."

"Okay, girls, comin' right up." Rebecca turned on her heels and headed toward the kitchen.

"So how do you feel about staying with Becca?"

"Well, I guess it would be okay. She's nice and very pretty. I like her laugh, and it would be nice to have a roommate. I guess I can try it for a couple of days."

"Okay." Not wanting to show her tremendous joy at her response, Kathleen kept it low-key. "Yes, let's just see how you feel in a few days. Oh, I got you a new bed and bed linens, so you get a fresh start. How's that?"

"Thanks, Kathleen. I don't know what to say."

"Just say you'll take care of yourself and get some rest and some decent food in you. That's all I ask."

"I can do that."

"Okay, ladies, here's your lunch. Now if you want anything else, just let me know."

"It looks really good, Becca, thanks."

"You're very welcome, my dear. I'll be back. Oh, Kathleen, would you like some coffee?"

"Yes, I would. Thank you."

"Black, I know. Be right back."

"No, I think I'd like some cream and sugar this time."

Becca's brow raised as she studied her.

"A girl can change her mind, can't she?"

"Of course. I'll be right back."

Emily had already eaten half her sandwich and drunk a third of her milkshake.

The girl must be starving, Kathleen ruminated.

They finished eating, and Rebecca hadn't had time to sit and talk with her about the wedding or anything else. Rebecca told her that she had tomorrow off and Kathleen should come to the apartment and spend a few hours with her and Emily.

Kathleen agreed and promised to come around ten. But, first, she had to take Emily upstairs and let Rebecca show her around the apartment. Rebecca assigned someone else to take charge, and they all trooped upstairs.

Rebecca guided Emily around the apartment and showed her to her room, where there was a bed, side table, lamp, dresser, small desk, and chair, waiting for her, which all matched and were new.

"Becca, this is beautiful. Thank you."

The bed was full-size with a headboard and footboard in a dark walnut. A beautiful handmade quilt in rose colors, and pale greens and blues, graced the top of the bed, feminine, but not too frilly. There were regular pillows, and pillow shams that were made from the same quilt fabric. The lamp, a ginger jar in a medium blue with a rose-colored shade but still gave off plenty of light where it stood. The rectangular dark walnut end table had been placed next to the bed.

"Don't thank me. This is all Kathleen. I hadn't even had time to furnish this room yet, so Kathleen did it for us."

Emily didn't know what to say. "Thank you, Kathleen. I can't get over what you're doing for me. You've been so nice."

"Emily, it's been my pleasure, but you might want to get your clothes out of those boxes and hang them up. There are hangers in there already."

"Let me guess. You did that too."

"Yes. I want you to be comfortable, feel better, and take care of yourself. Well, Becca, I should probably go. Frank will be getting worried about me, but I'll see you both tomorrow morning." She walked over to Emily and kissed her on the cheek. "Goodbye, Emily. Get a good night's sleep, okay?"

Emily stood and hugged her. "Kathleen, thank you for everything. I've never had anyone care about me the way you have today."

"I'm glad you're happy with this. You don't have to thank me. It was fun. I'll see you two tomorrow. Bye."

Both Emily and Rebecca said goodbye, and Kathleen walked downstairs, where her driver waited for her.

Exhausted, Kathleen leaned against the window in the back seat and fell asleep. It had been an extremely long and tiring day.

Chapter 6

The Next Day

Lincoln had been on the street long enough now, he had learned how to pick pockets—rather, he'd watched it done ample times. It seemed simple enough. Just walk up to someone, bump into them, and slip out their wallet. Easy. Of course, afterward, you try to get lost in the crowd and run and hide under the boardwalk until everyone stops looking for you unless the mark never discovers it's gone. If you're good, that's the way it's supposed to go.

This would be his first time and he was nervous. *No need to be nervous,* he reasoned. *I got this,* trying to bolster his bravado.

He tenuously walked into the street and found his target. An older man who he figured would be slower on his feet if something went wrong, and the man ran after him. He came closer to "the mark" and looked around to see exactly where he kept his wallet.

There it is. In his jacket pocket.

He bumped into him and deftly slipped out the wallet—until it got caught in the zipper. Lincoln pulled hard and it came loose, but the man was on to him now. As Lincoln ran so did the man. The old man tripped over someone's foot and fell to the street, which gave Lincoln the chance to get away.

He couldn't believe it. He pulled it off. It may not have been perfect, but he ended up with the cash. After congratulating himself, He pranced down the street feeling quite proud. Unseen, three older and wiser street kids caught up with him. They seized the wallet and beat him senseless. They kicked him in the ribs and kidneys as their final action.

"Listen, Link. No one takes over our territory. This wallet is ours. It's our money. You need to move on." His voice took on a syrupy sweetness. "Or you could work for us. We'd take only 70 percent of everything you steal, and you'd get thirty. We'd protect you from getting caught. Take the deal or work on your own. What do ya say?"

Lincoln couldn't speak, but he nodded. His eyes closed. They left him in the alley and walked away. Hours later, he tried to get up, but he hurt everywhere and dizziness overwhelmed him. He tried to move. Nothing worked. He struggled to sit up, but he couldn't. He attempted to recollect why he felt so awful and tried to orient himself to his new circumstances.

What am I doing here? he questioned. That was his only thought. Everything turned black while he floated into oblivion.

Right before dark, a man approached the alley, viewed Lincoln in the street, and grasped what had happened. He'd seen it before— the code of the street. He tried to talk to him, but Lincoln didn't stir. Gathering him up, he transferred him to his car and drove him to the hospital. When he arrived, he picked up the kid and carried him into the emergency room.

Kathleen's father, Peter Brennan, had left money in his will to add a wing to the hospital and dedicate it exclusively for emergencies. It was a relatively new idea, that would eventually take hold across the country. In the meantime, they learned the ambulances owned and operated by the hospital were basic, and the crew was untrained in first aid. Therefore, the hospital board made the unanimous decision to add a registered nurse to the team in an effort to raise the survival rate transferring the patient to the hospital. When the Emergency Department was officially opened, the medical personnel held their collective breaths, hoping this would indeed fulfill the requirements for survival. The naysayers didn't see the need for it—no surprise there. Change came hard to a small town. Since they found it unusual for a town this small to possess the most up-to-date medical equipment, it would remain to be seen if it would be successful.

"Oh my goodness." One of the nurses ran over to him. "What happened to him?"

"Looks like he got beaten up pretty badly. When I found him, he was unresponsive, so I brought him here. He's breathing but not awake."

"I'll call Doc Anderson."

The orderly ran off, wheeled back a gurney, and gently placed the kid on it.

Doc Anderson's name came over the loudspeaker and he arrived in short order. The nurse turned to the man and thanked him for transporting him.

"Sure thing. Just send the bill to my office, okay?"

"Okay, Mr. Strattford, will do."

"I think he's a street kid, so he has no one. Can I call and check on him?"

"Sure, that will be fine."

"If anything happens, please call me. You have my number at home and the office."

"We do, Mr. Strattford. We will keep you informed."

He thanked them, while he walked out the door.

Chapter 7

February 1951
Atwood Residence

Kathleen hadn't been feeling well for a while now. She'd fainted twice and been vomiting. After watching her and getting some history from Hettie, Franklin pleaded with her to see Doc. Of course, she protested, but Franklin insisted. On the day of the appointment, Franklin couldn't go with her. He had promised Raff he would take a look at his farm and then take him to The Café for lunch. Knowing that Raff had a lot on his plate and probably needed to talk, Kathleen went alone.

There were advantages to having staff at the estate. All she had to do was call, they would pick her up, and drive her anywhere she wanted to go. She knew they would be discreet, so no worries about them telling anyone she may be ill. Having a driver freed Franklin up to be able to use his truck if needed.

Kathleen didn't tell him, but she had seen this kind of sickness before and became concerned that it may be cancer. It's a horrendous disease, and she didn't know how she would ever be able to tell Franklin if that was the diagnosis. She asked God to eliminate her fears while she'd been driven into town. He dropped her off at Doc's office.

* * * * *

FROM SHADOWS TO DAYBREAK

Doc Anderson's Office

"Hi, Kathleen," Doc greeted her while she opened the door and walked inside. "Please come on in. Let's talk in the patient room. Sit over here." He motioned to the exam table. "Now tell me what's going on."

"Well, I haven't been feeling well for a while now. I've been vomiting and fainted twice. I don't want to eat. I'm delighted to be married to Frank, but I feel so awful. I've seen this before, and I'm afraid I might have cancer."

"Now, Kathleen, we don't know anything yet, so please don't jump to conclusions. Is there anything else you can tell me?"

"Frank's worried, and I hate that. I don't want to hurt him. He's already lost Pearl, and I don't want to put him through that again," she articulated, with flooded eyes.

"Kathleen, like I said, before you work yourself into a dither, let me examine you and see what I find out, okay?"

"Okay, Doc. I'm sorry."

"No need to apologize. I understand those fears, but let's see what we find. Okay?"

She nodded. "Okay."

"Now undress completely and put this gown on, and I'll be back in a few minutes."

He did a thorough examination, then told her to put her clothes back on, and he'd be back to talk to her in a few minutes.

She sighed. "It's bad, isn't it?"

"Just get dressed, and I'll be back in a few minutes."

"Okay, Doc."

After a few minutes, Doc returned.

"Okay, just be straight with me. Do I have cancer or something worse?"

"Kathleen, calm down. Breathe."

She drew in a big breath and blew it out. "I'm sorry, Doc."

"It's okay. Sometimes health, or the lack thereof, can be a little frightening."

"So is it good news or bad news?"

Cheryl Fosnot Bingisser

"That depends."

"On what?"

"On what *you* think."

"Doc, whatever do you mean?"

"Kathleen, you're not ill. You're pregnant."

"That's ridiculous. How could that happen?"

"Well, when a man and a woman love each other—"

"Doc, I'm serious."

"I'm sorry." He chuckled.

"I'm too old. My monthlies are few and far between. It's impossible."

"It doesn't happen often, but sometimes, during menopause, it can happen."

"A baby?"

Using his hands as measuring tools, he clinically stated, "Yeah, it's about this long—"

"Doc, you're teasing me."

"I am, and thoroughly enjoying myself." He laughed. "Kathleen, how do you feel about it?"

"Shocked."

"I'm sure. I know this is unexpected, so to speak, but there is so much joy in bringing a human being into this world and bringing him up in the nurture and admonition of the Lord. This is a good thing, Kathleen."

She smiled. "I put that all behind me years ago and never thought it possible. This is so—"

"Wonderful?" Doc offered. "Amazing?"

"Scary."

"You and Franklin will be great parents."

"Frank." Suddenly the fear of telling Franklin welled up within her. "What do I tell him?"

"Oh, I don't know. Something like this: 'Franklin we're having a baby.'" He laughed again.

"Doc, I swear you're just as bad as Frank is with all the jokes."

"Why, thank you. I like Franklin very much." He smiled. "I know him well, and he will be thrilled with this. He's waited a long time for a baby, and he and Pearl could never have one. Believe me. You have nothing to worry about."

"A baby. That's the last thing I expected you to say."

"It's a lot better than cancer, isn't it?"

"Oh, for pity's sake!"

He laughed. "Take a few minutes if you need to and come out when you're ready. When the shock wears off, the joy will more than replace it. Trust me."

"Thank you, Doc."

"You're very welcome. I love giving news like this. There's too much bad news in this world. This is good news." He instructed, as he opened the door and walked out, closing the door behind him.

Kathleen dressed, then sat and stared at the walls for a while. "Pregnant. I'm pregnant. I'm going to have a baby. I'm having a baby. I'm having a baby." She smiled.

She strolled out and regarded Doc with disbelief. "I'm having a baby."

"Yeah, I know."

"I don't believe it, Doc. I'm having a baby."

"Yes, you are, and I'm so happy for you two." He laughed, shaking his head.

"Such good news."

"Thanks, Doc." She breezed through the door, suspecting that her feet never touched the ground. The driver got out, opened the door for her, and closed it after she scooted in. She rested her head against the window.

"Are you okay, Miss Kathleen?"

"Yes, I'm fine." She couldn't cease smiling. "Now how do I tell Frankie?"

As soon as I get home, I'll have Hettie cook one of his favorite meals. I'll dig out the candles and use every one of them. I'll bring out some wine, Frankie loves that, and maybe I'll even have a swallow or two. It might help settle my stomach. The new china and new cloth napkins will add to the look on the table. The crystal stemware will reflect the candlelight. It'll be beautiful. I do wish the Christmas lights were still up. The colors are so cheerful and would help with the romance. We loved all that color, but the candles will help a lot. I can't wait. Frankie will love all this. She had it all thought out.

But then fear gripped her heart like a vice, and she gasped for breath. The "what ifs" began whirlling around her head.

But what if he doesn't want kids now? What if he's angry with me? What if he even hates me? We're older now. I know it was a real shock for me. Raising a child now will be much harder. Oh, God, please help me say the right thing so that Frankie will be okay with this. I love him so much, and we'll have another person to love that we created together from the deepest love we could possibly possess. Her thoughts tormented her.

Chapter 8

February 1951
Mayfield Residence

The house began to take shape but still so much left to do. Raff had done enough in the living room that he thought maybe he could ask Maddie to help him do the painting. They could choose colors for the living room, bathroom, and kitchen. After all, it would be her house too. Maybe it would make her feel more at home to choose the colors *she* wanted.

It was Saturday, and Raff knew she wouldn't be working today. Maybe this would be the day. He slid into his car and drove to Maddie's. Knocking on the door, he hoped Maddie would be okay with this. Time was growing short, and he wanted to get the house finished before their honeymoon.

Maddie opened the door. "Raff, it's good to see you. Please, come in."

"Happy to." He took her in his arms and kissed her. "Maddie, I have a great idea. How would you like to go to town with me and choose the colors to paint the walls of our house? It's not my house anymore. It's ours, and I want you to be happy with it. Would you do that with me?"

Placing her arms around his neck, she kissed him. "I would love to. I will help you paint too. Anything I can do to help get our house ready on time, I'm willing to do."

Cheryl Fosnot Bingisser

"Well, let's get moving then. We're burning daylight," he replied, laughing.

"Right behind you, cowboy." She grabbed her coat and followed Raff out the door.

At the General Store, they looked at all the different colors, and Raff wondered how in the world someone could ever choose one. There were at least thirty colors of blue, green, yellow, white, red, and everything in between. Maddie proved to be more focused. She knew what she liked; it was just a matter of finding the right shades.

"Raff, how about blue for the living room, more of a pale blue. What do you think?"

"I don't care. I want whatever makes you happy. I want you to love our home that we will live and love in for a long time—especially *love*," he said, teasing.

"Well, I want you to like it too. It's our house—*ours*. Okay?"

"Maddie, I'll love whatever you choose, so don't worry. Just find something you like."

"Alright. I like this Robin's egg blue. What do you think?"

"That is the ugliest color I've ever seen! Why on earth did you choose that one?" He broke into an uproarious laugh. "I'm teasing, Maddie. I like it. I think it will be pretty in that room. It's light."

Scowling, she faced him with her hands on her hips. "Raff, that was not nice at all."

"I know. I'm sorry. I just couldn't help myself."

"I was thinking maybe a two-tone look in the bathroom, like white on the ceiling and halfway down the walls, then a dark blue the rest of the way to the floor. What are you putting on the floor in there?"

"Either a tile or linoleum. Which would you prefer?"

"Tile would be pretty, but I think linoleum would be more cost-effective and maybe easier to clean. I think we could find one that would work with those paint colors. What do you think?"

"I like it. That's a good idea. We can always tile it later if we want to. We have a tub in there, but I think I can plumb in water for shower faucets too. I like showers. How do you feel about it?"

FROM SHADOWS TO DAYBREAK

"I like showers too. Here's the white enamel for the bathroom, and they have it in a sapphire blue for the bottom part too. I can get new towels, a shower curtain, a mirror, a laundry basket, and a wastebasket to complete the look. It would be nice to have a cupboard in there for towels and stuff. Maybe add a medicine cabinet. In the kitchen, I think I'd like a pale turquoise color for the walls and white for the cupboards. Then we need curtains, new kitchen towels, and other things."

"Well, so far, it sounds good. We can paint our bedroom and then quit until after the wedding and do the rest later. If we get these rooms finished, this house will look completely different. It'll be like walking into a new house, which is what I wanted for you. What about our bedroom and the bath upstairs?"

"Maybe I should pick out the bed linens and spread first and that will give me more ideas."

"How about red for passion?"

"Raff, that's awful, but kind of funny—in a deranged sort of way. We will need draperies in there and in the living room. Honestly, passion in the bedroom sounds awfully good right now," she whispered.

"Why, Maddie Henderson, you surprise me."

"Really? Well, cowboy, you've got a whole lot more surprises ahead of you. So just you wait!"

"Wow! I can't, but I do love surprises."

"Wait until you see what I pull out of my trousseau."

"What's that?"

"It's clothing used for the honeymoon. The best part is my nightgown. Trust me, you're going to love that."

"Oh, I see. Now I really can't wait!"

He kissed her, then took a deep breath. "Okay, enough of that, or I won't be able to concentrate. Back to work, my sweet."

Smiling, she looked the colors over again. "I like restful colors for a bedroom. You know, like blues or greens or lavender."

"Lavender. Isn't that purple?"

"Well, it's a very soft purple. Like this." She handed him a paint chip. "Or we could paint it white and let the bedspread or comforter carry the color. Maybe hang a little wallpaper."

"I guess that would be okay if you like it."

"Shall we get what we want, and go home, and get started?"

"Which room do you want to paint first?"

"Well, you've got the living room finished, so why don't we paint in there?"

"Okay. Let's get it mixed and find out how much we need, then get all the supplies to get this painted. We may as well get the paint for the bathroom too, before I put in the new floor. Let's get those rooms finished first, then the bedroom. As soon as I get the kitchen finished, which will take a while yet, we can get that painted and be done. Moving you in will be the happiest day of my life."

"Oh, really? What about the wedding day, and then there's the wedding night? But if you think moving me in is better than that Mayfield, you are sadly mistaken." She threw him a flirty smile with an arched eyebrow.

Raff grinned. "I think I just changed my mind. I'll hold out for the wedding night. Course, seeing you in that wedding dress I'm going to enjoy too."

"You should. It's one of the most beautiful wedding dresses I have ever seen and is costing me a small fortune. But cowboy, it will be worth it to see your face when you see me in it." She ran her fingers across his jaw and then kissed his cheek.

"Wow, that good, huh? And you're flirting with me." He smirked, thoroughly enjoying himself.

"Oh, yeah. There's more where that came from, cowboy."

He threw his arms around her and kissed her. "Maddie, I love you so much. I can't wait to marry you. But I do have one question. Do you want to travel that first night after the wedding, or maybe reserve a swanky hotel in Denver and spend the first night there before we go to California?"

"Oh, Raff, I would love to go to a luxury hotel for our first night. I think that would be the most romantic thing ever. We could even order our dinner and champagne in our room."

"Maddie, that sounds wonderful. We wouldn't have to go anywhere. We could spend our whole honeymoon there if you wanted to. I can afford it, and by then, your house will be sold, so we'd have a backup. What do you think?"

"That sounds like a fairy tale, and neither one of us has ever enjoyed anything like that. I think we would feel like a prince and princess, and I would adore that."

"Then, that's what we'll do. I'll do a little research into it and find the best one, and we'll just love each other for a whole week. Maddie, I can't wait. This will be a once-in-a-lifetime splurge that we deserve after all we've been through. And sometimes people give money at the wedding too, so that will help us get a few things you want for the house. I know we need new furniture for the living room. We can do this, Maddie."

"Now I'm even more excited. I still have some things to plan for the wedding, but Kathleen has been a big help. Hey, why don't we ask them out to The Café so we can be together and talk about the wedding, and you guys talk about whatever it is you talk about? We're not in a hurry to go home, are we? Or do we want to start painting today?"

"I'll leave it up to you to decide."

"I don't know. My better self says we should probably get some work done. I think it will make us feel better in the long run, don't you?"

"You're probably right."

"Let's pick up the stuff, take it to the register, get it home, and gitter done."

"Yes, ma'am."

Chapter 9

February 1951
Atwood Residence

    Hettie watched as Kathleen hustled about, putting up candles and placing all the china, linens, stemware, wine, and everything else she desired on the table and in the room. She danced while she worked. She didn't ask Kathleen about it, but she figured whatever the occasion, it had to be good news, and a lot of romance would be taking place too. But she would wait until Kathleen wanted to tell her. She already had an inkling, and if that were the case, she would be beside herself with joy. Kathleen lit all the candles. There were three on the table, seven on the mantel, and five on either side of the sink.

    Kathleen got all "gussied up," as Hettie called it. She changed into a beautiful, floor-length, satin, gown. It had a sweetheart neckline and was fitted down past her hips. There was a slit on the side, extending from the floor to her knee, and she wore red high-heeled shoes. At the waistline, there was an inch-wide rhinestone belt, and wore long, diamond earrings. Stunning. It fit Kathleen like a glove. Red had always been her favorite color, and knew Franklin would love it too. She also knew she wouldn't be able to wear it much longer. Choosing to wear it tonight had been a good decision. Inspecting herself in the full-length mirror, she turned and looked at the backside too. Her cheeks were blushed, and her lips were red. Her natural, curly, auburn hair fell like a waterfall below her shoulders. She placed her hands over her stomach and pondered what she would look like in a few months.

She walked into the living room and sat in the wingback chair. Questioning how much longer it would be before Franklin would be home, nerves began to overtake her. She paced, then sat, paced, then sat.

With dinner prepared, all Hettie had to do was serve it. She'd already decided as soon as she had served theirs, she would take hers into her room to give the two of them all the room they needed. She had made one of Franklin's favorites. Roast beef, mashed potatoes, gravy, corn, and apple pie for dessert. She was fussing around and humming. Suddenly, she burst into song.

I've got joy like a river.
I've got joy like a river.
I've got joy like a river in my soul.
Oooh, I've got joy like a river.
I've got joy like a river.
I've got joy like a river in my soul.

She laughed the most jovial laugh, and Kathleen joined her. She loved Hettie more than anyone but Franklin. There was a lot of joy in the house tonight! No doubt about it.

Franklin limped through the door, hung up his coat, and took off his boots. He turned and saw Kathleen. Dumbstruck, he stared at her. His jaw gaped. The dress was the most spectacular thing he had ever seen. Definitely form over function, but nonetheless absolutely incredible! Then he let out the longest wolf whistle Kathleen and Hettie had ever heard. His eyes danced and were as wide as silver dollar pancakes.

Kathleen smiled that flirtatious smile of hers.

Franklin walked over to her and said softly, "How is it possible that you just get more beautiful every single day? You are *stunning!* That dress is amazing, and you look magnificent in it."

He took her in his arms and dipped her, then brought her up and kissed her with so much love he thought his heart would rupture. He kissed her again. "Kathy, you are incredible. You look fantastic. You're positively glowing. I still wonder how I got so lucky to snag you to be my wife. I love you so much, my darling."

"Oh, Frankie, I hope you always feel the way you do right now. I love you beyond anything I could imagine."

"Oh no. Suddenly I feel underdressed. Did you want me to change and go out somewhere?"

"No, I want to stay right here tonight."

"Okay, even better. Would you like to dance, my dearest?"

"Alright, you two. Dance later. Food first. I'm going to dish up your food and take mine to my room, then leave you two to do… whatever." She snickered.

"Hettie, you don't have to do that," Franklin reacted.

"Ya, I do. I'm tired. I'll take care of the dishes later, either after my nap or in the mornin'. Jes' leave everythin' alone."

She dished up their meals and then hers. She took her plate into her room and closed the door.

"Shall we eat, Kathy?"

They sat down at the table and he kissed her again. "I love you, Kathy." Since he believed her to be the most gorgeous woman upon whom he'd ever rested his eyes, he longed to hold her close and dance with her.

"I love you too, Frankie."

Franklin said grace. He poured the wine, and they began their meal. Franklin kept his eyes on her, and noticed her fork had just been circling the plate, but not eating or drinking. She seemed distracted.

Franklin finally asked, "Are you okay? You're not eating at all. Are you not feeling well?"

"No, I'm fine, I'm just not very hungry. Will you please turn the radio on so we can dance? I just want to be close to you."

"I would dearly love to. I need to wrap my arms around you and hold you. You're so beautiful."

She offered him her hand; he took it and helped her up. He kissed her hand and then her cheek.

Turning the dial until the radio played romantic, excellent, dance music, he took her in his arms. They mostly swayed back and

FROM SHADOWS TO DAYBREAK

forth, but he spun her a couple of times with a suave flair, and she rewarded him with giggles.

"Frankie," she whispered.

"Yes, my dearest?"

She rested her head on his shoulder.

"Oh, you can't be serious. You're going to fall asleep on my shoulder while we're dancing? That's the rudest ever." He chuckled.

She hit his shoulder, and he responded with a laugh, then a belated, "Ouch!"

"I have something I have to tell you, and I'm so afraid you're going to be upset with me."

"Kathleen, my darling, it doesn't matter what it is. You must know by now, I'll still love you. You never have to worry about my love—ever."

"Are you sure, Frankie?"

"Of, course I am. What is it that has you so worried?"

"I don't know how to tell you. What if I tell you and you hate me afterward?"

"Just say it. I could never hate you. Please tell me."

"Well, I'm not sick."

"That's great. Why was that so hard to say? I'm very relieved you're not sick."

"I'm not sick, exactly. I'm…I'm…well…I'm pregnant, Frank."

"Excuse me?" He pulled back. "You're what?"

"I'm pregnant. We're having a baby."

He stopped, then shaking his head, he said, "How in the world did that happen?" He flopped into the rocker.

"Well, Doc explained it this way. When a man and a woman are in love, they—"

"You know what I mean. I thought we were too old for all that."

"Well, apparently not. I'm in shock too. Are you okay? Are you upset? Maybe you don't want kids now. Too late in life."

Franklin was stunned and couldn't find one word. He only stared at her.

She burst into tears. "I was so afraid of this. I was afraid you'd be mad at me and hate me. I'm sorry, Frank. I'm so sorry." She walked into the bedroom, slammed the door, threw herself on the bed, and sobbed. *What am I going to do now? Frank doesn't want kids. Maybe he doesn't want me either.*

Franklin limped through the door and sat on the bed.

"Just go away. I get it. I do. You don't want kids. You probably don't want me anymore either. Just leave me alone, Frank. I don't know what else to say."

He took her in his arms. "I didn't think it was possible to be any happier than I am already. You just proved me wrong. Yes, I was shocked. I mean, that's some unbelievable news, but, sweetheart, a baby is what I've always wanted and thought it would never happen. I couldn't be more surprised or pleased. Please stop crying. I love you."

She fell against his chest. "Oh, Frank, do you mean it?"

"Of course, I do. You must admit it was a gigantic shock. I was afraid you were dying, and then you tell me you're pregnant." He took her in his arms and kissed her. He moved from the bed, limped into the living room, and knocked on Hettie's door.

He shouted out the glad news. "Hettie, we're having a baby! We're having a baby!"

Hettie came out of her room. "Land sakes alive. My baby's havin' a baby! I'm as happy as a tick on a dog. This's amazin' news."

Kathleen rushed out of the bedroom and hugged Hettie. "I'm so happy for ya honey. 'Member I'll always be here for ya and that new little Atwood babe." She hugged Frank. "I'm happy for ya both. Excitin' news."

Franklin went over to the front door and flung it open. "Hey, world, we're having a baby!" he shouted.

Both Hettie and Kathleen laughed.

Franklin came back inside and strutted over to Kathleen like a proud rooster, swept her into his arms, and kissed her long and passionately. "I love you so much, darling." He stood her up and placed his hands on her stomach.

"Hettie, there's a baby in there. We made a baby."

"Ya sure did. Course it's not too surprisin' considerin' how much time you' spendin' in that bedroom." She grinned, then cackled.

"Hettie!" Kathleen shouted.

That only made them laugh louder and harder.

"A baby." He felt her stomach again. I can't believe it. We're having a baby. A boy."

"A girl," Kathleen retorted.

"Who cares? It's a baby, and I'll love it no matter what it is."

"Well, Doc said you'd be happy, but I never expected this. I'm so relieved."

Hettie praised God with one of her infamous hallelujahs and headed for her room.

Franklin swept up Kathleen, took her into the bedroom, closed the door, and kissed her. He whispered, "May I help you off with your dress, Mrs. Atwood?"

"Yes, I would love that, Mr. Atwood." She stood up, allowing Franklin to unzip her dress. He kissed her shoulder and her neck, then touched her back sending shivers up her spine. He kissed her lips, and Kathleen let the dress fall to the floor and lay down on the bed. Franklin went to the other side of the bed, took off his shirt, undressed, placed his prosthetic on the chair, and then turned out the lamp.

"Come here, Mrs. Atwood." He took her in his arms again and kissed her with fervor and gratitude. "You, Mrs. Atwood, are a remarkable woman whom I love with all my heart and soul."

"And you, Mr. Atwood, are a man that I will love with every fiber of my being, every moment, for the rest of my life. We made this baby out of the deepest love a person could possibly have for another. This baby will be the most loved baby on this earth."

"Yes, *he* will."

"*She* will."

"Whatever."

They laughed together.

Chapter 10

February 1951
General Hospital

After two days, Lincoln finally opened his eyes, and they darted around the room. *Where am I*, he questioned. *How did I get here?* Then the excessive pain he was experiencing invaded his consciousness. He tried to move, but everything hurt. *What happened to me?* His thoughts were jumbled. Nothing made sense. He tried to sit up, but the movement hurt even more. *Wait! This is a hospital bed.* He tried to recollect what happened. His head throbbed, and he blacked out.

Kristina, the registered nurse on the floor, drew close to check on him and take his vitals. Everything looked okay there, but she'd become concerned he hadn't awakened yet. The doctor would arrive in about an hour or two to see him; she would know more then. For now, he looked comfortable, and his vitals were good. She covered him up and walked out the door.

* * * * *

Miles Strattford hadn't heard anything from the hospital at all, so he assumed no news was good news. He considered dropping in tonight after he finished with his last few prescriptions. It had not only been a quiet day but also a long day. He'd become tired and wanted nothing more than to go home, sit by the fire, and read.

Unfortunately, lately, every time he got his nose into a book, he fell asleep. He couldn't figure out why that kept happening. Still young at fifty in the scheme of things and hadn't been sick, so why had he been so tired?

Just a few more prescriptions and he could head home, but far too tired to cook. Maybe he'd call The Café and order something he could pick up and take home. After dinner, he'd go directly to bed. When he reflected on it, he reasoned, *What a boring life I live. Get up, go to work, come home eat, and go to bed by eight-thirty. Is that even normal?*

He called The Café and ordered some chili and a ham sandwich. Time to turn out the lights and head home. He stopped by The Café and picked up his order, then headed home. He had planned to stop at the hospital but was just too tired tonight. He'd call them in the morning and catch up on Lincoln then.

He pulled into his driveway and started to get out of the car. Every ounce of energy had drained from his body. He didn't possess the energy it took to move. *I'll just rest here for a few minutes and then go into the house,* he decided. He lay his head back and fell instantly into a very, deep sleep.

When the sun came through the window, Miles awakened. He tried to focus on his whereabouts. He had slept all night in his car. *What in the world is wrong with me?* He asked. The fatigue seemed to be getting significantly worse in a hurry. He shrugged it off and walked into the house. Both he and his house were cold. He started a fire and sat in his chair. Since the fatigue had become such an issue, he considered making an appointment with Doc just to discover if there was anything seriously wrong. But he didn't feel sick, just exhausted. He rested his head on the back of the chair and went to sleep.

Chapter 11

End of February 1951
Connors's Apartment

    A month had passed now, and Emily and Rebecca seemed to be getting along well. Emily started to work part-time for Rebecca. She liked the work and found the customers to be friendly and kind to her. She acknowledged she liked it in this town and very grateful for Kathleen and how she'd done all those wonderful things for her. She'd become content living with Rebecca. They explored makeup together, nails, shopping—all those girly things that Emily hadn't done in a very long time.

    But there were times at night when the nightmare of *that* day replayed through her mind like a horror movie and she would awaken sweating, tangled in the sheets and blankets, and breathing heavily. Then taking deep breaths and turning on the light, she would finally go back to sleep, leaving the light on. The light seemed to make the dark nightmares and thoughts dissipate. During the day, she'd been busy enough she could keep those frightening visions tucked away but were always close by. Would they ever go away completely? Would she ever get past it?

    Rebecca and Emily had long conversations at night after work, and Emily liked those the best. More than a few times, Emily saw Rebecca reading her Bible and questioned why she would do that. She thought it an ancient book that had nothing to do with today,

FROM SHADOWS TO DAYBREAK

but since they got along well together, Emily decided it wasn't worth getting into an argument about a God in whom she didn't believe. She held her tongue.

Kathleen promised to come for breakfast this morning, so they were both looking forward to spending some time with her. Emily changed into one of her new dresses that Kathleen had purchased for her and pulled her hair back into a ponytail. She saw her image in the mirror and took pleasure in the newfound, healthy person looking back at her. Pink on her cheeks, eyes sparkling. Gratefulness filled her, upon reflecting over her new friendships, who were such a large part of the success she'd been experiencing.

Sitting at the table in The Café, the three of them were relishing their conversation. Kathleen had been especially appreciative to Rebecca for taking Emily in, and everything seemed to be going well. Kathleen, still dealing with morning sickness, which somedays lasted all day, had been pleased that Rebecca and Emily were forming a friendship—truly, a blessing. Thankfully, today seemed to be a good day, which brought relief. The waitress came to take their order.

"I'll have two eggs, sunny side up, hash browns, bacon, white toast, and some orange juice." Emily rattled her order off to Sharon since she'd recently memorized the menu.

"And I'll have two eggs over easy—no, on second thought, change that to scrambled eggs, with whole wheat toast and some tea." Kathleen revised her order, with a new appreciation for her current circumstances.

"Becca, what's on the menu that you want?" inquired Sharon.

"I think I'll have eggs over medium, sausage, and whole wheat toast too."

"Okay, I'll be back with your tea, Kathleen. Becca, did you want coffee?"

"Yes, thank you." Rebecca looked up at Kathleen with a brow arched. "What's with the tea?"

"I just thought it sounded better than coffee this morning."

"Uh-huh. You ordered coffee with cream and sugar last time."

"Did I? Maybe I'm switching. Coffee was getting boring, and there are lots of kinds of tea, you know."

Cheryl Fosnot Bingisser

"I guess so." But Rebecca wasn't buying it.

"So," Kathleen asked, "how are you doing, Emily? You look adorable in that dress and much healthier. I'm glad to see that."

"Yes, and I'm working for Becca part-time too."

"We're doing great. I love having her with me. It's kind of like a slumber party every night. We do a lot of laughing and talking. It's sure working for me. Spending every night alone isn't much fun."

"I'm glad to hear everything is working out so well."

"I'm having a lot of fun. I love staying with her. We do laugh a lot and have some good talks too."

"That's wonderful. It's so good to see you both happy."

"Okay, ladies, here's your breakfast," interrupted Sharon when she placed the plates on the table. She brought the tea, coffee, and orange juice on the second run.

Kathleen took one look at Emily's eggs and gulped out an, "Excuse me," put her hand to her mouth, and hurried to the restroom. She barely got there, before last night's dinner made a reappearance. She rinsed out her mouth, took a few deep breaths, and hoped she could face those eggs now. Certainly, she would have to change seats. Those eggs were just too close. After a few minutes, she walked back to the table, appearing a little pale.

"Are you alright?" Rebecca asked.

"Yes, sure, but I think I'd like to change seats and sit with you if it's okay with Emily."

"Sure. That's fine." Emily broke the yokes, and Kathleen took her second trip to the restroom.

When she got back to the table, she drank her tea and ate some toast. "I guess I'm not feeling very well this morning."

Rebecca studied her. "Uh-huh. Not feeling good, huh?"

"Nope. I think I'll head out early, go home, and go to bed. Maybe sleep it off. Must be the flu or something."

"It was the eggs that got you, huh? Two seconds later, Rebecca blurted, "Kathleen Atwood, you're pregnant, aren't you?"

"Shh. I don't want anyone to know."

"Well, if you keep running to the restroom every three seconds, it won't take long before the whole restaurant knows."

46

FROM SHADOWS TO DAYBREAK

"You're pregnant?" Emily asked.

Kathleen exclaimed with sarcasm, "Okay, yes. Happy now?"

"Yes, Kathleen, I'm ecstatic for you. This is wonderful! Aren't you excited?" probed Rebecca.

"Yes, Frank and I are so excited it's just silly at our house. Every five minutes, he asks me if I need to sit down. He won't hardly let me lift a plate, for goodness' sake. He's so sweet to me and so incredibly happy. Neither of us ever dreamed this could happen at our age."

"It must have come as a bit of a shock."

"That's an understatement. Frank and I were both stunned, but that quickly turned into so much joy and love that you would think there would be a great, big, red heart with an arrow through it and a cupid plastered on our front door."

They all laughed.

"Kathleen, I'm so happy for you. It's going to be a big change, but you guys have waited so long for this, I think you'll be just fine. Besides, Hettie's there too, and she will be a great help."

"She will, indeed."

Emily giggled. "Could I babysit once in a while?"

"Why, of course, you can. That would be wonderful. It would give Frank and me some time to ourselves—go out to a fancy dinner or something. That would be great. Thank you for volunteering."

"I can't wait," responded Emily. "This is so exciting."

"Just how far along are you?" Rebecca enquired.

"Truthfully, I think I got pregnant on our wedding night, so only two months. Not long enough to get rid of this morning sickness that seems to last all day some days."

"I'm sure that's hard."

"It is, but I'm fine, just very tired. Doc says that's all part of it, so I nap a lot. Frank seems to like that part." Kathleen giggled and noticed that Emily was staring out the window.

Rebecca laughed.

"Well, speaking of napping, I think I'm going home. Hey, you guys should visit me out at the cabin sometime soon. Becca, you need to see all the changes we made, and I know Frank and Hettie would love to see both of you."

"I'd like that. How about it, Emily? On our next day off would you like to visit Kathleen at the cabin? What do you think?"

Emily turned back to the conversation. "I would love it."

"Okay, it's settled. Just call me ahead of time so Hettie can have a meal ready."

After those words were spoken, she walked to the door opened it, stopped, said goodbye, then left.

"Goodbye," they said in unison.

"Well," said Rebecca, "that was quite the visit." She giggled.

"Yes, it was, and an exciting one too."

"Emily, is there anything wrong? You became awfully quiet the last few minutes."

"No, just thinking. I guess…"

"About what?"

"I don't know. I've never been able to watch a pregnancy up close like this before. I guess I'm kind of excited for them. It will be fun to babysit."

Shaking her head, Rebecca declared, happily. "I can't believe it. She's going to have a baby. God blessed this marriage from the very beginning."

"You really believe that? God does stuff like that?"

"I sure do. He wants us to have real joy, and that only comes from him. God gave them this baby—something Franklin had wanted for years. That's the ultimate joy! Happiness is fleeting. Joy is around even in the worst of times. When my friend died, I cried and grieved, but not like people who don't have Jesus. I knew I would see him again in heaven and be there forever. I missed him. We miss anyone who leaves this earth. But life doesn't end in death because our souls live on forever. Your choice is where your soul is going to live—heaven with Jesus or hell with Satan. And no one can ever make that choice for you."

"Is that stuff all in the Bible?"

"It is."

"There's so much in the Bible to experience. Never a waste of time. You know the girl from the bookstore, Maddie?"

"Yeah."

"She's a Christian and is getting married in April. Her fiancé just came to Christ a few months ago, and Franklin just came to the Lord on the day of the wedding. He stopped the wedding to do that first. There are a lot of people in this town who are coming to Jesus. Maybe you should come to church with me on Sunday. All four of them go there too, and Pastor Ryan is really good. You'd like him."

"Well, maybe. I don't think it's really for me, but thanks anyway."

"Think about it."

"Okay, I will."

Chapter 12

End of February 1951

Miles barely got to work before he needed a rest. His throat was scratchy and sore. This is crazy. *I think I need to make an appointment and get in as soon as possible,* he decided.

Miles called Doc and set an appointment for that afternoon. But how could he get through most of the workday without needing to sleep? It was nearly impossible. Maybe he'd call the other pharmacist to come in because he just wouldn't be functional today at all. He strode over to Doc's and waited. He struggled to stay awake. Acknowledging the abnormality of the illness, he used Doc's phone to call the other pharmacist to sub for him. He lay down on the bench and fell asleep.

Doc tried to wake him, but it became difficult. Finally, he sat up.

"Miles, come back to the patient room. Sit here on the table and let's talk. What's going on?"

"I keep sleeping. I'm so fatigued. The other night, I was in my car and was going to walk into the house, but I decided to rest a little first. I didn't wake up until morning. I can't seem to get past this fatigue. I couldn't even finish a shift today. This morning I woke up with a sore throat, but other than that, I've been okay."

Doc checked his eyes, nose, throat, and lymph nodes. He asked him a slew of other questions. Afterward, he sat down and scruti-

FROM SHADOWS TO DAYBREAK

nized him seriously. "Miles, I think you have mononucleosis. They call it mono."

"What's that?"

"They call it the sleeping disease—well, kissing disease really. It most frequently comes from teenagers, but adults get it too, so who've you been kissing, Miles?"

"I haven't. No one. Not that I wouldn't like to. Have anyone in mind?" He smirked.

"I'm only teasing."

"I'm not."

Doc laughed.

"You can get it other ways too, but it's rarer."

"What am I supposed to do?"

"Mostly, you just rest. No work, no anything. Just sleep. There's no real cure, but plenty of rest, lots of fluids, aspirin, and hot tea for the throat. That's about it. I think you caught it early, so just go home and go to bed. Is there a relative around who can look after you, and cook for you?"

"Not really."

"A neighbor, maybe?"

"Raff is close, but he and Maddie are working on his house so they can move her in after their wedding. Other than that, no."

"Maybe we should put you in the hospital for a few days to give you a head start. That way, you would get the care you need, and I'd be looking in on you too. It might be a good idea. If you're alone, you could fall asleep standing up. You have good insurance. Let's admit you for a few days and then assess the situation."

"Okay, only because I do fall asleep without warning, and cooking could be problematic."

"I think that's a good idea. I'll call ahead and get your paperwork finished so you won't have to struggle through filling it out. We can either call you a cab or send for an ambulance. The cab might be cheaper. "Ah—let me see if I have any more patients. If not, I'll take you over. Be right back."

Doc checked his schedule and found it cleared for the rest of the day. "Miles, I can take you over." *He's out again. Okay, I'll get someone from next door to help me get him in the car*, determined to hospitalize Miles as soon as possible.

He slept all the way to the hospital, where they admitted him immediately. Doc filled out all the paperwork, including insurance info. He was all set. Before Doc left the hospital, he peeked in on Miles to make certain he was all right. He'd fallen asleep.

Doc, aware that Raff knew Miles, resolved to call him and let him know Miles had been admitted to the hospital. He hoped Raff and Maddie could visit him in a day or two, depending on how he's doing.

Chapter 13

End of February 1951
Mayfield Residence

Maddie and Raff were knee-deep in paint when the phone rang. Raff put down the brush and trotted into the office to answer it.

"Hello?"

"Raff, this is Doc Anderson."

"Yes, Doc, is there anything wrong?"

"No. I know that you are acquainted with Miles Strattford. I admitted him to the hospital today. He needs a lot of rest, but I wondered if you and Maddie would consider visiting him in a day or two. He has no one, and I think any face would be a good thing for him. It's a long recovery time, so I thought a few days in the hospital in the beginning would give him a kick start."

"Sure, we wouldn't mind visiting with him at all. Is he going to be all right?"

"Yes, but it might take weeks or maybe months."

"Wow. We'll do what we can. He's been nice to us, and we like him. He's only a mile from me too, so we're close. I do have a question."

"Yes?"

"If he gets well enough to sit and be somewhere other than home, could he be with us during the day? That way, we could watch him and make sure he eats and rests. I'm at the house most of the time trying to finish it, and Maddie's over here when she's not working. If we can help, we would like to."

"I think that would be fine, but check with the hospital, me, and with him. I think it would be good for him not to be alone all the time. When you're sick, it can get depressing."

"Okay, I'll clear it with Maddie, but I think it might be good for him."

"Sounds good. Let's see how it goes. Hopefully, he can get back on his feet quickly."

"Yes."

"Raff, thank you. You can call me anytime. Bye."

"No problem. Goodbye." Raff hung up. He told Maddie about the conversation, and she agreed they should help however they could.

Raff walked across the room and cupped his hands under Maddie's chin. "Maddie, you look so cute with paint on your face. I have to say it's your color." Raff laughed and then enfolded her in his arms and kissed her sweetly. "I love you, Maddie Henderson, with all my heart and soul. I can't wait to make you my wife."

"I love you too, cowboy, but right now I think I'll wash the perfect paint color off my cheek. Thank you very much for pointing that out," she added sarcastically.

"No problem. Any little thing I can do to help. I'm nothing, if not helpful," he added, chuckling.

Chapter 14

End of February 1951
Atwood Residence

Kathleen's days seemed to drag by. Between her frequent trips to the bathroom and the naps that she'd been required to take, she wondered if all pregnant women felt like this or just the old ones—at least when it came to the fatigue. Franklin watched her like a hawk and wouldn't let her do anything, but for now, it seemed like common sense because she didn't feel like doing anything, anyway.

The door opened, and Franklin came in, hung up his coat, took off his boots, and immediately went on the hunt for Kathleen. Her chair sat empty, so he assumed she'd be in the bedroom. He opened the door just a crack, and he didn't see her there either. He hadn't seen her outside but hadn't looked in the back. Maybe she went for a walk. *I'll give her a while before I start looking for her. She's fainted before, and I don't want that happening outside because she could freeze to death*, he reasoned.

He sat in his rocker, watching the door. With his pipe lit, he inhaled. Sometimes, nothing but the pipe calmed him. He closed his eyes. The vision of Kathleen in that red dress flashed across his mind with a great deal of pleasure. He smiled. She looked fantastic in that dress. Their time together afterward was stellar, and he loved her more every single day.

How is he ever going to get through the next few months without suffocating her? He didn't want to. But he couldn't help worrying about her. The last thing he wanted to do was overreact or let her know how concerned he could become. She still has a normal life to live, just like he does. *Lord, please help me through this and calm my heart. I don't want her to run because I'm holding on too tightly. She's much too independent for that. I don't want to change her. I love her the way she is. But where is she? Calm down, Franklin. She's fine*, he tried to make himself believe those words, while he took another puff.

Kathleen walked into the room looking drawn, pale, and fatigued. She hung up her coat and took off her boots.

"Oh, Frank, your pipe." She put her hand over her mouth and hurried to the bathroom.

After a few minutes, Kathleen came out and sat in her chair. "Frank, would you mind putting out your pipe? It's making me sick."

"I'm so sorry. I didn't know. Sure. I had no idea that it would make you sick. Pearly used to love the smell of it. I'm sorry."

"She never went through pregnancy, did she?" she asked rather icily.

Kathleen noticed a wounded look covering his face and immediately recognized what she'd said that hurt him. "Frank, I didn't mean it like that. I'm so sorry. Please forgive me."

"I understand. It's okay. All's forgiven. Kathleen, why don't you come over here and sit with me?"

"Are you sure? You called me Kathleen, and you only do that when you're upset with me. Really, I love you, Frankie, but I think I'm too tired to get up."

"Okay, then. I'll come to you." He limped over to her, swept her up in his arms, brought her to his chair, and sat her on his lap. "I'm not upset. You just caught me a little off guard, is all. I didn't know that the pipe bothered you. Now this is better, my dearest," as he cuddled with her. "Darling, I love you, so very much." He kissed her on the cheek. "Have you had a rough day?"

"Not particularly. I just don't like feeling this tired. I know it won't last forever. It's just that I'm not used to feeling like this. I'm sorry to complain, Frankie. I do love you and our baby."

FROM SHADOWS TO DAYBREAK

"It's okay to complain when you don't feel well. I want to know. Just tell me what I can do for you without smothering you to death—which is what I think I'm doing."

"Ah, Frankie, no, you were just being concerned and wanted to take care of me. I understand. But I don't want you to think you have to jump up every five minutes to do everything for me. I'm not sick really. I'm just pregnant, and I won't feel like this forever—at least, I hope not—but I promise you, if I don't feel like getting out of this chair to get something or do something, I will ask you. I'm not being a martyr. So please don't worry about that. Deal?"

"Deal. Is there anything I can do for you now?" He kissed her lovingly.

"Yes, Frankie, my love, there is."

"And just what might that be?"

"You can kiss me like that again, please. I missed you."

"Well, maybe. If you do what I want you to. There is a cost, my dearest." He smirked.

"Really. What exactly is the cost of keeping those from me? You brute!"

He laughed. "Brute? That's what you called me the day you ran into me."

"You ran into me, and you know it." She smiled.

He laughed. "Is that really the way you remember it?"

"Of course, it is."

"I believe you said to me that day, something about needing glasses. Remember that?"

"Yes."

"Well, my dearest, not only do you need glasses, but your memory can use a little refresher too."

Kathleen punched his shoulder.

"Ouch! Now see here, these kisses can be withheld depending on what you might want to do for *me*, Mrs. Atwood. So you see, it's your choice."

"What exactly do you have in mind, Frankie?"

"It also depends on just how much energy you would like to expend, Mrs. Atwood," he whispered.

"Well, Mr. Atwood, I am very tired. Very tired…but…not so sleepy." They tried to hold back the laughter, but it spurted out in snorts and giggles instead.

"Well, since Hettie seems otherwise occupied, how about I save your tired bones a few steps and just carry you in."

"Why, Rhett, aren't you just the most charmin' thing I have ever seen," she said in her Southern accent, fanning herself with her hand.

"Scarlett, you have no idea."

"I do believe I'm going to swoon." She giggled as she placed the back of her hand up to her forehead and threw her head back.

"That's all right, Scarlett. I'll just heave you over my shoulder like a sack of potatoes, throw you on the bed, and have my way with you." He laughed.

"I was right in the first place. You are a brute!"

He chuckled. He walked through the bedroom door, closed it, and positioned her on the bed.

"So, Scarlett, what's your pleasure?"

"Oh, Rhett, just kiss me."

"I would be delighted, Scarlett."

"I just want you, Rhett—only you. Just kiss me."

"Frankly, my dear, I don't give a—way my kisses to just anybody."

Kathleen hit him in the shoulder.

"Ouch!"

Chapter 15

End of February 1951
The Café

The Café was serving the lunch crowd, and the place was almost full. Rebecca had all her staff working, and Emily had been taking orders. She had just gone back to the kitchen and came out with two plates of food. She turned to the table by the window to put the plates down when she froze—and dropped both plates. She stood there staring at this one man.

Then she collected herself. Turning to Sharon, she said, "I'll be right back to clean this mess up."

Sharon could tell she was upset. Emily's face had drained of color, and her eyes revealed fear.

"No. Go back to the kitchen and I'll take care of it. She knew something had gone wrong but didn't have time to talk right then."

Emily rushed back into the kitchen and her body shook with violence. She didn't know what to do. Run? Hide? She stood there, taking deep breaths, until she calmed down. Rebecca came in to check on her.

"Are you all right?"

"Yes, I'm fine. She lied while she tried to hide the import of the incident. The plates just slipped out of my hand. I'm sorry, Becca. You can take it out of my check."

"Don't be silly. Things happen. Are you sure you're okay?"

Cheryl Fosnot Bingisser

"Yeah, I'm fine. I'll just take this garbage out back and be right back."

"Okay, sweetie, but don't get upset about dropping plates. There's a lot worse things than that."

"I know, thanks," she uttered. She turned, picked up the garbage, and headed out the back door. She threw it in the garbage can and pivoted to go back inside when she was grabbed from behind.

"So you recognized me, huh?"

His breath stunk with the smell of liquor.

Did you tell anyone?"

"No."

He put his hand over her mouth. "I don't believe you. This time I'm gonna finish the job I started and just kill ya."

She bit his hand and started to run.

"Ouch! Why you little—"

He grabbed her arm again.

She turned and kicked him hard in his most vulnerable place. He fell to the ground, which slowed him down, and he groaned in pain.

She ran again. He caught up to her and grabbed her arm. She screamed.

A gunshot rang out. He froze.

"If you value your manly parts, insignificant though they must be, I strongly suggest you let her go."

He released her.

"Emily, run back to The Café!" Rebecca ordered. "Now don't you dare move a whisker. You can test me if you want to, but you should probably know that my daddy taught me to shoot when I was only three and I haven't missed a bullseye in twenty-seven years."

"Okay, lady. I'm not moving. Now put that gun down."

"Not likely. You don't seem to appreciate your situation here. I'm the one with the gun, and so far, I've let you stay in one piece. That could change in one second. Move, and I'll change you from a stud to a filly and take a whole lot of pleasure in doing so."

Raff heard the gunshot and ran around the corner to find out what happened.

FROM SHADOWS TO DAYBREAK

"Becca, are you okay?"

"Raff, go get the sheriff. I got this."

"You sure?"

"Yep."

"Okay."

He ran around the block and out of sight. Just a minute later, the sheriff and deputy came trotting around the corner, put the handcuffs on him, and started to escort him away. They stopped right by Rebecca.

"You wouldn't really have done it, would ya, lady?" asked the attacker.

"Let me put it this way: You're very fortunate the sheriff showed up when he did. The rifle was getting a little heavy. I wouldn't let go of it until you were either wiggling around on the ground like the worm you are—screaming like a little girl, or the sheriff came and rescued you."

The men all laughed, except for the attacker in handcuffs.

The sheriff added, "She got you good!"

They laughed again.

"Becca, you were magnificent!" Raff said, dumbfounded. "Spectacular! That was better than any scene I've ever seen in one of those cowboy movies. How did you learn to shoot?"

"My daddy taught me when I was only three years old. We were on the rodeo circuit when I was a kid. I was a sharpshooter. Never missed. Not one time."

"Wow! Maybe you could teach me how to shoot. Now that Maddie and I are getting married, I'd like to have some protection for her. And when I have more time, I want to hear that whole rodeo story. It sounds mighty interesting."

"I'd like that, Raff."

"You know, maybe you should teach the women around here, so scum like him won't come to this town."

"Maybe."

"Can we talk later? I need to get back to Maddie. We're painting the house, and we ran out of paint, which is why I'm here in the first place."

"Sure thing."

As he turned to walk away, she heard him say while shaking his head, "That was something. Maddie will never believe this one."

Rebecca took the gun and placed it back in the pantry, then went to look for Emily. She was in the kitchen shaking like the proverbial leaf. Rebecca put her arms around her and held her until she stopped shaking.

"He'll never hurt anyone again. You don't have to be afraid anymore. The sheriff took him to jail. There's just one more step you might have to take."

"What's that?"

"You might have to testify at his trial."

"You mean tell my story in front of people?"

"Yes, that's right, but you don't have to be afraid because I'll be with you every step of the way, and so will Kathleen. He's likely to have done this before, and we might be able to get others to step up and testify as well. In fact, every woman in this town will be behind you. There isn't anything we can't do when we stick together."

"Thank you so much, Becca. You saved my life."

"Listen, you fought back hard, and I'm proud of you. Don't you ever forget that. You're a lot stronger than you think. What do you say we forget all that and get back to work?"

"I'd like that. I'm so glad I met both you and Kathleen. You've done so much for me and changed my life completely. I'm so grateful."

"Nothing to worry about. It was my pleasure." Then under her breath, she added, "Really, my pleasure. I just wished he'd moved."

Rebecca walked back into the seating area and began to take an order when all the people in the room stood, clapped, and cheered.

She glanced around the room and blushed, then took a bow. They cheered louder, and some even whistled. She had to admit that it felt pretty good to put away that creep.

Chapter 16

End of February 1951
General Hospital

As soon as Lincoln was able to get out of bed without excruciating pain, he traipsed out of the hospital without being noticed. He had no idea how long the trek back to town would be because he'd never been any further than town. Staggering and struggling to stay upright, after about a quarter mile, he passed out and fell to the ground.

A runner glanced down the path and saw a kid face down in the dirt. He ran to his side and tried to wake him. Lincoln didn't move. He gazed at his battered and bruised body and tried to guess how he got there. Looking around, he didn't see anyone. Great. *What do I do now?* He deliberated. He was too weak to move on his own. In the distance, there was a red pickup traveling toward him. He jogged to the road and waved him down.

The pickup pulled off the road, and Jake told him about the kid. Franklin got out of the truck. His heart sank as he grasped the extent of the kid's injuries.

"I think this kid needs to go to the hospital. He's been beaten badly and isn't anywhere near healed."

Franklin picked him up and carried him to the pickup. "Hey, thanks for getting my attention. What's your name?"

"Jake. Jake Stevenson. This is the path I run almost every day, and I saw him lying there and didn't know exactly what to do. I was relieved when I saw your truck coming, especially when you stopped. Thanks."

"No problem. I'm glad I did too. Well, I better get him to the hospital. Have a good day."

"You too."

Pulling into the parking lot, Franklin parked, carefully placed his arms under the boy's little body, and carried him inside. "Nurse, I found this boy on the street and it looks like he's been beaten, and not too long ago either."

The nurse gave him a quick once-over. "That's the kid who ran away. He was here for three days, then he ran away. I don't think he has anybody. Mr. Strattford brought him in after he found him. He thought he was a street kid from town. I don't know how to keep the kid from running away. We can't tie him down to the bed. He's only seven. I'll have to go to Doc and see how we can contain this kid without hurting him, but we can't have him running out of the hospital. You can talk to Mr. Strattford about it if you want to. He's just down the hall in room 108. I'm sure he wouldn't mind the company."

"He's here? As a patient?" he asked, surprise written all over his face.

"He is."

"Sure, I'll peek in and see if he's up for visitors. Thanks for telling me."

"No problem."

Franklin ambled down the hall and found the room. He knocked quietly on the door and didn't get an answer, so he opened the door and scanned inside. He appeared to be sleeping, so Franklin turned to walk away.

"Franklin, is that you?"

"Yes, are you up for a visitor for a couple of minutes? I don't want to disturb you."

"Nonsense. I've done nothing but sleep all day. Flappin' my jaw isn't any work at all."

FROM SHADOWS TO DAYBREAK

Franklin laughed. "How are you feeling?"

"Tired."

"If you don't mind me asking, is there anything I can do to help you? How long are you going to be here?"

"I don't know. Doc says I have this disease that makes me want to sleep all the time, and he thought if he put me here for a few days, we'd get a jump start on it and maybe get over it faster. It's a long-term thing. He says it could be weeks or months. Apparently, there's nothing that can be done except rest and fluids."

"Oh, Miles, I'm so sorry. Is there anything I can do? What about your house? Can I check on it for you? Please, I'd like to help."

"Franklin, you've always been so kind to me. If you wouldn't mind, would you stop by the house and make sure I locked it up? I don't even remember if I went home before I got here or not."

"Sure. Anything else?"

"No, not right now anyway, but if you don't mind, I might have to impose on you farther down the road."

"Of course. Anything."

"Oh, by the way, congratulations on your marriage. Kathleen's a great catch. You're a lucky man."

"You have no idea exactly how lucky I feel. She's the sun and the moon to me. Well, I better let you get some rest since that's the doctor's order."

"Thanks, Franklin. You have no idea how much this means to me."

"Please, don't worry about a thing. I'm happy to do it," he answered, while he walked toward the door. "Oh, I almost forgot. Do you know anything about the kid you brought in who had been beaten up? He'd been found face down in the dirt, and I brought him in here. The nurse said he had run away in the middle of the night, but he sure didn't make it very far."

"No, I found him in the alley in town, almost dead. That's why I brought him in. I'm pretty sure he's a street kid," he offered. "Oh, you might need a key to my house. It's in the locker there in my trousers' pocket. Would you mind getting it? I'm way too unsteady to get out of bed."

"Not at all. Please, Miles, don't worry about a thing. I'll check in on you in a day or two, and if there's anything else you need, I'll leave my number at the front desk so you can have it."

"I appreciate it."

"Please, just rest easy, okay?"

"I will, thanks."

Franklin left, limped to the desk, and gave them his number in case he needed anything or something untoward happened. Then he headed toward Miles's house. He pulled in, checked the house, walked around the outside, locked the doors, and headed home.

Chapter 17

March 1951

Maddie arranged for Kathleen to meet her at The Café to work on wedding plans. The wedding date had been set for April twenty-first and approaching fast. She still hadn't picked out her flowers, what colors were important to her, or even any bridesmaids she wanted to stand with her. She thought Raff could go with her and help pick out the cake style and flavor. The reception would be held in the basement of the church, but the guest list and other arrangements still needed to be made. She had an appointment at the bridal shop for a fitting later this afternoon and hoped that Kathleen could go with her.

The to-do list kept multiplying and she didn't want to bother Raff because he'd been working so hard on the house. The deadline was essential if it were to be finished before the wedding. He already felt tired and pressured, so Maddie tried to take the rest of the wedding plans on herself. But between work, helping Raff with the house, and the wedding plans, she found herself stretched thinly. Usually, she was the practical one, but lately, her emotions were becoming fragile, and Raff's weren't a whole lot better. They needed time away from the house, but time was at a premium, and it seemed the fun had flitted away from their relationship. Maddie believed they were in a precarious position, but Raff was too busy to even notice, which disturbed her even more.

Rebecca had tried to clear some time to sit with Kathleen and Maddie and catch up on the wedding plans. But it also depended on how many people were part of the lunch crowd. She'd been a little shorthanded because one of the waitresses was out sick. She seated Maddie over by the window and noticed Kathleen coming down the street. She took their order and then passed it off to Emily.

Kathleen came in, immediately saw Maddie, sauntered over, hugged her, and sat on the chair across from her.

"It's so good to see you, Maddie."

"It's good to see you too. I think I've only seen you once since you got married. How are you?"

"I'm fine. Frank and I couldn't be happier and we hate being apart at all. Kind of silly for old people like us to act like kids. I guess, in a way, love brings out the youth in you. Gives you more energy— more vitality maybe." Kathleen said dreamily. Her eyes danced, and she glowed like a candle in the darkness.

"Well, you certainly look happy. You're actually glowing, for heaven's sake."

"Oh, don't be silly. I am not."

"Ah, Kathleen, I beg to differ, but you are glowing."

"I sure don't know how. I'm pretty tired."

Rebecca finally arrived at the table. "Hey, girls, what do you want for lunch? I'll take your order back to the kitchen and then hand it off to Emily."

"Kathleen, what sounds good to you? Eggs, sunny side up, maybe?" She stifled a giggle.

Kathleen swallowed hard and sent a warning look to Rebecca.

"Sorry. Couldn't resist. So what do you see?"

"I don't know. I'm not very hungry."

"You have to eat something. Do you want me to surprise you?"

"No, I don't trust you, Becca."

Rebecca laughed. "I wouldn't do that to you."

"Hey, what's up with you two?" Maddie asked, with a furrowed brow.

"Nothing. She's just being silly," Kathleen reacted, with irritation.

FROM SHADOWS TO DAYBREAK

"Yeah, that's it," Rebecca quipped, with just a hint of sarcasm. "Well?"

"Ask Maddie while I take a closer look."

"I think I'll have the chili and half a pastrami sandwich—oh, and coffee.

Rebecca looked at Kathleen, who suddenly looked a little pale. The corners of her mouth started to curl up, so she quickly turned away so Kathleen couldn't see her until she regained control.

Rebecca, obviously amused, turned toward Kathleen. "Okay, it's your turn. What do you see?"

"I know I want tea. What's the soup of the day?"

"Chili and chowder."

Kathleen gulped again.

"Maybe just some scrambled eggs and toast? How does that sound?"

"I think that would work. Could you bring the tea first, please? Thanks, Becca." She threw her a grateful glance, along with a "don't you dare" face.

"No problem. I'll be right back."

"Okay, tell me what's going on with you," pleaded Kathleen.

"I don't know. I just wish Raff and I were like you two."

"Oh, sweetie, what's wrong?"

Maddie's eyes flooded. "It's just that we're working so hard on the house, I'm still working at the bookstore, I'm doing all the wedding plans, and I feel like Raff doesn't even care." Everything came out of her mouth rapidly as tears dripped down her chin before she could wipe them away.

"Oh, honey, I'm sure Raff cares. They sometimes have one-track minds. Don't take it too seriously. Besides, I've been told by other people that couples get so stressed out planning the wedding they start to take it out on each other. They're too tired to cope well."

"Really?"

"Really. Some even break up before the wedding until they realize it's just temporary stuff. Then they're back on track, the wedding goes on as scheduled, and everyone's happy as clams."

"Oh, that makes me feel so much better. It sure sounds familiar."

"Trust me. Raff loves you, and you can see it every time he looks at you. You have nothing to worry about. We'll get those plans knocked out today—at least as many as possible. How does that sound?"

"I'm so relieved, and I have a fitting today. I was hoping that maybe you could come with me?"

"Oh, Maddie. I would love to. That's so exciting."

Rebecca drew closer and sat next to Maddie. "Lunch will be up in just a few minutes. Now what did I miss?"

"Maddie was just saying that she has a fitting today. Isn't that exciting?"

"I think that would be the most exciting part of the wedding—finding the perfect dress and then making it fit the very best on you. That's wonderful. The only thing better than that would be the honeymoon." They all giggled.

"We're ready for that part. Raff made reservations at a fancy hotel in Denver that was built way back in 1891. I guess it's beautiful on the inside, and he booked a suite. There's a restaurant and a bar, and Raff said we would never have to come out of our room the whole week if we didn't want to. He assured me that we needed the rest."

"Rest? It doesn't sound like rest is on the agenda at all," Kathleen added quietly." They all giggled.

"Well, you would know, Kathleen," remarked Rebecca.

The laughing continued.

Emily brought the plates full of food. She placed them on the table—the chili and the sandwich in front of Maddie, and the scrambled eggs and toast plate in front of Kathleen. Rebecca had decided on a ham sandwich, potato salad, and coffee. With the next trip came the tea and the two coffees.

Kathleen smelled the chili and the pastrami sandwich.

"Excuse me," she eked out as she put her hand over her mouth and hurried to the restroom.

"What's the matter with her?" Maddie asked. "Is she sick?"

"Don't tell her I told you, but she's pregnant. Still in the sick and tired stage," she said conspiratorially. She giggled. "She's trying to keep it quiet until she gets past the three-month period."

"That's wonderful. No wonder she is glowing."

"That's right, and I think your order was what sent her to the restroom this time. Last time, it was Emily's eggs sunny side up order." They laughed.

"So that's why you said that."

"Yep."

"You're terrible."

"I know, but it's so much fun, and I'm happy for them. They waited a long time to have kids, and even though this was quite the shock, these two haven't touched the ground since they found out, except for all the trips to the bathroom." They laughed.

Kathleen returned and looked at the two of them. "You told her, didn't you?"

"Yes, sorry, but it was pretty obvious. I think you should sit over by me to get away from Maddie's chili."

"I'm sorry, Kathleen. If I'd known, I wouldn't have ordered that."

"Don't worry about it. It happens all the time, and Becca enjoys it way too much."

Rebecca grinned. "I do. I really do."

Kathleen moved over next to Rebecca.

"Okay, Becca, you can say grace, just for that. I think you need to pray about it." Kathleen teased.

They laughed.

"You do understand at some point, this will happen to you, and then I get to sit by and tease you," Kathleen retorted.

Rebecca replied, "You need to find someone for me to marry first, then I'll think about pregnancy."

They each looked at the other and giggled. They ate the rest of their lunch and talked about the wedding. Maddie had decided on purple and yellow for her colors since it would be early spring. She also decided who would stand up for her, and that included the two of them. They were honored. Then it was time for the fitting, and

Maddie thought she'd pick out the bridesmaids' dresses at the same time.

The seamstress helped Maddie put the dress on and then guided her to the full-length mirror, where Kathleen sat, waiting.

Kathleen gasped. "Oh, Maddie. I have never seen a dress so beautiful, and you look stunning in it!"

The dress had a sweetheart neckline with beading and rhinestones. It was fitted to the waist and then flowed out into a full skirt that was all lace. Her veil was Italian lace and was crowned with a small rhinestone tiara.

Maddie studied herself in the mirror. She turned, looked at the back, and studied herself some more. She embodied a European princess.

"It's so beautiful."

"You think so?"

Kathleen rolled her eyes. "Maddie, seriously, I have never seen a dress that is so beautiful, and you, my dear, look drop-dead gorgeous in it. Raff is going to faint."

"You think so."

"Are you kidding me? Every man who has a heartbeat is going to think so—and most women, for that matter. Raff won't be able to speak. He'll be stunned. You remember how Frank looked at me?"

"Yes."

"Well, my dress can't hold a candle to this one, and it fits you beautifully. It's amazing."

"I don't ever want to get out of it. I feel beautiful in it," she said shyly.

"You should because you look incredible."

Maddie ogled herself until she glanced at the clock. Reluctantly, she said, "Okay, I'll go change. I still would like to pick out bridesmaids' dresses, and while you're here, you can choose what you want to wear."

"Okay, I'd love to." Kathleen waited while Maddie changed.

"Let's go to the bridesmaids' section." They walked into a different room and saw several racks full of all styles and colors of dresses.

"Maddie, you want to stick with purple and yellow, right?"

FROM SHADOWS TO DAYBREAK

"I was just thinking, maybe purple dresses and then use yellow roses for the flowers you, girls, carry," she said thoughtfully.

"I think that's a great idea. Purple and yellow look great together. Do you want a purple with more red in it or more blue?"

"I think blue, like iris or crocus."

"I think that's perfect. Hey, here's a dress that has a straight-across neckline, sort of like a sweetheart, but without that little dip, and an empire waistline, and the length is just below the knee in the front, and longer in the back. What do you think of that? It will work for me if I start showing by then—although it's probably a little early."

"I like that. It's so pretty and it looks like it comes in the perfect color. That's it. That's the one. Do you like it?"

"I love it. It's a dress that I could wear outside the wedding when Frank takes me somewhere special, and I can still wear it for a few months. I think it's perfect. I think the other girls will like it too."

"Okay, all I need to do is get the bridesmaids in to try the dresses on and get them ordered. I can't tell you how happy this makes me."

The salesgirl appeared and told them that the dress she chose was so popular she might even have them here in the right sizes, but they would have to come in right away before they were sold out.

"I'll go back and tell Becca. It should be easy for her since she's right down the street."

"Easy for me too. I'll tell you what, why don't I stay and try on a dress now and just get that done?"

"It would be wonderful."

Kathleen told the salesgirl her size, and she went to the back room and pulled two different sizes for her to try on.

She tried one on and it fit perfectly. She paid for it, and the saleslady covered it with a plastic bag and handed it to Kathleen, ready for her to take it home.

Maddie took all her wedding regalia with her, and Kathleen carried her shoes and dress. They walked to Raff's car, placed the items inside, and closed the door.

Kathleen turned to her. "I know I said I'd talk to Becca, but would you mind if I just went home? I'm exhausted."

"Not at all. You head home and get some rest, and we'll talk later. Thank you, Kathleen, for all your help. I can't tell you what a relief it is to get it done."

"Oh, it is an honor. Believe me. I thoroughly enjoyed myself. Don't you worry about a thing, okay?" Kathleen hugged her and headed for the car that had been waiting for her just a few yards away. After the driver opened the door, she put her dress inside and scooted in on the seat.

Maddie's heart was soaring. She couldn't wait to tell Raff all they'd accomplished today and how much help Kathleen had been. It had been a great day. She quickly headed to The Café, met with Rebecca straightaway, talked briefly, and then left.

Chapter 18

March 1951

Raff knocked on the door and waited for Maddie to open it. He'd been excited about what he planned for their evening. They needed a break from all the work they had done. Frayed nerves were taking a toll on them.

She had been working at the bookstore, working at home, and taking care of all the wedding plans, and Raff hadn't even asked her about it. He knew she'd been tired. They both were and had begun to take it out on each other. They needed a break. They needed to have fun. They needed to laugh together.

He hoped that this would make a difference. Maybe turn things around. The pressure had been too much.

Maddie answered the door and looked beautiful and irresistible. "Maddie, is that a new dress?"

"It is, and I'm so glad you noticed." She twirled around for him with a flourish.

"It's beautiful, but you are even more beautiful."

The dress had a square neckline and short sleeves. It hugged her waistline and had a circle skirt with pink flowers on a white background.

"Come over here." He wrapped his arms around her, and with a depth of love that almost surprised him, he kissed her. "Maddie, I love you so much. You are stunning. I'm sorry that I haven't taken the time to genuinely notice you and appreciate who I'm receiving as my wife." He traced her jawline, and her lips, and touched her nose. He kissed her forehead, her nose, her cheek, and her lips. He lengthened his kiss and reveled in who she was and how happy they would be when they married in just a few weeks. "Do you have any idea how much you mean to me? I couldn't live without you, my sweet. You've helped me become a better person, and I know you will help me become the husband God wants for you. I can't wait for that part."

"Mayfield, I've missed this. I love you more each day. I'm more excited about marrying you today than yesterday. Kiss me again, cowboy."

"Sure, ma'am." He bent down and gave her a sweet kiss.

"Hey, we need to go because I have planned an evening I think you will enjoy, and if you don't, you can plan the next date."

She grabbed her coat, stomped into her boots, opened the door, closed it, and bounded down the stairs toward the car. Raff let Maddie in and ran around the other side and scooted in behind the wheel. The car turned over and off they went.

"Where are we going?"

"Are you hungry?"

"Do you want to eat first or go to the movie first?"

"What movie?"

"*The African Queen.*"

"Raff, that's wonderful. I do want to see this movie. It's romantic."

"Oh, there she goes." He laughed. "I know you love romantic movies. Some would call this a chick flick, but since there's so much adventure in it, I think I can handle it. Humphrey Bogart and Katharine Hepburn are the stars, and I know you like them. Do you want to eat first?"

"Sure, let's eat first."

"We can't dawdle because there's only one showing, and it starts at seven-thirty."

"How about eating at The Café and then going? The movie's here, isn't it?"

"Yep. Right down the street and to the left."

"Okay, let's move, Mayfield. I don't want to miss a single second of this movie."

They walked into The Café, and Emily seated them. "What do you want, Maddie?"

"I think I want the pork chop dinner with mashed potatoes, beef gravy, and corn. Oh, and coffee please."

"Raff, what's your pleasure?"

"I'll have the meatloaf dinner, with the mashed potatoes, beef gravy, green beans, and coffee."

"Okay. I'll be back in a few minutes. How ya doing, Maddie? I wanted to sit and listen to the wedding plans, but I had to work. Maybe another time?" asked Emily.

"Of course. Next time I'm back here, we'll set aside the time because I'd like to tell you what we've decided."

"That would be great. I'd like that a lot. Thanks. Okay, I'll be back in a few."

"Maddie, you haven't told me about your lunch with Kathleen and Becca. What did you guys come up with?" asked Raff.

"It was great. Our colors are purple and yellow. The bridesmaids' dresses are purple. Kathleen already has hers, and Becca's going in tomorrow to try hers on, then maybe, we'll be done. I talked to Marybeth, my very best friend from high school, but she said she couldn't come. Do you think I should ask Emily?"

"That's up to you."

"Who are you going to use?"

"I was thinking of Franklin and Miles, but it sounds like Miles isn't going to be up to it. The only other person I can think of is Jake. I haven't seen him in years, but we could get together and see where we are, friendship-wise. It might work."

"Better find out soon because you guys are going to need to buy tuxes. We'll have to go to Denver to do it because there are no places here locally."

"Oh, I didn't think about that."

"Exactly."

"Okay, I get it. I'll get with Jake this week, talk with him, and see how it works. I really don't have any other friends. Kind of pathetic, huh?"

"You've just had a lot on your plate. You could do it with just Franklin, and I'll have Kathleen and Becca. Maybe have Becca and Emily as candlelighters, and wear the same dresses that Kathleen wears. Do you think that would work, and not upset Becca?"

"Better talk to her. She's in the kitchen right now. Talk to her, and then you can ask Emily tonight too."

"Good idea. I'll be back in a second."

Maddie found Rebecca in the pantry. She whispered, "Becca, I need to talk to you, quietly."

"Okay, what's up?"

"I hope you'll understand. Would you be terribly upset if I asked you to be a candlelighter with Emily instead of a bridesmaid, and wear the same dress?"

"Maddie, I'm honored just to have any part in this wedding. It will be nice getting to walk down the aisle with Emily, and I think she'll be thrilled. Don't give it another thought. Oh, I already bought my dress, so that just leaves Emily."

Maddie hugged her. "Thank you so much. You're so sweet to do this."

"Not at all. That's an easy one. Don't give it another thought."

"Thanks again, I'd better get back to Raff." She breezed out of the kitchen and into the customer area.

"It's all set. Becca's fine with it. Now I just need to ask Emily, and here she comes."

"Well, here are your orders. Anything else? Oh, I forgot your coffees. Be right back."

She put both cups on the table.

"Emily, I have a question to ask you."

"Okay."

"How would you like to be a candlelighter in my wedding?"

"You really mean it?"

"Yes, I do. I would like you to, and you'll walk up with Becca."

"Oh, I'm so excited."

"But I need you to try on the dress and make sure it fits. Can you maybe do that tomorrow?"

"Sure. Becca won't mind."

"Good." Emily walked away, jumped in the air, kicked her heels, and yelled out, "Wahoo!"

They laughed.

"And just like that, problem solved, and you don't have to ask Jake now either."

"Good girl. She seems happy about it. Not having to ask Jake is probably a good thing too."

"Okay, let's get dinner eaten before we miss the movie."

When they finished dinner, they walked to the theater. They found their seats in short order and sat. Raff placed his arm around her shoulder and drew her closer to him.

Maddie spoke in his ear. "Raff, how about some popcorn and drinks?"

Expecting more like sweet nothings—whispered, Raff shook his head in astonishment. "Maddie, you just ate a huge dinner."

"I know, but once I smell popcorn, it's already too late. Besides, it's a movie, and I need movie food, remember? A huge bucket of popcorn with extra butter and some Milk Duds. Oh, and a 7UP. Got that, cowboy?"

"You're kidding, right?"

Raff stared at her, then rolled his eyes. "You're not kidding." He shook his head. *Unbelievable! That girl can eat.* He smiled.

Fifteen minutes later, Raff returned. "I'm back. Here you go, just what you ordered."

"Well, in my defense, I get hungry at movies. A girl must eat, you know."

They laughed.

"Maddie, I love you."

"I love you too. Oh, you should have seen Kathleen when I put my dress on today. She said it was the most beautiful dress she had ever seen, and I looked stunning in it. She said that you would probably faint."

"She did, did she?"

"Yep. Really, Raff, it is an amazing dress."

"You look beautiful in anything you wear." He kissed her on the cheek. "Quiet. The movie's starting."

An hour and a half later, they walked out of the theater with Maddie's eyes sparkling like dew on a fresh new morning. She obviously loved the movie.

"Well, what do you think? Did you like it?" Maddie inquired.

"I did. All the adventure scenes were great!"

"Yeah, a little scary at times, but the romantic parts were fun, although it wasn't like they dressed up and went dancing or anything."

"Nope, they were filthy. I think my favorite part was when the German ship was sunk accidentally. That was hilarious. Someday I'd like to see it again. I think it was excellent."

"Okay, Mayfield, I think I'm ready to head home. I'm beat."

"Yeah, me too."

They sauntered to the car, got in, and left.

"Maddie, scoot over here and let me put my arm around you. I want you much closer."

"Okay, I like that too." She rested her head on his shoulder and kissed him on the cheek.

"Honey, I can't wait until we get married. I hate having to take you home. I want you with me all the time."

"I know. Me too. But very soon, we can."

He dropped her off, gave her a very long, passionate kiss, and drove home—alone.

"Lord, I'm so tired of being alone. I can't wait for Maddie to be with me. Please give me patience because I'm losing mine, and I can't afford to. I love her so much. Thank you for your grace, strength, and love. Amen."

Chapter 19

March 1951
Atwood Residence

Hettie was in the process of preparing dinner when Kathleen straggled in. She looked pale and exhausted. She hung up her coat, took off her boots, and sat in her chair.

"Hi, Hettie. I think I'm going to take a little nap." She passed out.

Hettie didn't like seeing her that tired. It concerned her. She knew pregnant women were tired in the first few months, but this seemed extreme.

Franklin limped through the door, and Hettie shushed him right away. He took off his coat and boots and walked over to Hettie.

"She's sleepin'. Hardly got through the door before she sat down and was sleepin'. I don't like it, Frank. She's too tired."

"I know. It concerns me too. I hate seeing her look like she's run a twenty-six-mile marathon or something. Do you know what she did today?"

"Nope. Didn't even git to say hello before she was out cold."

Franklin shook his head. "Do you think I should take her into the bedroom or leave her there?"

"Leave her. Sleepin' good right now."

"Hettie, I wonder if I should take her to the doctor. I mean, is this normal, or does she need more rest? I'm worried. I want to make sure she's okay. Nothing's more important to me than she is," he spoke with furrowed brows.

"Don't know. I don't think she'd let you take her to Doc. She hates that."

"All I want to do is hold her and make sure everything is all right."

"Frankie," Kathleen said sleepily, "is that you?"

"Yes, my dearest. It's me." He went to her side. "How about you and I just go take a little nap—and I mean sleep?" He smiled.

"Oh, I'm fine Frankie, just a little tired." She offered, more than a little drowsy—almost like she was drugged.

"I insist." He picked her up in his arms, carried her into the bedroom, lay her on the bed, and covered her with a blanket. He lay down next to her and put his arm around her.

"I love you, my darling," he whispered.

She was already asleep. He got out of bed, kissed her on the cheek, and went into the kitchen to talk with Hettie.

"Hettie, I don't think this is normal. I'm scared."

Hettie put her arm around him. "If yer that worried, Frank, call Doc and see if he can come out and examine her."

"That's a good idea. I'll do that right now."

He dialed the phone and waited for it to ring. It rang six times before he answered.

"Doc Anderson."

"Doc, this is Franklin."

"Oh, hi, Franklin. It's good to hear from you. Everything okay?"

"I don't know. It's Kathy. She's extremely fatigued, and I'm worried about her. She barely sits down, and she's out cold. I know I'm probably overreacting, but honestly, I'm scared. Could you please come and see her?"

"Franklin, she's probably fine. You need to remember that she's older than most pregnant women, and it might take more of a toll on her, but if it'll make you feel better, I'd be glad to come and look at her."

"Oh, thank you, Doc. It *would* make me feel better."

"Okay, I'll probably be out in about half an hour."

FROM SHADOWS TO DAYBREAK

"Oh, thanks. She must be okay."

"I'll be right there. Goodbye, Franklin."

"Thanks, Doc. Bye." He hung up. "Doc's on his way right now. I just hope Kathy doesn't kill me."

"No, I think this was a good call."

"Thanks, Hettie. I'm so glad you're here."

"Me too, Frank. Me too."

Thirty minutes later, there was a knock on the door. Hettie hurried to the door. "Please come in, Doc. Thank ya so much for comin'."

"No problem. Where is she?"

"She's back here." Franklin showed him back to the bedroom, where Kathleen was lying sound asleep.

Doc sat on the bed and took her vitals. "Pulse is fine. Blood pressure's high—real high. I don't like that." Doc shook her a little. "Kathleen, wake up for me, okay? This is Doc Anderson. Can you wake up for me?"

Kathleen didn't stir.

"Franklin, come over here and talk to her."

"Kathleen, please wake up. It's Frank. I love you, sweetie. Please wake up. Doc, what's wrong with her?"

"I'm not sure, but it's imperative that she wakes up."

"Kathleen, please wake up for me. Please." Franklin shook her. She didn't move.

"Franklin, we need to get her to the hospital immediately. I can't do anything for her here, and she needs medical attention that only the hospital can give her."

"What's wrong with her? Is she going to die? I can't lose her. Doc, please do something."

"Let's get her out to the truck, and I'll follow you to the hospital. She just may need mandatory rest. We'll know more in a few minutes, but you need to stay calm. She needs you to be calm and collected."

"Okay, I'll try." Franklin put her in the truck and put her head close to him so he could talk to her and try to awaken her. He started the truck and sped all the way to the hospital.

He pulled into the parking lot, opened her door, and lifted her into his arms. Closing the door behind him, he hurried into the emergency department.

"Please, help me. It's my wife. I can't wake her. Doc Anderson should be here in a minute. He's right behind me." Franklin's raised voice drew everyone's attention.

"Sir, how long has she been out?"

"I thought she was just sleeping, so I don't know for sure. She looked so tired and it worried me. She's two months pregnant. Please help her."

Doc walked into the hospital and told the emergency doctor what he'd found. His fear was a miscarriage, although he didn't see any blood. Her blood pressure was high—way too high.

The doctor began an exam immediately, and the nurse told Franklin to fill out all the hospital forms, including insurance. They took her clothes off, tied a hospital gown around her neck, and placed her in a bed. Franklin followed her instructions. He couldn't sit still one more minute. He paced down the hall and back. Doc Anderson stayed with the emergency doctor, so he knew they were taking care of her, but that didn't ease Franklin's fears at all.

"Nurse, what's going on? They've been in there for over a half hour, and I haven't heard a word," Franklin declared, more frightened and excited than even he expected.

"Mr. Atwood, that's not unusual at all. They will come out and talk to you as soon as they identify the problem. You must be patient," she said, in what Franklin thought was a condescending tone.

"Patient. That's my wife and baby in there. I love her. I love them. Please, find out what's going on!" He felt helpless. Fear crept in and covered him like a blanket.

"Mr. Atwood, as I said before, you must calm down. The doctors will be out as soon as they know something. You need to sit in the waiting room down the hall. There's reading material there."

"Reading material." He took a deep breath. "Okay, I'll try, but as soon as you know something, will you come and tell me?"

"The doctors will talk to you directly. Just stay calm. Your wife will need you to be calm and steady. Not nervous and upset."

FROM SHADOWS TO DAYBREAK

He took a deep breath and breathed out slowly. "Yes, you're probably right." He rubbed the back of his neck. "Is there a chapel here?"

"There is. It's on the second floor."

"Will you tell them that if I'm not in the waiting room, I'll be up there?"

"I will, Mr. Atwood."

"Thanks." Franklin took the elevator and found the chapel. A large, darkly stained cross stood in the center front. Created from a roughly hewn log, it brought to memory some pictures he had seen of crucifixions. The windows contained stained-glass pictures, and there were ten short pews, five on each side, for comfort and prayer. There were candles available for lighting. The walls were painted a very light blue, and there were quiet hymns playing through the sound system. Franklin sat on the front pew.

"Dear, Lord Jesus, I don't even know what to pray. I'm so scared. Please don't take her. I'm not ready to lose her. I can't live without her. She's carrying our baby. She's everything to me. I've never been happier. You brought us together. I can't believe you would take her from me so soon. Please, God. Please." He wept. "Please, God, bring her back to me. Please?"

He stayed, still unable to move. There was nothing left to say, but he didn't want to leave the chapel. Somehow it made him feel closer to God. He listened to the music: *"All to Jesus I surrender, All to him I freely give."*

It was one of his favorites, but could he do that now—when it might mean she could be gone? Surrender all? Would God ask him to do that? Lose Kathy? Lose their baby? Let her go? He didn't know how. Why would God take her? *You don't need her as much as I do.* He thought, resenting the loss already.

Tears streamed down his face unheeded. He pleaded aloud, "God, no. I can't. I can't give her up. Please don't ask me to. Please let her stay with me. I can't do this. I love her more than my own life."

I gave my Son's life for you, Franklin—because I love you so much. Will you surrender your wife and son to me?

Franklin looked around. He saw no one, but he knew he heard those words, even though they were whispered. He didn't move. He barely breathed. He ruminated if those words were spoken by God. Maybe he was just imagining it because he was so distraught. It couldn't be, but somewhere in his heart he knew they were, and he asked the impossible. He couldn't. He wouldn't!

"Dear God," he said aloud, "what you're asking me to do is impossible. I can't."

My son, I'm here.

There—that same voice.

Franklin shook his head. "No. No. Don't make me do this," he pleaded.

Nothing. No voice. "I Surrender All" was still playing. *That song should have changed minutes ago,* he groaned, irritated.

Franklin spoke aloud. "God, answer me. I can't do this. You understand. You know how much she means to me." He waited. No voice. Just the music. "Someone change that song!" He cried, angrily. He stared at the cross. "I understand what you're saying. I do. But…"

Franklin stared at the cross.

Then he studied the stained-glass windows—so many pictures of Jesus ministering to those in need. Pictures of the disciples with Jesus. The cross pictures fascinated him. Those down around the cross were few, but one was Mary, his mother. For a mother to watch her son die such a painful death, must have been like a knife in her heart and sensing the life-blood streaming from her own body. She had to be emotionally tormented by the tremendous load of grief she carried. Did she know God's holy wrath poured out on Jesus, his perfect Son, had been required for our sin? Did she know he was God wrapped in flesh? Did she know he would rise again in victory over the grave? Did she know she would be with him again someday? He did tell people, but most didn't understand him. In fact, when the women came to tell the disciples Jesus had risen, they had locked themselves away in fear and didn't believe them.

I'm so tired, Lord. I don't want to fight with you. Those who do often regret it. Why do you need her? Why? God, I love her more than I ever thought I could. She needs me too. She needs me to take care of

FROM SHADOWS TO DAYBREAK

her, protect her, and love her. I do that, Lord. Let me do that. Franklin beseeched God.

At last, Franklin stopped talking. He said everything he could say, and still God was not relenting. He just stared at the cross for another fifteen minutes. No words came. Drained, but feeling like it wasn't over, Franklin didn't know what else to say.

"I'll give my own life instead." *That sounds reasonable, doesn't it?* One last try. "Please? Will you please take my life instead? Leave my wife to raise our son. Please." He took a deep breath and sighed. He dropped his head in his hands. "How do I do this? I can say it, but I don't think I can ever mean it. So how do I mean it? How? It's going to hurt so much. Will the pain ever go away?"

I'd like to see our son before he dies. Can I please see him? My son. Lord, let me see him before you take him. He's my only son. The only one I will ever have, he argued. Then he stopped. *It was your only Son too.* He raked his hand through his hair and closed his eyes. That stupid song was still playing! *I'm beginning to hate that song,* he clenched his teeth. He sat on the pew for another few minutes. He held his head in his hands. He sighed and spoke aloud.

"Okay. Okay. I give up. I don't like it. In fact, I hate it! But I give them to you." Franklin uttered, resigned to offer his family to God.

My son, I will never leave you or forsake you.

There it was again—that voice. *He won't leave me. He can get me through this.* "It will be the hardest thing I've ever had to do, God, but I give them into your hands. I know I will see them again." He finally finished bargaining with God.

Suddenly, through all the tears, there came a peace he was surprised to feel—a peace he knew hadn't been manufactured by himself. God was with him here, in this room, at this moment. He had peace. He would take the peace and make it through. God promised he would not leave him. The peace that passes all understanding only comes from God. He stood and noticed the song had changed. He even knew the words:

Peace, peace, wonderful peace,
Coming down from the Father above;

Sweep over my spirit forever, I pray,
In fathomless billows of love.

The song held the answer. Perfect peace could only come from his heavenly Father. He smiled. *He always knows exactly what I need and when I need it,* he grasped the truth and held on tightly to it. "Thank you, Father." Limping out of the chapel, he rode the elevator downstairs. At this point, walking seemed like an unnecessary expense of energy he no longer possessed. He braced himself for what might be coming. Doc strode toward him.

"Franklin. Let's go sit down. We need to talk." He took a deep breath. "I'm afraid the news isn't good."

"Just tell me, Doc. I'm braced for it."

"Well, she will need to stay in the hospital for complete rest for several days. We must bring her blood pressure down. That concerns me, but you should take her home in four or five days…if all goes well and she does what I tell her to—namely staying in bed."

"That's great news! She's not dying?"

"Goodness, no. She's anemic so we're giving her iron intravenously, and we're giving her a blood transfusion to bolster her red blood cells. She needs to stay off her feet for a while, and honestly, I can't trust her to do that at home, so I'm insisting that she stay here. Her blood pressure is the most concerning. It's imperative that it comes down and quickly. Now if you want to, we can bring in a bed and you can stay with her…"

Franklin was already halfway down the hall. The nurse called out the room number, and he arrived there before Doc finished his sentence.

"Kathy."

Drowsy, she whispered softly, "Hi, Frankie."

He sat on the bed close to her careful not to disturb her wrist, where she lay connected to the IV. "Oh, my darling, how do you feel?"

"Just tired, I guess."

"Frankie, you look terrible."

"Gee thanks, my dearest." He smiled weakly.

"You okay?"

FROM SHADOWS TO DAYBREAK

"I'm fine, just worried about you. Do you know what happened?"

"No, the last thing I remember, is you picking me up. I don't remember anything else until I woke up here."

"Oh, Kathleen."

"Kathy."

"Whatever." They lightly chuckled, neither having a lot of energy to expend.

"Doc said they could bring in a bed so I could sleep in your room with you, so that's what I'm doing. I'm not letting you out of my sight."

"Frankie, will you please lie down next to me and hold me?"

"I would love to." He lay down beside her and carefully took her in his arms. "I love you so much, my darling."

"Oh, Frankie, I love you too. I'm so sorry I worried you. I didn't mean to."

"Kathy, please don't worry about me. I'm so relieved that you're okay. You have no idea just how relieved I am. Doc said you need to stay here for a few days and rest. *Rest*, Kathy. Please do what they say."

"I will. I promise. They don't know for sure what happened, but they think I've been doing too much, and my blood pressure is too high. They think part of it is because I'm an old lady." She giggled.

"Nonsense. You're not old," he added, smiling. "You're mature."

"That's not a whole lot better, you know."

He smiled. "I don't care how old you are. You will always be the most beautiful woman in the world to me," he kissed her cheek. He tenderly pulled her hair off her cheek and tucked it behind her ear. She looked so tired and fragile. He hurt for her. "Kathy, I need to call Hettie and give her an update. She'll be worried."

"Yes, please do. I think there's a phone over there by the window."

He found the phone and dialed. It rang three times before Hettie picked up.

"Atwood residence."

"Hettie, it's Franklin. Kathy is doing well. They are concerned about her high blood pressure, and she's anemic, so they're treating her with iron and a blood transfusion to raise her red blood cell count. Doc is going to keep her here for a few days to get the rest

89

she needs. I'm spending the night here with her. I'll call you if I hear anything else. And, Hettie, please keep praying. I know you were."

"Ya, Frank, I surely was. I felt God's call, and I was on my knees prayin' for both of ya."

"Believe me, I felt it. Thank you. I'll talk to you tomorrow."

"Okay, Frank, thanks for callin'." She hung up.

Frank put down the phone and lay down by Kathleen again. She had fallen asleep. He caressed her hair, ran his hand over her face, and kissed her cheek. He didn't want to leave her side. He took her hand and kissed it. *Oh, God, thank you so much for saving Kathy and my son. I love you, Father. I'm so very grateful for your love and to know that you will never leave me. I know I heard you today. Thank you. Thank you for everything. Amen.* He prayed silently.

Franklin bent down and whispered in her ear, "Kathy, I am right. We're having a boy."

Chapter 20

March 1951
Mayfield Residence

Having completed the painting in the bathroom, Raff thought he might be able to start on the small bathroom upstairs. If he finished it, the only room left to paint other than the kitchen would be their bedroom. Certain he could knock out the bathroom in about an hour, he grabbed the paint and headed upstairs.

With the bathroom completed, he examined the flooring and believed they should probably replace it too. So three floors in all—both bathrooms and the kitchen. All three rooms were fairly small, so it shouldn't be too costly. He cleaned up and went back downstairs.

He was drying his hands when he heard a knock on the door. He used the towel and walked to the door. Opening it, he discovered Maddie on the other side.

"Hey, what are you doing here? I thought I was seeing you tomorrow night...not that I mind."

"I just missed you, Mayfield. Are you going to let me in?"

"Of course. Come here, my sweet." Maddie sauntered over to him, and Raff took her in his arms and kissed her.

"Hmm, I needed that, Mayfield."

"There's more where that came from."

"Good, but first, I have a proposition for you."

"Hmm. Sounds shocking. I kind of like shocking." He grinned, flirting.

"Oh, you have no idea, cowboy."

They laughed.

"No, it's late, and I just wondered if you'd eaten yet because I haven't, and I'm starving. I wanted to know if maybe we could go out to dinner."

"I would like that. I haven't eaten either. I want to show you something first. Come and look at the bathroom."

"Oh, Raff, it's so beautiful. It's our bathroom. I can't believe we get to live together in this house. I'm so excited."

"Me too, babe, but there's more. Follow me upstairs. He guided her into the other bathroom. What do you think?"

"I love it. It's charming. The colors we chose are perfect. There's not that much left to do, is there? I mean, just the kitchen and our bedroom, right?"

"That's right. I hired some of Franklin's guys to do the countertop, so we just need to do the painting, unless you want to add wallpaper or something."

"I hadn't thought about it. Maybe it's something we could do down the road when I have time to look for it."

"Okay. Then the two bathroom floors and the kitchen floor, and we're done! Really done."

"I can't wait. It looks so amazing. Coming back from our honeymoon and walking upstairs to our bedroom will be wonderful. The two of us in our own home and then being able to go to bed together."

"Yes, it will. Maddie, I love you. I'm counting the days when my dream of being with you comes true. It's so hard waiting."

"I know, but right now, you're going to feed me, Mayfield. Let's go."

"Maddie, do you ever think of anything but your stomach?"

"Not this time of night. Get moving, cowboy."

"Yes, ma'am," he declared while he tipped his pretend cowboy hat, and ran down the steps to the car with Maddie right behind. "I suppose you already know what you want to eat."

FROM SHADOWS TO DAYBREAK

"Of course. The sooner we order, the sooner we eat. Figure it out, Mayfield. We have the menu memorized, for goodness' sake. Or at least, you should."

"Fine. I'll think about it on the way there."

"Hey, I heard that Kathleen is in the hospital. We should probably visit her maybe tomorrow evening," Raff suggested.

"Kathleen's in the hospital? What for?"

"I'm not sure, but she's supposed to be there a few days, and you knew Mr. Strattford is in the hospital too."

"My goodness, what in the world? Kathleen and I were just together a couple of days ago when we were working on the wedding. She said she was tired, but I figured it was just because she's pregnant."

"She's what?"

"I guess I forgot to tell you. Yep, they're having a baby and are both on cloud nine. Kathleen said the way Franklin's taking care of her is funny. He's continually making sure she's okay and jumping up all the time trying to do things for her. She hardly needs to get out of her chair. It's very sweet."

"Yeah, I bet it was a bit of a surprise."

"Shock, really."

"I can understand that."

After a few seconds, Maddie turned toward him and asked, "Raff, when would you like to have kids?"

"Well, not for a while. I want to have you all to myself. I don't want to share you with a child right away. I just want you. I want to love you."

"That's okay. I want to be with you too, but I don't want to wait too long. I want to have a family with you, Raff. I want kids—your kids."

"Maddie, scoot over here and sit next to me. Let me put my arm around you. I love you. I want to have a family too. I do...but not right away. We need some time to be together. Some private time to...love each other. You understand, don't you?"

"Of course, I do. I guess you're right. We could use some time to get used to living together and enjoying each other. I can see that. It would give us time to make a foundation for our marriage, so when we are ready to have kids, it won't be a question, right? We'll be ready for that extra person in our family."

"That's right. I want to see little Maddies running around someday, but not right away."

They reached The Café and Rebecca seated them.

Raff took Maddie's hand, laced his fingers through hers, and kissed her hand.

"I wish I could tell you what you mean to me. I can't imagine my life without you in it. I promise you; we will have a family, and we'll be great parents."

Maddie smiled. "I know. Right now, I just want to get married and take that fantastic honeymoon you have planned. I have dreams about us—having you with me always. Just the two of us away from the world, together the way we've wanted. That's what I'm looking forward to."

"Me too. I wish we could elope and go directly to the honeymoon, but we still live in the real world and have just a few more weeks before all that can happen. I can't wait." He kissed her hand again.

"Mayfield, will you marry me?"

"Not a soul on earth can stop me. Marrying you will be the happiest day of my life—seeing you in that beautiful dress you'll be wearing, kissing you at the end of the wedding, taking you from the church to that hotel, and being with you completely. Oh yes, I will marry you, Maddie Henderson, and I promise you it will be a day we will never forget!"

Chapter 21

March 1951
General Hospital

Exhausted, Franklin's leg was fiercely aching. He'd lost his leg from below the knee when he stepped on a land mine during World War II in the South Pacific. He wore a prosthetic, but it had been cumbersome and almost archaic. They hadn't progressed much since the war. Only a wooden stump attached by leather straps and wires being all there had been to the construction. In some cases, you could add a wooden shoe, but he decided to leave well enough alone. He'd been holding out for something that would be more aesthetically pleasing, but no one knew how long that would take.

Sometimes the pain had been dreadful. He walked with a limp and he hated that. It made him feel exposed and vulnerable. But physically, he was a tall, strong man with a muscular chest, arms that were well-developed and attractive, and a slim waist. Beautiful brown eyes, a gorgeous head of chestnut, and wavy hair with a strong jaw, made him extremely handsome, and were features that were desirable to most women. He was quite a catch at forty-two, but most didn't pay too much attention once they saw his leg. Kathleen had been different. She didn't care.

This, his second marriage, since Pearl had died three years ago. He had loved her and missed her, but the way he felt about Kathleen was significantly different. He almost couldn't breathe without her.

They had only been married since Christmas Eve, so they were much like young lovers with all the happiness and fun young lovers experience. Although there had been a feeling with these two, it would never change. Their love was one for the ages.

Even though fatigue had overwhelmed him before he lay on his bed in Kathleen's room, he knew he should check on Miles. It wasn't too late yet, and maybe there had been some improvement.

He knocked on Miles's door. Since only silence came from inside, he turned and initiated his walk back when Miles asked him to come in.

"Miles, how are you doing?"

"Well, I'm still sleeping a lot, so the days go by quickly. My only concern now is that I could lose my job because I don't know how long I'm going to be off work. I was in the middle of a deal to buy the drugstore, but I don't know if I can swing that and be off work at the same time. The timing of this is not good."

"Miles, I'm so sorry. Is there anything I can do?"

"I don't know what that might be. I guess I need to talk to the broker and see if I can hold him off for a while, but if I try to talk to him and fall asleep, that's not a good impression."

"No, it's not. Maybe I could sit in on a meeting with you. Find out if he would come here, and I could help fill in the blanks if you think that would help."

"I couldn't ask you to do that."

"You didn't. I volunteered."

"Okay, I'll see if I can set something up. Thank you, Franklin. I don't know how to ever repay your kindness."

"It's no problem. I need to be here anyway. Kathy's here on mandatory bed rest. She'll be here a few days, and I won't leave her unless it's just long enough to shower and change clothes. Maybe to have one of Hettie's wonderful meals, knowing the reputation that hospital food has," he voiced, chuckling.

"Yes, I've heard about her cooking. She's known all over this town. I'm so sorry to hear about Kathleen. Is she going to be okay?"

"We haven't told anyone yet, but she's pregnant and the strain has been a little too much for her. Her blood pressure is way too high, and she just doesn't get enough rest, so Doc decided to admit her to keep an eye on her. I agree. She sure doesn't listen to me."

"Well, congratulations on your new little one coming. I'm very happy for you two. I know you've wanted a child for a long time."

"Yes, I have, and so has she. It was a shock at first, but now we're over the moon about it."

Miles chuckled. "I bet you are. Look, are you sure you want to take on anything else with Kathleen being here?"

"It won't take that long, and I'm right here if anything happens."

"Thank you. You have proven to be a good friend I can count on, and I'm so grateful."

"Well, that's what friends are for. So get some sleep, and I'll check in on you tomorrow."

"Thanks, Franklin."

"See you later," he spoke, while he turned and headed out the door. He considered going upstairs to talk to Lincoln, but he didn't think he had it in him tonight. He'd try tomorrow and see if he could get the kid to talk—be his friend, but not now. He just wanted to see Kathleen and go to bed.

Franklin hobbled back down the hall, his leg continuing to plague him, and stumbled into the room. Kathleen lay resting, and he could see that his bed had been set up. As much as it called to him, he knew how satisfying it would feel to lie next to Kathleen. He needed to hold her close—even for a short while. He sat on the bed and slid in next to her. He placed his arm around her, careful not to interfere with the IV. She felt so good. He loved how she felt next to his body. He savored that feeling and drank it in like cold water on a blistering, hot day. They fit together so well.

She opened her eyes and looked at him. "Frankie, I love you. Hold me please."

"My dearest, you can't keep me away. I'm supposed to sleep in the bed over there, but I don't think I can sleep without you anymore. You've spoiled me."

"Frankie, stay with me here. I don't want you to go. I need your arms around me."

"I don't think they'll let me, but I promise I will stay with you until you fall asleep, or they kick me out—whichever comes first. Is that okay?"

"I'll take what I can get. Just stay close to me." She snuggled into his body.

"I'm right here. I'm not going anywhere." He kissed her cheek.

Chapter 22

March 1951
General Hospital

The hospital staff had finally determined that they would lock Lincoln in a room so they wouldn't have to tie him down. Even after he had been locked in, Lincoln had already tried to escape. They had to be extra cautious he didn't skirt around them and run.

Lincoln, at length, relaxed and never attempted it again, but he hated that they had control over him. He had been used to living on his own, but after the beating he had been given, fear of working with them was worse than the fear of not working with them.

Now that he had made that deal, he knew if he tried to break it, they could kill him. The code of the street demanded nothing less, but if he did work for them, he wouldn't make enough to survive. *So what am I s'posed to do?* He had no answers. He tried not to let the fear consuming him conquer his indomitable spirit.

The first thing on the agenda: He had to escape, but how? He sure didn't get very far the last time he tried. He still didn't know how far he was from town and too afraid to ask because then they would know that he would try to leave again, and they weren't giving him any openings.

He fell asleep, and the nightmare began again.

Stealing the wallet, almost getting caught, and then believing he had been successful. After patting himself on the back, those bigger, mean boys stole it back and beat him till he couldn't breathe. The pain he felt while they kicked and punched him had been dreadful. It seemed like it lasted forever. He tried to scream, but no voice came. Terror seized his heart. *Where was Momma? Why didn't she help me?* He speculated. He couldn't remember anything except wanting a full belly and the warmth of a fireplace. Blackness blissfully covered him. He tossed and turned, and every time he moved, his body retaliated. *"What is wrong with me?"* He queried.

A nurse came in the door, closed it quietly, and locked it, not wanting to wake him. She took his vitals and everything looked good, except for messy bedding and a shivering body. She pulled up the blanket and tucked him in, turned and left, locking the door behind her.

In the morning, Franklin asked the nurse to open the door and lock it behind him. She advised him to knock on the door when ready to leave, and she would open it for him. Since Lincoln lay sleeping, Franklin sat and started to pray—silently.

*Dear Lord, I just pray for Lincoln here. This boy is so lost and has no one to care for him. Right now, he wants to be on his own. He's so young and fragile, and he's the only one who doesn't know it. Lord, please help me establish a relationship with him to help him somehow. Give me the words to say. Thank you again for saving Kathy and my son. I love you. Am*en.

Lincoln's eyes opened and he saw Franklin sitting next to the bed. "Who are you, and what are you doing in here?" he asked gruffly.

"Well, good morning," Franklin said cheerily. "My name is Franklin, and I've come to visit you. I'm the one who brought you in the last time. A friend found you face down in the dirt, out cold."

"So?"

"So I thought I'd come and see how you're doing."

"I'm fine. You can leave now."

"I could, but I'm not going to."

"How come?"

"Because I want to talk to you."

"Don't want to talk."

FROM SHADOWS TO DAYBREAK

"Okay, then just listen. I know you're on your own, and I also know that some kids beat you up pretty good. I'd just like to be your friend if you'll let me. I'm a nice guy, you know." He smiled.

"Big deal."

"It's a big deal to me. I have some friends, but there's always room for one more. You can learn a lot from a good friend, and there are always benefits."

"Yeah, what's that?"

"Depends on the friend."

"Don't need no more friends."

"Oh really? How many do you have?"

"'Nuff."

"Where were all your friends when you were left in the alley almost dead a few days ago?"

"Almost dead?" He turned and studied Franklin.

"Yep. That's what my friend who brought you in here told me. He couldn't wake you. He picked you up, carried you to his car, and drove you here. He's committed to paying your bill and has also been admitted here."

"What's he doing here?"

"He's sick and will be here for several days with a very long recovery. That's the only reason he hasn't been up here to visit you."

"He didn't have to do that."

"You're right, he didn't. That's why he's so special. He could have left you there and let you die, but he didn't."

"Just leave me alone. I'm tired."

"I told you I would like to be your friend. Are you interested?"

"I'll think about it."

"Okay. I'll be back soon."

"Why?"

"I told you because I don't give up easily, and I want to be your friend. So what do you say? Friends?" he asked, holding his hand out for Lincoln to shake.

"Maybe. I'll think on it." He turned away from Franklin.

"Okay, I'll see you later. Get some rest. You'll need it to heal," he commented, while he walked to the door and knocked.

The nurse came right away, unlocked the door, let him through, and locked it afterward. "Well, how'd it go?"

Franklin shook his head. "I'm not sure, but I'm not going to quit trying. This kid may be stubborn, but he needs someone. I'll be back, maybe tomorrow. Right now, I need to get back to Kathy."

"Okay, we'll see you later. Oh, how's she doing?"

"I guess alright. It's just hard to see her so tired and fragile. I mean, that girl is a spitfire. That's one of the many things I love about her. I just want her to be okay, you know?"

"I'm sure she will be, with enough rest. Don't worry, she knows you love her and that's worth a lot. You have no idea how many patients we get in here who have no one to visit them. It's sad."

"You mean like Lincoln?"

"Exactly."

Franklin turned and walked down the hall to the elevator to see Kathleen. She had awakened.

"Hi, my dearest. It's good to see you awake."

"Yeah, they just gave me a sponge bath."

"Oh, I'm sorry I missed that. Next time maybe I can give it to you, huh?"

Kathleen hit him on the shoulder.

"Ouch. Will you stop doing that?" He laughed.

"Nope. Not ever. A girl's gotta have something for defense."

"Oh, please." He rolled his eyes.

Kathleen laughed. With that irresistible little pout, she kissed him on the cheek, saying, "I love you, Frankie."

"There you go again, cheating, knowing I can't say no to you when you do that. So what do you want now, you malcontent?"

Laughing, Kathleen said, "I was hoping you could scare up a sandwich for me. I'm starving, and apparently, I slept through lunch."

"It's always something with you, isn't it?" he teased.

"That's right. So get moving."

"Okay, okay, I'll get right on it, General Atwood," he snapped to attention and saluted.

She laughed. He left, found a nurse, told her what to get for Kathleen, and then asked her if she could get something for him too.

102

FROM SHADOWS TO DAYBREAK

She said she'd make sure the kitchen would bring them something within a half hour or so. He thanked her and went back to the room. Kathleen had disappeared.

"Kathleen. Where are you?"

No answer. He looked in the bathroom, and she seemed extremely weak. He caught her just before she fell, swept her up in his arms, and placed her back in bed. Her face had become devoid of color.

"Kathy, what are you doing out of bed? You're not supposed to get up without someone with you. You could have gotten hurt. Please, Kathy, I'm begging you. Please wait for someone from now on."

Much to her chagrin, he called in a nurse to check on her and take her vitals.

"Mrs. Atwood, your blood pressure plummeted, which is why you became so weak. I'm surprised you didn't pass out altogether. You cannot get out of bed without at least one person to help you. We have got to get you stabilized. With your blood pressure unstable, it's very unpredictable. Please use your call button if your husband isn't here—even if he is. It's better to have someone here who can help you medically if you need it."

"I'm sorry, everyone. I just had to go, and no one was around. I didn't think I would be so weak."

"Really? Why on earth do you think you're in here? You're on mandatory bed rest.

Do you know what that means? You can't do that," he said, clearly annoyed, and sharper than he intended.

She sighed. "I'm sorry. I promise it won't happen again. Just please don't be mad at me," she pleaded, her eyes watering.

"I'm sorry. I'm just worried about you. I don't want anything to happen to you. Forgive me?" he asked.

The nurse checked her IV, warned her again about getting out of bed, and left the room. "I forgive you, but only if you kiss me, and I mean *really* kiss me. None of those kisses on the cheek types," she directed, with that pout.

"Oh, for goodness' sake." He rolled his eyes at her. "You're doing it again."

He took her in his arms and kissed her the way he had wanted to for hours.

"How's that? Mrs. Atwood?" he asked, grinning from ear to ear.

"Oh." She arched her brow and stuck out her lip. "It was okay, but not one of your best. I think you should do it again and try a little harder this time." She smiled, flirtatiously.

"You do, do you? Not sure I should. After all, you broke the rules. I think that kiss is all you should get until you learn to follow the rules, Mrs. Atwood."

"Mr. Atwood, I'm afraid I must insist. I am the general, and I believe you're just an enlisted soldier. Isn't that the situation?"

Laughing, Franklin said, "I think you lost your rank, private."

Kathleen, thoroughly enjoying the banter, pulled him close to her. She whispered, "Frankie, kiss me now. That's an order!"

He kissed her. "That's much better. You're dismissed!"

Franklin chuckled. The nurse walked in with their belated lunches, and Franklin sat up.

She quipped, "All right, you two, get a room."

Smiling, Kathleen said, "I do believe we already have one."

The nurse laughed. "I guess you got me there." She dropped the tray on the table and left. "Those two are crazy in love," she added, shaking her head while she left.

Chapter 23

Mid-March 1951
General Hospital

Franklin, sitting next to Lincoln waiting for him to awaken, had been praying for Kathy, Miles, and Lincoln. Then, the Lord nudged him to add Raff and Maddie, and he acknowledged their need for prayer as well. They still had weeks before their wedding, amid planning one and refurbishing their house. That's a lot to handle.

Lincoln stirred. "You're back. Thought I told you I don't want to be your friend."

"No, I believe you said you had enough friends, and then we decided that maybe you didn't. Turning down someone who wants to be your friend, that you can trust, would be just plain stupid, and I don't think you're stupid. In fact, I think you're a little too smart for your own good."

"How do I know I can trust you."

"You don't, but I'm telling you that you can. I will always tell you the truth, always care about you, and always be your friend. Now what do I have to do to prove it to you?"

"Don't know."

"Then come up with something because I would like to count you among my friends. I don't have many, but the ones I do have, I can count on 100 percent. That's what I'd like to do for you. Now what do you say?"

"I don't know. I guess it would be okay. How's that guy who's sick here in the hospital? Is he going to be, okay?"

"Why, do you want to know?"

"Just 'cuz."

"Because he cared about you enough to bring you here?"

"I s'pose," he said, playing with his hands.

"I just talked to him. He can't get out of bed, and he will be in bed for a very long time."

"Could I talk to him?" he asked with just a hint of gratitude.

"Well, you might be able to talk to him on the phone. I can talk to the nurse and see if we can set something up for you. I'm sure he would love to hear from you."

"Really? You think so?"

Nodding his head, assuring him, "I know so. Who knows, you might just make another friend you can trust—with your life."

"Friends?" Franklin held his hand out again for Lincoln to shake.

Lincoln thought for a few seconds and studied Franklin's face, then suspiciously replied, "I guess we can try and see if it works out," while he put his hand out and shook Franklin's.

Together, they said, "Friends."

Chapter 24

March 1951
General Hospital

"Doc Anderson to emergency. Incoming ambulance is two minutes out," blared the announcement over the PA system.

What, now? Doc shivered. His shift nearly over, he had been looking forward to going home, eating his usual PB&J then flopping into bed—except he just ran out of peanut butter! Drat! Well, toast and jam will have to do, but even the kind of energy he'd have to summon to accomplish that small task seemed long gone. He prayed this emergency would be simple and swift.

The ambulance pulled up to the doors which automatically swung open as the ambulance crew pushed the gurney forward toward the emergency room. Doc quickly caught up with them while they raced down the hall. "What have we got?"

"Female, thirty-eight years of age. Pain in the right lower quadrant. Fever a hundred three degrees, BP one sixty over ninety, pulse one hundred ten. Probably appendix, but you're the doctor, so she's all yours now. I'm just a nurse," retorted Brooke.

"Does she have a name?"

"Patricia Hammer—friends call her Pat," she says.

A sharp pain sliced through Pat's body like a knife, and she groaned, curling into a fetal position with her hands over the affected area.

Cheryl Fosnot Bingisser

"Miss Hammer, I'm Doc Anderson. I'm sorry that I need to do this, and I will warn you that this will hurt, but please try and stay calm, okay?"

She responded with a nod because talking seemed like more effort than she could muster since most of her energy had been wrung from her body in extreme pain.

Doc pressed down on the lower quadrant, and she squealed in agony.

"I'm so sorry, but I need to make sure of what is going on. Miss Hammer, I'm afraid you have acute appendicitis. We will need to prep you for immediate surgery to have them removed. I'll get the nurse to give you a little morphine so you can relax a little, and then the anesthesiologist will take it from there, okay?"

Filled with pain, she nodded again. Her deep, green eyes showed a depth of understanding he didn't usually see in emergency. She was stunning. Her face was pale and the way her wavy, long blonde hair fell shoulder length around her, with the appearance of silk, she imitated an angel—at least what his imagination believed an angel would appear like. His hand almost strayed to touch her hair, but he resisted. Her sweaty brow didn't detract from her porcelain skin, cute little button nose, or those full, pink lips. *Kissable lips.* He closed his eyes for a second to regain control of his senses. Everything within him longed to touch her. *What on earth is the matter with me?* He questioned.

"Miss Hammer, I promise you that this is a simple procedure and you'll be right as rain in no time. Try to relax, let the pain med take hold and I'll see you in a few minutes before surgery. Nurse, morphine stat," he called.

"On it, Doc," Kristine said, leaving the room.

Pat weakly replied, "Thank you," as sweat poured off her brow.

Several minutes later, Doc returned to her room for one final check before surgery.

Doc examined her. She seemed to be relaxed for the first time since he'd seen her. She looked at him dreamily and she slightly slurred her words as she spoke to him slowly and deliberately. "Are you an angel? You look sooo handsome." She smiled coyly, while her eyelashes fluttered.

Doc grinned. "No, I'm afraid heaven isn't ready for either of us just yet. I'm only your doctor that's tethered to the earth for a while longer. You seem to be feeling a little better since last I saw you." He chuckled.

"Oh yes, I *looove* you, guys!"

"Why, thank you, Miss Hammer. We're quite fond of you as well. I'll see you in surgery in a few minutes. In the meantime, just relax and get some rest. It'll all be over before you know it." Doc turned to leave.

"Goodbye, Doctor Angel," she whispered, waving to him as she floated off into Neverland.

Doc walked away chuckling. He couldn't say why, but his heart pulsated wildly. She was so beautiful! Like a china doll, he wanted to hold and protect. Why is she distracting me so? She's a patient—albeit a drop-dead-gorgeous one, but still a patient.

He checked on her again after surgery and she lay sleeping. Kristine reported she had been doing very well, so with his shift over, he walked through the doors to his car to head home. Driving home, he couldn't shake the beautiful woman from his thoughts. He smiled recalling her comment about him being an angel and so handsome. Oh, how wonderful it would be to have someone like her to love. Stop it! What did he have to look forward to tonight? Just another night in a cold house with toast and jam because he forgot to pick up his usual peanut butter. His fists clenched the steering wheel. Sharing his life with someone, he admitted, had become a dream he had given up on—until tonight. Is there still a glimmer of hope out there that it might still happen?

Feeling his heart open to that possibility, he knew instinctively just how dangerous and unachievable that dream would be. At the age of fifty, he again resolved to completely close himself off before his traitorous emotions did irreparable damage to his aching and lonely heart. Besides, he reasoned, he had no time for a relationship. He hardly had time to socialize with his friends, let alone nurture a loving relationship for a possible marriage.

Fine then! All settled! That's it, Sherman. Get your head on straight. "Now on to that toast and jam. I'll have to buy the peanut butter tomorrow morning," he muttered bitterly.

Chapter 25

Mid-March 1951
General Hospital

    Wanting to walk him a little way down the hall, the nurses helped Miles out of bed. Leaving in a few days, they needed him to be able to get himself to the bathroom and in and out of bed. Being very weak, they brought a walker in for him for a little more stability. He only walked a few yards before they had to take him back. They'd be back in a few hours to try again. They might even try physical therapy if this didn't work.

    Still sleeping more than he would like, his distaste for inactivity disturbed him. He wanted to get back to work and live a normal life, but according to Doc, he needed to release that notion altogether. He was thankful for Franklin's, Raff's, and Maddie's visits. It had been a bright spot in an otherwise, dull and boring day—except when he lay sleeping.

    Miles had talked to Lincoln on the phone a couple of times and hoped he might be getting somewhere, but he wished he could see him in person. Maybe he would try and see if a nurse could wheel him up there so he could talk to Lincoln. He wanted to have a relationship with the kid.

    He hated to think about what might happen to him when they released him from the hospital. Maybe he could do some research on foster families, and find him a family, so he wouldn't have to go back to the streets. Now if only he could stay awake long enough to do it.

But someone needs to do something, and he couldn't ask Franklin to get involved anymore with Kathleen being pregnant, and not in the best of health. No, Franklin needed to spend his time helping her. He couldn't ask Raff or Maddie. They had their own lives that were just beginning. Who else is there? And with those thoughts buzzing around in his head, he drifted off to sleep.

Chapter 26

Mid-March 1951
General Hospital

Kathleen had been napping when Franklin limped into the room. Exhausted, he had hoped he could lie next to her without waking her. He just wanted to feel her body next to his. Kathleen stirred when Franklin put his arm around her.

"Frankie?"

"Yes, my dearest."

"I missed you."

Franklin smiled. "You did not. You were asleep."

"I always miss you when I don't feel you next to me."

"Not nearly as much as I do. I could have crawled over there in that bed, but I needed to feel you close to me. I love you, Kathy."

"Oh, I love you so much. I miss us being together."

Franklin grinned. "My darling, so do I. I miss that too, very much, but you need to get better. You need rest and believe me, that is not resting."

Kathleen laughed. "Maybe not, but I still miss it. Will you kiss me?"

"You'd be pretty hard-pressed to stop me." He took her in his arms and kissed her, showing her just how much he loved her.

"Okay, you better rest now."

"Oh, come on. That's all I've been doing. Just kiss me."

"You know, we don't have a lock on the door, and there's only so many kisses I can dish out before we need one." He laughed.

She giggled. "I know. I feel like I did before we got married. Always doing the 'we can't' dance. How many days do I need to stay here before I can go home and sleep in my bed?"

"Patience, my dearest. I know that's not your strong suit."

"That's for sure." She laughed.

"You need to get your strength back. I can't go through that again. You scared me, and I was afraid I'd lost you. We can wait. I want you better."

"I'm sorry, Frank. I just want our lives back the way they were, you know?"

"I know. Once you're stronger, we can be semi-normal again, but you've got a ways to go before that happens. Maybe I should go home and let you rest. I'm probably pretty ripe and could use a shower."

"I can rest with you here, but if you would feel better being clean and smelling good, then I guess I can let you go. Though, you do know I love that aftershave you put on. It kind of drives me crazy," she said, flirting. "You may even have to kiss me a few more times."

"Kathy, you're flirting with me."

"You noticed. I can flirt with my husband, can't I? Can't do much else."

He chuckled. "Sorry, but that's the way it has to be until you get better, and we can go home. Now is there anything you want me to bring back for you? Maybe some of Hettie's cooking?"

"How about my robe and nightgown that I wore on our wedding night?" She pouted flirtatiously.

"Oh no, you don't. I could never handle that. Your robe and nightgown will stay at home in the closet until we're home. Got it, Mrs. Atwood?" He laughed.

"Chicken," she teased.

"Yep. I sure am." He responded with a chuckle.

"Okay, I'm going home and taking a cold shower. I promise I'll bring back something special from Hettie. Anything else I can do for you?"

"Yes, but you already said you won't do it, Mr. Atwood."

He laughed. "That's right. Now I'll be back in a few hours, and the only thing I want you to do is rest. Please, can you do that without me nagging you? And please stay in bed!"

"Not sure. What do I get in return? If I'm required to follow the rules, Mr. Atwood, I really think I deserve a reward. So what do I get out of it?" She giggled.

I'll tell you what you'll get if you don't follow the rules. How's that?"

"Oh, you're no fun at all."

"Good, boring means you'll get rest. Now turn over and get some sleep. I'll be back soon. Follow the rules, or you'll be in big trouble!"

"Really? What kind of trouble, Frankie?"

"I don't know yet, but I'll think of something while I'm gone. Now go to sleep. That's an order! You're not the only one who can hand out the orders, General Atwood."

Chapter 27

March 1951
Connors's Apartment

With Emily in bed for the night, Rebecca finally had time to herself. Not that she minded Emily's company, it's just sometimes she needed some time to read her Bible, pray, and think. There's not much time when you're running a restaurant to have any downtime. This is the time she tried to set aside for herself. It helped recharge her for the next day.

Tonight, however, she'd been having a hard time concentrating on anything. Memories were engulfing her, and she didn't know what had triggered them. When she couldn't seem to shut them down, and too tired to fight them, she decided she'd just go with them. She allowed them to wash over her like waves on a lake.

* * * * *

Her years in the rodeo with her father came into view. Fun and exciting at times, but mostly just setting up, taking down, practicing, and moving on to the next town. Her father had become the go-to guy for all emergencies, which left little or no time for her at all. Her dad taught her to shoot, and she loved that, and shooting in front of the crowds while so young had been exhilarating. She lived to enter-

FROM SHADOWS TO DAYBREAK

tain and loved hearing the roar of the crowd every time she hit the target. She ate it up.

As she got older, she had to do more trick shots—riding the horse backward or standing on the horse. So not only did she have to be a perfect shot, but she also had to be a trick rider, which usually took years to perfect. But not for Rebecca. She took to it like walking on a sidewalk, and the people loved it.

Her father seemed proud of her too, but never told her that. He watched her with a smile and a nod, but that had been about all she ever received from him. Her mother ran off with a neighbor years before, so she didn't even remember her. Nevertheless, she loved what she did and she considered herself powerful and confident. She knew she could tackle anything, which translated well into a strong and self-assured young woman—pretty much fearless. Not too many women possessed that quality, so she gave credit to her father for the opportunity the rodeo had given her.

He'd been helping with Rebecca's horse one day, in his stall, when a loud noise scared the horse, and he freaked—stomping her father to death. No one heard the screams, so in a matter of seconds, survival became an impossibility.

At only five years of age, Rebecca grieved deeply. The rodeo people cared for her and protected her, but it would never be the same as having her father around. She became unresponsive. She no longer sought the crowds or their roaring applause. The entertainer's heart died with her father. It just wasn't in her anymore. Their only option—finding a relative who would take her in and raise her. Reluctantly, when her grandparents came to pick her up, her rodeo family gave her to them. They were all there and hated to see her leave. They were a family, and they loved her so much. The loss of Rebecca would be with them for a long time.

She thrived with her grandparents, and Papa, as she called her grandfather, kept her shooting. He took her hunting with him and target shooting. It became almost like having a piece of her father with her.

School came easy like everything else did for her. She graduated from high school with honors and had been accepted into the

University of Colorado School of Business, with a full-ride scholarship. Everyone loved her, both students and faculty. No one ever had an unkind word about her. She treated everyone the same and, as a result, had so many friends that everyone on campus knew and admired her.

They loved her sense of humor and straightforwardness and knew her to be always truthful. Her confidence stood out among the women, and the young men were just a tad apprehensive around her. Most girls on campus were either forward and flirty or shy. She was an enigma. The men didn't know how to handle that kind of confidence in a woman. They were nice to her, but being her boyfriend was much too intimidating.

Until Brad. When Bradly Steven Crawford walked into her economics class, Rebecca's heart started beating like a drum, and her pulse quickened. Strikingly handsome, he had the deepest blue eyes she had ever seen. You could see the ocean in them, for goodness' sake. He had blond hair, parted on one side and combed back in a fetching wave. His deep bass, velvet-smooth voice soothed her very soul. She loved it when he had a report to give in front of the class. She didn't hear any real words, but she loved the sound of his voice. Kindness and respect were his evident traits to the faculty and all the staff. The students, especially the women, were in love with him—all of them, or so it seemed. And why not? Perfection was difficult to find—if not impossible. She couldn't think of one negative thing about him. But there were so many girls wrestling for his attention that she knew that a relationship of any kind with him absurd.

Eating her lunch outside on a bench near the front entrance, Brad sat down beside her. Shocked, she almost dropped her lunch on the ground.

"Is this seat taken, Rebecca?"

Her jaw dropped, her eyes were as big as silver dollars, and she was dumbfounded. No words escaped her lips, but she nodded when she finally came to her senses.

He laughed at her awkwardness but not in a negative way. He thought it kind of cute, and had been quite taken with her. Maybe

FROM SHADOWS TO DAYBREAK

because she seemed about the only girl on campus who didn't target him.

Beautiful, with long, blond hair that curled on the ends, and gorgeous green eyes which reminded him a lot of the beautiful greens he'd seen in Ireland. He knew her to be smart, and he liked intelligent girls. He had grades that were comparable to Rebecca's, so they had that in common. Dressed impeccably at all times because he'd grown up in wealth, and "the clothes made the man," his mother drummed those words into his head at least a thousand times.

His mother focused on social standing and status. Not much else interested her. It had always been about the next big social event and what new, formal dress she could buy. The whole county would be talking about her the next day. She would customarily be in the newspaper—sometimes complete with a picture, which she hoped would be the case.

"Call me Becca, my friends all do."

"Okay, Becca. I wondered how you'd feel about having coffee with me sometime," he said, with that irresistible smile that reached all the way to his eyes.

"A…a…what?" *He is way out of my league*, she already acknowledged that truth.

"Would you like to have coffee with me sometime?" he repeated.

Still stunned, she tried to make sense of what he'd just said. She hadn't stopped staring since he'd sat beside her.

"Becca, is that a yes, or no?"

"Ah…yes," she answered, in surprise.

"Okay, how does tomorrow sound right after economics?" he asked, rather amused by her response.

"Fine…fine. I think it's—"

"Fine?"

"Yeah. That."

"You sure are a woman of few words," he said, with a smile.

"Not usually, it's just you surprised me a little."

"Oh. Well, maybe there are more surprises to come. So may I walk you over to the coffee shop after class?"

"Yeah, sure. I think I'd like that."

"Okay, Becca, I'll see you in class. Take care. I gotta run." He walked off leaving her with a look of astonishment on her face, which he recognized as the cutest thing ever.

"Yeah, you too."

What did I just do? I didn't have one intelligent word to say to him. What makes me think I can carry on a real conversation with him? she asked herself. *I wish I hadn't done that. He's going to be bored stiff.*

Captivated by her beauty, and her inability to converse, he couldn't wait to spend more time with her. He smiled while he thought about how awkward she seemed, and it amused him greatly, but, oh, so endearing. He was looking forward to seeing her tomorrow and hoped this to be the beginning of a lasting relationship.

Chapter 28

Mid-March 1951
General Hospital

Franklin and Kathleen were both asleep on the hospital bed when a knock on the door awakened him. Franklin rose to open it.

Emily and Rebecca walked in.

"Hey, it's good to see you," Franklin said.

Rebecca whispered, "How is she?"

"She's fine. Just weak and tired. She's been in here longer than we thought she would be, but I'm hoping to take her home in the next few days. Doc just doesn't trust her to stay off her feet at home, so they keep her here. We're both getting tired of it, and Hettie and I will keep an eye on her when she's home."

"Kathleen, darling, you have some visitors."

Kathleen turned over. "Oh, Becca and Emily. You don't have any idea how good it is to see you two. I've missed you so much," Her hands went up to her hair. "Oh, I must look a fright. I haven't even looked in a mirror for a while. I must look dreadful."

"Nonsense. You couldn't look awful even if you rolled in the mud."

"No mud. I get sponge baths."

They laughed.

"Well, we've been missing you too. How are you feeling?" asked Rebecca.

Cheryl Fosnot Bingisser

"Like I want to get out of here. I'm tired of the hospital and hospital food. I miss Hettie's cooking, and I want to sleep in my bed again. Plus, anyone who tells you that you get a lot of rest in the hospital is a liar. Nurses in and out fifty times a day, taking your vitals and talking with you to make sure you're still kicking—very little rest. Then the doctors make their rounds. Okay, I'm exaggerating a little. I'm just homesick."

They all laughed.

"We just saw Raff and Maddie visit with Mr. Strattford, so I think they might be by in a couple of minutes. We've all been worried about you," Rebecca sympathetically said.

"Hey, honey, I think I'll go to Miles's room and stay there with Raff, and then Maddie can come and talk girl stuff with you two. This is the last place I want to be. Way too much estrogen in here for me," he made a goofy face and headed toward the door.

The girls all laughed.

"I'll send Maddie down." Franklin crossed back over to Kathleen and kissed her on the cheek, whispering, "Don't get overtired now, okay? I love you."

"Frank, you worry too much."

He gave her a raised brow with a warning look. She nodded and smiled.

Just a couple of minutes later, Maddie walked in. All of them were so excited to be together again. It had been way too long.

Kathleen was overjoyed to see them. "Maddie, any new plans for the wedding? I'm sorry I've been AWOL."

"Think nothing of it. The guest list is written and sent out. All the flowers are ordered. We're going to use lilacs and yellow roses, even if they have to get them from another part of the country. So the big arrangements up front will be full baskets of those flowers and other purple and yellow flowers. I ordered yellow rose wrist corsages for you two, and Kathleen, you have a beautiful, yellow—and purple—rose, cascading arrangement, with some baby's breath and leaves. Should be gorgeous. I have the same roses with some lilacs, that come halfway down my dress. Might throw in some stephanotis too, which would be amazing with the purple and yellow."

FROM SHADOWS TO DAYBREAK

"Wow! I can't wait to see it. It's going to be a showstopper," announced Rebecca.

"Thank you so much, Maddie, for including me in your wedding. It means so much to me. I've never been in a wedding before. I have the dress now and I can't wait to wear it. I love it!" exclaimed Emily. "But the only flowers I recognize are the lilacs and roses. Can't wait to see what they all look like together."

Kathleen chimed in. "I think this wedding will be absolutely stunning! Wait until you see Maddie's dress. Beautiful doesn't begin to do it justice. I have never seen a wedding dress close to this one. It's gorgeous, and she is amazing in it. It's quite something."

"I do feel wonderful in it. Like a princess. But between you and me, I just want to get on with it and get to the honeymoon."

The girls laughed. Kathleen added, "Believe me, I understand that tug-of-war. Frank and I fought those feelings for a short time. But as hard as might be, I will say, the reward is definitely worth it. God honors it, Maddie. You will be glad you waited."

"I know, and I am looking forward to it. Thankfully, keeping busy has helped. Now it's only a little over a month away. We're still working on the house, but it's almost done. I can't wait until Raff doesn't have to take me home anymore and all we have to do is go upstairs to our bedroom."

"So what's going on with you, Emily?" Kathleen inquired, wanting to change the subject.

"Well, you'll be surprised to hear that I enrolled in school and will start on Monday. I have two years before I can graduate, but the teacher said that if my test scores are good, she might be able to advance me."

"Isn't that great?" asked Rebecca. "I'm so proud of her. She's doing so well and look how beautiful she's become. She's turned into quite the young lady."

"Yes, she has." Both Maddie and Kathleen nodded in agreement.

"We're certainly proud of you, Emily. You look lovely, and I'm glad you're motivated to go back to school and get your diploma. That's great," Kathleen added.

123

Cheryl Fosnot Bingisser

Rebecca took a closer look at Kathleen. Her face was pale, and there were bags under her eyes. She appeared weary and drawn.

"So is there anything I can get for you, like eggs sunny side up or something?"

"Becca, you're terrible!" exclaimed Kathleen.

They laughed.

"I know, but it's so much fun. It's not nearly as bad as chili and pastrami, is it?"

Kathleen swallowed. "Okay, you brat. Stop it this minute!"

They laughed again.

"What's going on in here? We can hear the ruckus clear up and down the hall," teased Franklin.

"It's always like this when we get together. Rebecca declared.

"She's right," added Kathleen. "I have the best friends in the world and feel so very blessed. And we're multigenerational. You don't see that very often. We all learn from each other, and it's remarkable."

"Yeah, I'm kind of jealous of you ladies. I've never had close friends, although I'm becoming close with Miles and Raff, and if I can, I'm trying to forge a relationship with young Lincoln. He isn't making it easy, though," Franklin declared, shaking his head.

"Isn't he the street kid I heard about? Didn't he get beat up or something?" Emily queried.

"Yep, and he's right upstairs. He'll be here a while. I'm trying to get to him before they let him out of here because after that, who knows what will happen to him." Franklin snapped his fingers. "Oh no! I promised him that I'd have a nurse set up a phone call between him and Miles. He wants to talk to him because he knows Miles brought him in and he would have died if he hadn't. I think he's feeling a bit grateful, so I need to see this through. I'll be right back."

Franklin went to the nurses' station and told her the situation. She knew there was a way. The next time he visited Lincoln, he would be able to tell him that they could hook up the phone to Miles's room, which should make things easier for Miles too.

Walking back to Kathleen's room, Rebecca, Emily, and Maddie were just coming out.

124

FROM SHADOWS TO DAYBREAK

"Hey, thanks guys for coming. It was a real treat for her. She misses you."

Rebecca studied him before she proceeded with the question. "It was good to see her too. Do you honestly think she's getting better?"

"I do. You should have seen her when we brought her in. I thought I had lost her. She'd been out for quite a while and no one knew what was wrong with her. I had Doc come to the house and she wouldn't wake up. It was terrifying, and I thought she was going to die. It was an awful night." He shook his head.

"I'm so sorry, Franklin," said Maddie, sympathetically. "It must have been a nightmare."

"It was. I did a lot of praying. I don't even want to think about it because I never want to go through that again."

Rebecca added, "I'm sure. I'm so sorry Franklin, I love her too, and I can't imagine not having her around. She's such a joy and a great friend."

"I'll tell her you said that. She's like that with everyone—even me. I think we're best friends besides being husband and wife. I can't tell you how much I love her. When she's not with me, I miss her." He nervously chuckled. "I guess that doesn't sound very masculine, but that's the kind of love we have for one another. I am so grateful and blessed beyond belief."

"You know, that's how I want Raff to love me. I know how I feel when I'm not with him. It's so difficult."

"Maddie, I've seen him when he's not with you. There's no doubt in my mind that He loves you and can't wait to be with you permanently. We even talked about it tonight. He does love you like that. No need to worry."

"Thanks, Franklin. That's so good to hear from someone who's a little on the outside. It means a lot."

"No problem. You can talk to me anytime. Kathleen too. She loves you. You have a wise woman for a friend."

"I know, and I don't take it for granted. Well, I better get back to Raff. See ya later."

She left, and Franklin walked back into Kathleen's room. She had fallen asleep. He considered getting into the bed they brought in for him, but he just couldn't do it. He wanted to be next to Kathleen. He climbed onto the bed and lay next to her.

Whispering, she said, "Frankie, I love you."

"Kathy, I love you so much. I'm staying right here next to you. Can you go back to sleep?"

"I don't want to sleep. I want to love you."

"Mrs. Atwood, nothing would make me happier, but you need your strength. I promise when we do get together, it will have been worth the wait. We'll get your wedding night robe and nightgown down and—"

"Promise?"

"I promise, then Hettie will have more fodder to tease us with."

They chuckled.

Chapter 29

Mid-March
Atwood Residence

Hettie was working around the house when the phone rang. "Atwood residence."

"Hi, Hettie. I just wanted to give you an update on Kathleen. You know, my daily check-in."

"Yeah, Frank. I know. How's she doin'? I miss her."

"You know, Hettie, I could come and pick you up so you can visit with her if you want. I wouldn't mind."

"That's way too much trouble."

"It is not. Besides, I know she misses you something awful. She would love to see you. I don't know why I didn't think of it before. Although, she's only going to be here another few days."

"I can wait, Frank. It's no big deal. Besides, then I can figure out what I wanna make for her welcome home dinner. Any ideas?"

"She likes everything you make. Trust me. Hospital food is getting to her. You could give her Cheerios and she'd be happy. She's starting to turn green every time they bring in the green Jell-O. So anything will work."

Hettie laughed. "Yeah, I know hospital food ain't the best, so I'll think of somethin'."

"Just know she doesn't eat a lot right now, although with your cooking she might, and if not, I will. I've missed your food somethin' fierce."

Hettie chuckled, "You like everythin' I cook. You're easy, Frank."

"Well, after eating my cooking for three years, I'd eat anyone's—except for hospital food. No offense."

"Don't be silly. I love cookin' for ya. You eat anythin' and everythin'."

"I do, and completely enjoy every single bite of it."

"So how's she doin'?"

"I don't know. I guess she's getting better. She's still sleeping a lot, but Doc says she's doing okay, so I guess she is. I know just getting her home is going to tire her out."

"Frank don't ya worry none. If Doc says she's doin' okay, then she is. Ya gotta quit worryin' or she's goin' worry and that ain't good. So stop doin' it!"

"You're right Hettie. I just can't help keeping in mind how close she was to—"

"Frank. Stop that right now. Ya can't think like that. Give her to God, son. That's all anyone can do. He loves her more than ya do. So no more of that kind of thinkin'. Got it?"

Chuckling, Franklin admitted, "You're right, Hettie. What would I ever do without you?"

"Don't know. Be lost, I guess." She roared. "'Member, I still be prayin' for both of ya."

"I know. Thanks Hettie. We need it. Well, I better get back to her."

"Frank, ya gotta rest as much as she does. Better sleep while ya can."

"I'm fine."

"No, ya ain't. Do what I say and no arguin', okay?"

"Got it, General Blackstone."

"Good." Laughing, Hettie hung up.

Chapter 30

April 1941
University of Colorado School of Business

Brad walked Rebecca across campus to the coffee shop. The sun gleaming in the sky with its warmth, summoned everyone outside with bustling activities. Bicycles were everywhere, couples were out walking, the tennis courts were full, and cars were being washed. It had been a long, cold winter and the snow had stayed longer than usual, so the fast warm-up had been an invitation to the great outdoors, and everyone was taking advantage of it.

"Beautiful day, isn't it?" asked Brad.

"Yes. I love the sunshine and it smells so good outside," she said, taking a deep breath.

"I've been looking forward to this today."

"Really?"

"Of course. Aren't you?" he asked, surprised.

"Yeah, I guess I'm still stunned you even asked me. You're way out of my league and well…I'm just surprised."

"Why do you say that? I've wanted to get to know you for a long time. I just didn't think you were interested in me."

"I wasn't. I mean, you have so many girls throwing themselves at you, I didn't even think about a friendship with you. It wasn't going to happen, so I never entertained the idea at all."

"Those girls mean nothing to me."

Cheryl Fosnot Bingisser

"Well, maybe you should let them know because they seem pretty clueless."

"I don't care what they think. Most of them don't have a thought in their heads. They aren't here for an education. They're here to find a husband any way they can. That's not what I want. I want a girl of substance, who has real goals and achieves them. Someone I can forge a real relationship with, not a flirty, casual, empty-headed, half-wit. That's not for me."

"Maybe you should slap a sign on your back and forehead letting them know that because they think you're fair game."

"Well, can we just move on to a different topic? I'm tired of this one. Right now, my choice is you, okay?"

"Key words being 'right now'?"

"Wow, you're a tough nut to crack. That's not what I meant at all. I meant presently, not having to do with anything in the past. I just want a friendship with you, not any of them. Okay?"

"Okay, if you say so."

"Okay, moving on. Let's get some coffee, sit down and talk like normal people."

"So you're saying that you're not normal, or I'm not?"

Oh, for goodness' sake." He sighed. "Do you have to make everything so hard? Listen, to me. We're here. Let's just enjoy the coffee and doughnuts and talk, okay?"

"Okay." She nodded. "I would like that."

"Good, now we're getting somewhere."

She laughed. "I'm just being cautious for my own sake."

"Someone must have hurt you pretty badly for you to act like this."

"It's not like that. I lost people close to me, so it's hard for me to let anyone in. I guess you could say I'm cautious and skeptical of people's motives."

"I'm sorry to hear that. I don't have any other motive other than trying to get to know you. That's all. I will never lie to you or take advantage of you in any way. You should probably know that I'm a believer in Jesus Christ, so I'm held to a higher standard than those who aren't."

FROM SHADOWS TO DAYBREAK

"Ah, a religious guy, huh?"

"Not exactly. It's a personal relationship with a God who loves me."

"Well, that sounds better than a lot of other things I've heard guys say, so I guess, with that said, I think I can trust you."

"Okay. Can I write that down somewhere, so when this surfaces again, and I now believe it will, I have proof of what you just said?"

Rebecca laughed. "You might want to engrave it in cement." Her eyes twinkled.

How beautiful, he thought. *I like this girl. She fights back and isn't afraid to say what she thinks, and she seems to think a lot—overthinks, really. But we can change that down the road.*

Three college girls walked in and headed right to their table.

"Hi, Brad. What's on your schedule for today? If you aren't busy this afternoon, I have some time free. How about a picnic, a movie, or something?"

One of the girls leaned over the table and placed her face directly in front of Brad. Rebecca rolled her eyes and shook her head.

"Look, girls, I'm not interested, so please leave us alone, okay?"

"Fine, for now, but see you in class later, and maybe we can go for a walk or something, huh?"

"I'm trying to be polite here. I'm not interested. Please leave my date and me alone." He raised his voice minutely to again reveal his disinterest in them.

Rebecca looked at him with surprise.

They turned and walked away until they got to the door. They turned back with glazed-over eyes, and blew kisses to him, ignoring everything he'd just said.

He dropped his head and sighed. "I'm sorry, Becca. Really, I am. They just don't get the message and I don't know what to do. I don't want to have anything to do with them."

"This was a date?" she asked in surprise.

"Well, of course, it's a date, albeit a casual one. What did you think it was?"

"I don't know. I'm just surprised."

"I seem to surprise you a lot."

"Look, Brad, I don't know if I can handle all this if we continue to go out. It's just too much."

"I didn't figure you for one who would give up so easily. I thought you were a fighter."

"I am. I just don't know if I want to fight your entourage every time we walk outside. It's not just you I'm going out with. It's every other groupie on campus.

Just grab one or ten of them out of your harem and be happy with that."

"Harem?" His dimples deepened when he laughed. "Those girls have no idea what real love is."

"Look, just leave me alone. I can't do this."

"You might give up easily, but I don't. I'm not quitting. I'm going to keep asking you out, so get used to me being around because I'm not going anywhere. You don't scare me."

She rolled her eyes. "Just go away."

"See ya in class this afternoon. You might not recognize me. I'll be wearing a mask so the groupies, as you call them, won't see me."

"What, don't blame me because I'm beautiful?"

He tossed his head, "Something like that." He gave her the most wonderful smile she had ever seen.

"Whatever." She walked away without looking back. Oh, she wanted to but thought better of it.

Brad mused, *Hmm, I think I'm breaking her down*, shaking his head and smiling.

Chapter 31

March 1951
General Hospital

As the wheelchair rolled closer to Lincoln's room, Miles's mind had been reeling, trying to think of what to say to this kid. He didn't want to scare him off but thought he needed to push him a little so he could get this kid to trust him. The nurse unlocked the door, pushed Miles through, then pulled the door closed, and locked it.

Lincoln looked up with curiosity. "Who are you?"

"I'm Mr. Strattford, and I've come to see you."

"You're the one I talked to on the phone, right?"

"Yes, I am. I had to do some fast talking to get a nurse to bring me up here and she's not going to let me stay too long. She's afraid I'll get too tired, and I'm supposed to be resting. Anyway, I wanted to see you in person instead of using the phone all the time."

"Are you feeling any better?"

"I don't know. They tell me this might take months before I'm close to being back to normal."

"What's wrong with you?"

"I've got this weird disease that makes me very tired and sleepy. It's called mono. The only thing that makes it better is sleep and rest—a lot of it."

"Oh. How long ya goin' be here?"

Cheryl Fosnot Bingisser

"They're trying to get me home very soon, but I'm not strong enough yet. I can only walk a few feet. Might even need physical therapy."

"What's that?"

"They're very special exercises that work the muscles you need to strengthen you. Once you've been in bed for a while, you lose the use of your muscles, and they just don't work anymore. A therapist comes and helps you exercise, so you can walk at least far enough to get around your own house without falling."

"Oh, sorry. Um—how come you brung me to the hospital?"

"Because if I hadn't, you would be in a cemetery right now, *not* in a hospital."

"What do ya want from me?"

"Nothing."

"Everybody wants somethin'. What's your angle?" He tilted his head and studied Miles intently.

"Don't have one. I only want to help you. I'd like to keep helping you if you'd let me."

"No one cares about me. Why should *you*?"

"Well, first that's not true. Someone does care about you."

"Who?"

"Franklin. He cares a lot."

"Maybe. We'll see how it goes."

Miles smiled. "Oh, a skeptic, huh?"

"A what?"

"A skeptic. It means someone who's hard to convince of some things. You seem to be one of those."

"Maybe."

"They're not going to let me stay very long, so I was wondering next time I visit, if would you like to play checkers or something?"

"Really? I'm pretty good at checkers." His face brightened. "Used to beat my momma all the time. Sure, I'll crush ya." He smiled cheerfully.

Miles laughed. "Oh really. We'll see about that. Okay, so it's set. Next visit we'll play a mean game of checkers. I'll practice in the meantime."

Miles smiled. *Just the suggestion of something fun really turned his attitude around. Something else to think about. Maybe I can get through to this kid yet. I'll have to have Franklin try a game with him. It seems to disarm him. Now I need Franklin to get a checkerboard for me.* He sifted through his thoughts.

The nurse unlocked the door and came to retrieve Miles. Lincoln looked a little disappointed that he was leaving.

"Hey, when you comin' back?" He studied Miles's face.

"Don't know for sure, but as soon as I can, okay?"

His smile disappeared, his eyes flashed, and a pout entered his face. "Don't hurry on my account. I'm used to being alone. I like it that way. Don't need nobody."

"Lincoln, I will be back. I always tell the truth, okay?" he declared, trying to quell Lincoln's disappointment.

"Yeah, we'll see."

"Okay, take care of yourself, and I'll see you soon. Get ready because I'm going to beat you good."

"No, you won't. I never lose." Immediately, the joy returned to his face.

"We'll see." The nurse wheeled him out of the room and locked the door.

"Well, how'd it go?"

"Better than I expected. I think he's competitive, so I appealed to that side of him, and it worked. So next time I come, we're playing checkers, which happens to be his favorite game, that he never loses," he added, with a chuckle.

"I'm glad someone is getting to him. He's a tough kid."

"No, he isn't. He's scared and trying to act tough so no one sees it."

"Well, thanks for talking with him. He doesn't have visitors and gets lonely, but it's hard to get close to the kid."

"It is, but I think I've accidentally found something that just might work."

Chapter 32

Mid-March 1951
Mayfield Residence

Raff's life with Maddie seemed almost idyllic. He already believed at times he didn't deserve her, but God had graciously given Maddie to him to be his lifelong partner, and he couldn't be more thrilled about it. Beautiful, amazing, intelligent, and kind—the perfect wife for him. He just wished he had the same innocence about him that she did, but he had already explored the physical side of love with more women than he could count. He now regretted those choices. Maddie had kept herself pure for her husband, for which he was very grateful, but wished he could offer her the same purity.

He'd had some troubling dreams of late but couldn't remember much—except the feelings he had upon waking—feelings of doubt and unworthiness. God had forgiven him for that lifestyle and now he would be moving on to a life with Maddie that they both looked forward to. But still—

Sleeping peacefully, Raff suddenly felt a strange heavy, oppressiveness hover over him and a hissing sound he couldn't place. A sulfur smell entered the room. There were voices—dark, hissing voices that seemed to pull and try to drag him down into a smoky pit of misery and horror. Fighting back, he wrestled with his blankets and sheets. He tried to awaken but couldn't.

FROM SHADOWS TO DAYBREAK

One terrifying voice shrieked at him, "Maddie couldn't love you. She's innocent and beautiful! You're a sinner, a womanizer who will never be happy with one woman."

Another voice picked up where the last one left off. "She'll limit your experience. You weren't meant for one girl," he squealed. "You'll seek out other women eventually and crush that sweet, innocent girl."

Another higher-pitched voice screeched. "You have unique physical desires and passions that can't be satisfied with a girl who has no experience!"

"Go back to what you know you love! There are so many beautiful women out there who would love you the way you pursue—with the passion, pleasure, and experience you eagerly desire."

"Let some strait-laced boy take care of that boring little housewife you think you want and go and do what makes you happy. Spread the love around!"

Each voice hounded him. He fought to get away but to no avail. He was trapped and screamed for help, but he couldn't open his mouth. He couldn't fathom what was happening to him.

Terrified, he cried out to God to release him from this horrific nightmare. "Save me, dear God!"

He immediately awakened and everything was peaceful again. Had this been some kind of demonic attack? What happened?

I'm not the man the voices accused me of being. Not anymore. I love Maddie with all my heart and my desires are now to please her—not myself. I have changed, Lord. You have changed me. Please take those voices away. I have no doubt about Maddie. You have given her to me as my bride and I will always cherish and love her. Lord, please take all those fears and old doubts away and fill me with all the joy and love for her that a man can possibly possess. Thank you, Lord, for making the darkness flee and bringing light into my life again. I will continue to trust you and the two of us will walk with you, together. I love you, Lord. Amen.

Relief and gratefulness washed over him. God had spared him from that disturbing and terrorizing nightmare. He had never experienced anything like that before and prayed it would never happen again. He believed he should share this with Maddie because keeping secrets is never a good thing. He wanted a truly loving marriage with honesty always at the forefront. He'd talk to Maddie tonight. He hoped she would still trust him to be the husband she wanted. He could, couldn't he? Of course. God would give him the strength to be the kind of husband Maddie wanted and needed. He could never do it on his own, but God would provide whatever Raff needed to be the husband he wanted to be for her—for Maddie. Besides, he couldn't allow his past life to affect his future. He could not—would not—let that happen.

Chapter 33

Mid-March 1951
General Hospital

    Sleeping peacefully on her hospital bed, Franklin limped quietly into the room not wanting to disturb Kathleen. Besides, he loved just gazing at her, even though she looked tired and fragile, she was still the most beautiful woman he had ever seen. He still had a hard time believing she had chosen him for a husband—a cripple that most people dismissed because he wasn't *normal* just didn't bother her at all. Incredible.
    He still hadn't told her how he'd been injured and knew that day would come soon. He just hoped it wouldn't be until she felt better. He didn't want to upset her. He didn't know what his horrific story would do to her, so he avoided that conversation. It would be okay for now because they were both caught up in her health and their baby—their son. He still couldn't believe they were having a boy. He hadn't revealed to anyone his time in the hospital chapel, what he had gone through that night, and not sure he ever would. For God to tell him they were having a boy was special. Extraordinary. He couldn't tell Kathleen, at least not until after the birth.
    The biggest problem was how to keep Kathleen from overdoing and maybe risking her life or the baby's. With spring fast approaching, he knew he would be spending more time away from her preparing the orchard and he'd become fearful that she would resent it.

It had been difficult being away from her and she felt the same way. If resting was something she would have to do the better part, or all, of her pregnancy, which he feared Doc would order, she would be bored to tears and want him there with her. He didn't know how he could do both. He had to make a living unless he let Kathleen pay for everything. They'd already had that discussion once, but it still didn't sit well with him. It would be okay if they had to but not consistently. He couldn't.

He walked over to her bedside and watched her breathe. "Oh, God, how I love her." Even words couldn't describe the profound feeling of love he possessed. He didn't know it was possible to love another person this much.

She stirred a little, and he smiled at her.

"Good morning, darling," he said lovingly, moving some hair off her face and kissing her forehead.

"Good morning? Good grief, it's three o'clock in the afternoon. How long have I been asleep this time?"

"I don't know. I've been out for a while. I brought you something, my dearest, Mrs. Atwood." His eyes danced, and his smile always melted her heart.

"My wedding robe and nightgown?" She smiled, flirtatiously.

Franklin laughed. "I told you that's staying in the closet. Do you recall that conversation?"

"Yeah, I'm afraid I do. I don't like it though." She pouted.

He rolled his eyes. "There you go again. Stop that!" He kissed her on the lips long and lovingly.

"Okay, Mr. Atwood, what wonderful gift did you bring your wife? Did Hettie pack some food for me?"

"I wish. I didn't get home, just a couple of places in town."

"Okay, let's see it."

Franklin handed her the most exquisite red-and-white rose arrangement she had ever seen. The bouquet consisted of three dozen red and white roses, in a beautiful crystal vase, with plenty of eucalypti and tall ornamental grasses. It was spectacular.

"Oh, Frank, they're absolutely gorgeous. I love them."

FROM SHADOWS TO DAYBREAK

"Well, I figured you liked red roses and eucalyptus, so I just went from there."

"How observant of you to notice that. Most men wouldn't have."

"Well, I guess that proves it."

"Proves what?"

"That you married the most wonderful man in the world!" Kathleen hit his shoulder.

"Ouch!"

"Well, I have to admit you are pretty wonderful. But you'll never get me to say that again. A girl needs leverage, you know."

Chuckling, he said, "Leverage, huh?"

"Yep. Very important. Men have all—"

"Yeah, yeah, I know, all the advantages. I believe we've had this conversation before. I didn't agree with you then, and I don't agree with you now. So save your breath."

Kathleen laughed. "Well, whether you agree with me or not, Frankie, it's true."

"Whatever." He rolled his eyes at her.

Kathleen laughed.

"On the good news front, Miles was sitting up when I saw him, but he said that when he can leave the hospital, living alone doesn't seem the right thing to do. Cooking would be out because he could fall asleep, and then a whole list of horrible things could result, but he doesn't have any family or anyone to stay with him. I suggested a nurse and cook combination in one person."

"Well, I can see why he feels that way. It's scary being alone, especially if you're feeling weak and vulnerable."

"Speaking from experience?"

"Well, not exactly, but it's no fun feeling weak. It's hard, and I hate it."

"I know you do. I wish I could change things for you. I know this is hard on you."

"Oh, Frankie, I'm so sorry. I shouldn't be complaining like this. I know you love me and want me to come home. I can see what a toll this has taken on you, and I'm sorry."

"Kathleen Atwood, you stop this right now. You don't have to worry about me. I'm fine, and I can take care of myself. Right now, it's you I'm concerned about."

"Doc says I'm getting better and he'll probably send me home in two days. Can you handle that?"

"Can I? I can't wait! But I'm sure you will still have to be careful, so I just want you to be prepared to hear that from Doc. I have a hunch it's coming."

"I know. I hate the thought of it, but I know you're right. Please, Frankie, can we…at least get my robe and nightgown out of the closet?"

Franklin laughed. "My dearest, no one would like that more."

Chapter 34

Mid-March 1951
Weaver Residence

    Marianne Weaver had just taken a phone call from foster parents whose child had run away for the third time and wanted her to place him with someone else. Her heart broke for them both, but what could she do? This kid had been in several foster homes, always belligerent, always fighting, always destroying things, and begging to leave. He wasn't just an angry kid; he was filled with rage. Rather than living in a foster home, he would prefer the streets.
    She had listened to almost every story possible about those kids who had been placed in homes where every kind of abuse imaginable took place. It had happened to some she had placed. She had nightmares about them. How were you supposed to know exactly what these parents were like when you couldn't be with them twenty-four hours a day? Some of them lied to you constantly, but no way to know until it was too late. They were properly vetted, of course, but again, you only received so much information, and it never told the whole story.
    The system never worked the way it had been designed to, but no other organization came close to it either. So what should a social worker do? She loved her dreadful career when she knew she'd placed a child in a loving home, where he would thrive. Unfortunately, they were few and far between.

Cheryl Fosnot Bingisser

Today had been a difficult day and she needed to go home and put her feet up. The *Hallmark Hall of Fame* movie she wanted to watch aired tonight, and she just wanted to relax and get lost in a story that took her away from the real world. Sometimes reality is way overrated. She had reached the place where she barely watched the news anymore because evil was rampant, politics were nauseating, and corruption spread everywhere. Crime had become unbridled, and no one felt safe just walking down the street in the big cities anymore. Life was hard, and fluff a delightful change.

Social work was supposed to be the answer to some of it, but the problems with the children had gotten so big and widespread, the social workers couldn't keep up. Even when she did find a great home for kids, who had been taken from their parents for drug abuse, or other major offenses, at a moment's notice, the judge could reverse the decision. Then take them back to the parents they knew would reoffend. A cycle that never ended. Challenging and at times, depressing. There weren't any answers except one: Only Jesus could change the hearts of people. Short of that, these things would continue, and, in most cases, worsen. There were so many times when she felt like quitting, but there had been no one to take her place. She couldn't just desert the place and leave yet another hole in the system that was already full of them.

The hospital had called and said they had a kid there who lived on the streets and had been beaten very badly. He would be there for a few more days. They wanted to know if there might be a home in which he may fit. He wouldn't be an easy kid, but once you broke through, she thought he would turn into a good one. He had a tough exterior, but underneath a little boy who'd been horribly hurt. They didn't have any other information on him but knew he had been living alone. If they didn't find a good home for him soon, he would be living on the streets at the ripe old age of seven.

She promised she would investigate but knew for sure at this point there were no homes available. She was too tired to cook, so she looked in the freezer and found a chicken pot pie that she liked and popped it into the oven. It would be baked in time to sit with her dinner and watch the movie. Surprised at how much she looked forward to it, she sat and relaxed.

Marianne, at forty-eight, tired earlier than she used to, and with less sleep, and longer hours, it all led to a less-than-healthy lifestyle. She had a family, but none lived close by, so she rarely saw them, and her grandchildren hardly knew her. Even when they came to visit, Marianne either had to work, or some disaster would happen that would take her away. There was no time for friends or relationships, so getting lost in work suited her. But the older *she* became, the harder *it* became. They tried to tell her to take a vacation and get away from the whole business for a couple of weeks, but there just didn't seem to be any time to do it. Her short vacations had become chicken pot pies and *Hallmark Hall of Fame* movies.

Chapter 35

Mid-March 1951
General Hospital

Franklin hobbled into Miles's room, glad for his upright position and seemed more alert. He thought it had to be good news—at least maybe hopeful news.

"Miles, it's so good to see you sitting up and looking a little more lifelike."

"How are you feeling?"

"They're trying to help me get strong enough to go home, so they're taking me on short walks with a walker to exercise my legs. I guess my stamina is increasing, but it's still a long road ahead." He took a deep breath and blew it out.

"I'm sorry, Miles. Hey, the nurse said you'd been up to see Lincoln. How did it go?"

"I think I'm starting to get somewhere. I told him that the next time I came, I was going to play checkers with him, and apparently, he thinks he'll *crush* me because he never loses."

Franklin chuckled. "It sounds like you may have cracked him."

"I don't know, as soon as he knew I was leaving, he covered himself with that tough exterior and acted like he didn't care if I came back or not. He's not fooling anyone. He's scared to death to trust or need anyone."

"You're exactly right. I've started to break him down, but he's not cracking easily. Your idea of playing games is a good one. It breaks down his defenses. I should probably do that as well."

"Which is one of the reasons I asked you to come. Would you be willing to buy a checkerboard for me? I don't have any way of getting one."

"Not at all, and since I'm already looking, can you think of any other game he might like? Maybe Parcheesi or something like that?"

"That would be a great game for him. A little different from checkers, but still the same idea. I can give you some money to purchase them."

"Don't be silly. I'm happy to do it. I need to see him today as well. Kathleen will be going home in a few days so he won't be as accessible to me as he is now."

"She's doing better, then?"

"Frankly, Miles, I don't see much of a difference, but Doc says she's better and her blood pressure is back down, so I guess that's progress. She's still so tired and sleeps a great deal. I'm still concerned about her. I've prayed so much for her, and I've only been home about three times since she was admitted. I can't be away from her for too long. She gets a little cranky when I'm not here with her."

Miles studied him. He looked nervous and tired. "Franklin, I'm a little concerned about you. You look exhausted. Are you okay?"

"Yeah, I'm fine. I'm just a little worried about Kathy. I don't want to lose her now that we've found each other. I'm trying to 'be anxious for nothing,' but it's challenging when I see her so exhausted and fragile."

"Was that a quote from the Bible?"

"Yes, it is. I recently came to the Lord very recently, at my own wedding." Franklin saw the surprised look on his face. "Yeah, it was a bit of a showstopper. He made a huge difference in my life and I'm learning new things every day."

"Your wedding, huh?"

"Yeah, it's a very long story."

"I bet it is. Someday I want to hear all about it. It sounds interesting."

Chuckling, he admitted, "It was that for sure."

"Well, if Doc says she's doing better, she must be. I think maybe you love her so much that the thought of losing her is coloring your assessment of the situation."

"Wow. That's very insightful and might be true. I'm going to chew on that one for a while. I'm glad I got a chance to talk to you about it. Miles, you've become a good friend to me and I want you to know how much I treasure our friendship."

"Franklin, it's pretty much the other way around, but I'm glad if I brought a little perspective to it. Sometimes someone who isn't so close can see things that you can't. Part of friendship is being objective when necessary."

"Well, thank you very much because you might have just hit the nail on the head. With that, I need to get out of here, get those games for us, and get back to Kathy. Truthfully, I don't know if I have the energy to tackle Lincoln today."

"You know what? Why don't I set up another phone call with him and maybe that will let you off the hook for today."

"Are you up to that? I don't want you to wear out."

"Yeah, I think I can do that. You can take the rest of the day and spend it with Kathleen. She needs you."

"Thanks, Miles. That's kind of you. I'll get to the toy store and get those games, and then we'll see how young Lincoln responds to that. I hope it breaks down some of the walls he's spent so much time building."

"Me too. He needs someone he can depend on."

"Get some rest. I'll see you later."

Chapter 36

April 1941
University of Colorado School of Business

Rebecca had tried to avoid Brad when they were on campus. She hated watching all those girls fall all over him. Some even wrote their phone numbers on paper and put them in his shirt or trouser pockets. It was disgusting. To his credit, he didn't seem comfortable with it either. He didn't lead these girls on, so he'd been innocent in that respect. She just couldn't be certain about the rest, so she studied how he handled it.

True to his word, Brad hadn't stopped asking her on a date. He told her when his father was young, he used to be a salesman, and they were taught that with every no, you were closer to a yes. Brad had been determined not to let her get away. There was something special about her, and he wanted to get to know her. After weeks of being asked every single day, she'd finally given in, and they were to meet off campus a few blocks away by this famous brick building. He'd pick her up and take her to their destination.

Nerves were plaguing Rebecca. She liked him a lot more than she cared to admit—so handsome and sweet. Believing him to be genuinely interested in her, she still felt hesitant about meeting him and having his entourage appear. She couldn't take that on a regular basis. It would drive her nuts, besides being rude and ridiculous.

Cheryl Fosnot Bingisser

She didn't know what to wear on the date. She hadn't asked where he'd be taking her, so she wore a white blouse, with short sleeves, and a bow at the neck, a red full skirt, and a wide, black belt around the waist. Black pumps and a black bag completed the ensemble. Her hair, pinned up in a French roll, with tendrils along her face, and a flower in the center of the roll, Rebecca gave herself one last look in the full-length mirror. She turned around and believed she passed muster. All she had to do was grab a jacket and head off campus. It hadn't been a long walk or dark outside yet, so she didn't feel unsafe, although she would be a little concerned about the walk back, if it became dark before they left.

She walked quickly and arrived at the building five minutes before six-thirty. She didn't want to be late. Once this date was over, she wouldn't have to worry about any further contact with him, and he'd be gone permanently. On second thought, did she really want him out of her life? Of course, she did. No more girls hanging around them. No, just this one date and it would be all over. She wouldn't have to deal with him anymore.

Six-thirty had come and gone and still no sign of him. Maybe he just set her up for a joke. Maybe he just wanted to humiliate her and wouldn't come at all. Maybe she should just walk away. Deep down inside, she couldn't help being disappointed. She really liked him, but if this is what he did to girls he likes, she would label him a miscreant, and wanted no part of him. Just five more minutes and she would be heading back. From behind her, she felt a tap on her shoulder and she screamed. Turning around, he was standing there looking, well, looking so utterly handsome. She had trouble opening her mouth to say anything. The red started from her neck and went all the way to her cheeks. She felt the heat.

He smiled at her. "Hi, Becca. Are you ready for our date?"

"Yeah, sure. Where are you taking me?"

"I don't think I want to tell you yet. My car is right over there. I'll walk with you. I've been looking forward to this. I hope you have."

"I have some reservations about it, but I hope we have a nice time. I want to see what you're made of, Brad Crawford."

FROM SHADOWS TO DAYBREAK

"Oh, I see, so this is a test."

"Of course, it is. Isn't that what we talked about?"

"I don't think the word *test* was ever used, but if that's what you want, I'll try to pass it. Does that work?" He smiled, so sweetly.

No sarcasm or meanness, just the facts. It was a good first impression for the evening. Maybe this wouldn't be so bad after all.

"I guess."

Brad led her across the street to the car and walked her to the passenger side, opened the door for her, and closed it when she had seated herself. Then he walked around to his side, closed the door, and started the car.

"Well, are you ready for this?" he said, with a smile, while those blue eyes seemed to dance.

He was so easy on the eyes and so wildly handsome. She was beginning to relax and guessed that she might even like this evening, but did she want to? "I am. Let's see what you got. Impress me." She smiled while she threw down the gauntlet.

He believed her to be so beautiful, and her smile like the sunrise. She had the cutest nose, and her mouth had beautiful, full lips that screamed to be kissed, so he rapidly moved his eyes back up to those emerald greens and took a deep breath.

He started the car, and they were off. An awkward silence covered them for a few minutes like neither of them could or would speak. It seemed like first dates always started that way. You wanted to turn around and go home before it got any worse, but sometimes it took a few minutes, so she would try to be patient. Maybe she could think of a conversation starter.

"So do you have a part-time job or anything?"

"I was working at the bookstore, but they laid me off because business seemed to slow down, which makes no sense to me at all. It's always busy. Maybe I did something wrong and they just didn't tell me."

"I'm sorry. That doesn't seem fair. So where are you from?"

Well, I was born in Boston, but we moved from there to New Jersey, then New York, then Pennsylvania, then California,

Washington, and finally Colorado. So I guess you could say I'm from everywhere."

"Wow."

"How about you?"

"My early childhood was spent with a rodeo. I was a sharpshooter. My daddy taught me to shoot at the age of three, and I never missed one target after. By my fifth birthday, I was tricking on horses and still never missed a bullseye. My dad had been stomped to death by my horse that same year, so they sent me to live with my grandparents. Papa was a shooter too. We hunted together and went sharp shooting together—like I still had a piece of my dad with me." She stopped. Maybe she'd said too much. "Sorry, that was a lot of history you probably weren't looking for or needed."

"Not at all. It's very interesting. A sharpshooter—I didn't see that one coming. I'm sorry about your dad. That had to be hard as a child."

"Yeah, I didn't want to entertain anymore. I just didn't feel like it without him with me. It was difficult."

"I'm so sorry. What about your mom?"

"She ran off with a neighbor when I was little and never came back, so it was just dad and me."

"Wow! Sounds like you had a pretty rough life."

"Not really. I loved the rodeo and my grandparents. They stayed with me until I went to college, and they moved to Florida to get to the warmer weather. Gram has terrible arthritis, and the warmth makes it easier to move. What about your family?"

"We moved all the time. My parents are into the social scene, so money and status are their thing. My mom loves it when she's in the paper on the society page, and she's over the moon if she is in a picture. I was never into that kind of stuff. When I came to know Jesus, I just didn't have any interest in fame, power, or any of that stuff. I just wanted a quiet life with real love in my life and a true life, not one lived for society. To me, that is a fake life. There's nothing fake about Jesus, and that's who I follow now—not my parents and their bid for success and money. Well, we're here. I hope you like it. It's my favorite restaurant."

FROM SHADOWS TO DAYBREAK

Helping her out of the car, Brad offered her his arm. They walked a block and then crossed the street. The beautiful, old brick building, constructed in the 1890s, had been turned into an Italian restaurant to which people seemed to flock.

"Brad, this is great. I love this building. It's beautiful. I love architecture and old buildings."

"Well, I didn't know that, but at least I'm passing the test on this part."

Becca smiled. "Yes, you are. I love it."

"Let's go inside. You'll like this even better."

She walked in, and her eyes darted around the room. The walls were replete with original brick, and the tables were for four, with beautiful candles and red tablecloths. All around the room were lush green plants and old wine bottles. The waiters were all dressed in tuxes for an upscale restaurant, and everything just perfect.

"So is the food as good as the environment?"

"Better, if you can believe that. You're going to love it. Everything is perfectly done, and I've never had a bad meal here. Not once."

The head waiter led them to a table in the far corner that seemed quieter and darker. The candlelight was beautiful, and it danced off the stemware that had already been placed. He had reservations and asked for this particular table. It also had a beautiful vase full of red roses and white carnations with baby's breath. And since it wasn't on any other table, she knew Brad had ordered those for her too. How sweet. *I don't want to like this guy, but he seems to like romantic evenings, and that's my soft spot. So watch it, Becca!* She cautioned herself.

The host said he would be back with the menus and would take their drink order. Drink order. *Do I dare have a glass of wine? Maybe since he's a Christian he doesn't drink at all so I won't have to worry.*

Brad slid her chair under the table and took her coat. He hung it up around the corner, then came back and sat. "Well, what do you think so far?"

"I think you went to a lot of trouble for me, which makes me just a bit uncomfortable."

"Why?"

"Maybe it's too soon for all of this."

"All of what? It's just dinner. I told you I won't take advantage of you, and I'm not trying to well…you know. I don't do that. This is dinner, just to have some fun. So please break down those walls and let me in."

"Okay, I guess I just made a snap judgment, and I'm sorry. It won't happen again. Can I start over, please?"

"I'd like that."

"Hi, I'm Rebecca, but my friends call me Becca."

"Hi, Becca, I'm glad to know you. Would you like to have dinner with me tonight?"

"I would, thank you so much for asking me."

They both laughed, and in a second, all the barriers were gone, and they both relaxed to enjoy the evening.

Rebecca thanked him for the beautiful flowers.

They had a great dinner and each had a glass of red wine. The candlelight and roses on the table just added to the romance of the evening, and Rebecca and Brad had a wonderful time together. They both liked each other and knew this would not be the last date for the two of them. Brad couldn't be happier about the way it turned out, and neither could Rebecca, except it irritated her just a bit that she felt that way. She didn't want to. He was so hard to resist. Downright irritating—in all the *right* ways.

Chapter 37

Mid-March 1951
Mountain View High School

Back in school, Emily had been enjoying her first few days. She'd received the classes she wanted, which made her very happy. She took home economics, biology, US history, math, and choir. It was a full schedule, but she loved it. She'd even found some girlfriends with whom she felt comfortable.

Emily had run away from her parents who disregarded her and were involved in Washington society and the DC political arena. They tried to groom her for society, but she never quite fit in, and even though she strived to earn her parent's love, they weren't interested. She'd become nothing more than yet another hindrance to the path of success they desperately labored toward. Although their endeavor was close to unproductive, they never ceased struggling to attain the luxury and notoriety they craved. Emily became a barrier to all they coveted. Knowing she wouldn't be missed for several days, she left home with little but determination and enough cash to get her far from there. She never looked back.

Heidi, who had a background similar to hers, was warmhearted and congenial, and they understood each other. Currently living with her grandparents, giving her a much better situation than her home life had been, and she couldn't be happier. She loved them, had stability for the first time in her life, and had been thriving here.

She loved school, but a little shy like Emily, and quieter than Rosa. Likable and fun, and Emily loved being with her.

Rosa—funny and beautiful. Sweet but a little boy crazy, which had not been Emily's mind-set. Smart and likable, Rosa and Emily gelled right away. They were already talking about a sleepover, which Emily had never experienced before and she became quite enthused about it. It sounded like the ultimate girls' fun time.

The three of them were always together like they were joined at the hip. They found each other after classes, ate lunch together, and walked home together. They already put the date on the calendar for the sleepover. Emily was looking forward to it, and it couldn't come fast enough for her. Rosa wanted to invite more girls at first, but the other two talked her out of it. They believed the three of them together were all they needed.

Their first slumber party would be at Rebecca's apartment. Emily was thrilled and even asked Rebecca if Maddie might want to come and help Rebecca with all the food and games, or whatever else they might want to do that night. Rebecca thought it a great idea and invited her.

Maddie attended slumber parties a few years ago and knew how much fun they could be.

They decided on Friday night and it seemed like the hours at school dragged by.

The final bell rang and the girls couldn't wait to start their evening together. Maddie picked them up so the girls wouldn't have to walk with all their gear. The first thing on the docket was an early showing of *Casablanca*, which would start in an hour and a half. They still had time to get to Rebecca's, stash their gear, set up their beds, laugh, and talk, while Maddie and Rebecca started dinner that could be completed after the movie. They knew there would be popcorn at the movie, so they didn't fix too much for dinner.

The girls talked about all things girly—fashion, movies, boys, school, magazines, foods they liked, and anything else that came to mind. Emily had the time of her life. She'd finally found a life where she fit in, people cared about her, and she loved all of it. She'd never been happier.

FROM SHADOWS TO DAYBREAK

Then the nightmare would intrude, but it seemed it didn't happen as often, and she thought she was finally handling it well. The happy times outweighed the nightmares, which gave her hope for a future—a good future.

* * * * *

Brent, who was captain of the football team, had set his sights on her. He talked with her in the halls and walked her to her classes. He wanted to walk her home, but Emily hadn't been ready for it. There were crowds of people in the halls and she felt safe there, but not walking home. Too many things could go wrong, and uncertain if she would ever trust a boy completely again.

She thought him to be dreamy, and all the girls wanted him. But he had chosen her and even though boys weren't high on her list, Rosa had persuaded her to walk with him to the soda shop just two blocks down the street. It was right after school, so darkness had not yet descended, and there would be a lot of people on the street, so nothing to worry about.

Brent met her after the last bell, and they started walking toward the soda shop. He carried her books for her, which proved just how gentlemanly and impressive he could be.

"So how was school today, Emily?"

"Fine. Mrs. Benson picked at us in Home EC, but it was okay. I got an A on my US history test today."

"That's great. I hate that class. I like biology better. We get to dissect a frog in a couple of weeks, so that should be fun," he said, with a laugh.

"Yeah, fun for you maybe, but I'm not crazy about the idea. It's just icky!"

"That sounds like a girl, alright. They don't like the blood and guts part of biology. I like all parts of biology," he said, with a raised brow and a flirty behavior that Emily didn't recognize.

"Oh, we're here." They found their booth and sat while a young man came and took their order.

"I'd like a strawberry shake and fries, please," said Emily, shyly.

Cheryl Fosnot Bingisser

"And I think I'll have a chocolate shake and fries."

"Okay, comin' right up," he replied, then he went back to the kitchen.

Brent stared at her and Emily looked away, feeling very uncomfortable. "Do you have any idea how pretty you are?" He took her hand that had been on the table, and Emily ripped it away and placed it in her lap.

"What's wrong? I'm not going to hurt you or anything. I just wanted to hold hands with you. Everybody does it. I'm just telling you the truth. You are pretty."

"I'm sorry, I just don't want to hold hands right now, okay?" Her face flushed, and she wanted to go home. This just didn't feel right. "I think I'd like to go home now."

"Why? We haven't even eaten our food yet. It should be here in a minute. Please don't go. I like you a lot, and I just want to get to know you better. That's all. Please stay and eat and talk with me. Then I'll walk you home," he pleaded.

"Okay, I'll stay." She relented. "I'm sorry. It's just that I've never had a boyfriend or anything before."

"Wow. You've *never* had one?"

"No. I really would rather not talk about it if that's okay."

"Sure, I'm sorry. I don't want to hurt you or make you feel uncomfortable. Relax, and we'll change the subject, okay?"

"Okay. What do you want to talk about?"

"About you. You haven't been in town very long, have you?"

"It's been a while, now. I like it here, and I like school. I know you play football. Doesn't that hurt when you get tackled?"

"Why, do you worry about me?" he asked, flirting.

"I was just wondering how you do that every week. You must be bruised and cut up pretty bad some nights."

"Yeah, but you get used to it. We practice all week, so we get strong and can take a hit pretty good, but there are those that I don't see coming, and they can hit a kidney or something like that, and then I'm sore for a few days, but I love football."

"Really, it seems so...so...brutal!"

158

FROM SHADOWS TO DAYBREAK

"Brutal? he shook his head. "I guess it could be called that. We're trained for it, though, so it's usually okay. Just a soak in an ice tub, massage, or something, and we're right back at it the next day."

"I think I'll stick to choir, thank you. Much safer." She giggled.

Brent laughed. "I guess it is. Are you finished? I can walk you home now if you'd like?"

"No, that's okay. I need to go back to school. I forgot my math book, and we're having a test tomorrow," she argued, beginning to feel a little nervous.

"Well, okay. I'll walk you back to school then."

"I guess it's okay. Thanks." Still a little jittery, but she viewed a lot of people so, it seemed safe enough.

They walked the first block, and he pulled her into the alley. "Kiss me. Come on, Emily. Everybody does it. It's no big deal. It's just kissing. Besides, I know you want it. You're just playing hard to get." He tried to kiss her several times and pulled her toward him.

She fought back. He tried to kiss her again. She kneed him in his most vulnerable place, and she turned and ran all the way home, leaving him on the ground, moaning in pain. She was hysterical by the time she got to The Café, and Rebecca understood straightaway that something was wrong. She motioned for Emily to go upstairs, and she'd be right up. Emily lay on the bed, sobbing. Rebecca quickly walked into her room and lay down beside her with her arm around her.

"Emily, what's wrong? What's happened?"

"I feel so stupid!" She sobbed. "I walked to the soda shop with this guy, who seemed nice and said he liked me, and then on the way back to school, he pulled me into the alley. He said he knew I wanted it, and tried to kiss me several times, and even tried to pull me close to him. I kneed in his male parts just as hard as I could and ran all the way here. I'm stupid. I'm never doing anything with a boy ever again!" She couldn't stop crying and shook from fear, and the nightmare just seemed to continue.

"Oh, Emily. I'm so sorry. There are nice boys out there. I promise. But there are also boys who intend to take advantage of girls too."

"How are you supposed to know the difference? 'Cuz I sure don't."

Rebecca took her in her arms and held her while she cried.

"What's wrong with me that guys want to do that to me? What did I do wrong?"

"Oh, sweetheart, you didn't do anything wrong. Boys like this are just full of themselves and are used to getting anything they want. This is not your fault. Please don't think that. You did absolutely nothing wrong. This is evil and sinful pure and simple. It's not you!"

"Then why does it keep happening?"

"I don't know, Emily, but I'll tell you again. It's nothing you did wrong. It's not your fault. I want you to give me this worm's name, and I'm going directly to his parents, the principal, or both. No one does this to a friend of mine and gets away with it. Do you remember the last incident? I can still shoot and still hit."

"No, I don't want you to go after him. Just let it go. I just want to forget it."

"Emily, that's the problem. Guys like this get away with it because we're afraid to speak up. We can't continue to let them do this to us. Someone needs to stop them, and it might as well start with us. Please tell me this kid's name. I'll take care of this my way."

"No, Becca. I won't let you. It would get all over school, and then it would just get worse. Please just forget it. I shouldn't have told you."

"Yes, you should have told me, and I always want you to tell me. I'm your friend and guardian, and I love you. I'm supposed to protect you and I didn't. I'm so sorry, Emily. But this isn't your fault or mine. It's his, and he should get his comeuppance for it. If you're positive you don't want me to go after him, I won't, but it's against my better judgment."

"Thanks, Becca. Can I stay up here tonight and not work? I don't feel up to talking to people tonight."

"Of course, sweetheart, but please don't believe the lie that you did something to deserve this or you're at fault somehow because you're not. Okay?"

FROM SHADOWS TO DAYBREAK

"Okay. I'll try." Tears were still falling, but not as badly. She was calming down and Rebecca had to get back to work.

"I'll be right downstairs if you need me. I can get someone to cover for me if you'd like me to stay with you, or you can call me on the phone, and I can be up here in a few seconds." She held her again. "Maybe you should rest for a while. I'm so sorry this happened to you, but I'm here for you, okay?"

"Yeah, I'm kind of tired. I think I'll rest." She lay down and tried to relax.

Rebecca kissed her on the forehead and said she'd try to get off early. She was only a phone call away.

Chapter 38

March 1951
General Hospital

Playing checkers wasn't exactly the way he wanted to spend this afternoon, but he knew he had to. After a round of physical therapy, Miles had become weary. But he thought he would have time for a nap before he went up if the nurse would wake him, so Lincoln wouldn't be disappointed, or lose whatever trust had just been initiated between them. The nurse promised to do that, so Miles lay down for a quick nap. He awoke and checked the time to see two hours had passed.

"Oh no. I overslept." Why hadn't the nurse awakened him like she said she would? Lincoln would never believe he just took a nap and it turned into a lot more. *What do I do now?* He hesitated, as he mulled over things.

He called for a nurse and asked her to take him upstairs so he could work with Lincoln. Believing that Miles needed more rest, and not entirely on board with the whole idea, she finally relented and mandated that he only stay a half hour. Miles knew it wouldn't be long enough, but it was better than nothing. He grabbed the game and off they went.

Sitting in the chair by the bed, Lincoln looked a little healthier today. Miles studied him while she wheeled him into the room. He

FROM SHADOWS TO DAYBREAK

worried about what it could mean in terms of leaving the hospital. For Lincoln, this could be bad news, and that concerned him.

"Hey, Lincoln, ready to play? I've been practicing."

"You're late."

"I know. I took a nap and overslept. They gave me physical therapy today, and I guess it wore me out. The nurse promised to wake me up but didn't. As soon as I did, I had a nurse bring me up here. She gave me strict orders that I could not stay longer than a half hour. So are we just going to talk today or do you want to challenge the king to a game of checkers? Your choice."

"How do I know you're telling me the truth?"

"You don't. I told you that I would never lie to you, and I won't. It's up to you whether you choose to believe me, but I don't intend to spend the next half hour jawing with you about whether I'm lying or not. So do I stay, or do I go?"

"Fine. Bring the board over here and let the massacre begin."

"Massacre? That's a hard word for a seven-year-old. I'm impressed." Miles laughed.

"Yeah, my mom used to give me vo-cab-u-lary words all the time, so I learned a lot."

"Where is your mom, Lincoln?"

"I don't wanna talk about it."

"Okay."

They played the game for the next forty-five minutes and Miles was exhausted. He needed to go back to bed, but without the nurse coming, he had become a fixture. Lincoln won three out of four, but he still exhibited unhappiness. He expected to win them all and became a little upset over the one loss.

"You know Lincoln, no one wins them all. Losing is just a part of life. We learn more when we lose or fail than we ever do when we win or succeed. That's just a fact."

"I don't like losing."

Miles chuckled. "No one does, but it happens. A good loser is every bit as important as being a good winner. It's called being a good sport. Losing is always hard, but we need to learn that it's a big part of life and try again next time. We learn from it and move on. That's the best way to handle it. If you get all upset or mad over a loss, no one will ever want to play with you."

"You mean *you* won't want to play with *me*."

"No, I don't. My brother used to become angry when he lost. We would play Monopoly late at night after our parents went to bed, and we would only play a full game if he was winning. If he started losing, the game and all the hotels and houses would be flipped all over the floor. That not only ended the game, but it also brought my mom in, and we both got into trouble."

"Hmm. So who had to pick up the mess he made?"

"Who do you think?"

"You?"

"Nope. We both did. Waking her up was not a smart thing to do. I learned that playing with him was not going to be any fun unless I lost. I didn't want to lose all the time. So I quit playing with him. He was a bad sport. It's not something you want to be. Being a good sport in any game or sport is very important. Even a team sport. A team must display good sportsmanship. They aren't going to win them all, so they must know how to take a loss and try to win the next one."

"I think I get it. I still don't like it, though."

Miles laughed. "I don't either. How about next time you let me win?"

"No way. That would be being a bad sport, wouldn't it?"

"I knew you were smart."

They both laughed as the nurse came in to take Miles back. Trying not to let out a sigh of relief in front of Lincoln, he told himself to calm down and not show how tired he felt.

"Okay, Lincoln, I'll see you when the nurse lets me out of my room. Sometimes I feel like there's a lock on my door too. They're always telling me I need to rest. I have to follow Doc's orders, or I'll never get out of here. I'll be back, and next time, I'm going to beat you. No more Mr. Nice Guy for me."

Lincoln laughed, while the nurse wheeled Miles out the door.

"Bye, Lincoln. Get some rest and mind the doctors and nurses, okay?"

"Okay, I'll try. I promise. Do you know if Franklin's coming to see me soon?"

"He will, but his wife has been sick, so he's been staying with her. I know he has a game he wants to play with you, so he'll be here."

"He does?"

"Yep. See ya. Take care, kid."

"Bye, Mister."

Chapter 39

Mid-March 1951
General Hospital

Walking down the hall with a nurse on each side and using a walker, Kathleen became exhausted. She hadn't gone very far before they had to take her back. They were barely able to get her back into bed before she fell asleep. Franklin had no idea they were going to get her out of bed, so he was shocked when the nurse stopped him to tell him what had happened. Concerned about her weakness, he limped directly into her room and lay on the bed with her. She didn't even stir when he put his arm around her. The nurse took her vitals, and her blood pressure had plunged again. She told Franklin she would talk to Doc.

Lord, why isn't she getting better? Why is she so tired? What am I supposed to do to help? I don't know anymore, Lord. I don't know what to do, he silently prayed.

Doc says she's getting better, but I don't see it, and I'm scared. I'm tired, Lord. I know I'm not supposed to be anxious, so I guess I'm asking you to give me peace and strength. Please tell me what to do to help her. Please, Lord. I'll do anything—except give her up. Please don't ask me to do that again. I don't think I can. I love her so much. I need her. Please give me the strength to give her what she needs. Let the doctors figure out what's wrong and heal her. You gave her to me in the first place. Please help us both. I love you, Lord. Give me grace, peace, and strength to han-

FROM SHADOWS TO DAYBREAK

dle what's next. I can't pray anymore. Just help me. Help us. I ask this in the name of Jesus. Amen.

He pleaded with God, something he didn't think he would ever have to do again. This had become all too familiar, and he didn't like it.

Franklin wiped away the tears that escaped his eyes while he poured out his heart to his Lord. Was that the right prayer? Is there a right or wrong way to pray? He decided to stop with the introspection. He was too tired. Exhausted, he fell asleep.

"Frankie, are you okay?" she whispered.

Fast asleep, he didn't hear her. A few minutes later, Kathleen turned over and kissed him on the cheek. She loved him so much. She knew exhaustion had overtaken him and felt guilty that he spent so much time at the hospital. She just wanted to go home. She missed her husband. She missed loving him. She wanted to be healthy again, but she didn't feel better. She wanted a full life with him, but maybe she would never get better. Maybe she wouldn't survive this after all. Maybe she needed to prepare Frank for her passing and help him move on with his life. The tears began to flow. She didn't want to wake him, and she tried not to make a sound, but the sobs came anyway—hard and fast.

Lord, I don't want to leave him. We're going to be a family. We are a family. Please help me get better so Frank can have this child. Even if I don't survive after childbirth, please let him have this baby. He's waited so long. Please, that's all I ask of you. Please make me strong enough to bear his child, she prayed silently.

"Kathy, are you okay?"

"Please, Frank, hold me." She sobbed. She didn't want to but she couldn't stop.

"Oh, darling, tell me what has you so upset? Why are you crying? Are you sick? Do I need to call a nurse or doctor?"

"No, I'm just scared, Frank. I'm afraid I'm…I can't. Please just hold me."

He took her in his arms and held her tightly. "Kathy, my darling, I love you so very much. Please tell me what's wrong."

"I can't. It's too…I can't."

"Please, tell me. I'm here. I'm not leaving you."

"I know. I'm afraid…afraid I'm leaving you. It's too hard to think about it. I don't want to leave you, Frank. I love you and our baby. Please don't let me go. Please stay with me forever. I can't…I don't want to leave you."

He held her tightly. Then he stopped. A renewed hope, strength, and a peace that was so unexpected—but probably shouldn't have been—took hold of him. "Kathy, I won't let you leave me. You *must* get better. I just prayed about this, and for the first time since you came in here, I believe the Lord has answered my prayer. You are going to get better. You are going to have our s—baby. God is giving us a miracle right this very minute. I'm telling you. It's as if he reached down and took hold of my heart to tell me that he heard me. You are staying with me. Now believe it, Kathy. Embrace it with all your heart. God is giving you renewed health. Trust him. Please? It is going to happen."

"Really, Frank?"

"I know it. I believe it, and I want you to believe it too."

"Would God give us this miracle?"

"He *is* giving us this miracle. He wants us to be a family, and we will be a family.

"Frank, if you believe it, then I'll believe it too. I'm going home to be your wife and mother to our baby. I do, I believe it!"

Thank you, Lord, for answered prayer. Thank you for saving my Kathy and our son. I believe you are going to do great things through our child, and I trust that you will let us live long enough to see some of them. Thank you for the miracle you are giving us, though undeserved. Thank you for renewed faith, peace, and strength that we know only came from you. We are so grateful and love you, Lord. Amen. Silently, he thanked God for the miracle that he believed with all his heart would begin soon.

Chapter 40

Mid-March 1951
Weaver Residence

Sighing, as she hung up the phone, Marianne's head dropped. Would this job ever get easier? She already knew the answer but believed she had to keep trying. Placing Lincoln in a foster home had become more difficult. There simply were not enough families to take a young boy. Most wanted a baby, not a child with a checkered past. They were already stretched to take an infant. It was difficult to induce families to foster children at all. There were legitimate reasons. One, the children didn't usually stay; they hoped to eventually adopt their foster child. When that didn't come to fruition, they soon became disillusioned and stopped the program altogether. It was too easy to become attached, just to have them taken away later.

If the child became difficult, with a background that included some kind of abuse, that made it challenging to communicate effectively. Assuaging the anger and rage that were either right below the surface or right on their sleeve, ready to explode at any second became impossible. Belligerent, argumentative, destructive, running away—all these things were so complicated for anyone to deal with, but especially for those without counseling training, or any kind of training, for that matter. Most are ordinary families that are ill-equipped for a child that is so damaged and broken.

This kid had to go somewhere. There had to be someone out there who could handle a kid who had such potential, yet unable to break through and live up to it, at least at this point. She needed to talk to someone who might know a little about him, which might help her find a family for him. She called the hospital and asked if they knew if Lincoln had any contact with someone who might know him, even a little. The nurse gave her both Franklin's and Miles's names and said they were both at the hospital currently. Marianne concluded that it was time to go to the hospital and see what she could find out about this kid, praying that the Lord would help her discern what this kid needed and who could best give him those things.

Chapter 41

Mid-March 1951
General Hospital

Marianne scheduled a meeting with both Franklin and Miles at the same time in Miles's room. She wanted to hear what they had to say.

"So, Mr. Strattford, can you tell me anything about Lincoln? I understand you were the one who brought him into the hospital in the first place."

"First, call me Miles. Yes, I brought him in. I found him lying in the alley beaten so badly he was almost dead. I picked him up and brought him straight here. I know that he lives on the street, and I suspect he was beaten by others who were probably older than him for whatever he had just stolen. I know enough to know there's a code on the street. Those boys will do anything to get the younger ones to work for them at a huge cost. The beating is so bad, that the kid easily would agree to do what they ask, then they leave him in the street, not caring if he lives or dies."

Marianne sighed. "It's so awful what happens to those kids who have no place to go. Do you know anything about his parents?"

"I tried to ask him about it yesterday, but he said he didn't want to talk about it. I'm trying to build a relationship with him. Yesterday we played checkers, and he responded very well to the competition.

It kind of broke down his defenses a little. We talked about sportsmanship, which was a brand-new concept to him."

"That's great. Board games are good for bringing out a sense of family, and some of the good things that may have existed in his family setting. It does lower the walls a little, a least for a while, which shows that there may be hope for him yet."

"Do you feel the same way about him, Franklin?"

"I haven't had too much time with him. I've been spending most of it with my wife who's admitted here as well. I am attempting to build a relationship with him and have been up to talk to him. I bought a game to play with him, but Kathleen took a turn for the worse, and I've been staying with her. Although I believe she will get better. Meaning, I may be freer to spend a little more time with him. I think he's a good kid who's been broken by circumstances that he's had no control over. I don't believe he's a hardened criminal or anything. He might respond positively to a family that can circle around him and just let him be a little boy, without having to try to survive on his own, and love him."

"I'm so sorry that your wife is ill. That must be difficult for you."

"Thank you. I believe she'll get better."

"I'm glad to hear that. Any other information you can give me?"

"Not really. Kathleen and I are newlyweds and can't take in a little boy. If circumstances were different, we might have been able to, but certainly not now."

"Unfortunately, I'm single, and the illness I am currently struggling with is supposed to take months to recover, and there's no real cure. It's just rest and lots of sleep. Can't do that with a kid. Honestly, I've never even thought about bringing a child into my home, but I'm starting to take a liking to him, and I think underneath it all, he's a good kid. He just needs someone who cares and is willing to take the time to nurture and love him.

"I think Miles is right. Lincoln needs a lot of love and acceptance, and to know things are permanent, and it all won't be ripped away from him once he allows himself to feel something good."

FROM SHADOWS TO DAYBREAK

"Well, thank you for taking the time with me today. I think this information may help me locate a family that might work for him. It's always a dicey thing, and knowing that Jesus loves every one of those kids helps me put them into his hands and try to let go, so I can sleep at night. Otherwise, it's practically impossible. I've had nightmares about what has happened to some of my cases. God is the only reason I can do this job at all."

"Well, Marianne, I'll be praying for you. This has got to be one of the most challenging jobs there is. There's so much tragedy and pain in this world and people who don't care about their kids. I don't envy you at all. I sure couldn't do it."

"Me either. I commend you, for taking such a difficult job, and it sounds like you are doing it to the best of your ability. Keep on keeping on. I'll continue to work with Lincoln, and we'll see what happens."

"Thank you, gentlemen. We'll be in touch," she added, as she walked out the door. Both men bid her goodbye and began their conversation.

"What do you think, Franklin?"

"I guess, I think she'll do the best she can. I'm glad I'm not her."

"Yeah, that's for sure. Now tell me about Kathleen. What's happened that you said she took a turn for the worst?" He queried, concern covering his face and eyes.

"They tried to walk her just a few feet, and they had to bring her back and put her to bed. She fell asleep before they could get the blankets on her. I got up on the bed with her and put my arm around her, and she didn't even stir, not even a sigh or anything. I was so scared, Miles. I fell asleep because of exhaustion, and when I woke up, Kathy was sobbing and telling me that she was leaving me—dying—and she didn't want to leave. She wants us to have the family we're supposed to have.

"Miles, I have never felt so helpless before. I held her tightly. Then, this miracle happened. I felt a peace and strength that weren't there just moments before, and I told her she was not going to leave me. God had answered my prayer. I knew he was going to heal her, and we're going home, having our child, and watching him grow up.

We both believe it now, and we have put ourselves and our family into his hands to watch this miracle happen."

"Wow! I'm so sorry you've been through that. But I have to say I admire your faith in God and the way you're holding out for that miracle. You said you were sure you were going to watch *him* grow up. You think you're having a boy," he said, with a *gotcha* smile.

"Just a feeling, I guess." Franklin's grin exposed his assurance.

"Well, I'm just glad that you're feeling better about things, and I hope you're right about the miracle. It sounds like you two are due for one."

"Thanks, Miles. I'm going to let you get some sleep. Would you mind taking on Lincoln again without me today? I need to be with Kathy."

"Sure, think nothing of it. He's looking forward to it anyway, and I think I'm finally making inroads with him. If not, I can set up a phone call, and I'll let him know that you are dealing with your wife's illness and will be up as soon as leaving her isn't a hardship for either of you."

"Thank you. I appreciate it. I need to be with her, and I don't have enough energy to spread it around so thinly. I'm exhausted, but I try not to show it in front of Kathy. I don't want her to take on any guilt that could hamper her recovery."

"Do not worry. I got this."

"Thanks. Well, I better get back. Is there anything I can do for you before I leave?"

Not today, but I would like to talk with you soon about something. But for now, go to her. She needs you, and from the looks of things, I think you need her too, so go."

Walking out the door, he waved goodbye and thanked him again. He headed to Kathleen's room, hoping he could finally get some rest.

Chapter 42

April 1941
University of Colorado, School of Business

Waiting by the brick building for Brad to pick her up, Rebecca's excitement grew. As usual, he wouldn't explain their destination, but was always a wonderful surprise. He was so attentive, attractive, kind, exciting, truthful, honorable, and trustworthy, and she was falling in love with him. He almost sounded like a Boy Scout. He had had an innocence about him that allured her. Always relaxed, their conversations were easy and stimulating. They talked about so many things, including current events and school. She believed she knew him well and was completely comfortable around him. Like Jericho, all her walls had completely crumbled, but she had no fear or reticence about the relationship at all. Even that fact didn't incite alarm.

Today, he told her to dress casually, bring a jacket, and wear shoes in which she could walk comfortably. Usually, their dates were dress-up affairs, but not this time, so she couldn't wait to see what he had up his sleeve.

He sneaked up behind her and put his arm around her shoulder.

"Oh, Brad. You startled me, but at least you didn't scare me this time. I must be getting used to this routine."

"Probably. Are you ready for this date? I promise we haven't done this before, and I hope you're up to it, Becca," he added, with a smile on his face and a raised brow.

Cheryl Fosnot Bingisser

"Listen, Mr. Blue Eyes, I can handle anything you can dish out. So yes, I'm more than ready."

"Let's go. Where are we going?"

"Now really? With all the dates we've gone on, have I ever told you ahead of time where we're going or what we're doing?"

"Well, no, but I thought this might be different." She giggled.

"Not likely, my friend," he said, tilting his head and grinning. "Get in the car, oh, curious one. We've got a bit of driving to do."

"Okay. I'm ready!"

After an hour, Brad parked the car alongside a country road in the middle of nowhere. The questions Rebecca had were many, but she held her tongue. Brad's face was fairly glowing with excitement and hopeful contemplations, rendering her knees weak.

"Okay, Becca, grab your jacket and let's move," he commanded. "I just have to get a little something out of the trunk."

He pulled out a bag that he slung over his shoulder, and he placed his hand on the small of her back, moving her forward. Brad led her down a small, worn path. After about a mile, most of which happened to be uphill, he stopped. Rebecca gazed out over the scenery in front of her and took a deep breath.

"Oh, Brad, it's beautiful up here." She pointed to a massive waterfall off to the left as tons of water fell over the rocks totally unencumbered with amazing power and ease. There were all kinds of wildflowers in pink, white, yellow, blue, and lush greens on both sides of the fall that almost made it look tropical.

Brad watched her enjoy the beauty around her, and his heart soared at her delight.

"It's so beautiful, isn't it?"

"Not as beautiful as you," he murmured softly.

She looked at him and studied his face and eyes. There was something there that she hadn't seen before and she liked it. Could it be love? Could he be falling in love with her?

She dropped her eyes and smiled shyly. "I don't know what to say to that."

"You don't have to say anything. It's only something that I've observed for a long time and never told you."

FROM SHADOWS TO DAYBREAK

"Well, thank you."

He turned away, grabbed the bag, and opened it. Pulling out a blanket, he threw it on the ground, then he brought out some fried chicken and potato salad, plates, silverware, and napkins. Next were two champagne glasses and a bottle of champagne.

"Well, what do you think?"

"Brad, this is wonderful. Thank you for this. I don't suppose you fried the chicken or made the potato salad, so just where are you hiding your cook? Is she in the bag somewhere?"

Brad laughed. "No cook, just take out, but I wish I had a cook. My roommate's cooking is as bad as mine. We'd starve if we weren't on campus."

Becca laughed. "Yes, I know what you mean. We have one cook in our room, but she's out all the time, so she never cooks, leaving us to our own devices. Not a good plan. Campus food, while not my first choice, is better than no food at all."

He laughed, as he brought out the food and put it on the blanket, then opened the champagne and poured each of them a glass.

He held his glass up, as did she. They clinked, and both said cheers at the same time. They gazed into each other's eyes and didn't look away for several seconds. A spark of electricity struck them.

Brad said grace over the food, something she hadn't seen anyone else do, but he did it every time they ate together. She had become used to it and had begun to listen intently to what he was saying to his God. Becoming interested in who this God was and what he had to do with people personally—with her personally; she needed to know. Was he an intimate God? Did he care about people enough to listen to their prayers and answer them, or did a simple recitation spoken like so many other religions, appease his god? But his prayers seemed so personal like God was sitting next to him instead of millions of miles away. She hungered to know the answer but was afraid to ask.

They finished eating, and Brad took some pictures of the scenery and the scenery that was seated next to him on the blanket. He couldn't take his eyes off her. He took a deep breath and blew it out. He had to find something else to think about.

The sun had already set with brilliant colors of orange, pink, and yellow, but twilight trailed right behind. Time to pack up and head for the car. They walked down the path where he had parked the car, but it had vanished. Maybe they were looking too far north or south. They walked both ways. Nope, the car was nowhere in sight, and they were stranded.

Rebecca looked at Brad wondering what he must be thinking.

"Becca, I can assure you that this was not part of the date."

"I can believe that. What are we going to do?"

"I guess we start walking. Whoever stole my car must be having a good laugh at my expense."

"Our expense."

"Right." He dropped his head and sighed. "Becca, I'm so sorry about this. We're a long way away from anything or anyone. If you're more comfortable making a shelter and spending the night together, we can do that. I don't mean together, together. Just with each other."

"I knew what you meant. There doesn't seem to be any light on the road at all. Do you think we can find a place to hunker down until morning?"

"Sure, I am a Boy Scout you know. Eagle Scout, actually," he explained to her while he recited the Boy Scout salute, and then the Boy Scout mission.

Becca laughed. "Well, Boy Scout—"

"Eagle Scout," he corrected her with a grin.

"Yes, Eagle Scout. Well, I suggest we *scout* out a place to stay so we don't freeze to death."

"Yes," he said chuckling, "I think you're right."

They hiked back up the trail until Brad found the perfect spot for the night. He didn't have anything with him to start a fire, but he could do it the old-fashioned way—rubbing two sticks together. He had done it before and knew it would get too cold not to have some source of heat. They gathered some small twigs and things that would catch fire easily.

Brad knew he needed to get everything set up before darkness overtook them. He found some soft leaves and branches for the floor, large branches to lean against, and a huge tree that had to be at least

178

FROM SHADOWS TO DAYBREAK

thirty feet high. They could crawl back inside that area and be safe. He did have the common sense to bring a flashlight, so at least they had that. He supposed they could have used it to walk down the road, then dismissed the idea, believing staying here was the best option. He took himself to task for the fact that he had no matches with him. He couldn't have been more stupid. *Be prepared.* Yeah, he messed that up really well.

They still had food left over, so something good there. There was lots of champagne, but getting drunk, while keeping warm, probably not the best idea when they were so close together—alone. Brad went to work on a fire, and before too long, the fire roared, kept animals away, and kept them nice and warm.

Contented, Rebecca sighed. Since Brad was with her, she harbored no fear. She instinctively knew he would take care of her and protect her. She felt loved—a foreign feeling, to be sure, and almost afraid to trust it. Maybe it's what she desperately wanted, but before now hadn't realized it. How would she know for certain? Even though she knew her grandparents loved her, she ached for something outside that—something special. Something she couldn't identify until today. She wanted a relationship with a man who loved her. Is Brad the one? Is that the glimmer she observed in his eyes? Did he feel that way about her?

Making everything on the ground as comfortable as possible, he asked Rebecca to come and try it out.

"Is it comfortable enough for you?"

"I think so."

Brad got the blanket out of the bag and covered her with it. She kept her jacket on and had worn warm socks, so at least she'd done that right.

"I think you need to get under this blanket too, Boy Scout," she teased, grinning.

"I'm fine. The fire's here and I'm strong and masculine," he proclaimed, with his arms up and hands fisted like he was lifting weights.

"Right. If I need a blanket, so do you. So stop arguing with me and get under here."

"Becca, I'm fine."

"Come on. The blanket's big. There's plenty of room."

"Becca, do I have to spell it out for you?"

"What do you mean? I just want you to stay warm."

He took a deep breath. "Look, I don't know how to say this delicately, so here goes: I'm afraid that if I get under that blanket with you, I will want to do more than I should. Now do you understand? I hope I didn't offend your sensibilities, but you pushed me, and I guess I'm not very good at being delicate."

"Oh. I'm sorry." Heat flooded her face. I wasn't even thinking that at all."

"I know, but I am. I don't want to do anything that would hurt you or me. I'm keeping myself for my bride. If that's you in the future, that would be great, but in any case, I can't give that up to anyone but her, and on my wedding night—not before. The temptation would be too great, and I'm only human. You are a beautiful woman and I...I...never mind. I probably should have kept that to myself. I'm sorry."

"Don't be. I'm sorry. I'm so thickheaded that I made you say it out loud. Forgive me for being so stupid."

"No, you're not stupid. In fact, it's rather endearing because all the other women are thinking about that all the time. It's quite refreshing, but I'm sorry I had to spell it out like that."

"No apology needed. I guess I'm going to try to get some sleep. You gonna be, okay?"

"Yeah, I'm fine. I'll keep the fire going so we both stay warm and keep the animals away. Get some sleep. We still have quite a hike to take tomorrow. And thinking about tomorrow, we're likely to face a lot of flak for not going back to campus tonight. No one, including the faculty, will ever believe that we didn't sleep together. We could face suspension or something worse, not to mention what some of the students are going to believe and gossip about. I hope you're prepared for that."

"I never thought of that, either. Listen, Brad, I'm sorry about all of this. I feel like it's kind of my fault because I persuaded you to stay, rather than walk back."

FROM SHADOWS TO DAYBREAK

"Becca, this is not your fault. The car being stolen isn't my fault either. Life sometimes isn't fair, and we've hit one of those spots. Don't blame yourself for any of this. We can weather this storm together. If we get suspended, we'll handle it like adults and figure out our next move. We'll be fine. A lot worse things could have happened to us, and who knows, maybe they'll even believe us. Stranger things have happened."

"I guess so, but I feel awful about it."

"Well, don't. We had a good day, didn't we? I mean, we had fun and we saw God's beautiful creation, ate a good meal together, and drank some champagne. I enjoyed myself, and I'd do it again. A great day indeed."

"When you say it like that, I guess that's true. Thank you for taking care of me in—several different ways. I appreciate it. I'm proud of you for thinking of both of us like that and I feel—"

"What?"

"I feel...well, closer to you for this. I'm sorry if that's too blunt, but you've been honest with me, and I'm being honest with you."

"I'm glad you told me that. Becca...I think I'm...I'm so afraid to say this."

"Please say it. I need to hear it tonight."

"I'm falling in love with you. I don't know how you feel. I just hope you won't walk away from me now."

"No, you don't understand. I'm falling in love with you too."

"Really?"

"Really."

Brad walked over to her and cupped her face in his hands. He gazed into her eyes and kissed her forehead.

"Okay, now that we know that, we have to be even more careful. It's going to be harder, Becca."

"I know. But I promise, I'll try not to make it any harder on you. Now that we both know, maybe that makes it easier in a way. We don't have to speculate on what the other one is thinking."

"I couldn't tell you what I was thinking, anyway." They laughed nervously.

"Together, we can figure this out. We'll do this right. I promise you."

"Yes, but only with God's help."

Chapter 43

Mid-March 1951
Mountain View High School

Emily finally felt brave enough to go back to school. It was wonderful to see her friends again. She missed them. She loved being back in class. Choir was so much fun and, probably her favorite class. At lunchtime, the girls all headed to the lunchroom together.

Suddenly, out of nowhere, one kid grabbed her and started to pull her away from the other girls. Two more accomplices joined him and assisted in pulling her into the boys' restroom. The girls rushed after her. The young men started ripping her clothes off.

"We know what you want, and we're just the ones to give it to you. Stop fighting and playing hard to get and let us do what we know you want." They pulled at her hair and threw her down on the floor. The girls rushed in, kicked them, and pushed them away. A cold, mocking laugh escaped from the young men. "It's okay. We'll be back. She's begging for it. Brent told us she was easy. We just want some of the action. It's all just a game to her and playing hard to get is a part of it."

Traumatized, Emily couldn't move. Shaking violently, the girls helped her get up from the floor. They tried to call Rebecca, but she didn't answer the phone. They weren't sure what to do. Emily begged them not to go to any teacher or the principal. She just wanted to go home. They paid for a taxi to get her home safely and walked her upstairs. With Emily in shock, she could hardly communicate at all. They stayed with her as long as they could, but they didn't know what else to do. They made certain they tucked her in bed and covered her, so she would stay warm. They hugged her, said they would call her later, and left.

Emily tried to sleep. Every time she closed her eyes, she saw them and the attacker from months before. They were all together, clawing at her, laughing at her, and treating her like nothing—a zero. Just like garbage that no one cared about. She sobbed uncontrollably. *Why does this keep happening to me?* She was only trash to be used and thrown away. Boys didn't care for her. They just wanted to use her. *Used. Trash. Garbage.* My only reason to live. Her parents never wanted her, and now the boys just use her. *I'm worthless. I'm an awful person! I don't belong here. I don't belong anywhere!*

* * * * *

Rebecca had been running errands and then set off for the school. She kept her word. She didn't go to Brent's parents or the principal, but she did go to the coach of the football team to tell him exactly what happened.

He grieved for Emily and what the kid did to her. Livid with the young man, he asked Rebecca if she would mind taking some time and praying with him about this, to determine exactly how to handle the situation. It unquestionably needed severe punishment.

Encouraged by his reaction, she said she would be happy to pray with him. She confided in him what had happened to Emily earlier, and why this had been so upsetting. He understood. He had teenage girls at home and as a father, this would be his worst nightmare. This should not have happened. They spent about a half hour in prayer for wisdom on how to proceed. He needed to talk to the principal before he did anything else, but he promised to keep Rebecca's confidence about Emily and Brent's pass at her.

In the meantime, he would be praying for her and Brent, the football star who would be punished. Those who were Christians on the team needed to know what happened and what the consequences

FROM SHADOWS TO DAYBREAK

were so they could pray for the team regularly. Contemplating his next move, he considered starting a Bible study during lunch. No law would be broken here, and these kids could obviously use it. It's not like he needed anything else on his plate, but this was serious and needed to be dealt with on many levels. He fell to his knees.

Oh, God, I feel so inadequate to do this. This boy, and boys like him, lack direction, and they apparently aren't getting it at home. Help me do this right. Direct me so this is taken care of in a way that honors you and helps this boy do the right thing. And, Lord, for Emily, I hurt for her. Help her heal from those awful wounds she's carrying around with her. She's so torn up by this, and this kid has no idea what he's done. Help me, Lord Jesus. Give me your grace, love, strength, and especially wisdom. Amen. While he prayed, he felt God's presence with him.

* * * * *

Rosa and Heidi had decided to go back to school and talk to the principal about the act perpetrated by the three boys on the football team this afternoon. They knew they could be betraying Emily's trust, but they couldn't stand by and do nothing. There was still an hour before school ended, so they knew he would still be in his office. They asked the secretary if they could talk to him. He had just hung up from a very difficult parental phone call and seemed quite agitated. The secretary said no, there was no time on his schedule, but the girls insisted it was extremely important they see him, and they weren't leaving until they could. At last, she relented, and they walked into his office.

The girls shared the whole story.

Principal Jackson bellowed. "Gloria! Get Coach in here, immediately! It's an emergency!"

"Yes, sir, Mr. Jackson. I'm on it."

The girls left to go home. Their parents had to be informed of the situation, and if they needed to meet, Mr. Jackson was willing to do it. But he told them they should be proud of themselves for

185

fighting back and preventing what could have been a tragedy of epic proportions.

* * * * *

Rebecca knew she'd done the right thing and had been pleased that Coach not only acted swiftly but also was a Christian and very sympathetic to Emily. Maybe she should have reported it earlier, but she argued with herself for far too long. Coach's reaction vindicated Emily, and Rebecca had been relieved to leave it in his hands.

She would remain in prayer about it, but now knew it would be handled correctly. She thanked God that he had put Coach where he did, maybe just for this reason.

She parked her car and scurried upstairs to talk with Emily. It would remain a secret as far as the coach was concerned—at least for now. She knocked on the door. Emily didn't answer. She slowly opened the door. Rebecca's scream split the silence.

"Oh, God, no!" She ran to Emily, then swiftly ran to the bathroom, grabbed washcloths and small towels, wrapped Emily's wrists as tightly as she possibly could, then tried to wake her. Fear rose in Rebecca's heart. Had she lost Emily? Her face had drained of any color and her lips were a ghastly shade of blue. Blood dripped from everywhere; the bedding, the floor—her hands. She recalled the last horror movie she had watched and a shiver ran up her spine. A real life could be ebbing away. Rebecca ran to the phone to call Doc and never had been more relieved that his office was right downstairs. He arrived in just a minute.

He promptly examined her. "Becca, it would have only been a minute longer, and she would have been gone. We need to get her to the hospital now. I'm calling the ambulance because someone needs to be with her who can give her medical attention while she's on her way there. I'll go directly to the hospital and meet you at emergency." She heard the sirens in the background. "I'll direct them to this room. They will know what to do. You can ride with them if you want to, but time is of the essence. We could still lose her. Do you have any idea why she would do such a thing?"

FROM SHADOWS TO DAYBREAK

"Yes. But I had no idea she was so devastated. She seemed healthier and handling things better. Oh, this is my fault. I should have known she was this fragile."

"Becca, this is not your fault. But she is going to need you if she survives this. Pray for strength and wisdom because you're going to need them."

The ambulance crew ran in, the nurse checked her out, and understood her to be stable, for the moment. They started an IV, lifted her onto the gurney, and took her downstairs to the ambulance. They allowed Rebecca to come with them, but only if she kept out of the way. They may use her to talk to Emily since she was there, but their main task was to keep her alive until the hospital staff could take over.

They rushed her directly to emergency and they expeditiously worked on her. Doc Anderson hastily entered and apprised them of the situation. He ordered a blood draw stat, for her blood type, then ordered the blood.

They asked Rebecca to fill out insurance forms and all those mundane details, but she couldn't keep her hands from shaking long enough to write. She endeavored to pray, but all that passed her lips were the loud sobs that shook her shoulders. She needed someone here with her. Someone who could sit with her and pray with her. She thought of Kathleen but arbitrarily dismissed the idea. Maybe she could get a hold of Franklin, at least to tell him, so he could be praying. Then Maddie came to mind. She hurried to the phone and dialed, praying that she would answer. It rang four times before she heard Maddie on the other end.

"Hello."

"Maddie, this is Becca." She couldn't hold the sobs back.

"Becca, what's wrong? Is Kathleen, okay?"

"I don't know. I haven't seen her. It's about Emily. She slit her wrists today, and she's in the hospital. Could you please come and be with me? She could still die. There was so much blood. It was awful. Maddie, I'm so scared. Please come."

It was difficult for Maddie to fully understand Rebecca since the sobbing muffled some of her words. She did distinguish enough to know there was an emergency, and it included Emily. "I'll be right there. Hang on, Becca. I'll be praying the whole way. Should I bring Raff?"

"I don't know. Maybe not yet. I'm trying to keep the suicide attempt as quiet as possible. Thank you, Maddie. I'll see you in a few minutes."

She reached the nurses' desk and asked if they could get a message to Franklin to come to emergency. "It's important, and I don't think I should leave right now." The nurse explained that she could page him, but Rebecca didn't want to disturb Kathleen or worry her. "I don't know. I just need to see him."

"I'll send someone down right away."

"Thank you. I'd appreciate it."

One of the younger nurses left and returned in a few minutes. She spotted Franklin coming around the corner, and Rebecca ran to him and hugged him.

"Becca, what's wrong?"

Rebecca relayed the events of the last half hour. "Emily slit her wrists this afternoon, and I found her barely breathing. I'm so scared, Franklin. I didn't want to bother you or Kathleen, but I needed someone with me, and I knew you were here."

Franklin held her. "No, I'm glad you got a hold of me. I'm so sorry, Becca. How is she?"

"I don't know. Doc said she lost so much blood she still might not make it. It's my fault, Franklin." Her eyes flooded.

"It's not your fault. Something like that is never your fault. Do you know why she did this?"

"Yes. She was almost attacked again. He tried to, and Emily kneed him in the groin, and she was able to get away. Franklin, it hurts, what he did to her. She was devastated, but I didn't know it had become this bad. I never dreamed she'd do something like this. I should have stayed with her." She sobbed.

Franklin kept his arms around her and walked her to a nearby bench. "Let's sit down over here. Now look, this is not your fault. That young man did this to her, and I hope they punish him harshly for it. It's awful, especially since that girl was already so vulnerable.

Why don't we call Pastor Ryan? I think it would be good if he were here for you and Emily. What do you think?"

She nodded. "Would you mind doing that? I'm having a hard time keeping it together at all."

"Of course, you are. It's okay, and I don't mind at all. I'll also tell Kathy. She can pray when she's awake. She would be furious with both of us if we didn't tell her."

"True." She smiled. "Thank you, Franklin. Maddie's coming as soon as she can. Maybe we can talk to Raff too. We need as many people as we can get to pray to help Emily through this."

"I agree. We can get a prayer line going at church too, if you would like. They wouldn't need to know the details, just that she needed prayer."

"That would be good. I'm sorry, Franklin, but I just can't seem to focus on anything. Will you do that for me?"

"Of course. Don't worry about a thing. I'll get things moving, and you just keep praying. I'll call Pastor Ryan to get the prayer line moving forward and ask him to come. We probably need to give him the details, though. Do you want to do that? I can stay with you if you want me to."

"I should let you get back to Kathleen."

"She's fine for a while. I can help. That's what friends are for. Besides, Maddie should be here in a little while, and I'm sure she'll take over from here."

"Okay. Thanks. I didn't even ask you how Kathleen is doing. Is she getting better?"

"I finally think so, yes. I think she's going to be okay. She has a way to go yet, but at least I am starting to feel like there's improvement. God is going to give us the miracle I've been praying for. It's taken a long time to get here, but it's going to be okay."

"I'm so glad, Franklin. I've been so concerned about her. She just didn't look good at all the last time I saw her."

"I know, and it got worse, but she turned a corner and it's getting better. I'm going to get my wife back yet." He smiled.

"That's so good to hear. I've been praying. Look, there's Maddie."

"Becca, I'm going to go do those things for you, and if there's anything else you need, just walk down to our room and let me know. I want to do what I can, okay?" He waved at Maddie and went back to Kathleen's room to make the calls. *If she's awake she'd want to know, and if she's sleeping, she'd want me to wake her, so I might as well make the calls from the room.* He smiled. He was beyond relieved that Kathleen felt a little better, but right now, his thoughts turned toward Emily and all that poor girl had yet to go through for healing. He prayed while he walked back to Kathleen. Praise God, he's still in the business of healing—body and soul.

Chapter 44

April 1942
University of Colorado, School of Business

    Poets write about beautiful days like this one. Puffy, white clouds floated by in stark contrast to the azure blue sky, even though the temperature remained a little cool. Brad had been so excited about their date tonight. He had asked Rebecca to dress formally because he would be wearing a tux. She had gone shopping with her roommates and bought a gown that Brad couldn't wait to see. She was stunning. They'd been dating now for over a year and had enjoyed every moment they had together, but graduation grew closer and he wanted to take the next step in their relationship. He believed Rebecca might be ready for it, and he knew he'd been ready for quite some time.
    Everyone on campus knew that the two of them were dating, so he hadn't been bothered by all the girls anymore, which meant he could pick Rebecca up on campus and walk with her to the car. Now that their dating had become common knowledge, and the need for the cloak-and-dagger stuff had come to a merciful end, Brad could now walk her to the car.
    He knocked on the door, and Rebecca leisurely opened it. Wearing a floor-length, emerald-green taffeta dress, with narrow straps and a sweetheart neckline, fitted to the waist, and then opening to a full skirt, she looked incredible. Silver high-heeled shoes

with a silver bag, and long diamond-looking earrings completed the formality of the dress. The emerald color of the dress made her eyes sparkle and dance and appeared perfect with her hair color.

Brad's jaw gaped. "Wow! You look spectacular. Stunning. Wow. I almost feel underdressed."

"On the contrary, Boy Scout, you look very handsome. The girls are going to fall all over you when they see you. I know I would, if you weren't already mine."

"My angel, you look so beautiful—not that you don't always, but this is beyond anything even in my dreams." He wrapped her in his arms and kissed her.

"Wow. Scout, you haven't forgotten how to kiss me since the last time I saw you. You're amazing. You steal my breath. Do you know that?"

"I try." He grinned.

"Well, you don't have to try too hard. So where are you taking me this time?"

"Okay, after all this time, I shouldn't have to recount the rules. You know I don't reveal anything until we get there."

"Yeah, but I spent all this money on my gown."

"Well, I can tell you that it was absolutely worth it. You look gorgeous!"

Laughing, she thanked him. "Fine. No more questions, but it better be worth it."

He chuckled as his eyes spoke of the love he held in his heart for her. "Oh, I think you'll find it worth your while."

"You know, when I was a kid, I was a tomboy, what with the rodeo and all, but this grown-up girl loves playing dress-up." She giggled.

"Well, I, for one, am very glad you grew up." He smirked with a side glance. "Just a few more minutes, and we're there, so you won't have to hold your tongue anymore. I know it's killing you." He chuckled.

"How did you know?"

"Because I know you, my angel."

"We're here."

FROM SHADOWS TO DAYBREAK

"This is the famous Oxford Hotel, isn't it?"

"Yes, it is. You are going to have an unforgettable evening, at least I hope it is."

"You don't have to worry about that. I'm already enraptured by all this. You're so wonderful, do you know that?"

"Yes, I do, but I'm glad you acknowledge it. I worked hard. I went to the School of Romance and Unforgettable Evenings. Didn't I tell you? It's right on my resume."

"I must have missed that part."

"Well, that's too bad because I got straight As."

He exited the car, walked around the front, and opened her door. He offered her his hand, and she stepped out of the car onto the ground. He gave her his arm and she slipped her arm through his.

"Such a gentleman," she said.

"All part of the excellent service, my angel."

"Hmm. I like this service. More, please," she flirted, with a smile and raised brow.

Brad laughed. "Trust me. There's more." He kissed her on the cheek.

"Is that all I get?"

"Later, angel. Just hang in there a little longer, okay?"

"I guess if I have to."

They walked up the stairs to the hotel, and the doorman opened the door for them. She glanced all around, stunned by the beauty of the place. *What did Brad have in mind for the rest of the evening?* Her mind tossed around several ideas. So far it had been lovely.

He placed his hand on the small of her back and led her into the restaurant. He left her standing, to speak to the head waiter. The waiter looked in the reservation book, found it, and led them back to a table in the corner which had been beautifully decorated. There were rose petals all over the white tablecloth, and a large vase full of red and pink roses with baby's breath and ornamental grasses. The lead crystal vase reflected the light that came from all the candles of different sizes on the corner of the table. It was beautiful and romantic, and Rebecca loved it.

He reached over, took her hand in his, and kissed it. "You're so beautiful, my angel. You do know I'm in love with you, right?"

"I thought so." She smiled flirtatiously. "I'm certainly in love with you."

"Really? I did not know that." He teased.

The waiter appeared. "Would you like a wine list, sir?"

Brad whispered in his ear, "I would like champagne for a very special occasion." He grinned conspiratorially.

Nodding, the waiter smiled. "Ah, yes, sir. Very good, sir. I shall return shortly with the very best we have. I believe you will be pleased." He returned with the glasses and champagne and poured it for them. "I will bring back a menu in just a few moments, sir."

"Thank you."

They sipped their champagne, and Rebecca was flying. It just couldn't get any better than this. She'd never been happier. Brad took her hand and laced his fingers through hers.

The waiter returned with the menus, and they both studied them. They chose their dinner, and the meal was outstanding. They drank more champagne and were both lost in their little world of romance and love. Suddenly, Brad stood up and walked to Rebecca's side of the table. He knelt on one knee.

Her hands flew to her face and her eyes grew larger.

"Becca, I love you. I have loved you since the night we got stranded on the mountain. But tonight, I want you to know that I can't live without you, and I ask you if you would please spend the rest of your life with me. Grow old with me, please? I love you, my angel."

She stood, wrapped her arms around him, and answered, "Yes, yes. Oh yes, Brad. I love you so. If I didn't have this gown on, I would have jumped into your arms." She laughed, and he laughed with her.

Everyone in the restaurant clapped as the two of them held each other. Suddenly, he became aware of the ring still occupying his pocket. He pulled it out and gently slipped it on her finger. The restaurant rang with laughter in celebration.

He led her to the dance floor. They danced to several tunes like, "Dancing in the Dark," "Let's Get Away from it All," "All of Me," and more. They danced the rest of the night. She rested her head on his shoulder and imagined how that would feel after they were married. Married. She would be marrying him and soon. Her heart took flight. She couldn't imagine being any more blissful than at this moment. Rebecca loved him, and he loved her. They were getting married and a whole new life would soon begin. Just the thought of marrying Brad seemed almost impossible—if it weren't true.

Brad was so full of joy that he thanked God for the miracle of love. He loved her so much, and they were about to be married and, in the future, start a family together. Happiness saturated his heart. The whole thing seemed surreal, but real it would be—very real—and their love would make this the happiest of marriages. It would last a lifetime. Although they hadn't set a date yet, neither of them could wait for that day to begin. They did know it would be after graduation.

Chapter 45

Mid-March 1951
General Hospital

Sitting in the chair by the window, studying Lincoln, Marianne tried to get to know this kid to find him a family. Something south of thrilled would describe his demeanor, and she wondered how to approach the subject.

"So what are you going to do when you leave the hospital?"

"Don't know."

"No plans then."

"Never needed 'em."

"Hmm. I see. What if I tell you that you need them now? The hospital is not going to release you until you have a place to go. Where are you going?"

"I told you, I don't know."

That's too bad. Your next stop could be juvenile detention."

"What's that?"

"Jail for kids."

"I didn't do nothin' wrong. Why would they put me in jail?"

"Because you have no place to live. They won't let you live on the street."

"I don't want to go to jail. I can take care of myself—just like always."

FROM SHADOWS TO DAYBREAK

"Yeah, I saw how well that worked for you. How long do you think it will be before they beat you up again if you don't do what they tell you, or if they just feel like it? They don't play by the rules, you know. Just because they tell you they'll protect you, doesn't mean they can't change their minds in a second, and you'd find yourself right back here again. Is that what you want?"

"At least they feed me in here and I have friends. I play checkers with Mister, and Franklin plays games with me too."

"You can't stay here forever, and neither can they. They'll go home. What home are you going to?"

"Maybe Mister will let me live with him. He likes me."

"I'm sure he does, but he's sick, and will be for a long time."

"Then I'll take care of him till he gets better."

"Sure. Are you going to cook for him and do his laundry?"

"Don't know. Just leave me alone. I don't need nobody." Lincoln turned toward the wall.

"Right. Well, what if I can find a family who would like you to come and live with them, just until something else comes up?"

"What if I don't like 'em?"

"We can talk about that later."

"Don't know. What if they don't like me?"

"Then we make different arrangements."

"'Rangements?"

"Different plans."

"I'll think about it. I'm tired. Leave me alone now." Lincoln turned toward the wall.

"Okay, Lincoln. I hope you will let me help you. I'll be back in a couple of days. Take care of yourself and be good to the doctors and nurses. They're here to help you get better. We all want that for you. Goodbye." She knocked on the door, and the nurse let her out and relocked it.

Mashing his face into the pillow, Lincoln cried. "Momma, where are you? I miss you so much. Please come and take me home. Please, Momma. Please, find me." He sobbed until he fell asleep.

Two days later, Marianne came back as promised. There were still no smiles from Lincoln to greet her. Fear of what the future held for him began to mount. He had been comfortable in the hospital and knew everyone now. Where would he go, and would Mister and Franklin come to visit him? Would he go to the kids' jail? Where could he go? Would a new family like him? Would he like them? What if it didn't work out and they didn't want him anymore? Then where would he go?

All the questions made him long for his momma, but she hadn't been to see him for so long. Maybe she didn't want him anymore either. They told him she had died, but that didn't mean she couldn't see him anymore, did it? Why hadn't she come to see him? He couldn't tell anyone he missed her; not sure what would happen if he did, but he didn't think it would be good.

"Lincoln, I found a family for you that wants you to come and live with them," Marianne explained. "They don't have any other kids and want to take care of you. They've always wanted a little boy like you. They own a farm with lots of room for you to run and play. They have sheep and goats, and you can play with them. There's so much for you to do. They will love you like their own and take good care of you. What do you say? Would you like to meet them? Once you meet them, if you don't like them, you don't have to go with them, but I hope you will at least try to make it work."

"I don't know. I want to stay with Mister." Tears started streaming down his cheeks.

"I know you do, and I wish you could, but you know he's sick, and he can't take care of you. I'm sorry Lincoln. I wish I could wave a magic wand and make it all better, but I can't."

"Can Mister and Franklin come and visit me?" He wiped his face with his hands.

"I'll make sure they can. I promise you that you can see them. I'll give you their phone numbers too so you can talk with them. I'm sure they would like that."

"Can I see them before I go?"

"Sure, I'll set it up for you. So what do you think?"

"I guess I could take a quick look at 'em. Maybe then decide, okay?"

"Okay, Lincoln. You know, you are a good kid, and I'm very proud of you for trying this. It takes a lot of courage, and it tells me you're very brave."

"I am, huh."

"Yes, you are. Would you shake my hand so I know that you will be my friend? I need another one."

"I guess I could. I don't got girl-type friends."

They shook hands. All Marianne wanted to do was hold him and let him know she would care for him. It wouldn't work! Why wouldn't it? She couldn't believe she was even entertaining the idea. She had no room for a kid in her life. There was no way it would work. Maybe it was time to think of someone else besides herself. She had to work. She couldn't take care of a kid. All these mental gymnastics were staging a coup.

"Goodbye, my friend. I will see you soon. Now be good and do what the nurses and doctors tell you, okay?"

"Everybody tells me that. I'll try."

"They just want you to get better." Marianne left Lincoln, walked down the hall to the ladies' room, and cried. *What am I thinking?*

Chapter 46

Mid-March 1951
General Hospital

Praying while he walked through the emergency doors, Pastor Ryan made his way down the hall until he saw Rebecca and Maddie sitting in the waiting room. He looked weary and concerned. He walked over to them and sat beside Rebecca.

"Becca, I'm so sorry. How is she doing?"

"I don't know. I haven't heard anything yet. It's so awful!"

"Do you know why she did this?"

Rebecca reported the story that Emily had told her earlier.

"This girl has been through so much and now this. She was more fragile than I thought. I shouldn't have left her alone."

"Becca, does Emily know the Lord?"

"No. That's the part that frightens me."

"Her soul is our first concern. We need to pray she survives this, so she has a second chance to meet Jesus before it's too late. Let's pray together that God preserves this girl's life and that she gets the help she needs to heal from all those wounds. She's going to be dealing with this for a very long time and will be quite fragile. She's going to need a lot of counseling. I've seen this before, and it's a long and painful process. Sometimes the counselor is chosen by the state, but sometimes they will allow a clergyman or pastor to do it. I hope it is the latter in this case because she needs the spiritual element to get

FROM SHADOWS TO DAYBREAK

past this. Only Jesus can heal her psychological wounds as well as physical ones."

They prayed together. They still had no word from the doctors, and Rebecca had become anxious. The prayers hadn't brought her peace, and she kept wondering if Emily would survive this violent act, she'd committed against herself. She ached for the girl, knowing how desperate she had to feel to consider implementing such a plan. Rehearsing the scene in her mind brought tears all over again.

* * * * *

Coach Johnson and Principal Jackson were in Jackson's office when the phone rang. Doc Anderson had called. When the principal got off the phone, the color drained from his face.

"Coach, this story just keeps getting worse." He shook his head. "After Emily's attack, she tried to commit suicide by slitting her wrists, and she's in the hospital. They're still not certain she's going to make it."

"Oh, God," the coach cried. He dropped his head in his hands. There were tears in his eyes while grief over this girl's pain seized his heart. "I can't imagine what she must be going through."

"Coach, I think we need to take a trip to the hospital and find out what's going on. Becca has to be worried sick."

"She was apprehensive before she even knew of the attack. No wonder Emily did this. She just wanted out. This has happened too many times, and I'm sure she believed by now that she deserved it somehow and couldn't handle it one more second."

"Sam," replied Coach, "I must tell you, for that kid to go back to the football team and tell them that Emily had been easy, and they could have fun with her too, is absolutely cruel. I think expulsion for these boys and for the one who started all this is the least we can do. The three who did the act should be brought up on charges. We can't let this go unpunished. A girl's life is at stake, and they think they are just playing around. They had no idea of the consequences." He rubbed his forehead. "This cannot be accepted behavior, and the punishment should be swift and severe."

Cheryl Fosnot Bingisser

"I agree with you. We might have to alert the school board, but her name must be preserved at all costs. She could never handle this becoming common knowledge. The embarrassment could kill her," expressed Principal Jackson.

"You know, this is what angers me. It's the men who do these things, and yet it's the women who feel ashamed and embarrassed. Their names are the ones that are dragged through the mud instead of the creeps that did the vile act. It's backward," added the coach angrily.

"I'm telling you now that the shame will not rest on her head. Somehow these boys will be called out and will face this with the community knowing what they did. The school will not allow this to happen again. The boys will face stiff consequences, and everyone will know why, even if it must be *leaked* somehow. I'm sick and tired of the women taking the blame for the men's behavior!" exclaimed the principal. "The courts will try to seal their files because the boys aren't eighteen. But not this time. Somehow it will get out before the court can keep it quiet. It might not be entirely ethical, but it will be just."

"I have no problem with that at all. It's time the men took a stand on this issue. Standing, Coach Johnson sighed. "Well, I think we'd better get to the hospital."

* * * * *

Pastor Ryan, Maddie, and Rebecca were still in the waiting room when Coach Johnson and Principal Jackson walked through automatic, sliding glass doors.

Becca introduced them and asked why they were there.

"Becca." Coach sat on Rebecca's other side. "We're so sorry to hear about Emily. How is she doing?"

"We don't know yet. All I know is that she could still die, and I haven't heard anything since we got her here over an hour ago. Mr. Jackson, how did you find out?"

"Doc Anderson called me. They must let the school know when something like this happens. The boys who did this to her will be

202

punished severely and may even be brought up on charges. I'm so sorry this happened to this poor young lady."

"I don't understand. What are you talking about?"

"You don't know?" asked Coach.

"Know what?"

The coach and the principal looked at each other, and both took a deep breath.

"Becca, three boys dragged Emily into the boys' restroom and attacked her. Rosa and Heidi were able to stop them, but Emily was so traumatized she couldn't even get up off the floor without the girls' help. They came back to school and told us what happened," Coach recapped the story, his eyes flooded with tears.

"We're so sorry. Is there anything we can do here?" Principal Jackson asked sympathetically.

Becca burst into tears. Maddie held her while she wept. Pastor Ryan introduced himself and said they had been praying for her, but they didn't know anything about the attack. This just became much worse than they thought. It was no wonder Emily did this. They pushed her over the edge, and she may never come back.

Maddie called Raff and then Franklin. They both came to the waiting room. They all prayed together over this girl, who had endured so much. The original rape with a knife to her throat, and the second threat with a knife; Brent, who tried to physically coerce her into kissing him, and fed the team false information; and now the attack in the restroom by three boys. This is more than any child should have to endure. Her innocence had been stolen. The fear and trauma with which it left her, would take an extended period of time, and a painful journey to emotional, physical, and spiritual health—if she even survived.

Chapter 47

Mid-March 1951
General Hospital

While sitting in chair by the window and reading her Bible, Kathleen noticed Franklin limping into the room.

"Do you have any idea how good it is to see you sitting up and reading?"

"I think so, Frankie. Come over here and kiss me. I'm getting stronger and kissing always makes me feel even stronger." She tilted her head and smiled.

"You are such a flirt, Mrs. Atwood." He lifted her chin and kissed her. "I love you, my dearest. It's so good to see you seated in a chair with a little bit of pink in your cheeks."

"How are you feeling?"

"A little better today. I'm getting better every day. Very soon, I can go home. Oh, I can't wait for that. I have plans—big plans for you, Mr. Atwood."

"Slow down, little filly. You've got a way to go before any big plans are made with anybody—even me."

"A little exercise never hurt anyone," she stated, with a flirtatious smile and a raised brow.

"Okay, I can see I'm going to have to *rein* you in." He laughed.

"Frank, not to change the subject, but how's Emily?"

FROM SHADOWS TO DAYBREAK

He dropped his head. "The news is not good. The coach and the principal came to support Becca and then told us that Emily had been dragged into the boys' restroom, and three boys attacked her. Her friends kept it from getting worse, but she had been clearly traumatized. That's why she did this. It all had become too much."

"Oh, Frank, that poor girl." Tears pooled in Kathleen's eyes. "This is awful. She may never recover from this." She shook her head and the tears flowed, unheeded.

Franklin took her in his arms and let her cry. "Sweetheart, please don't get too upset. I know you love her and are worried about her, and we all should be, but you can't let this make you sick again."

Kathleen sat with a straight spine and renewed strength. "Frank, you listen to me. You can't shield me from everything. I will not allow it. I'm getting better. Emily, Maddie, and Becca are my friends, and two of them are in trouble. Now what do you think I'm going to do about it? I can't sit by and do nothing."

Frank took a deep breath and blew it out. "Of course, you can't. I guess I forgot for a minute who I was talking to. I just worry about you. The one thing you can do is pray for her. She needs that most of all."

"Yes, that's true, but, Mr. Franklin Atwood, hear this: You are the one who told me in no uncertain terms that God was going to heal me completely and I am to embrace and believe that with all my heart. I did. Did you?"

"Wow. *Mister*, even. You must be upset." He chuckled, sighing. "Okay, you're right. You do know I hate it when you're right." They laughed. "I do want to shelter you. It's part of my job description as your husband, but I promise I will try to let you be you and do those things that you deem necessary and helpful. I'm also warning you. If I see you getting overtired and worn out, I *will* put a stop to it, Mrs. Kathleen Marie Atwood. Now do I make myself clear?"

"Crystal. You must be upset. It's the first time you've ever used my middle name like that. Impressive." She giggled.

Franklin shook his head. "Okay now. I'll talk to Becca and have her come to the room. I know that Pastor Ryan and Maddie are here too, but if you want them all in here, you will have a time limit imposed upon you. Got it?"

Kathleen rolled her eyes, "Got it, Mr. Franklin Mason Atwood."

"Touché," Franklin added. Franklin asked a nurse to send a note to Rebecca, and within minutes Maddie and Rebecca entered the room. Both had red eyes, the telltale signs of crying.

"Oh, Kathleen." Rebecca walked over to her and they hugged each other. "It's so awful. There was so much blood and I was terrified. She's gone through so much and now this. I can understand why she felt she had no alternative, but it makes me so sad, and I wish I could take all her pain away."

"Becca, how is she physically? Is she going to be alright?"

"All I've heard is that she's stable, but it's still touch and go. She lost so much blood, that when Doc examined her, he said just one minute more and she would have been gone."

"I'm so sorry, Becca. Maddie, get over here. We need a group hug." Maddie walked over to her, and they hugged each other and cried. "We need to keep praying for her. Those boys, if you can even call them that, should get what they deserve!"

Rebecca found her voice. "It sounds like both the coach and the principal are right there with you on that. He said what upsets him about this kind of thing is that it's the victim who bears the shame and embarrassment instead of the men who do this. I think it's time for the men in this community to stand and let the rest of these men know this will not be tolerated anymore."

"You know what?" Kathleen spoke. "If that is something they're thinking about doing, we need to get the women together."

Maddie chimed in, "You're absolutely right. This should never happen again. I think we should talk to the coach and the principal and bring this community together. We must care for one another to work toward this common goal. At the trial, we all come to show our support for them. I'm sick and tired of women being taken advantage of, and it's time we stopped it. And if we can get some men to stand with us, that will make a statement to the men in this town that it's over."

FROM SHADOWS TO DAYBREAK

"Okay, girls, I, for one, am with you, and I know most of the Christian men in this community should and will stand with us. So I say let's get the ball rolling and set something up. We'll get Pastor Ryan involved too. Bringing in the spiritual aspect of this won't hurt either," explained Franklin. "However, right now, our focus must be on Emily and her fragility. If she survives this, she will have a long journey ahead for her physical and emotional health. Since she doesn't know the Lord, we need to pray about that too because healing does come from him. I have personal knowledge of that." He looked over at Kathleen.

"Yes, you do. Thankfully, you look so much better than you did the last time we saw you," offered Maddie. "We're all so relieved."

"Thanks, girls. It's been a long haul, but God is healing me, and I'm feeling a little better every day. Hopefully, I can go home soon. I guess you could say I'm getting very homesick. I miss our bed, Hettie's cooking, the fireplace, and Frank. I miss the way things used to be."

"I'm sure you do," said Maddie, understanding what Kathleen didn't say.

Franklin, looking at the clock, sent a "time's up" look to Kathleen who ignored him. Then he glanced at his watch and up at her with a raised brow and a warning expression. Still trying to ignore him but thinking better of it, she nodded.

"Well, girls, Frank is giving me the 'look.' He wants me to cut this short, so instead of me making him the bad guy, I need to shoo you out of here before he decides I can never have visitors again."

"She's right. I did warn her. I just don't want her to get too tired. You know what's she been through, I want her well. We're both tired of being in the hospital and ready to go home but can't, till Doc says she's ready. So I need to let you ladies say goodbye. Becca, please keep us informed because we both still want to help and will be praying for all of you through this process. Let us know as soon as you hear anything about her condition, okay?"

"Yes, we don't want to tire her out either, and I need to check on Emily and see if there's any news on her condition. I just pray that whatever the news is, it's good. I don't think I can take any more bad news today. I've pretty much had it."

"It's understandable. Just the trauma of seeing her like that would be difficult. I'm so sorry you had to go through that. We will continue to pray and please do not be afraid to come into my—our room to fill us in," said Kathleen.

Franklin looked at her and gave her a knowing smile. The girls hugged each other and walked out of the room.

"Okay, Mrs. Atwood, it's time for you to rest."

"I know, but I need you to lie down beside me, okay?"

His brow raised, "Are you sure that's all you want from me, Mrs. Atwood?"

"I know it's not all I want from you, but that's all you'll give me, so I'll try to be satisfied with that, if you don't mind."

He raised her head and kissed her passionately.

"Come on. I'll help you get back into bed." He chuckled.

He helped her walk over to the bed and lifted her to lay her on the bed. He covered her up and kissed her on the cheek.

"Oh no, you don't, Mr. Atwood. A kiss on the cheek is not going to work. Not this time."

"Really, just what are you going to do about, Mrs. Atwood?"

She pulled him down and kissed him on the lips with amazing love and affection.

Franklin leaned into her and kissed back with a passion he'd been holding back for several days. Oh, how he missed this. Missed her, and now she would be coming back to him. Franklin had not forgotten who had brought her back to him from the brink of death. He inhaled a big breath and blew out.

"Just where is that lock when you need one?" he asked, laughing.

Chapter 48

Mid-March 1951
Atwood Residence

    Hettie returned from the mailbox with the letter that included a small flower drawing in the right-hand corner at the bottom of the envelope. She recognized the flower from decades earlier. Could it be? After all these years? Would she finally get in touch with her? Was there something wrong? It's been what? At least twenty-five years. Why now?
    She wished she could read her daughter's mind, but that had always been a difficult task. It wouldn't help her at all to open the letter since she'd never learned to read, so she'd have to wait until either Franklin or Kathleen could read it to her. How could she possibly think of anything else until then? When would Franklin return? She couldn't ask him to come home. It wouldn't be fair to him or Kathleen. She'd simply have to wait. Maybe someday she should learn to read. *That's ridiculous. I'm jes' too old to learn anythin' like readin' or writin'.*
    She hadn't heard from Franklin for a few days, but the last time he'd spoken to her, he'd said there was improvement, and things were progressing well. She thanked God, especially when he told her how critical her health had become. Hettie prayed fervently that God would spare her, fully aware that he could take her at any moment. She would have dealt with it if it happened, but she had been so grateful that God had chosen to bring her back and give her not only

her life but also the life of the precious child she was carrying. She hoped it was a boy, but no way to know for certain.

Wishing they were home so she could cook a real meal, she appreciated anew how empty the house had become without them. She missed them and missed cooking for them. Without them, there had been no entertainment (and they were very entertaining) and very little to do. Maybe she should return to the estate. There were always things to do there. Franklin could call her if they were coming home. It had been the first time she could ever recollect being bored. She could call Billy. Maybe he could take her for a drive or something. No, she couldn't keep him from his job. What would she do at the estate? No one to cook for except the staff, and they already had someone for that.

Kathleen had hired another person to take her place. Maybe she should go visit Kathleen in the hospital. Billy could drive her there. She still didn't know when they were coming home, and Franklin had said he'd take her. But if Billy drove her, then Franklin wouldn't have to leave the hospital. It had been weeks since she'd talked to Kathleen, and she missed her. Hettie looked over her dress and decided to gussy up a little. She called Billy and asked if he could come and drive her to the hospital.

"I'd be glad to Miss Hettie. Be there in a few minutes. Be good to see ya. Been a while. See you in a bit."

"Okay thanks, Billy."

She quickly got two meals ready to take to them and bagged them up.

William arrived in twenty minutes. The knock on the door drew Hettie's attention. Standing at the open door with a smile on his face, stood William. He grabbed her bag, the bag of food, and walked out the door. William opened the back door for her and waited for her to get seated, then closed the door. He walked around the front, opened his door, placed the bags on the passenger side, and slid behind the wheel. He glanced in the rearview mirror and asked if she was ready to go. She nodded, and they sped off down the road.

"So how's Miss Kathleen doin'?"

"Franklin said she's gittin' better fin'lly, but it's been real hard on 'em both."

"Glad to hear she's gittin' better. Been prayin' for 'em."

FROM SHADOWS TO DAYBREAK

"Thank ya kindly, Billy. Means a lot."

They tried to make small talk, but Hettie couldn't keep her mind off the letter. Just in case one of them felt up to it, she had it with her. William let her out in the driveway of the hospital, and Hettie walked up to the nurses' station.

"Yes, may I help you?"

"Mrs. Atwood's room number, please."

"Are you a family member?"

Hettie stopped to think for a second. "Yep, I am. Raised her myself."

The nurse raised a brow and looked Hettie up and down, then looked up the room number. "She's in room number 104, right down the hall."

"Thank you." Hettie turned and walked down the hall. She knocked on the door, and no one answered. Disappointed, she started to walk away when Franklin opened the door. Surprised to see her standing there, he threw his arms around her. She was a sight for sore eyes. She walked in and noticed Kathleen asleep.

She looked at Franklin and whispered, "Is she okay? Can I talk to her?"

"Kathy, my dearest, you have a very special visitor." He smiled knowingly.

"Hmm...I do?"

Hettie walked around the other side of the bed and gazed upon her.

Franklin watched with amusement as Kathleen spotted her.

She gasped. "Hettie, it's so good to see you." They hugged each other, and Kathleen did not want to let go of her. "Oh, Hettie, I've missed you so much. Did you bring us anything?" She smiled.

"Now, girl, do ya think I'd come all this way without somethin' to warm up your insides?"

"Hettie. I'm so tired of hospital food I could scream. You are a lifesaver."

Franklin laughed. "Me too. If I see one more bowl of green or red Jell-O, well, let's say that the breakfast I had this morning might come back and make an appearance in a totally different form—one no one would enjoy."

Everyone laughed.

Opening her bag, she pulled out slices of roast beef, mashed potatoes, gravy, and a green salad. Franklin began salivating before she even pulled out the gravy. It smelled like heaven in that room, and they dug in using the silverware and plates she brought with her.

She set everything on the countertop by the sink, dished up two plates of food, and handed them to the two of them.

They dug in like they hadn't eaten in a month and enjoyed every single bite.

"There's more if you wantin' seconds."

"Hettie, I couldn't eat another bite," said Kathleen, licking her lips. "It was wonderful."

"I could. I would take seconds."

"Ah, Frank, I miss cookin' for ya. Ya always eat like ya love my food. I like that 'bout ya."

"I like that you like cooking for me. I love eating your food. I miss you, Hettie. Hopefully, we can come home soon. Kathy's starting to feel better finally."

"Praise God! So good to hear. Been prayin' like crazy. These ol' knee bones are plumb tired out." She laughed.

"We felt it, Hettie," declared Kathleen.

Hettie collected the plates and put them back in the bag. "Kathleen. Can I ask a favor?"

"Of course, anything. You know that."

Hettie handed her the letter.

"This come today. I think it be from Jessie, but not sure. Could you read it to me?"

"Jessie? You haven't heard from her since she got married and left, have you?"

"Nope. That's why I want ya to read it. Don't know if somethin's wrong or what."

Chapter 49

April 1942
The Oxford Hotel, Denver

Almost dancing to the car after a fantastic evening, Brad had his arm around his fiancée, and they were floating on air. He took Rebecca in his arms and kissed her with a fervency he hadn't before expressed. She responded in kind and felt the angels must be singing because she was on cloud nine.

He opened the door for her and gave her his hand to steady her as she slid in and seated herself. He kissed her on the cheek before he went around the front, opened his door, and slid in. They gazed into each other's eyes. He just didn't want this evening to end which had exceeded all expectations. The joy and happiness bubbling inside them were remarkable, a feeling neither had experienced before. He reached over, pulled her to him, and ardently kissed her.

Then after starting the car, they took off down the highway and headed for school.

"Becca, would you sit next to me? I want to put my arm around you and hold you. I love you so much. I can't believe you are going to be my wife. God has blessed me so much by giving you to me."

"Brad, can I ask you something?"

"Sure, anything, my angel."

"You talk about God a lot. Can you tell me about him? Why do you believe in him and what is the personal relationship you keep talking about? If this isn't the time, I can wait, but it's been on my mind a lot lately."

"I'd love to tell you about him. The only pathway to God is through Jesus Christ, God's Son. God sent him to earth to die on the cross to pay the penalty for our sin so we could have eternal life with him. He died and arose on the third day. He's alive and dwells within all those who believe what I just told you."

"He died for me?"

"He did for me too and for the whole world. That's how much he loved us. He wants us to spend forever with him. It's simple, but I guarantee you it will change your life completely."

"Is all that in the Bible?"

"It is, and a lot more—the history of the Jewish nation, part of Jesus's life on this earth, Paul's ministry throughout the Mediterranean, and some of the disciples' letters. It's a huge history lesson with all the instructions you can imagine on how to live a Christian life."

"If I believe that, what do I do next?"

"Do you believe you've ever sinned?"

"I guess."

"Okay, let me ask you another question. Have you ever told a lie?"

"Sure, hasn't everyone?"

"Yes. But the Bible says that lying is a sin. So when you lied, you sinned. There are all kinds of sins, and we've all done them. Therefore, you and I are sinners. Jesus came to save sinners. We all need a savior, and he's the one that God sent to do that for us."

"Okay, I know I've done a lot of things that are wrong. That's sin?"

"Yep."

"So Jesus came to take my sin away?"

"That's right. Then God sees us through his perfect Son, so we are pure and blameless. We don't have to pay for our wrongdoing, Jesus already did. We just have to ask for his forgiveness and ask him into our lives to live forever, and he does."

FROM SHADOWS TO DAYBREAK

"Brad, I'm so sorry I sinned and he died for me. What do I do next? I want Jesus in my life. I want what you have and to live according to what the Bible teaches. What do I have to do?"

"You've already done most of it. All you have to do is to ask Jesus into your life to live and to help you become the person he wants you to be."

"How?"

"Just pray. Just talk to him like you talk to me."

"Jesus, I want you to live in me and help me live like you teach in the Bible. I'm so sorry for my sin and that you died for me. Please forgive me, take all my sin away, and make me a new person. Thank you. Amen."

"Was that right? Did I do it right?"

Brad laughed softly then, hugged her tightly. "Becca you did it perfectly. You are now God's child. You belong to the family of God. You're in my family now. I couldn't be happier, my angel. I love you so much."

"Will you teach me about the Bible?"

"I will be happy to. This day will be one I will remember forever!"

* * * * *

Max had spent most of the evening in a bar and had more drinks than he could count, but he knew he could drive safely. He never got drunk, and there were only a few miles to his house. The barkeeper tried to take his keys, but Max won the fight. Barreling around the corner on the highway, flying about thirty miles an hour faster than the legal speed limit, Max lost control of the car. Driving at seventy miles an hour, he nailed Brad's car broadside. The severe impact forced the car across the road, into the ditch, and wedged up against the hill. Rebecca's head had been thrown through the window and then thrust back toward Brad. Her head bled profusely from shards of glass that had lodged deep in her skull. Her left arm had been twisted up under her shoulder blade and blood dripped from her right leg which landed in an awkward position. The impact killed Brad instantly.

*****

Rebecca awoke the next day in unfamiliar surroundings. *Where am I?*

It's sunny. Wasn't she out with Brad? Didn't Brad just propose to her tonight? She tried to move her left arm to see her engagement ring, but instead there was a cast restricting her movement. The pain began to register, and she blinked her eyes and tried to focus. She tried to remember how she broke her arm. A cast surrounded her right leg, and her right shoulder hurt badly. A cervical collar restrained her neck. Nothing made sense. Trying to evaluate the rest of her body, she found that she hurt everywhere. Her head pounded, her mind reeled, and dizziness consumed her. She tried to sit up, but the severe pain prevented it, and she lay back down.

A doctor came in at that moment and looked her over. She attempted to speak, but nothing would come. She studied him and finally whispered, "What happened?"

"Rebecca, do you know where you are?"

"She started to shake her head, but it hammered. She whispered, "No."

"For now, I think you need to rest and we'll answer your questions later."

"No," she whispered. "Tell me now."

Rebecca, I'm going to give you something to make you sleep. Right now, that's the most important thing." He filled a syringe and stuck it into the IV that hung off to the side of her head. She fought it for a few seconds, then drifted off to sleep.

Chapter 50

Mid-March 1951
Mountain View High School

The team had been sitting in the locker room with no idea what was coming. The families of the boys involved had been notified and even though they weren't looking forward to the fall-out, they were all in agreement that the punishment fit the crime. They had tried everything they knew how to do to discipline these kids, but nothing worked. This would be their last chance until the prison system took over, and depending on how this went tonight, they may have charges pressed against them that could mean some jail time anyway.

Coach expected some flak, but even the dads were sympathetic to the girl. All but one had girls of their own and were outraged that their boys could do something so cruel to another girl. Would they have let another boy do that to their own sister? This punishment needed to happen, as hard as it would be to watch.

The principal and the coach both walked in together, and the boys all glanced around at each other questioning what was going on. Unusual procedure must be the title for this meeting.

The principal started first. "Gentlemen, this is a subject I never believed I would need to approach in this school. Not only does it grieve my very soul, but I am outraged and have never been more disappointed in any of my students than I am right now. I've been here a long time and have seen a lot of things, but this is beyond my scope of understanding. I am shocked that any of my men could have had anything to do with it. Coach and I have talked, along with the parents involved. The men who were involved in this will pay dearly for what they have done. Not only that, but it also will be in the school paper with the names, and if it goes to trial, it will no doubt be known by the community. This is a tragic incident that will never be repeated.

"It has come to our attention there is one man who lied to incite and inflame this and three who were directly involved in an attack on one of our female students here in one of the men's restrooms. This would be a sexual act conducted by the three of them together. They ganged up on her and tried to convince her they were just doing what she wanted and begged for. They were told by one man that she'd been so easy, and they could have her too. She played a good game of 'hard to get,' which meant nothing—in the end, she gave willingly. Nothing could be further from the truth. This girl had been completely innocent, and if her friends had not intervened, I have no doubt the act would have been completed, maybe three times over.

"This disgusting behavior will be punished swiftly and severely. These men who are here tonight have no idea what they have done or the consequences they have put into motion. But at some point, it will probably leak out because these things almost always do. It may be weeks or months, but people will find out. Oftentimes, it is the women who face the shame and embarrassment of these acts. I'm saying right here the shame is not hers to bear. It is here in this room with these men. They will be shamed and embarrassed, which is appropriate for what they have done.

"So right here, right now this is what will happen: The four men who were involved either passively or aggressively in this vile act, as of tonight are expelled and will never be allowed on campus again. You men can get up right now and leave. In fact, if you don't, there is a security officer standing by right outside to escort you out. I will wait until you leave the premises before we continue."

The four of them stood and walked out the door with their heads down. When they opened it, the security officer could be seen by all the men who were in attendance.

FROM SHADOWS TO DAYBREAK

Most of those who were left were in shock.

"I hope this picture stays in your minds for a long time. Now for the rest of you who are left, Coach has something he wants to say."

"Men, with everything Principal Jackson said, I completely agree. This has been a day that I will never forget and I hope you don't either. I am a Christian. Beginning next week, I am starting a Bible study during the lunch hour. It is strictly voluntary, but those who would like to come are invited. Those who want to see what it's all about are also invited.

"Now the reason for this is because I see the evil all around us, and what happened yesterday is a classic example of it. I know on this team there are Christians who want to honor the Lord. I am asking you to get together as a group and start praying for this school, for its students, for the girl who was attacked, and for the men who were just expelled. Let me say it again: all this is voluntary. I'm not asking anyone to do anything that is against what they believe. From now on, I do expect us to always act as gentlemen, on campus or off. Conduct yourselves as men of integrity, dignity, and respect for all, especially women—your mothers, sisters, aunts, grandmothers—all women. They are the ones who raised us. They are the ones who love us no matter what. If that's not your story, I'm sorry, but that does not excuse bad behavior. Respect, gentlemen. That's what I expect from all of you starting tonight, and hopefully for the rest of your lives.

"Men, you have a responsibility, a higher calling, if you will, to protect our girls, our women. That's what we are supposed to do—part of our job description as men. Therefore, if you ever see any girl being hassled or mistreated in any way, I trust from now on you will intervene to stop it. We need to stand and let our girls and women know that we will protect them. This community will be different if we start right now. We can change this school, this community, this state, and maybe this country, if we stand together as men who respect all people regardless of race, religion, sex, or economics. Football is a great game, but in the end, that's all it is—a game. What you saw tonight is real life. Things that matter—respect and integrity, gentlemen. That's what I require from all of you from now on. Now do I make myself clear?"

They all cried out in unison, "Yes, Coach!"

Chapter 51

Mid-March 1951
General Hospital

Hettie handed Kathleen the letter she thought came from Jessie. Hettie hadn't heard from her daughter since she had married and left town—not a word in twenty-five years. She had no idea if she had children, what her husband did for a living, or if Jessie had been happy with her life. She couldn't be certain she was still alive—until now. But now with the letter in front of her, she wondered, why write now after all these years. It could be really dreadful news, and Hettie wouldn't have any way to help her. Fear, concern, and happiness flooded her all at one time.

Kathleen looked at Hettie. "Are you ready for me to read this to you?"

"Not sure, Kathleen. I'm afeared that somethin's wrong, but I have to know."

"Okay. Take a deep breath. It's going to be okay."

"Hettie, I can step out so you two can have some privacy. I don't mind," Franklin remarked.

"No, Frank, I purty much know all 'bout you, guess it bein' okay you knowin' about me and mine."

Franklin nodded.

Cheryl Fosnot Bingisser

Dear Mama,

I know it's a shock to hear from me, but before you get scared, everything is fine. We're all okay. I'm so sorry that I haven't written before. I know you must worry about me, and I've been a horrible daughter for not taking your feelings into account. I was thoughtless, rude, unfeeling, and selfish. Mama, I'm so sorry. Please forgive me. I promise I'll keep you up-to-date from now on. I'd like to tell you a little about my family and me so you can get to know us.

Theodore is a doctor and half-owner of a clinic in Nashville, Tennessee. It's in a colored neighborhood, and a lot of his work is pro bono, but we are doing well financially, and I'm very proud of him. The community is delighted to have a clinic so close. Most of the patients walk there. They get care they couldn't afford any-where else. It's wonderful, and he is really making a difference.

Shandra is fourteen and a bit of a handful. She's always had a bundle of energy and runs at one hundred miles an hour. I've never had the energy to keep up with her, so we were both glad when she got involved in sports. She plays softball, soccer, and basketball and has her eye on playing professionally, but that's years away. Choir and English are her favorite subjects, and she gets excellent grades. She has many friends and is well-liked. She's beautiful and looks like you when you were her age. Cooking and baking are her favorite pastimes, but I'm not that great of a teacher, so we hope she'll take Home EC this year. She's a beauty and has boys falling all over her, which is a big concern for her father and me.

FROM SHADOWS TO DAYBREAK

Teddy is just fifteen. He's not crazy about school. He does like science, math, and music, but other subjects just don't hold his interest. He loves the trumpet and is in the band. He's second chair but wants to try out for first chair, and by the way, he's practicing, I have no doubt he'll make it. He is nothing, if not determined. He loves the tree house he built in the backyard. It's not perfect, but it stays together, and that makes him very happy. He often takes his trumpet to the tree house and practices out there, much to the chagrin of the neighborhood. But he doesn't care and plays anyway. Actually, I kind of like it.

Tosha is seventeen and will be graduating next year. She is focused on her grades and getting ready for college. She loves science, math, history, and music. She's in the girls' choir and loves it. She has your voice, Momma. She sings like a bird. With her wanderlust, we are sure she will go far away to college. She's still researching where that might be. Since she loves research, she wants to be a scientist in the medical field. We're very proud of her.

Well, that's it, Mama. Those are our children whom we love and of whom we're very proud. You are a grandma, and someday, I hope you can meet them for yourself. Me, I'm busy being a mom, and I love it. I can't cook like you, but the kids have never tasted yours, so they think I cook just fine. Are you still working for Kathy? I was thinking about her and wondering how she was doing. Did she ever get married? Does she have any kids? I didn't do right by her either. I'm assuming she's reading this to you, and if that's true, Kathy, I'm sorry I broke up our friendship.

I miss you. Maybe someday I can come and visit you and Mama.

I go to church with the kids on Sundays. Theodore doesn't go but says it's good for the kids. Mama, I gave my heart to Jesus just a few weeks ago, and that's when I realized what an awful daughter I had been. I had to repent and tell the Lord I wanted to change and honor my mama like I should have all along. Mama, I hope you can forgive me. I'm so sorry.

I love you.

Your daughter,
Jessie

Kathleen looked up, and Hettie had tears in her eyes. Kathleen bent over and hugged her tightly.

"Hettie, this is such good news, and like you always say, 'Hallelujah, there's another one for the kingdom!'"

Hettie laughed. "You're right 'bout that, girl."

"It sounds like she wants to come home and visit you. I would love that. If she couldn't come before, how about we invite her to come here after the baby's born so we can introduce her to little Bella."

"Wait. Bella? Isn't that a girl's name? You do know that we're having a boy, right?" Franklin teased.

Both Hettie and Kathleen laughed.

"Hettie," Franklin asked, "how are you feeling about all this?"

"I jes' as happy as a daffydil in March. My darlin' girl wants to see her mama. Praise be to Jesus."

"Yes," Kathleen said, "we're so very happy for you. Now as soon as you want to, we can write a letter back to her. How about it?"

"Ya, that's the best idea ever."

"No, I think I have an even better one. Frank and the Doc are already conspiring against me to make me rest most of the afternoon every single day, but they didn't say I had to be in bed. How would you feel about me teaching you to read?"

"Kathleen, I jes' too old for such nonsense."

"You're never too old to learn, Hettie. Besides no one I know is smarter than you are."

"Kathy's right. You slay me with all that good stuff you say. You are wise and smart, way beyond your years. I think that's an excellent idea, and while she's teaching you, you have a front-row seat to watching her, making sure she stays off her feet. You'd be doing me a favor."

"Ya surely do make it sound good. Okay, but if it don't work out, don't be upset Kathleen. It jes' means I can't learn no more. That's all."

"Nonsense Hettie. You will pick it up so fast, you'll be shocked. I don't know why it never occurred to me before. In fact, I should apologize for not thinking of it before now. I'm sorry, Hettie."

"Now that's jes' plain silly. No need for 'poligizin'. We all jes' busy that's all. Now don't ya worry none 'bout that."

"Okay, when I get home, school will be in session. You game, Hettie?"

"I guess I am."

"It's a date then. Watch out world, here comes Hettie!"

"Hey, I have just one little question," Franklin declared, with a furrowed brow. "Jessie calls you Kathy?"

Kathleen looked at him and smiled, "She's the only other person I allowed to call me that. Well, actually, it wasn't that I allowed it. It's more like she insisted, and I finally gave up telling her not to."

"Here I thought that was my privilege alone." He sighed. "My life's crumbled into a million pieces. I thought that was my special name for you. I wonder if that means I need to find another one, 'cuz I could, you know, and it wouldn't be nearly as nice." He grinned.

They laughed. "No, Kathy is just fine, don't go digging any further than that, please?"

"I feel a little limited now, but I guess it'll be okay, *Kathy*." He chuckled.

Chapter 52

Mid-March 1951
General Hospital

Lincoln had won the last three games in a row and Miles only one. Lincoln celebrated. Miles, not so much, but he took it in stride and had been just about played out when Marianne walked in.

"Hi, Lincoln."

"Hi."

"This is Mister."

"Yes, I know, we've already met. Hello. How are you doing?"

"Well, I've managed to stay upright for the last hour, so I guess that's some improvement."

"I guess any improvement is better than none, right?"

"Yes, just slow and frustrating, but Lincoln is helping me out by beating me at checkers constantly. Personally, I think he cheats, but he denies it."

"I do not. I don't know how to cheat at checkers. You're just not a good sport, that's all."

Miles laughed. "You got me there, kid."

"Lincoln, I'd like to talk to you alone, unless you'd like Mister to stay."

"Mister, could you stay?"

Miles looked at Marianne, trying to perceive what she wanted him to do.

FROM SHADOWS TO DAYBREAK

"Really, it's okay if you want to. Maybe it would be better."

"Okay, Lincoln. I'm pretty tired, but maybe you can nudge me if I fall asleep and start snoring. What do you say?"

"Okay. I'll hit ya if you fall asleep."

"Not too hard, okay? I might fall over." They all laughed.

"Lincoln, I have set up a meeting with your new family for tomorrow. They will come here, and I will be here too."

"Can Mister or Franklin be here too?"

"I don't think that's a good idea. They want to meet you alone, talk with you, and get to know you a little. See if you like them and if they like you—that sort of thing."

"But if I don't like them, I don't have to go, right?"

"That's right, but I hope you will at least give them a chance. They are excited about meeting you."

"Mister, can you and Franklin come and visit me if I move?"

"I can't right now, Lincoln, but when I get better, I can. You'll have to talk to Franklin about it, but I think he can work something out for you. He likes you a lot. So do I."

"What if they don't like me?"

"Then you won't have to do anything, and we'll look for another family, but I don't think that's going to happen. I think this is a good fit for you."

"Okay. See you tomorrow."

"Goodbye, Lincoln. I'll see you tomorrow, okay?"

"Yep."

Marianne knocked on the door, and the nurse opened it. She left and locked it up again.

"Lincoln, how do you feel about this?" asked Miles.

"I guess it's okay. I just wish I could live with you, but she said you're too sick. If you weren't sick, could I live with you?"

"I told you I would always tell you the truth, remember?"

"Yeah."

"The truth is, I don't know. I work all day, and there wouldn't be anyone there to take care of you."

"I can take care of myself."

"I believe the squirrel's already climbed that tree. You know that doesn't work. But since I'm not well, there's nothing to talk about. If that home doesn't work out, and if I'm well, then we can talk about it. Is that fair?"

"I s'pose. Don't like it much though."

"I don't blame you. Sometimes life just isn't fair. Look at me. I don't want to be sick. And what about Franklin's wife, who's been so sick? That's not fair either, but that's the way life is. Sometimes it's just plain hard."

"Yeah, but it doesn't seem right."

"I know, but you still have people who care about you, and we'll still see you and talk to you on the phone. We're not going to forget about you, Lincoln. You don't have to worry about that at all."

"Is that the fair part?"

Miles laughed. "Maybe. I'll come over and play checkers with you when I get better, and in the meantime, I promise to call you, and you can tell me all the things you're doing in your new home. Would that be okay?"

"Yeah, I guess."

"Good. Now I'm about to fall asleep on you, so I think it's time that I went back to my room and went to sleep. Is that okay with you?"

"Don't like it, but I want you to get better, so okay."

"Good. I'll at least talk to you tomorrow if I don't see you, okay?"

"Okay."

Miles wheeled over and knocked on the door, and the nurse came almost immediately. She opened the door, let him out, and relocked it.

Chapter 53

Mid-March 1951
General Hospital

Lincoln had been dressed in a new blue suit, a white shirt, and a navy-blue tie. He looked every bit the gentleman and very irresistible. Any family would be proud to have a darling little boy like him. Lincoln seemed nervous, but Miles and Franklin had gone a long way toward crumbling Lincoln's walls. Being more vulnerable, and less angry, he wanted a fresh start, if he had his friends around for support.

Marianne assured him repeatedly that this meeting would be okay and they were going to love him. His future looked hopeful and he tried to believe that everything would be okay. But terrified that once he was away from his friends and the hospital, everything would change, and maybe things wouldn't be the way Miss Marianne kept reassuring him they would be. Then what would happen? Would he be able to come back? There were a lot of questions that he had floating around in his head, mostly because of fear.

Lincoln longed to understand where his momma might be. If he moved again, she may never find him. So what should he do? He couldn't say anything about his momma. He knew they wouldn't let him stay for that reason. Should he tell Miss Marianne he doesn't like the family?

He wished Mister was here with him. He would be able to help him decide what to do. He knew Mister liked him and would always tell him the truth. Just what is the truth? If only his momma would come and take him home, he wouldn't have to deal with any of this. Where is she?

They would be here any minute. His hands started shaking. His body shortly followed. He didn't know what was happening, but he couldn't seem to stop it. The shaking became steadily worse, and fear gripped his heart. Lincoln walked over to the corner and sat down. He blankly stared, perceiving nothing.

Marianne entered the room and noticed him sitting in the corner. She quickly walked over to him and bent down so she could see him eye to eye.

"Lincoln, what's wrong?"

Lincoln started kicking and screaming, biting her, and pulling her hair. She yelled for a doctor. He'd been a healthy kid. How could this happen? The nurse and doctor ran into the room and assessed the situation. They sprang into action instantly. He ordered the nurse to get *Haldol*, stat. Lincoln hadn't slowed down one bit—kicking, screaming, biting, and slapping. He'd become totally out of control. Marianne pulled back and got away.

The nurse quickly approached and the doctor told her exactly how much to use. She filled the syringe and injected it into his thigh. He still didn't slow down. He couldn't be fought with, and it would take a couple of minutes for the drug to take effect. It seemed to last forever. Then he stopped and looked glazed over—almost catatonic. *What on earth had happened to this healthy little boy?* Marianne questioned.

The doctor turned to Marianne and explained, "Mrs. Weaver, I'm afraid Lincoln has had a severe panic attack. There isn't anything more we can do for him today. We will keep him sedated and watch him closely. He could be okay tomorrow, or it could last several days. This could be the only attack, or there could be more. There's no way to know for sure."

FROM SHADOWS TO DAYBREAK

Marianne kissed Lincoln on the forehead and turned to leave. It had been heartbreaking to watch what Lincoln went through. What could she do about it?

Marianne talked to Franklin before she left the hospital and recapped what had happened to Lincoln. There wouldn't be a family to meet today—maybe not for a few days, until they knew for sure if he'd become completely stable. She asked Franklin to check on him to keep him calm tomorrow. Needing to ask the doctors who would be treating Lincoln first, Franklin agreed. Marianne echoed the concern she held for him.

But Franklin worried that something else was going on with the boy, and he didn't like the way this sounded. He sighed.

"What now, Lord?" It seemed he just plugged a hole and another sprung a leak. Kathleen was getting better, but now there were Emily and Rebecca. Miles was starting to feel a little better, but he still had a long way to go. Now just when the kid has a chance to be a part of a family, the kid has a panic attack.

Dear heavenly Father, I just don't understand, and I feel so tired, Lord. Both Kathleen and I just want to go home, and all these things happening at once seems like we're supposed to stay here. Lord, take care of Lincoln and help me find out what is going on in his head today. And Emily's situation is so grave, that it will take a long time before she gets over it—if ever. Then there's the coach and the principal, who will be dealing with all the fallout. It seems like the whole world is collapsing around us, and we can't do anything to stop it. Tell me what to do. Give me wisdom in working with these people. I need energy that I don't have now, and I need your strength. Please help me with all this. Thank you for always hearing my prayers. Amen. Silently Franklin prayed and gratitude for answered prayer filled his heart.

Coming out of the bathroom with a nurse by her side, Kathleen noticed Franklin's head resting in his hands.

"Frank, what's wrong? Is Emily okay?"

"I don't know. It's Lincoln. Marianne said he'd had a severe panic attack and went berserk. He tried to beat Marianne. He bit her and did all kinds of things that were so out of character for him. Kathy, I don't think I can handle one more awful thing. It seems like half the community is in this hospital, and then there's the thing that's going on at school. It's just so overwhelming, and I feel so drained. If Lincoln can have visitors tomorrow, they would like me to go up and spend some time with him to keep him calm. I'm not certain I'm equipped to handle it. Honestly, I just want everyone to go away, and for you and me to go home."

"I know, Frankie. I feel the same way. I want to go home so badly, but it seems like we are needed here. Maybe that's why the Lord still has us here. Maybe that's why I got so sick—so we wouldn't go home, and be here for Lincoln, Becca, Emily, and Miles—all of them. It does seem overwhelming, and I know I haven't been able to help with any of it. And you've been stretched so thin. I'm sorry, Frankie. I should have helped you somehow."

"No, Kathy, that's not what I mean. You are here because you are not well. Until you are well enough to go home, we'll both be here. I guess I'm tired and a little beaten down."

"I understand. I know you're tired. You've been taking care of me nonstop since I came in here. But God is using you to work with all these different people and will give you wisdom and strength to continue until he says we can go home. You can't do this in your own strength. Why don't you come up on this bed, lie down, and take a nap with me?"

Franklin raised his brow. "A nap with you? Really? You are talking about sleeping, aren't you?"

"Yes. I'm talking about sleeping, unfortunately. I'm tired and could sleep, and maybe you could too. It might give you a little reserve strength that you could use right now. What do you say?"

"You know, I think that sounds like a good idea, and I never turn down a chance to have your body next to mine. I need you, Kathy. I'm sorry I'm leaning on you right now, but honestly, I need you—in more ways than one. I need your inner strength too, and if lying next to you will help with that, you don't have to ask me twice." He smiled.

Kathleen giggled. "Just come over her and put your arm around me so I can nestle into your body and feel your strength, holding me, okay?"

"I got it and will gladly help in any way I can," he answered, teasing. "I miss us—in our bed, the way we used to be. I need you as much as you need me." Franklin's head dropped. "I'm sorry. I shouldn't have said that. I know you're struggling too, and usually, I can tamp you down, but today, it's me that needs it. Please forgive me for being such a brute!"

"Frankie," she whispered softly, her warm breath tickling his ear. "Do you have any idea how good it feels to know you want the same thing I do? We're newlyweds," her voice rose, "after waiting as long as I did, and you since your wife died, I think it's perfectly normal to feel the way we do, don't you?"

"I do. I just wish we could lock that door and be together the way we want." He sighed. "But we won't have to wait forever, I promise. Before you know it, we'll be able to bring that robe and nightgown out of the closet." He smirked.

Kathleen whispered, "Who needs a robe and nightgown, Mr. Atwood."

Franklin gasped. "Oh, my goodness. Mrs. Atwood, how shameful!"

Kathleen giggled.

"Please, let's get some rest. I really do need a nap—a sleeping kind, so don't get any ideas, Mrs. Atwood."

"Ah, you're no fun at all."

"I know, and I guess I need to stay that way for now. I love you, my dearest." He kissed her on her forehead.

"I love you, Frankie."

They both fell asleep, with Franklin's arm around her.

Chapter 54

April 1942
Saint Joseph's Hospital

Rebecca woke to sunshine streaming through the windows. Looking around and trying to get her bearings, she still couldn't make sense of anything. She tried to move just a little, and the pain from everywhere screamed at her to lie still. The collar kept her from moving freely. Where was she? The last thing she remembered was Brad slipping that engagement ring on her finger. They spent the rest of the night dancing, feeling so in love that there were just the two of them that mattered in the whole world—just them. They were getting married and would live happily ever after. But then, how did she get hurt, and where is Brad? Nothing made sense, and there were so many questions, but no one ever around to answer them. *Why can't I remember anything?*

She found herself getting sleepy again and that frustrated her. Why couldn't she stay awake long enough to talk to anyone? Maybe someone could tell her what happened. How had she been hurt? Could everything about Brad been a dream? Isn't he real? I can't remember if anything is real.

She tried to scream for Brad, but nothing came out. She tried again. "Brad!" But only a small voice slipped past her lips.

What is wrong with me? Where am I?

FROM SHADOWS TO DAYBREAK

The doctor walked in. "Oh, good, Rebecca, you're awake. How are you feeling?"

"Confused," she said, so softly it was little more than a whisper.

"Rebecca, do you have any family or friends around here we can call to come be with you?"

"No. Just Brad. Where is he? I was with him last night, wasn't I? Ow, my head is pounding, and I hurt from head to toe. What happened? Where's Brad?" Agitated, she began screaming Brad's name, but barely made a sound, "Brad. Brad, where are you? Please come and see me. What happened to me? I want to go to Brad. Please let me see Brad. We're engaged, and I want to see him!" Clearly distressed, the nurse, who was standing by, took her vitals. Her blood pressure had risen and her pulse was racing.

Dr. Samuels pleaded, "Rebecca, you must calm down. Please calm down."

"Please bring me Brad. Please, I love him. We're getting married. Where is he?"

"Rebecca, I'm going to sedate you so you can get some rest."

"No, please just answer my questions. Where is he?"

"Okay, Rebecca, you're going to relax now and fall asleep. You need your rest."

Rebecca fell asleep. The dreamy night came back crystal clear. They danced. He asked her to marry him, and she loved him with all her heart. She kissed him, and he kissed her. *We're getting married. We have a future.* Then deep sleep overtook her, and everything went black.

The doctors were nervous about explaining Brad's death so early in her healing, but she became so agitated, that something had to be done. They agreed to call the school and find out who Rebecca's roommates were and if they were close enough to be willing to stay with her. She had no one else.

Hearing the story, the grapevine at the college spread the news across the campus. Shortly, everyone knew that Brad was dead and that Rebecca had been badly injured. Those close to them knew Brad was popping the question. This was the worst tragedy to hit the school in recent memory.

Julie, Rebecca's roommate, said she would come to the hospital and stay a few days, but she needed to get back to school for finals. Rebecca was probably closer to Julie than any of the others. She had a myriad of friends, but few close ones, and with no family, the selection of people who could be with her were few.

The doctors had been through this kind of thing before, but it was never easy, and they dreaded it. Once she understood she had been hospitalized and Brad had died, the real work would begin. She'd have such a dreadful time with all that she'd have to process, and her life, as she knew it, was gone forever. They heard that the drunk driver was fine, but would be charged with negligent homicide and probably only serve one or two years at most. Sometimes, life just isn't fair. This would be a tough one to wade through.

Chapter 55

Mid-March 1951
General Hospital

Franklin was struggling. Maybe Miles could cut through some of the fog Franklin was feeling, fatigued as he had been. He wished he would have handled Kathleen better instead of telling her how he really felt. Pressuring Kathleen could be detrimental to her health and he wouldn't do it just because he'd been exhausted and needed to be with her. Kathleen's needs were legitimate, and he would focus on them.

He wished he understood what Lincoln's problems were. If things were different, maybe he and Kathleen could have adopted him. But that would never work now. He just wanted the kid to have a good life with a family that would love him and make him happy. The kid had simple needs, it wouldn't be that hard, but with Kathleen's weakness, she couldn't care for an active boy, and truth be told, he wasn't sure he could either.

But he genuinely liked him. He's a good kid. It's just too bad there are no family members around whom could take him in. When he reached Miles's door he knocked lightly, not wanting to wake him if he were sleeping.

"Come in, it's open."

"Miles, it's good to see you sitting up. The last few times I've come you've been upright. Are you feeling any better?"

Cheryl Fosnot Bingisser

"Some, but it's still very slow. There is improvement for which I am grateful, but I wish it were faster."

"Believe me, Miles, I totally understand how you feel. Kathleen and I were just having the same conversation. We just want to go home too. Frankly, no pun intended, I'm so tired I can hardly think. I want to take Kathy home and go back to our lives the way they were. Together. I miss being with my wife. That's probably more than you wanted or needed to know. Forgive me. I'm just in a strange state of mind right now. The world just seems to be closing in on me—on us."

"Franklin, you don't ever have to apologize for being honest or speaking your mind—not with me. With all that's going on around here, I'm not surprised. Everybody seems to lean on you because you're the only one who's not ill, but you are exhausted, and it's written all over your face. You need to rest. You can't try to solve everyone else's problems. You have some of your own that need attention."

"Look, I have some things I need to tell you that you're going to hear but aren't going to like, and none of it is good. First, Lincoln had a severe panic attack this morning. They're trying to figure out why, but he won't be meeting his family today. He attacked Marianne, but he didn't know what he was doing. They had to sedate him and don't know if I'll be able to see him today or if they will keep him sedated for another day or two.

"There's a girl upstairs who's a good friend of Kathy's who was attacked at school by some of the guys from the football team. And this part must be kept quiet, but she tried to commit suicide. This is not the first time this girl has been attacked. She'd been trying to get over the last one when this happened. She's a sweet kid and none of this was her fault.

"Those boys who were involved were expelled and their names will be published in the school newspaper. They are taking a very strong stand on this so it never happens again. None of them know about the suicide attempt and when it leaks out, and it always does, there will be more fallout, and those boys will be in even bigger trouble with the community and maybe the court. This girl will need years of therapy and maybe never go back to school. Miles, the whole thing makes me sick."

"Oh, Franklin, what a mess. I can't believe this. It is overwhelming, for sure. How is she doing?"

"They think she'll be okay physically, but the rest of it will take her a long time."

"It's no wonder you're feeling tired. All these people are relying on you to help them and you're having a hard time just taking care of Kathleen, which should be your priority. Franklin, you can't do it all. No one can. Now I can take care of Lincoln today. I'm feeling stronger, and we're getting closer. I like the kid. If things were different, I might have adopted him myself. But who knows how long this is going take?"

"Miles, you've taken over for me a few days now, and I don't want him to think I don't care because I like him too. I was thinking the same thing you were. Maybe if Kathy were healthy, we might have been able to adopt him, but she's not. It seems like the timing's off or something."

"Agreed. I just wish I knew more about this family he's supposed to meet. I know Marianne is trying to find him a good home, but there aren't many out there."

"Miles, if you think you're up to taking on Lincoln today, I might just go back to the room and get some sleep. Maybe my mood will be better tomorrow if I can get a few extra zzzzs."

"It's not a mood. It's being overtired and overwhelmed, both for good reason. Now go get some sleep and cuddle with your wife. That's the best medicine ever."

"Speaking from experience?"

Miles smiled. "Yep."

Franklin smiled and walked to the door, then turned back and looked at Miles.

"Hmm. That's mysterious. Care to share?"

"Nope."

Chapter 56

Mid-March 1951
Mayfield Residence

Maddie had been washing up after she finished painting their bedroom and very pleased with the results. The wedding date drew nearer but still seemed far away. Raff had concentrated his efforts on the kitchen and was very close to completion. Once the kitchen had been finished, the three floors would go in, and their home would finally be completed. It seemed to her that they had been working on it forever.

"Hey, Maddie, come and take a look at this and see what you think."

"Coming." She dropped the cleaned brush and rinsed her hands. Walking into the kitchen, her eyes sparkled.

"Raff, it's so beautiful. That countertop is amazing, and the paint we picked out for the walls is wonderful. Once the white goes on the cupboards, the look will be perfect. I can't wait."

"Me either, and we still have plenty of time before the wedding to get the furniture and lamps, plus all other stuff, and the bed linens. It will be fun to have it all finished, then we can come home and enjoy being together, living in our new home. You know, like adults—grown-ups."

They both chuckled.

FROM SHADOWS TO DAYBREAK

"We still need to go pick out our cake, and everything else we want to serve at the reception, and you and Franklin need to get those tuxes. Flowers are done, invitations are sent out, and honeymoon is scheduled—that's my favorite part. There's not much left to do. Wait! We forgot pictures. We need to find a photographer. They are usually scheduled months in advance. I hope we haven't waited too long. So cake, reception food, if we're having more than cake, tuxes, and pictures—I think that's it. But we better get on that right away. Maybe we'll even have time to rest before the wedding and feel fantastic at the wedding, instead of being so tired we won't even remember it."

"Oh, I don't think we're going to forget the wedding or the honeymoon. Our wedding is the event of the season, and we're not likely to forget it, nor is anyone else who attends. Just seeing you in your dress will be blazed into the memory of everyone who has a pulse. They couldn't forget it, even if they wanted to. It's simply not going to happen. Then there's me in that unforgettable tux with this handsome face and the bluest eyes in Colorado. No, no one is going to forget this wedding, and we're not going to forget our honeymoon."

Raff grabbed Maddie and kissed her playfully, then passionately and then deeper with rising passion.

"Okay," he said, clearing his throat. "Well, we're not on our honeymoon yet, are we? I think I should go take a cold shower, and then we can head out for something to eat. You game?"

Maddie laughed and elbowed him on the shoulder. "No, we're not on our honeymoon, but I could still use another one of those kisses again, Mayfield."

"I could too, but it'll have to wait. Grab your coat and boots and let's go get a bite to eat. We can go to the newly renamed Becca's Place unless you want to go somewhere else. The brand-new sign is up too. It's great."

"No, that's fine. Can I have a kiss when you take me home, cowboy?"

"Maybe. We'll have to see. I suppose I can give you a little one. Come on, my soon-to-be bride. Move it. I'm starving!"

On the road to Becca's Place, Raff had quieted.

"What are you thinking about?"

"Well, you know we never did solve two of the mysteries my dad left us. The prescription thing which might be nothing and the books and the chest. We still don't know where those came from, or why he had them and didn't use them to pay his debt. Instead, he waited for me to find the money in the book hidden inside the bookcase. I still can't figure it out. Doesn't make sense to me."

"I know. Me either. But does it really matter? I mean, the debt is paid. We've got money for the honeymoon and the farm and even for the shed remodeling. So who cares?"

"I don't know, it just seems unfinished. Unanswered. I don't like it."

"I know. You want everything in a box all wrapped up with a big red bow and with a note attached saying, *finished, finito, finale*, right?" They pulled into Becca's Place, continued their conversation on the way inside, while Emily seated them.

Their meals were delicious. They would expect nothing less. They made their way to the car, started it, and roared off.

Maddie giggled. "Getting back to our earlier discussion, Raff, you do want everything wrapped up in a box with a big red bow."

"Yeah," he said, nodding. "Something like that."

"Ain't gonna happen, cowboy. Real life doesn't always end with a box, a bow, and a note. Sometimes, it just blows in the wind. Sometimes we're just not supposed to know."

"Yeah. I don't like it much, but I suppose you could be right. Aren't you even curious?"

"Of course, I am, but if the answers aren't forthcoming, we ought to let it go and just enjoy the books, clean up the chest, bring it downstairs where it can be useful, and pretty up the joint a little. Does that make sense?"

"Yeah, I guess. I like the idea of cleaning up the chest and using it in the living room. That's a great idea. We can use it for blankets when we cuddle on the couch or any number of things, plus it will look impressive in the living room now that it's painted."

"I like the cuddling part." Maddie giggled.

He chuckled. "Man, you have a one-track mind tonight. You're going to be hard to say good night to. I'm going to have to kiss and run."

"Chicken."

"Yep. Afraid so. Kissing and running is all you're getting tonight."

He drove her home and walked her up the stairs to the front door.

"Be happy, I could run without the kiss. We're too close to the wedding for me to mess it up now. So good night, my sweet." Raff kissed her cheek, ran back down the stairs to the car, and drove home.

Chapter 57

Mid-March 1951
General Hospital

Although Emily had improved, the doctors found her primarily unresponsive. She didn't want to see anyone, and when she was awake, she stared into space or cried. Pastor Ryan had come and gone twice without seeing her but wouldn't give up. He might need to see her without her permission to begin the process of healing, whether she believed herself ready or not.

Even Rebecca had been turned away, which broke her heart. She wanted to hold her and let Emily know she loved her. But she, at least, had to be willing to see her. Maybe it's time to remove that decision from Emily. She didn't know what she needed, and lying in bed crying all day would not aid in her healing. Some tears were healing, but these probably were not.

Rebecca resolved that tomorrow, she wouldn't ask to see Emily; rather, she would walk directly into her room and take control. Emily needed her, and Rebecca knew that. Besides, no one else could visit.

Doc Anderson had talked to her earlier and told her she was getting slightly better physically but even more fragile emotionally than he originally believed. Her fragility concerned him, but he knew there were many people praying for her, and only God could heal a broken spirit. He studied Rebecca's face and didn't like what he viewed.

FROM SHADOWS TO DAYBREAK

"Becca, I'm concerned about you. You have dark circles under your eyes. I'm sure you're not getting enough rest, still running the restaurant, and anxious about Emily and Kathleen. You can't do it all, and you're not going to be able to help anyone if you collapse from exhaustion. I may put you in here for mandatory rest. Now do you hear me? I'm ordering you to go home now and get some rest. If needed, I will order something to help you sleep so you can cope better with everything you've got on your plate. I think you need to transfer some of the responsibility to someone else and take care of yourself. Let someone else manage the restaurant. I'm sure you've trained someone who can do it, and you get some rest. Do I make myself clear?"

"Yes, Doc. It's just that I'm so worried about Emily and I—" She burst into tears.

Doc put his hand in the small of her back and ushered her into the waiting room. He held her while she cried. When she raised her head, and the tears had stopped, she grabbed a tissue that lay on the table next to her.

"You see what I mean? You're spent, Becca. You can't help anyone in this condition. If I see you like this again, I will have you admitted. You're overwhelmed and beyond fatigued. The only thing you should do right now is rest. Now are you going to take care of yourself, or do I have to? Your choice."

"You're right. I can hardly put one foot in front of the other. I cry myself to sleep at night and feel so sad for what Emily went through and will go through. It breaks my heart, and I ache for her."

"That's because you're a very compassionate person, and even though you're a strong woman when one of your own hurts, you do too. Scripture tells us to do that, but it doesn't say it should break us because we're so concerned."

"I guess I never looked at it like that. Emily lost so much, and maybe what I'm feeling is everything I lost ten years ago. Maybe recalling that horrific time is coloring my feelings for what Emily is going through."

"Becca, I don't know what that loss is about, and you don't have to tell me, but I can tell you that you might very well be right.

Sometimes a tragedy will trigger feelings from another, more personal tragedy, and cause a bit of an emotional breakdown. This may be why your feelings are so intense. Please listen to me. I'm going to order something for you to sleep, and hopefully, you will sleep for at least twelve hours straight. Then I want you to take another one and sleep another twelve hours. Then I want to see you in my office. You do this, or the other option is that I put you in here and make you rest. It's your choice now, but if you continue down this path, you won't have a choice."

"Okay, I get it. I will do what you want. I know I'm headed over the edge, and in truth, it's a little frightening."

"I'm sure it is. Add a little panic to everything else I just said. I'll write you a prescription, and you can pick it up at the desk. I'm serious about this, Becca. You do this, or I'll act. You're teetering on the edge, and I don't want you to fall over. Got it?"

"I promise, Doc. I heard you loud and clear."

"Good. Now I have rounds to do. I need to see Kathleen and Miles before I go back to the office. I'll see you in two days at my office."

"Got it. Thanks, Doc."

"You bet. See you later." With his back to her, he waved to her over his shoulder, as he walked down the hall toward Kathleen's room.

Chapter 58

Mid-March 1951
General Hospital

Franklin lay beside Kathleen sleeping when there was a knock on the door, and Doc breezed inside. He was glad to see them both getting some rest, but Franklin awoke when Doc opened the door.

"Hi, Doc. How are you doing today?" Franklin asked while he rose.

"I'm fine. Been a bit of a rough one, though. I've come with good news and bad news."

"Really? This place can use a little good news. So far, it's been bad on all fronts. It's been difficult for everyone."

"But I finally have some good news."

"Franklin, if Kathleen keeps improving like this, I'll let her go home in just a few days."

"Okay. What's the bad news?"

"The bad news is that Kathleen, because of the blood pressure issue and a little protein in her urine, is going to have to stay off her feet for the rest of the pregnancy, or she could lose the baby."

"What's going on?" asked Kathleen, rubbing the sleep from her eyes as she awakened. "Oh, hi, Doc."

"Kathy, Doc has come with a bit of good news and not-so-good news."

Cheryl Fosnot Bingisser

"I'm ready for that. It's been all bad news for a while now, and I think Frank and I are a bit overwhelmed. What's the news?"

"Well, if you keep improving like you are right now, I'll let you go home in a few days."

"Really? Wait. How few?"

"Well, we'll see, but I'm thinking maybe three, but the not-so-good news is that I'm afraid staying off your feet, for the most part, will be something you will have to do for the rest of your pregnancy. We can't seem to keep your blood pressure regulated. It needs to come down and stay down, but not by plunging like it has in the hospital. There's also a little protein in your urine that could indicate some symptoms of preeclampsia. Now you don't have the severe symptoms, but I don't want you to either. Kathleen, I'm sorry, but I want you to have a healthy baby, and I think the only way we can assure it will happen is to keep you inactive."

"Oh, Frank, I can't believe it. I can't do that. Doc, really?"

"Kathy, we can do this. I know it will be hard for you, but it won't last forever, and I'll help you anyway I can."

"If you don't do it, you could land right back here for who knows how long."

I've already told Hettie the conditions of her homecoming, so we're prepared. It sounds like I need to get you an ottoman, that's the same height as your chair, to put your legs up.

"Yes, that would be perfect. Now can you promise me you'll do that?"

"Yes, I'll do anything to go home. I'm so sick of this place, and the food, and Frank not getting rest and worrying about me—"

"I get it." Doc put his hand up. "You want to go home."

They both laughed.

"I want to keep that little bundle you're carrying right where it is until it's big enough to see its way into the world, so it's not just you I'm concerned about."

"I know, and I want that too, but I do have a question." She glanced at him, shyly, then looked over to Franklin.

"Is it okay if Frank and me, you know, get together?"

"It's fine. Just be a little careful, Franklin."

248

"I will. Three days, huh? Anything I can do to make you subtract a day?"

"We'll take it one day at a time. But, Kathleen, you still need to rest. I'm going to have the nurses start walking you a little so you can get around some at home. But don't overdo it. Also, I'll need to see you once a week in my office, and if anything—and I mean *anything*—happens, you call me immediately."

"I promise, Mom. I'll be good."

Doc raised his brow at her and smiled. "Yes, well, mind you *P*s and *Q*s, young lady. Did your mom ever say that to you?"

"Actually, she did." They laughed, and Doc turned and waved over his shoulder as he left the room.

"Kathy, we're finally going home. I can't wait." He picked her up and kissed her. "I love you, darling. It will be so good to be home with you again. We sure haven't had much time at home since our wedding."

"No, we haven't." She kissed him. "I love you, Frankie. I can't wait to be home again. And before you say anything, I promise I'll follow all Doc's rules, okay?"

"Okay. That's good enough for me." He picked her up, placed her in bed, and lay down beside her. "I wish we were home this very minute," he whispered in her ear.

"Me too." She giggled. "Maybe if I'm really good, he'll let me go a day early."

"That sounds even nicer. The sooner, the better."

Chapter 59

Mid-March 1951
General Hospital

    Marianne had been sitting with Lincoln when the sound of the key in the door captured her attention. The door opened, and a man and a woman in their late thirties walked into the room. The woman had short blond hair and hazel eyes that looked a little glazed over and sunken, with dark bags underneath. She had a long face and a very thin body, and she seemed quite tall for a woman. Her countenance was a little dark—not bright, not happy. Norma. The name fit her—a little old. Even though young, she appeared much older than her age number would indicate.

    The man acted charming enough, with short curly brown hair, deep brown eyes, a friendly face and features, and about the same height as his wife—but a little more filled out. They really seemed mismatched. But opposites attract, and Ralph certainly appeared to be her opposite.

    Marianne's eyes narrowed and her brow furrowed. She hadn't personally seen Norma for a couple of weeks, but she seemed a lot healthier before. She questioned if she'd been ill. Something seemed a little off with her.

    Norma walked over to the bed where Lincoln was sitting and bent down to talk to him at eye level. "It's nice to meet you, Lincoln.

My name is Norma. I really am glad you want to come home and live with us. We've wanted a boy like you for a very long time."

"I've been waiting to meet you too. Miss Marianne says that you got sheeps and goats. Can I play with them when I move?"

"Of course, you can. They will love you."

"Ralph stepped over. So you like animals, huh?"

"Uh-huh. I used to have a dog when I was little, but he ran away."

"I see. Well, it's nice to meet you. How would you like to come home with us today?"

"I think I would. Do I get my own room?"

"Yes, you do."

"Okay. Is there a yard?"

"There's a whole farm—lots of room for you to play and run. What do you say? Would you like to come?

"Is it okay if Franklin visits me and Mister talks to me on the phone?"

Miss Marianne has already talked to us about it, and it's perfectly fine. I'm glad you have some friends to visit with you."

"Okay, I guess we can go now."

Marianne took him in her arms and whispered, "You call me anytime, okay?" She slipped her business card in his pocket and gave his hand to Norma. They walked through the door and down the hall.

Marianne walked down the hall into the Ladies' restroom and cried. Why didn't she keep this kid? She wanted to run after him. She could have taken him home. She felt unsettled. Maybe because she loved this little guy and wished she'd done things differently. Oh, well, it's over now.

Chapter 60

Mid-March 1951
Bankhead Residence

  Ralph stepped out of the car and took Lincoln by the hand. He bent down, looked him straight in the eyes, and clasped his hands roughly on Lincoln's shoulders. "Now you listen to me, boy. You do everything I tell you to do when I tell you to do it, or you won't be able to move for a week. I'm locking you in your room at night so don't think you can get away from here. You're not going anywhere. You're here to work, and if you don't, I'll beat you until you do what you're told. Do you understand, kid?"
  Lincoln started to cry. "Yes. Can I go to my room now?"
  "No, there's work to do. The barn is over there. I'll be in to show you what to do, and you better do it right the first time. Got it? Oh, and the next time I see you cry, you're gonna get a beating. You're a boy, and boys never cry. Hear me, boy?"
  "Yes." He nodded his head. "Can I call Franklin now?"
  "No. You're never calling anyone. Just do what you're told!"
  From a safe distance, Norma looked on with tears trickling down her cheeks.
  Lincoln was terrified. What had he done wrong? *Why doesn't he like me? Why is he so mean to me? Why can't I call Franklin? He said I could.* He didn't understand anything, except he wanted to leave. *Miss Marianne said I didn't have to stay if I didn't want to. Maybe I*

FROM SHADOWS TO DAYBREAK

could call her. Or maybe if I'm real nice, they will like me and everything will be okay. He reasoned. His worst fears were being carried out, and Lincoln didn't understand why.

The situation did not improve. Lincoln had been beaten every day, sometimes even kicked. He tried to do everything asked of him, but it was never enough. Lincoln could never reach Ralph's perfect standards. No detail would or could be overlooked. Since perfection was unattainable, physical retribution resulted—beaten, kicked, slapped—he experienced it all. Ralph never did anything quietly, he yelled, screamed, bellowed, and shrieked. Lincoln also witnessed Norma's regular beatings. But her screams pierced Lincoln's ears. He couldn't do anything. He knew if he helped or cried at all, it would only get more severe. He began wetting the bed and was beaten horrifically every time it happened. Ralph was merciless, and he'd been forced to sleep in it. He became more frightened than he'd ever been. It became so severe that Lincoln tried to run away. Ralph caught him, tied him to a chair, and wouldn't let him go to the bathroom, so he wet his pants. He was beaten so brutally that he couldn't move for two days. Failing to ask permission before grabbing a banana off the kitchen counter and eating it became the cause of his last and worst beating.

The knock on the door sent Ralph across the room to open it. Marianne had decided to do a surprise visit. It had been nine days, and it seemed like a good time.

"Hi, Ralph. May I come in?"

"It's not a good time."

"I'm sorry to hear that, but I'll come in anyway. You knew about surprise visits. This is one of those. Where's Lincoln?"

"He's not here. He's playing with friends."

"What friends? Which house? I want to see him."

"The house down the street. How should I know?"

Marianne looked at Norma and saw bruises and cuts all over her arms. She tried to hide them and looked down. She wouldn't raise her head or look Marianne in the eyes. Marianne knew something was drastically wrong.

"I'm going to Lincoln's room."

Cheryl Fosnot Bingisser

"You can't go in there."

Marianne walked back to the bedroom and tried to open it. It was locked.

"Ralph, you open this door immediately or I'll have the sheriff down here so fast you're going to wish you were in the next county. Now!"

Ralph got the key and unlocked the door. Lincoln was lying on the bed and was unconscious. She hurried into the bedroom and picked him up. The whole room smelled of urine, and he and his bedding were covered in it. She carried him to the car and yelled back at Ralph, "I'm pressing charges, and I swear I'll beat you within an inch of your life if you ever come near me or Lincoln again. Better yet, I'll shoot you. Norma, if you want out of here, now's your chance. He won't stop, you know. It will only get worse. If you come now, I'll help you, but it's your decision, and you've got about ten seconds to make it." Marianne placed Lincoln on the back seat, slid behind the wheel, and started it. Norma just stood there. "Norma? Now because I'm leaving."

She didn't move, and Marianne's heart broke again. She backed up the car and headed down the street toward the hospital. "Oh, God, I should have let him stay with me. I'm so sorry. Please let him be okay. I'm so scared. He looks half dead."

She sped toward the hospital and finally drove into the parking lot. She picked him up and slammed the door. She ran into the emergency room and yelled for help.

The nurse came running and looked at him. "Isn't that Lincoln?"

"Yes, his foster father beat him half to death. Please help him. I just found him like this."

The nurse got on the PA and asked for Doc Anderson to come to emergency. Doc showed up around a minute later.

"Marianne, what are you doing here?"

"It's Lincoln. His foster father beat him half to death. Doc, it's my fault. I never should have let him go." Her shoulders shook and tears streamed down her cheeks.

"Marianne, settle down. I'm going to examine him, and I'll be out in a few minutes. It's not your fault. You can't predict the future, and human nature being what it is, you never know what one person will do to another."

Doc stepped over to the nurse and told her to get a note to Franklin and have him come to emergency. She nodded and walked toward Kathleen's room. Returning, in a few minutes, Franklin followed close behind her.

He spied Marianne as soon as he rounded the corner, he noticed her distressed state. He walked up to her and sat beside her.

"Marianne, what's wrong?"

"It's Lincoln. His foster father beat him half to death, and it's my fault. I never should have let him go. I should have taken him home with me."

"Franklin," she asked fearfully, "what if he doesn't make it? He never wanted a child to love. He wanted to work him to death and then beat him when something didn't go his way. I should have vetted him better."

Franklin's head dropped, and he shook his head. His eyes flooded. "That poor kid. Marianne, I know you're scared, and frankly so am I, but the best thing we can do right now is pray that he wakes up, sees his friends, and knows this nightmare is over. And I promise you, Kathleen and I will take him in before I let anything happen to this precious little boy again."

"Franklin, I've already decided to adopt him. If he'll have me. After this, I wouldn't blame him if he hated me."

"He won't hate you. The best thing we can do for him right now is pray that the Lord protects him from the emotional beating he's taken, and maybe those who love him can somehow cancel out the last several days for him. We need to pray that the nightmare of those days won't linger."

Marianne nodded.

"Dear Lord Jesus, we don't understand why this precious little boy was hurt so badly again, but we know that you have a heart for children. We're asking you to please heal him emotionally and physically. Please keep him in your care and hold him in your arms. He needs you—we all need you. Please, Lord, you are the Great Physician. Heal those who are hurt and give the rest of us the strength and wisdom to help those who need us. Thank you for your love and mercy and for always hearing our prayers. Amen."

They both raised their heads in time to see Doc coming toward them.

"Well," he began as he sat beside Marianne, "he's going to be okay, but he's hurt very badly. His kidneys have been bruised. He doesn't have any breaks, but honestly, that's a miracle. He's been beaten several times, and we're checking for internal injuries, but so far, I think he's okay. There could be other issues, but for now, he's going to have to stay here for some time. I'm concerned about his emotional health as well. I'm glad to see you praying because he's going to need it. It took a while to clean him up. He must have been lying in urine for days. How anyone can do that to a child is beyond me. I'm going back in there, but I do think he will be okay."

"Should I stay with him?"

"No, I'm going to sedate him so he'll sleep. I think both you and Franklin should get some rest. Maybe one of you should bring Miles up to speed if he's awake. Lord, have mercy. Since you two are Christians, please keep us all in your prayers. These last couple of weeks have been the worst I've ever experienced in all my years of practice. The whole staff is exhausted and wondering what in the world is going on. The difference is that we know. It's just evil reigning right now, and only prayers and the Lord can rein it back in. It's not just the people we know, it's happening all over the county, and this is the only hospital. It's been one tragedy after another, multiple accidents, mostly caused by drunk driving or drugs, abuse of every kind, physical and sexual attacks, suicides, and even demonic activities. It's been dreadful."

"Franklin, there's more. I sent Becca home to rest for a couple of days. She's beyond exhausted, and I was concerned about her health as well. You two go get some rest, and if anything happens that I think you should know, I'll inform you."

Marianne and Franklin both nodded and said that was fine. Franklin turned to Marianne.

"Do you want me to talk to Miles? I don't mind."

FROM SHADOWS TO DAYBREAK

"Yes, I don't think I could even look him straight in the eyes right now. I feel so responsible."

"We've been over this. It's not your fault. Please don't allow Satan to let you take the blame for this. This is his fault. He *wants* you to believe that. But don't. I don't know about you, but I haven't even shared Jesus with Lincoln. He needs Jesus more than anyone or anything. So the next time I get a chance, that's exactly what I'm going to do."

"I agree with you. Okay, I'll go home and do a lot of praying until I get my head on straight. I'm also pressing charges against that animal who did this to him and is doing it regularly to his wife. I'm sick of this stuff."

"Me too. There's been a lot of talk like that lately. I believe soon there's going to be a community meeting dealing with this, and it would be nice if you could be there in the front row with me, Pastor Ryan, and others. We're hoping the whole community comes because this has got to stop, and we think we can do it if we all stand together."

"I like that idea, and you bet I'll be there. Thanks, Franklin. Whoever would've thought I'd find friendships in the hospital that may last a lifetime?" she expressed, shaking her head.

"I know. Same with me. It's funny how the Lord works. Maybe all this happened so we would come together and take a stand. We might look back on this night and say, "This is where it all got started.""

"I pray you're right."

"Yep, me too. Well, you go home, and I'll head to Miles, then I'm going to spend the night with my wife."

"All right. See you tomorrow."

Franklin waved as he headed down the hall. He sighed and shook his head. His shoulders slumped. He dreaded telling Miles. He knocked on the door. Miles didn't answer. Franklin peeked in and noticed he was sleeping, so he slipped back out and started to walk away when Miles told him to come in.

"I'm sorry, Miles. I hope I didn't wake you."

"I was dozing, but please come in."

Cheryl Fosnot Bingisser

"I'm afraid I have more bad news. Lincoln was beaten pretty badly by his foster father. Marianne did a surprise visit and found him locked in his room, unconscious, lying in days of urine. He was bleeding and in awful shape. The Doc said his kidneys are bruised, but no breaks that they saw."

"Oh no, not again. It's almost like he may have had a better shot on the street. I can't believe it. I don't know what to do. Franklin, I wish I could take him. I don't see how I can."

"Don't worry about that. Marianne is adopting him. She wanted to earlier, then thought she couldn't do it because a family would be better for him."

"That's ironic."

"Yeah. I would ask you to pray for him, but I think I'm barking up the wrong tree on that one."

"Maybe, although I wouldn't mind hearing what your take is on God sometime."

"I'd love to share that 'good news' with you. Just tell me when."

"I see another tragedy has taken place, and who did they call to help again? Franklin, go to your room and get some sleep. It doesn't look like it's going to get better anytime soon."

"I feel like my dad just sent me to my room." He chuckled.

"Hey, I'm not that old. No, I'm just telling you to go to your wife. I feel so helpless in this bed, not being able to help anyone or anything."

"Not true, Miles. You have helped me numerous times, and I don't know what I would have done without you here."

"I'm not sure that's true, but I'll take it. Get some sleep. I'll talk to you tomorrow. And please tell Marianne I'd like to see her. She shouldn't feel guilty about this, and I think I know her well enough already to know she will."

"You're right. She's pretty torn up about it. I'll give her the message tomorrow. But for now, I'm going to bed with my wife. Oh, I forgot to tell you. Doc said if Kathy keeps improving, she can go home in two or three days, but for the rest of her pregnancy, she will need to stay off her feet."

"That's almost good news. At least she gets to go home."

"Keeping her off her feet is going to be the hard part. She doesn't let much grass grow under her, and she certainly doesn't like being told what to do."

"Right. I can understand that. She's a strong woman."

"She is. Speaking of women and going to bed, want to talk about it? You have me very curious."

"Oh, maybe the day you tell me about your conversion on your wedding day, I'll share the days when love was mine a very long time ago."

"I can't wait to hear this. I guess for now, I'll head back to Kathleen and check in on you tomorrow. Let's hope we all get a good night's rest. Night."

"Night, Franklin."

Chapter 61

April 1942
Saint Joseph's Hospital

Rebecca awoke and saw Julie seated in a chair by her bed with a textbook in her lap. She was glad to see anyone other than the doctor, but she still didn't know why she hadn't seen Brad. *Where had he gone? Why had he left me? Did he change his mind and decide he didn't want to marry me? Did I do something wrong? Or had it all been a dream and not real at all?* She attempted to make sense of it and put puzzle pieces in their place, but it was like a montage that circled in her brain, mixing reality with dreams, and not being able to decipher which was which. *Why does my head hurt so badly? Why can't I move easier? When was I hurt and how?* All these questions, and no one would answer any of them. Her frustration mounted, and she became easily agitated.

"Julie," she said softly, "it's good to see you. Do you know where Brad is? I need to talk with him, and they won't let me see him. He is real, isn't he, or was I just dreaming?"

All the color drained from Julie's face. How in the world was she supposed to answer those questions? They told her to stay away from anything to do with Brad, and that became the first question out of her mouth. She walked to her bedside.

She asked tentatively, "Hi, Becca. How are you feeling?"

FROM SHADOWS TO DAYBREAK

"Awful. I think I'm in a hospital or something. Do you know why? What happened to me? And Brad is real, isn't he?"

"Yes, you are in a hospital, and Brad is real. He's just not here right now. The doctors say you need to rest. I'm just here to make sure you do it. So stop worrying and get some sleep, okay?"

"Why isn't he here? I think I remember him proposing. Did he change his mind? Did he decide he didn't want to marry me? Did he run away because I did something he didn't like?" Rebecca burst into tears. "Where is he, Julie? I need to see him."

"I'll be right back." Julie ran to the desk, told the nurse that Rebecca was in tears, and wanted to see Brad. She didn't know what to do. The nurse called the doctor, and he ordered a sedative so she would go back to sleep. The nurse came just a couple of minutes later with a syringe.

"No," Rebecca cried, "I don't want to sleep. Please tell me where Brad is. Please." She sobbed. "Why won't they let me see him? I need him to hold me. Please, please let me see him."

"Rebecca, you need to calm down. This is not good for you. Please calm down."

"No. I won't calm down, and her eyelids fluttered closed. She whispered, "Brad, tell me again you love me. Please." Everything went black, and she heard nothing.

Julie burst into tears. "I can't do this. She asked me questions that you guys told me not to answer. I didn't know this would be so hard. She's my friend, and I have to lie to her. How long are you going to wait to tell her that he's gone? They were in a horrible accident, and he didn't survive? Isn't it better to tell her than for her to think he left her and decided not to marry her, without even saying goodbye? She is in pain for goodness' sake."

"I'll talk to the doctor about it, but this is the most upset I've seen her. I don't know how she'll react if they tell her the truth."

"Well, in my opinion, the longer you wait to tell her, the more anxious she'll become. It makes sense to me, but I'm no professional. I do know Becca, and she is determined and won't quit until she learns the truth."

"I'll meet with the doctor and tell him what you said about her personality. It might help. We know nothing about her. She has no family, so it's hard to know just how to handle it. The poor girl is going to go through the worst kind of grief. I've seen this so many times, and it never gets easier. Each person handles it a little differently, but there are steps to go through, and even though people take them at different tempos and in different orders, they all need to go through them. It's painful, no matter how long it takes."

"Becca is one of the most compassionate, kind, and generous people I have ever met. She feels deeply for others, and I can't imagine that she's not going to feel deeply about this. I don't know if I can stand by and watch her go through it. It's so disturbing."

"Yes, it is, but she needs someone. If you know of anyone else, I'll be glad to get in touch with them. She has no one as far as we know. Would you like to go through this without anyone you know?"

She rolled her eyes, "Well no, but I can only stay a few days. I have finals next week and graduation, is just a couple of weeks away."

"I get it. It is your decision of course, but put yourself in her place. You just became engaged, and in one second, your life changed. How would you feel?"

"You're right. I don't know how I'd handle it, but how do I answer the questions she asks me? I can't lie to her. She always knows when I'm lying."

"She'll sleep for a while, and I'll get back to you after I talk to the doctor."

"Okay."

The nurse turned and walked through the door, leaving Julie alone with Rebecca and her thoughts, wishing she could be anywhere else but here.

Chapter 62

April 1951
General Hospital

Pastor Ryan walked into Emily's room. She glanced up at him and then turned away.

"Hello, Emily. I'm Pastor Ryan. I've come to visit with you."

"Well, you can turn around and leave now. Visit's over."

"I'm sorry, you feel that way, but I can't leave."

"Why not?"

"Because I've been ordered by the court to counsel you and help you get over the things that have happened to you. So I don't have a choice. Frankly, neither do you. Now it's up to you whether you want to get better or stay in here forever scared, lonely, and depressed. I'm not saying you don't have a reason to feel that way because you certainly do. You've been through some things that no one should ever have to go through. But what you have a lot of, most people don't."

"Oh, yeah? What's that?"

"There are people who love you and are worried sick about you like Becca, Kathleen, and Maddie, just to name a few, and also, your girlfriends from school."

"They know? The kids at school know?"

"Well, they know the boys who tried to attack a girl because their names were made known. Everyone knows who all four of them are—none of them know who they attacked, or that you tried suicide as an escape. They won't be hurting anyone anymore. The girls at school feel much safer now, thanks to your friends, who saved you—in more ways than one. They love you and miss you."

"Everyone knows who the boys are?"

"Yep. It was published in the school paper. As a result, Coach started a Bible study, and the Christian boys on the team are praying for the school, the staff, the boys, and the girl who was attacked."

"Wow. I didn't want anyone to get hurt."

"It's a *good* thing. I think people in the community are very upset and might just come together and make a difference so this doesn't happen again."

"But they don't know it was me, right?"

"Right, but truthfully, you are not the one who should be worried. There is no shame in this. You did nothing wrong. They are the ones who are ashamed and embarrassed—not you!"

"But people will laugh, and the boys will tease me."

"Not anymore. Things are changing, and it might all be because people are sick and tired of women getting hurt. It's going to be a different climate out there from now on. I believe God is going to change this town in a way that may spread to other towns all around us. Once they find out how it works here, they'll all want it in their communities."

"You think they won't laugh at me or think it's my fault?"

"I can't say that 100 percent, but I will say there are a lot more people on your side than you can ever imagine—both women and men."

"That's good. Do you think they'll find out...what I did?"

"Honestly, Emily, leaks always happen. Sooner or later, it probably will come out, but they also know how awful you must have felt in order to do something so desperate, so they'll still be behind you."

"I'm so sorry I did this, but I just couldn't take it anymore. I felt like it was somehow my fault...that...that I was worthless, garbage, trash to be used and thrown away.

I felt so desperate that I just wanted out. I didn't want to feel anything anymore. Dying was the only way I could think of to make it all stop—to just go away."

FROM SHADOWS TO DAYBREAK

"Those thoughts didn't come from you, Emily. Those thoughts came from the pit of hell itself. Satan wanted you to take your life. That's what he does. He wants people to die without ever knowing Jesus because they would spend an eternity without God, in a world of agonizing pain and darkness. Satan is a liar and he wanted you to believe all that disgusting garbage. God is light. Satan is darkness. Both heaven and hell are eternal. You do live forever. It's just about where you choose to live. I, for one, am glad you were not successful in carrying out the act. This way you get another chance to make the right choice."

"Becca talks like that too. In fact, she said much the same thing to me weeks ago, about living forever and having to make that choice myself."

"She's right. It's what the Bible teaches, and it is God's love letter to us. The Bible tells us why he sent Jesus."

"I don't know if I believe all that stuff."

"Okay. I get that. I'm never going to force you into anything. God loves you, more than anyone could, and he wants you to come to him. I'm just going to tell you what he tells me in his Word. It *is* true. You can trust God's Word."

"Becca says that too. Is she okay?"

"Not really. Doc sent her home to sleep because she's been so upset. She's not been sleeping or eating. She'd become very fragile and looked exhausted. She prays for you all the time. Seeing all that blood when she found you, severely affected her."

Emily hung her head. "Oh no. I guess I didn't think of that."

"Most people who attempt suicide don't consider what it does to all the people around them. They can't. They just think the same thing you did. They're desperate. They just want the emotional pain to stop."

"That's exactly what I was feeling."

"Kathleen and Maddie are praying, and so are Franklin, Raff, and Doc. They all know what a burden you've carried and they want you to feel better. They all love you and want the best for you."

"I didn't want them to know."

"Well, Emily"—he shook his head—"that's not always the way life is. People *do* find out, but these people care for you. Do not feel embarrassed. Instead, feel loved and cared for."

"Pastor, I'm kind of tired now. When are you coming back?"

"I'll be back tomorrow, Emily. Get some rest and think about what we talked about today, okay?"

"I will. I'll see you tomorrow. Pastor, can you bring a Bible for me to read?"

"Of course. I'll be happy to. See you tomorrow. Bye."

"Bye."

Emily turned over and felt a tiny ray of hope shine in the distance. Hope, something she hadn't experienced since the attempt. Her lips curled in a half smile.

Encouraged, Pastor Ryan went directly to the Mountain View Bookstore to find a Bible version Emily could read and understand. He chose one he knew suited her, and headed home, praying that God would bring this girl back to health—emotionally, physically, and spiritually.

Chapter 63

April 1951
Atwood Residence

Waiting for Franklin and Kathleen to arrive home, Hettie had become jittery. She had labored on this meal all afternoon and was excited to have both their favorites. They were certain to have plenty of leftovers, but she didn't think anyone would mind.

As soon as the familiar sound of the truck struck her ears, Hettie flew the door open to welcome them home. Franklin was lit up like a Christmas tree—so excited to be home—to stay. He'd already bought the ottoman—the right size and color, completely all ready for her. Lumbering around to Kathleen's side, he opened the door, swooped her up, carried her to the door, and over the threshold.

"Welcome home, Mrs. Kathleen Marie Atwood. I didn't get a chance to carry you over the threshold after we got married, so I thought this was almost as important an occasion." He kissed her with gratefulness and joy.

She'd become as excited as Franklin to finally be home. Fatigued but not willing to give into it or show it to either Franklin or Hettie, she feigned a healthy face and body. Celebrating home would be the theme for the night, and she would savor it for a long time.

Setting her down on her chair and making sure she rested those legs on the ottoman, he waited for her to notice and compliment him on how nicely the two pieces went together.

"And you didn't think I had any decorating prowess. Boy were you wrong!" They laughed.

"Yes, Frank, you did a good job. I'm impressed."

"Favorably?"

"Yes."

"Well, you should be. It took a lot of work—the color wheel, the size, the height, and the shape. Very hard indeed." He chuckled.

It is good to experience that sound again, thought Hettie, as she rejoiced. His laugh—not just a sound—it was an experience, and Hettie inhaled it like the smell of the lasagna in the oven. She walked over to Kathleen and hugged her, then she hugged him too. She couldn't be happier. The house seemed to take a deep breath while fresh, new life entered its door. Normality had returned to this once quiet cabin.

"Okay, you two, git yourselfs over here and git to eatin'. I didn't stand over a hot stove all day for you to get busy doin' somethin' else first. Frank, I got your fav'rite lasagna. Kathleen, I got your fav'rite Cheerios."

They all laughed.

"Nah, jes' teasin'. I made the fancy pork roast you like. Now git over here."

"Okay, Hettie, we can't wait to eat. We're starving." Franklin said, with anticipation. Kathleen walked slowly to the table and Franklin seated her before taking a seat himself.

Franklin bowed his head. "Father, we are so grateful to you for saving Kathleen and our baby and incredibly grateful to be home. Thank you for answered prayer, for saving grace, and for your loving mercy. Thank you for Hettie and the way she always knows exactly what we need. I'm grateful to know and love her. Thank you for the food on which she always does such a tremendous job—the best cook in the whole state—and for your many blessings. Oh, and thank you for your healing touch. Amen."

Hettie burst into song with her perfect pitch, perfectly clear, and beautiful soprano voice.

Praise God from whom all blessings flow.
Praise Him, all creatures here below.

FROM SHADOWS TO DAYBREAK

Praise Him above, ye heavenly host.
Praise Father, Son, and Holy Ghost.
Amen.

Both Franklin and Kathleen sang with her without one dry eye. Their thanksgiving to God had overflowed with joy and a new appreciation of God's love and his faithfulness to them.

Hettie served them, and they ate like they hadn't eaten for a long time. It felt so good to be home and be somewhat normal again. Hettie was humming in the kitchen, and Kathleen and Franklin just couldn't wipe the smiles off their faces. Franklin could tell Kathleen was tiring. He didn't want to look concerned, but he eyed her closely. She lay her head back on the chair, and he knew the time had come to get her to bed.

"Come on, Mrs. Atwood. I think you've had enough for today. It's time to get you to bed. Hettie, do you need me for anything?"

"No, ya all get on with livin' like normal. I'll see ya later. So good to have ya home," she said, smiling.

"Good to be home, Hettie."

Franklin took her arm to help her get out of the chair and into the bedroom. She was still a little unsteady but not quite as weak. He felt relieved and grateful.

Kathleen held tightly to his arm while they made their way into the bedroom, and Franklin shut the door. "Well, Mrs. Atwood, how are you feeling? Are you tired? Do you need to sleep?"

"Frankie, I've been waiting for this moment for weeks. What do you think?"

He chuckled. "Would you like me to get your robe and nightgown for you?"

She whispered, "Who needs a nightgown, Mr. Atwood? Just please help me get ready for bed." She pulled his head down and kissed him.

He smiled. "You're flirting with me, Mrs. Atwood."

"Oh no, I'm way past flirting, Mr. Atwood," she whispered. "I'm all the way to very serious." He helped her get undressed, and she slipped into bed without the nightgown.

He chuckled. "I like it when you feel better, especially when you're serious." He smiled and drew in a deep breath. "And you still steal my breath. Mrs. Atwood, I've missed you—missed us."

"Good, that's what I like to hear because you know how much I've missed it."

"Mrs. Atwood," he whispered, "I love you, my darling. Do you know that even when you were sick, you were still the most beautiful woman I have ever seen? Just let me hold you closely and feel you next to me without that stupid hospital gown!"

Kathleen giggled. "What, it wasn't fashionable enough for you? I rather liked it. Simple, easy to maintain, great length, didn't have to worry about wrinkles, in short—perfect." She giggled.

Franklin laughed. "Kathy, will you be quiet and just kiss me, please?"

"I'd like nothing better. Welcome home, Mr. Atwood. I love you, Frankie." She kissed him with all the depth of love she possessed. "I've missed this so much."

"I have too, my dearest. Welcome home, Mrs. Atwood." There were just the two of them. Finally—only his hands, his body, and the passion they had been missing for weeks.

Kathleen fell asleep, and Franklin kept his arm around her and cherished the love, mercy, grace, and healing power of God. He prayed that Kathleen would not fight staying down, but they were together again, and God had granted her this much health and the health of their son. He couldn't be more grateful, and joy filled his heart. He fell asleep with a smile on his face and a hymn of praise on his lips.

Praise to the Lord, the Almighty, the King of creation! O my soul, praise Him, for He is thy health and salvation!

Chapter 64

April 1951
Grace Community Church

    Principal Jackson, Coach Johnson, Pastor Ryan, Rebecca Connors, Doc Anderson, Marianne Weaver, Franklin, Raff, and Maddie, were together to plan the first community meeting regarding the events of the past few weeks and the fallout that occurred as a result. It was important to them that they all knew the importance of working together—the school, the church, friends, and both men and women in the whole community. If they were able to get everyone on the same page and most of them committed to being a part of this movement toward community safety and the consequences for those who committed crimes, they believed they could make a huge difference.

    They were all in agreement with the concept. It would take all of them to pull this off. They needed advertising, speeches, that included both men and women, refreshments, and a lot of prayer. All of them were Christians and were tired of the evil that had attacked the whole county with vengeance. This was their chance to stand up for what was right and just, and hopefully bring peace back to their town which had been sorely lacking.

    It was decided that Coach and Rebecca would give the speeches, Marianne would take care of the advertisements for the local paper, and she and Rebecca would get posters printed to put on all the windows of the businesses in town. Pastor Ryan, Doc, and Principal Jackson would be available to talk with anyone after the meeting and for anything else that might come up at the last minute or be needed. Pastor Ryan would get the Ladies' Aid to take care of the refreshments, and he would announce the meeting in church and put it in the bulletin for the next two weeks. He wanted the church crowd to take a big role in this, and he wasn't certain they would. They were also sure that there would be questions for Principal Jackson and Coach Johnson regarding the school events.

Then they spent nearly an hour just praying over this event, and God's reining in of the evil all around them. They prayed for the healing of the girl who was attacked, the boys who were involved in it, and the coach and the principal who had to deal with it, and the parents who were managing with the disfavor of everyone around them. The meeting had been set for Monday night, the sixteenth of April, at 7:00 p.m. They said good night, and they all said they would be in prayer for all who were involved and for a good outcome, for everyone's sake.

Chapter 65

April 1951
General Hospital

As Miles wheeled into Lincoln's room, he wondered if Lincoln would even want to talk to him. He'd been in the hospital for a few days and still in rough condition but hopeful that a visit might lift his spirits.

"Hi, Lincoln. I've come to see you."

Miles was aching for this kid, who'd been through so much. So little, so fragile, and so vulnerable. He hated seeing him like this.

"Lincoln," he said softly, "Do you feel up to seeing me today? I'd sure like to talk to you."

"Mister, I don't feel so good."

"I know, buddy. Do you think we can talk just a little before you need to go to sleep?"

"Mister, can I tell you somethin'?"

"I wish you would."

"I'm scared." Tears started flowing down his cheeks.

Miles put his arms around him and lifted him onto his lap. "Lincoln, I'm so sorry about what happened. I just want you to feel better, and I promise you this will *never* happen again. *Never* again."

"They said that before," he cried, trying to wipe away the tears.

"I know, but you know I never lie to you, right?"

"You said that. Is it still true?"

"Buddy, it's still true. It will *always* be true. I wish it had never happened. That bad man will never hurt you again. Has Miss Marianne been in to see you?"

"Yes."

"What did she tell you?"

"She said she brung me to the hospital and was so sorry that man hurt me."

"Anything else?"

"Yeah, she said she would never send me to a family again. She likes me, Mister."

"Lincoln, she loves you. There are several people in this hospital who love you."

"I guess so. I just don't know what to do. Momma won't come for me, and I don't have anyone else. I can't live with you because you're sick. Franklin's wife is sick, so I can't live with him. What am I going to do? Where do I go after I get better? I'm scared. I don't want to leave again. I want to stay here." He burst into tears.

"Oh, buddy, I promise you there is a person who loves you and wants you to live with them. I can't tell you. It's not my place, but you know I won't lie to you, and you love this person. She loves you too. She's just afraid that you don't like her anymore because you got hurt."

"You mean Miss Marianne?"

"I said you were smart. If I did mean her, would it be okay with you?"

"Mister, if I couldn't live with you, I would like to live with her. I like her. I don't think she meant to get me hurt. I think she likes me, right?"

"Yes, buddy, she likes you a lot. Would you like me to tell her that you would like to live with her?"

"Yes, could you tell her to visit me too?"

"I sure will. Now how are you feeling today?"

"I can't move very well, and it hurts pretty bad, but the doctors are taking good care of me, and I don't get locked up anymore either. I like being here."

"Buddy, I have to go get some rest too, but I will talk to Miss Marianne for you, and maybe tomorrow you may feel up to a game of checkers. What do you think?"

"I think I'd like to try, but I feel pretty tired right now. I think I'll go to sleep, okay?"

Miles sat him back on the bed.

"That's fine, bud. Just get some rest and get ready to lose at checkers. I've been practicing, and I'm pretty good now."

"I'll still crush ya. See ya, night."

Miles chuckled. "Good night, buddy. See ya."

Miles left the room thinking his heart had broken into at least fifty pieces. Lincoln's emotions were raw, but he didn't seem angry or blamed anyone, which brought relief. He knew he must have nightmares, but all in all, encouraged by his conversation with him. He couldn't wait to talk to Marianne to relay Lincoln's message about his feelings for her. He wished he could take care of Lincoln himself but knew it couldn't happen. Marianne would be good for him, and maybe when he could get around, he could visit them together. *Hmm... That's a really good idea,* he ruminated, *for more than one reason.* He smiled.

Chapter 66

May 1942
Saint Joseph's Hospital

"I think she's doing better. She has finally accepted Brad's death, and the counseling is helping. The chaplain has been doing a fine job with her, and Becca seems to like him. I think it's time we get a little more serious about her physical therapy. At some point, we're going to have to send her home unless she heads back to school and finishes. That's her decision. Let's get that leg and arm strengthened, and then the rest is up to her," reflected the doctor working on her case.

"Okay, Doc. I'll talk to her. She was doing better and even joked with one of the nurses the last few days. She still has to go through the grief process, but I think she's well on her way."

The nurse walked down the hall to Rebecca's room and saw her sitting in a chair, reading the Bible the chaplain had found for her, so she walked on.

She'd been reading it a great deal and writing down questions. The chaplain liked visiting with her because it challenged him too. It made him study a bit more than usual to answer them correctly, and Rebecca had made great strides in her spiritual walk with God.

She still cried when she thought about Brad, but that was normal. She had been growing and changing, and hope and joy seemed to replace some of the loss and pain that had enveloped her and captured her every thought.

Now working on the physical aspect and getting out of the hospital was her goal. She wanted to graduate and get her degree in business and thought she would start back up in the fall, or maybe even the summer quarter if her registration would arrive in time. She hadn't heard from any of her roommates since they graduated and acknowledged that she probably wouldn't. If she went back to school, she'd have to start over with new roommates and contemplated if she were really strong enough to do it.

Starting over seemed like way too much work, but she couldn't afford her own apartment, so she had no choice. She had enough for her schooling because of her scholarship, but paying medical bills was another thing altogether.

She did have insurance because Papa had taught her a long time ago about such things, so she had been prepared but didn't know if it would cover everything. So far, they didn't seem too worried about it. They believed she did have insurance, and they were willing to wait until she could get all the paperwork together. The lack of memory complicated things, but she had no control over it. She couldn't even remember the name of her insurance company. She'd forgotten a lot of things since the accident, and that was just one of them.

They said the reason for the memory loss was the blow to the head and all the glass that cut into her skull deeply in several places. But recovery had helped and details were returning. The accident was still a blur, but they said it may never come back completely. That was probably a good thing, so she didn't even try to recall those moments. She took pleasure in the rest of that wonderful evening, and even though difficult, it still brought joy because someone had loved her so much, enough to propose marriage, and maybe, just maybe, someday it would happen again.

* * * * *

Cheryl Fosnot Bingisser

March 1943

Chaplain Welty had just received a letter from Rebecca Connors and couldn't wait to open it. He stepped into his office, sat down at his desk, and slit opened the envelope.

Dear Chaplain Welty,

I'm writing this to thank you for all you did for me while I was in the hospital. I thought you might want to know how I've been doing lately. I'm feeling well. All those things that you taught me about the Bible are what keep me sane and spiritually healthy. You have made such a difference in my life. I will never forget you, which sounds a little weird since I couldn't remember much of anything while I was there.

I went back to school, obtained my business degree, and graduated with honors. I went to culinary school and found I had a talent for cooking, so I bought a little café in this little town, about a half hour out of Denver. If you're ever in the neighborhood drop in and visit me. I'd love to talk with you, and dinner's on me. I trust you are well, and the Lord is using you with other patients the way he used you with me. Again, thank you, and may God bless you richly.

In Christ,
Rebecca

The chaplain put down the letter and smiled. It never ceased to amaze him how God could take someone like Rebecca, who was in such bad shape, heal her, and then have her come back and graduate. Then buy a business, and carry on with her life. Not only that but also after becoming a new Christian, continued growing spiritually. He rarely received this kind of good news, but when he did, he rejoiced that God had put him in this position to be used in such remarkable and unexpected ways.

Chapter 67

April 9, 1951

    Franklin, Raff, and Maddie travelled to Denver to purchase the tuxes for the wedding—just for Franklin and Raff, to clarify. It wasn't that Maddie didn't trust the two of them to choose their tuxes without her. Okay, it was that she didn't trust them. Two men—never. Raff chose a formal white dinner jacket with a black bow tie and black trousers. A white shirt with black tuxedo buttons completed his wedding attire. Franklin bought a black jacket and trousers and a white formal shirt with a black bow tie. While they were fitted, Maddie whistled. "Wow! There's just something special about a man in a tuxedo," she exclaimed with a raised brow. Both men laughed and enjoyed the attention. Finished. Next stop, the photographer.

    They talked to Mike from "Mike's Photography and Memories" and made sure all the pictures they had ordered were finalized. Half the price was due today, and the rest was due when the pictures were picked up.

    The next stop—taste testing for the cake. They both wanted chocolate, but according to the baker, people believed that to be a bit overdone. The second choice was a three-layered vanilla cake with lemon filling. The idea of the lemon appealed to them because the yellow color went perfectly with the flowers. The baker said he would use the yellow and lavender roses on the cake for decorations, so the decision was made. Oh yes, and the flavor was heavenly.

FROM SHADOWS TO DAYBREAK

In addition, they added two chocolate sheet cakes. They also ordered different kinds of cookies, and mints, and even added M&M's and mixed nuts, at the last minute for the kids who would be there. The Ladies' Aid always took care of everything that had to do with the reception, so there was something they didn't need to think about, which became a huge relief. That took care of everything on their list. The last stop—Becca's Place—for dinner.

Sitting at the booth after their orders were taken, Raff took Maddie's hand and laced his finger through hers. He kissed her hand, thanked her for helping with all those plans, and apologized for not having everything completed the way he should have.

"Maddie, I'm sorry I didn't get everything done. But on the brighter side, everything's done in the house, and we can start moving you in now. It's only twelve days before the wedding, and I can't wait."

"Raff, I love you, and it's okay about the plans. I enjoyed working through them with you. They're done now, and we can just take some time to rest—after we move me in. I'm so excited about finally being able to relax. I do have some shopping to do as far as the linens for the bathrooms and our bedroom. Our bedroom—doesn't that sound great?"

"I can't wait. I want to just go home, go upstairs to our bedroom, and live like we've wanted to for months now. Everything's finally ready, and we're just days away from the wedding and honeymoon. It's going to happen, Maddie. After all this time, it's really happening."

"I know. My feet are hardly touching the ground. I'm so excited."

"We're close now, babe. Why don't we do some shopping tomorrow and then go to a movie or something, just have a little fun? I promise popcorn," he added, with a singsong voice.

"I think that sounds wonderful. I'm tired of all the work we've done, and it will be nice to just relax and have a little fun for a change. Popcorn and Milk Duds?"

Raff rolled his eyes. "I suppose that's the only way I can get you to go, huh?"

"Yep. C'mon, it'll be fun. You know you love it as much as I do. You can't kid a kidder."

Reluctantly, he agreed and then laughed. They were relaxed and enjoyed their time together without a list of things to do, squeezing their time away, but very excited for the events coming in the near future.

"I don't know about you, but I think after dinner I'll just go home and turn in. I'm tired."

"Me too, but could we spend just a few minutes cuddling and maybe a kiss or two? I've missed that, and I feel like I need that tonight."

"I don't know. That takes a lot of work and I don't know if I'm up to it after a very long, hard day," he teased.

"Work it out, cowboy, because your fiancée needs you."

He sighed. "Well, if I have to, I suppose I can. It'll be quite the endeavor, but I'll summon the energy from somewhere, I guess." He smiled.

Maddie rolled her eyes at him and laughed.

"Whatever you need, ma'am. I'm here for you."

"Good, now that's what a girl likes to hear. Took you long enough to figure that out! I'll never understand why men are so dense."

"Dense? Why do I feel that isn't a compliment?"

"Well, maybe because it isn't. You can't help it. It's part of the male makeup, but I'm sure in time, I'll get used to it, cowboy."

"You're right about one thing. I'll never understand women."

"The good thing is, Mayfield, you only have to understand one."

Chapter 68

April 10, 1951
Atwood Residence

    Hettie had gone shopping, searching for a dress for Raff and Maddie's wedding, leaving Franklin and Kathleen time to set up the perfect surprise in her room. She always fled after dinner and sat alone in her room to give the two of them the run of the house, but it never felt quite right. So now they had something they couldn't wait to show her and hoped she would enjoy it.
    They were both in their chairs and turned toward the door when she walked into the house. In her arms, she carried a dress in a plastic bag that was slung over her arm and a big box, and she carried another bag in her other hand. She was loaded down with her treasures.
    "Good grief, Hettie, did you buy out the whole town?" Franklin inquired, with a chuckle.
    "Maybe. Had me some fun, I'd say. Don't do much of that, so felt purty good."
    "I'm sure it did," Kathleen replied. "Show us what you bought. I see a dress. Let's take a look at it."
    "Yeah, I want to see it too."
    "Okay. I hope ya like it." Hettie pulled it out of the bag, her eyes peeled for their reactions.

"It's beautiful, Hettie. It's the perfect color too. You're going to look amazing in it," Kathleen said. "And guess who gets to walk you down the aisle to sit right up front, just like a very special person should."

Franklin stood, puffed out his chest, and acted like he was pressing down the lapels of his tux. "That would be me, and it will be my pleasure to take your arm and walk you down that aisle in that beautiful, fetching dress. All eyes will be on you, and they're going to forget all about the bride," he declared, his eyes dancing and a huge smile on his face.

"Oh, go on with ya now. No one's goin' be able to take their eyes off that bride. I already know she's goin' be stunnin', but thanks for the notions, liar."

"What's in the box?" asked Franklin, laughing.

"A hat."

"Can we see it?"

"Nope! Ain't goin' show ya. Girl's gotta keep some secrets."

"Okay. Speaking of secrets, we have a little surprise for you, Hettie. Wait until I can get Kathleen into your room and give me a couple of minutes, then come in, okay?"

"Okay, Frank. What on earth did ya do now?"

"Just wait, okay?"

"Okay. I don't know why ya gotta be so silly, but okay," she grumbled.

They laughed. Franklin helped Kathleen out of her chair and held her arm as she made her way into the room and helped seat her in one of the wingbacks.

Franklin set everything up and then called for Hettie to come in.

"I'm a comin', silly kids." She walked in the door and stared at the box in the corner. "Is that what I'm thinkin' it is?"

"That depends on what you think it is."

"It's that…that new-fangled TV thing!" She exclaimed.

Franklin turned it on, watching her reaction.

"How'd them people git in there?" she asked.

Franklin and Kathleen both laughed. Franklin explained, "It's funny you should ask that. I wondered the same thing. They're not inside the box. It's a technical thing, but what you see is movies taken earlier, and then put on the small screen, instead of a huge screen in the theater. You can watch it right here without having to pay for it. What do you think?"

"I think it's of the devil, sure as shootin'."

Franklin and Kathleen eyed each other, not knowing exactly what to say.

"Hettie, please sit down and let me show you something, okay?"

She took a deep breath. "Okay."

Franklin turned it on to a station that was playing *I Love Lucy*. He turned up the sound and watched while Lucy and Ricky were up to their usual antics and making the world laugh. Hettie watched in amazement and started laughing. She sat back and put up her feet. She started getting into it, and then she was glued to the TV. She loved it, and Kathleen and Franklin couldn't have been more pleased.

"Hettie, we bought this for you because you insist on going to your room after dinner, and we wanted you to have something to do while you're in here. We thought you would enjoy just putting your feet up and watching some good programs. There are a few different channels you can watch to see what choices you have, but we want you to be happy here. We love you and just want to do whatever we can to make that happen for you, okay?"

"Frank, you guys already make me happy jes' watchin' ya love on each other. That's bein' my fun. This…this is gonna be a diff'rent kind of fun. Thanks, you two. I love ya too. Now git out so I can watch my TV."

Please, Hettie, we still need you to cook for us. We'll starve otherwise."

They all laughed.

"Go on, now I'll be out in a bit. Gotta see what Lucy's goin' do next."

They both looked at each other. Franklin started laughing. "Kathy, I think we've created a monster."

Chapter 69

April 16, 1951
Grace Community Church

    Franklin, Marianne, Coach Johnson, Principal Jackson, Pastor Ryan, Rebecca, Raff, Maddie, and Doc were all seated up front waiting for the meeting to begin. There was an energy in the air that was electrifying. The anticipation for this event had been building for two weeks. Franklin turned around and noticed the church was packed, and people were standing all around the room.

    No one could believe the turnout. Most of the high school students were there. Most adult men and women of the community were there, as well as older women from the church and regular attendees. Obviously, God had his hand on this, and encouraging, positive things were about to take place. Rebecca deemed it challenging just to keep seated. Finally, the crowd sensed that things were about to begin, and a hush fell over the audience.

    The coach stood and faced the crowd. "Thank you all for coming. This is going to be a lot of straight talk. Even though this takes place in a church, we're not holding back too much on what needs to be said here tonight. If that disturbs your sensibilities, please feel free to leave now. It's okay to do so. We're not out to offend people."

    No one moved.

    "You all know by now what happened at the school just weeks ago. We know it happens often in our community. Most of the time,

FROM SHADOWS TO DAYBREAK

the men who commit these acts of abuse and violence are never prosecuted. If they are, most women are afraid to testify because of further threats to them or another family member, or out of embarrassment and shame.

"Most of us men have taken a 'boys will be boys' attitude, or 'they're just sowing their wild oats.' Those of us who have daughters and wives have a little different view. It's our girls, wives, girlfriends, moms, aunts, and even grandmothers, to whom they're sowing their 'wild oats.' I venture to say that most of us either know someone or were the victims of attacks both physically and/or sexually but were probably too traumatized to press charges. Most are too intimidated to tell her story in court because of the shame involved. *She* was ashamed and embarrassed—the victim. That's pretty typical, and the men who do these vile acts know this and generally get away with it, and then go back to reoffend. There are few, if any, consequences. Next time it might be your daughter. This is all going to change tonight."

"Before I go any further, I'm going to ask Pastor Ryan to pray and then Becca is going to speak to us, and then I will end the meeting. Listen up, people, because we're no longer playing games in this community. Old ideas need to change."

"Pastor?"

"I want to read this verse before I pray. It's 1 John chapter 3, verse 18."

"Dear children, let us not love with words or tongue, but with actions and truth."

"Dear heavenly Father, I just want to thank you that you love us no matter what our behavior but you also hate evil and sin and the consequences that always come as a result. So tonight, as we meet, I ask you to give us compassion, love, wisdom, strength, and a genuine feeling of a community that comes together because it cares for its people. Help us to love each other and because of that, take care of one another. We ask all this in the wonderful name of Jesus. Amen."

"Thank you, Pastor. Okay, Becca, you're up."

Cheryl Fosnot Bingisser

"Thanks. Thank you all for coming. I want to address all the ladies and girls here tonight. Well, men too, but it's the women right here who can begin to turn the tide.

"We traditionally lived exactly as the Coach Johnson already described. With God's help and the strength of the women who are in this room, that will end.

"We are women who are strong. Some of us have children, have raised them, or are grandmothers who had to be strong to go through the trials and joys of raising children. The rest of us have strengths that we are just learning about, or don't even know we have yet.

"These women who've been attacked are not to be blamed or thought less of because of it. They weren't 'asking for it' or 'begging for it.' They didn't 'deserve it.' None of these things, which we've all heard, and some have even believed, are true.

"The simple truth is that men do this because it makes them feel powerful. They love asserting power over someone who looks weaker than them. Sometimes they do it in gangs because there's more power that way. One may not accomplish it, but several together could. Others use guns or knives to threaten us to keep quiet and not tell anyone, or they will hurt us again or another family member. Or it's our word against theirs, and no one will ever believe us. Most of us back off, and the men who do these acts get away with it. Many of them are repeaters, and since there are no consequences, they feel emboldened to do it again. This is how this is going to change.

"When a woman is abused or attacked in any way, when she goes to trial, we will all come every single day until the trial is over. Girls, these men have been intimidating us forever. It's our turn. If you know the man on trial and he has attacked you, it's time for you to come forward and tell them. This increases his jail time and again shows the offender that we are standing together.

"If we do this and show each other that we care, we can change things.

"The boys who attacked the girl at school had their names printed in the school paper. That's how we end this. Put the shame where it belongs. No more wagging our heads and saying, '*Ah, isn't that too bad?*' and doing nothing.

FROM SHADOWS TO DAYBREAK

"Starting in a couple of months, we women are going to meet right here every other month to learn about each other and get to know one another. The older women will be with the girls and younger women, and we'll do all kinds of things to build community among us. We'll pray for each other and take care of each other. Once that happens, when one of us gets hurt, we will want to help and take care of her. That's what we need. Women, there isn't anything we can't do when we stand together.

"One other thing. This is something absolutely no one *ever* talks about, and it may be shocking to some of you: If you have been abused or are being abused currently, this is not your fault. If you have been attacked by someone you know—a boyfriend, a relative, a family member, or even a husband—make no mistake. This is not the way to demonstrate love. I know this is not easy to hear, but girls, it's the truth. Love cares more for the other person than for themselves. You don't deserve it. You didn't do anything wrong, even if he tells you that you did. You can report it. Tell someone. Tell one of us, and we will stand with you and support you.

"We will let everyone know when our first meeting will be. Girls from senior high and up are invited, but that's entirely your parent's decision. I pray all of you will come so we can change this community and make us feel safe and secure on our streets again. Thank you."

One by one, the women stood and clapped, until the whole crowd was on its feet.

Then the coach returned up front. "Thank you, Becca. I hope you ladies listened because she is exactly right.

"Men, the same thing holds true for you. First, we need to stand up and protect our women—all of them. We need to call out those who we know are preying on our women and girls and cut the 'good old boys' attitude.

"Some of you may not know this, and I wasn't going to say anything about it, but I feel that the Lord is leading me to do so. There is a girl in the hospital who attempted to take her own life because she felt worthless, heinous, trash, to be used, and thrown away. This wonderful, innocent girl has been attacked twice, neither time was it her fault, nor had she been asking for it. She'd been targeted because she was a girl who could be overtaken by a more powerful male. In the school, it took three of them to attack her. It was an act of violence, cowardice, and contempt.

"This girl will recover physically, but emotionally, it is going to take a very long time. She didn't want anyone to know anything about it because she's ashamed and embarrassed. Instead of her being ashamed, this community needs to come around her and let her know that she is loved and cared for, and none of this is her fault. She simply wanted the pain to stop and couldn't take the teasing, the laughing behind her back, the shaking of heads, and the whispering that she believed would come. She believed the lie that she did something to deserve it. That's why she did it. That's why girls rarely press charges because of the big lie.

"This girl deserves a life of happiness and joy. The need to be loved, friendship, and caring is universal. The kids in the school have a responsibility to take this girl under their wing and make her feel as welcome or more welcome than all the other students walking the halls. I have to say I've been a coach for a long time. I've never experienced anything like it in the time I've been here. She may never get over this. Men, this could have been your daughter, your wife, your mother, your grandmother, or your girlfriend.

"Stand with me in telling the rest of the male gender that it won't be tolerated in this town ever again, and the men who do these things will be held responsible and pay the consequences for their actions. Our attitudes must change. God has put us in a position of authority to protect our women and girls. It's part of our job description as men.

"Together, men and women, we can change our schools, we can change our community, we can change our state, and maybe even the country. We could become the template for the whole nation. This could be that effective, but it's all up to you. It depends on you. What are you going to do? We need all of us who are willing to work to bring about the change needed here."

Everyone in the church stood, clapped, cheered, and whistled. Becca burst into tears.

FROM SHADOWS TO DAYBREAK

Coach began to pray. "Thank you, Father. Now please give us the courage and strength to take the steps to really start a fire in the community that can be an example of what you can accomplish when we come together and are of one mind. God bless all those who are in attendance tonight. We pray for the girl who is so scared and fragile, the boys involved in the act, and their families. We also pray for Becca and me and all those up front here to continue to lead this community. God, give us wisdom. Thank you, Lord. Amen."

Again, everyone stood and clapped.

"Those up front here, please make yourselves available to anyone who would like to talk about anything we discussed tonight. I know we didn't ask before, but I think you can all handle it.

"Oh, one more quick aside. Marianne, who is a social worker, has seen the results of abuse in a hundred different ways to kids in our town. There is a seven-year-old in the hospital right now who was beaten half to death by his foster father. If you know anything about the abuse of children or would like to talk with her or are even thinking about becoming foster parents, I know she would like to talk with you. I hope you don't mind, Marianne, I didn't ask you ahead of time."

"No, that's fine. I would like that."

"Also, the Ladies Aid of the church has prepared refreshments for all of us, so feel free to go down to the basement and find everything down there. With that, the formal meeting is over. Thank you, everyone, for coming and listening."

Rebecca was shocked at how many women said they had experienced abuse or been attacked. But now, they were ready to fight back and not let this happen anymore.

The men decided that not only the women should attend the trials, but the men should too. It would show solidarity to intimidate offenders even further, and send a message that it simply will not be acceptable behavior. The days of "boys will be boys" attitudes were concluding. It might be a slow death, but at least the old ways were beginning to come to an end.

The meeting had been a complete success, and now the real work would begin. One meeting down, and who knew how many to go? They did believe a movement had begun, and the hope of it spreading meant everything. It would make a difference here and maybe even further, with God's help and blessing.

Chapter 70

April 17, 1951
General Hospital

Sitting up on the bed, Emily was reading the Bible that Pastor Ryan had brought her. He had asked her to start in the Gospel of John. She had started writing down her questions, and Pastor had been answering them. She came across this verse: "Whoever believes in the Son has eternal life, but whoever rejects the Son will not see life, for God's wrath remains on them" (John 3:36).

What did that mean? Did God send people to hell? Is there more than one way to God? Why does God get angry? She had a lot of questions to ask him today.

Striding into the room, Pastor Ryan was gratified to see her reading her Bible and writing down questions. God was working on her heart and pulling her to him, and it's remarkable to have just a small part in his work.

Emily started with her questions. "Why does God send people to hell?"

"Well, hello to you too, Emily. How are you feeling today?"

Emily laughed. "Hello, Pastor Ryan."

"He doesn't," he answered, as he sat on the chair next to the bed. "He gives you the choice to accept him or reject him. If you reject him, you end up in hell."

"So that means there's only one way to God?"

"Yes. Only one way, and it says that in the Bible."

"But what about all the other religions? Don't they go to God too?"

"No, there is only one way and it's through Jesus Christ, God's Son. There is no other way. No one else has paid the sacrifice for our sin. No other religion has bought you with the price of the cross."

"Wait, are you saying that Jesus died for my sin?"

"That's exactly right. When you get further into the book, you'll see the whole story of how Jesus died for you and me. It's not easy reading, but it means the difference between life and death for us. When we die physically, our souls live on. It's like Becca told you. When you choose Jesus, you choose life in heaven with him. When you reject him, you have chosen hell, which is eternal separation from God, pain, suffering, and total blackness forever. It's a very long time—no end. Suffering forever."

"Wow! Why would anyone choose that eternity?"

"Mostly because they don't believe it truly exists, and if they do, it's this skewed version of partying all the time, drinking, and having unlimited partners—all the things the world believes are pleasurable. The problem is it ends in a very different eternity than they thought. It's Satan's lie because he wants them to choose his eternity over God's.

"God's is light and golden streets, crystal seas, mansions built just for us, and worshipping the King of kings. It's very different.

"But that life of pleasure, really isn't fulfilling either. It leads to emptiness, despair, depression, and sometimes even suicide. They talk a good game and act like it's great, but inside, the truth is a very different scenario. It's searching for meaning, something outside themselves, but not knowing what or who that is. I can't tell you how many men and women I have counseled who had chosen that path and wished they hadn't. It almost destroyed them."

"So if I want to go to heaven what do I do?"

"I could tell you, and I would love to, but I think, in this case, I would like you to read it for yourself."

"I get it. Discover it on my own, like in school?"

FROM SHADOWS TO DAYBREAK

"Maybe. Besides, you might even find more questions. Now I have a few for you. How are you feeling?"

"I'm still tired, but I think there's a small sliver of hope out there. I don't feel desperate or frightened. It's like things are slowly changing."

"Where do you think the hope is coming from?"

"I see what you're doing there. You want me to say it's coming from God, right?"

"No, I just want you to tell me what you think."

"I don't know. Maybe talking to you has helped. I'm not so closed off, like some of the walls are coming down. Maybe it's okay to let some people draw a little closer. Does that make sense?"

"Yes, it does. Who do you think you'd like to get closer to?"

"I don't know, maybe the girls from school. I miss Rosa and Heidi."

"Would you like to see them?"

"Maybe. I just don't know if I want them to know what I did."

"Why?"

"Because they're going to think I'm weird."

"Emily, I can tell you, that they are waiting for you to tell them you would like to see them. They miss you too. They want to know that you're okay. Remember, they were with you right before you decided to take your life.

"I'm going to tell you this because I think you can handle it. A lot of people already know about you. They want to support you and they care about you. You don't need to feel bad or worry about what people think anymore because they think you're pretty great, and the boys who did this are not. Everyone is on your side."

"Really? Are you sure?"

"Trust me. I'm telling you the truth. I believe you're going to end up with so many friends, you won't know what to do with them all. They're going to love you."

Emily's face lit up.

Pastor Ryan was relieved that the Lord had told him how to handle Emily. She dealt with it well and was even more positive than she had been earlier. *We're getting somewhere. Thank you, Lord.*

With that, Pastor Ryan thought it was time for him to leave. Emily was tiring, and he wanted to talk to Doc to learn his opinion about Emily having her friends visit.

"Emily, I have to leave now. It's getting late and you're looking a bit weary. So get some rest, and I'll see you tomorrow. Keep reading. You're doing better, and that's exactly what we all want to see. Bye now."

"Bye, Pastor. See you tomorrow. Thank you for talking with me."

"Of course. Bye now."

Pastor Ryan turned the corner and found the doctor standing at the nurses' station. He asked to speak with him alone. They walked to his office, and both sat—Doc on one side of his desk and Pastor Ryan on the other side.

"What's on your mind, Paul?" Doc asked.

"I just left Emily's room and have a question. Do you think she might be ready to see a couple of her girlfriends?"

"The two who helped her?"

"Yep."

"Maybe. What do you think?"

"I think it might be good for her. She is progressing, reading the Bible, I got her, and writing down questions. She even said she had a small ray of hope in the distance, so I know things are more positive now."

"Well, that is good news. If you think so, I'm okay with it. You have a better handle on it than I do."

"Okay. Well, I'll talk to her about it tomorrow. I'll see if she considers herself ready. I did tell her that a lot of people already know, and she didn't freak out, so that's good."

"Yeah. That's huge. Well, you do what you think is best and then just let me know where she is and how she's processing things. I think that'll will work for me."

"Okay. Thanks, Doc. Wait. One more question. Raff and Maddie's wedding is just a few days away, and she's a candlelighter. Do you think we can let her do this? She'll be with Becca, even walking down the aisle with her. If she misses this, it could be devastating for her. She's never been in a wedding before, and she's really looking forward to it."

Doc answered him, with doubt written all over his face. "I forgot about that. I don't know." He shook his head. "This is a tough one because it could go either way. It might be too much if something is said. On the other hand, if she doesn't go, it could be worse for her. I tend to think it would be good for her, but her wrists will show her cuts, and I don't know if she's ready for that."

"Do you want me to talk to her about it tomorrow?"

"I think you should feel her out and see what direction she takes. You're probably going to read her fairly well but tread lightly, and you may have to bring up the wrists and see how she reacts. That's the issue that will probably determine her decision. I'll be praying. Let me know what you come up with."

Pastor Ryan inhaled a big breath and blew it out. "Sometimes I hate this job."

Doc chuckled. "I know exactly what you mean."

Chapter 71

April 17, 1951
General Hospital

Marianne walked into Lincoln's room, holding her breath. Miles had expressed to her that Lincoln wanted her to visit, and he didn't hold any grudges.

"Don't worry. It's okay. Lincoln loves you and wants to be with you," reassured Miles.

"Are you sure?"

"I just saw him. What I thought interesting, he wasn't angry or revengeful. He was sweet and kind. He even told me that he liked you and knew you didn't want that man to hurt him. So quit worrying and go talk to that boy who will be your son. He's also my buddy, so don't forget that. I love that kid too, and I want to be in his life as much as I can. Once I get out of here and can get around, I plan on visiting. I hope that's okay," he added, with a shy smile.

She enjoyed the little shyness she detected in his smile. Had she discovered a little interest in her? She did like him. If he could visit Lincoln, maybe they could have dinner, just to spend time with Lincoln, of course.

"I guess that would be fine," she replied, smiling. "I'm sure Lincoln would like that."

"Yeah, I think he would too." Then he stopped. *Should I say this? Would she think I'm too presumptuous? Go for it.*

FROM SHADOWS TO DAYBREAK

"How about you? Would *you* like it?" He held his breath, hoping he hadn't gone too far.

She studied him, then smiled. "I think I would like that."

"Good, because I would too."

"Okay, well I guess I better go see him."

"Stop by after you've talked to him and let me know how it went, okay?"

"Of course. Then we can discuss what we think about his demeanor."

"Right, demeaner." He smiled, and his eyes sparkled.

"Well, I need to go. Bye." She hurried out the door and down the hall. *What did I say? That was so stupid. Demeanor. He saw right through that. This is embarrassing,* she ruminated, rehearsing the conversation.

Miles chuckled. "Demeanor. She kind of blew that one. Kind of funny. Good to know she's not the only one who's a little nervous." *I really think she likes me.* He grinned.

* * * * *

"Hi, Lincoln. How are you doing?"

Lincoln turned and looked at her. He'd been crying. "I'm not feeling so good. My side hurts right here." He pointed to a place on his side that was badly bruised.

Marianne almost burst into tears herself, just seeing how battered he was. *He is so little and fragile, and I just want to hold him in my arms and tell him he's going to be okay.*

"I'm so sorry, sweetheart. Is there anything I can do to help you?"

"I think so." He nodded.

"What would that be?"

"Mister said you want me to come and live with you. Is that true?"

"Would you like it to be?"

"Why do grown-ups always do that when they don't want to answer a question?"

Marianne laughed. "You got me there. Mister told me you were smart. He was right. Yes, Lincoln. I want you to come and live with me. If you would like me to, I would like to adopt you so you can be my son and live with me forever. Would you like that?"

"I wouldn't ever have to go to another family? I could really stay all the time and never have to leave?"

"That's right."

"Mister always tells me the truth. Do you always tell me the truth?"

"I do, Lincoln. I will never lie to you. I never have. I just messed up badly and sent you to the wrong family. I'm so sorry, Lincoln. I can't tell you how much." Water pooled in her eyes.

"I know. You didn't know that man would hurt me, did you?"

"No, I didn't. I never would have sent you there if I had any idea he was like that. If it makes you feel any better, he's in jail now for hurting you."

"Is he in kid jail?"

"Nope, he's in grown-up jail for a very long time. He will never hurt you again."

"What about Norma?"

"I don't know about her, honey."

"He hurt her too, and she screamed a lot."

"I'm sorry, Lincoln. Now what do you say, do you want to live with me?"

"Will you be my new momma since my momma isn't finding me?"

"I will never take the place of your mother, but you could still call me momma or whatever you want to. It's up to you, Lincoln. Anything you want. Do you know what?"

"What?"

"I love you, sweetheart."

"Miss Marianne, I want to live with you. I love you too. When can I come? Can Mister visit when he's better? Can Franklin come? Can we have dinner? Can me and Mister play checkers? Can Joey, from school, come to see me?" His questions came like a run-away train, hard and fast.

FROM SHADOWS TO DAYBREAK

Marianne laughed. "That's a lot of questions, but it's yes to all of them—anything you want." She hugged him, and he cried into her shoulder while relief washed over him.

"Momma, can I sit on your lap and lay my head on your shoulder. Would that be okay with you?"

Marianne picked him up, placed her arms around him, and set him on her lap.

"Lincoln, I love you and love having you sit on my lap." They both cried together—tears of joy. The salt on his cheeks mixed with the salt on hers. It was impossible to tell whose salty tears belonged to whom.

"Momma, when can I go home with you?"

"When you're feeling better. They won't let you leave until you don't hurt so much."

"Can you stay with me. I see things at night that scare me. He yelled at me and hurt me. It scares me. I'm afraid he's here and is going to hit me again. Momma, please don't go. Please stay with me."

"Oh, Lincoln, if they'll let me, I'll stay with you. Don't be scared, sweetheart. I love you. I promise you that man will *never* ever hurt you again. I always tell you the truth."

"Will you please stay, Momma?"

"I will. I need to go home and get a few things, and then I'll be right back. Would that be okay with you?"

"Will you come back?"

"Lincoln, I told you I won't lie to you. I will come back, I promise. I need to talk to the doctor first to make sure it's okay. I'll be right back. You rest." She walked through the door.

Knocking on Miles's door, she hoped with everything in her that he wasn't asleep.

"Door's open. Come in." Miles glanced at her. "Marianne, you look upset. Is everything okay?"

"Miles, it's so awful. The kid is so scared. He's having nightmares, and he's afraid that horrible man is coming back to hurt him." Tears were trickling down her face.

"Marianne, come over here. You can cry on my shoulder."

She walked over to him, and the tears turned to shaking sobs. Miles held her and loved the way she felt against him. It had been years since he had held a woman in his arms, and he'd all but forgotten the feeling it stirred. He tried to concentrate on the subject at hand, but he could barely think of anything but how close she was to him and how fast his heart was drumming. "Marianne, did he say anything about living with you?"

"Yes, he wants to. It's just so hard to see him like that. He wants me to spend the night, so I told him I would, but I need to pick up a few things, and I'd be right back."

"He loves you too. He's already talking about having you come over to dinner to play checkers."

"I knew I liked that kid. I love food, you know. I bet you're a good cook too, huh?"

"Sorry, frozen chicken pot pies are my specialty," she offered shyly.

"Well, there's always Beccas's Place." He laughed.

She giggled. "I guess. Thanks, Miles. I feel better just being with you—I mean talking with you."

"You'd better pick up your stuff and get back to Lincoln. He's fragile, and staying with him is probably a good idea. I wish I could help you with that. I wish I knew when things would get back to normal for me. I'm sorry I can't help."

"You already did, Miles. Stop beating yourself up. Get some rest, and I'll see you tomorrow. Thank you for letting me cry on your shoulder. I guess it was kind of building up on me. I've been feeling so guilty, and then just seeing him like that again, I guess it made me emotional. So see you did help me. Thanks. I better go." She turned and walked through the door, but she looked back before the door closed.

"See you tomorrow, Marianne. It's going to be okay."

"I know. Bye."

"Bye."

Hmm...so she felt better just being with me. That's good news. It looks like that relationship I was thinking about earlier might already be on the way. I like her a lot. I liked having her close to me and her lean-

FROM SHADOWS TO DAYBREAK

ing on me the way she did. She felt better after that cry, and I was there to help her with it. I think this is going somewhere, and with Lincoln wanting to see me, that wonderful little kid may be the thing that brings me to a real relationship with a woman that I haven't had in decades. Things may be looking up for you, Strattford. Maybe the hospital was the right place at the right time after all, he mused.

* * * * *

Marianne returned to the hospital and walked directly into Lincoln's room. Waiting for her, he was sitting up, reading a Dr. Suess book.

"Momma, you came back!" His face was radiant as he closed the book and threw it on the table.

"Of course, I did. I told you I would."

"I'm going to be here for you, just like I promised. I'm next to you—nice and close."

"If I go to sleep and get scared and see that man hitting me, will you hold me?"

"Yes. I'll be right here. Don't you worry about a thing. I'm going to be your momma, and that starts right now. Is that okay?"

"Momma?"

"Yes, Lincoln?"

"I love you, Momma."

"Oh, Lincoln, I love you so much."

"Night, Momma."

"Good night, Lincoln."

Only an hour later, a scream split the silence. "No! No! Please don't hurt me. I'll be good. No! I need Floyd. Where's Floyd? Momma, where did he go? I need Floyd."

He screamed and cried till Marianne's heart broke into a thousand pieces. She jumped up, picked him up, and held him on her lap. He awoke to see Marianne holding him.

"Momma, you're here."

"I am. Lincoln who's Floyd?"

"Do you know Floyd?"

"I don't. Where is he?"

"I don't know. I think he's lost, but I miss him. He's my favorite friend. He always listened to me and cuddled with me. He's my panda. He needs me very much, and he can't find me. Do you know where he is?"

"You know, Lincoln, I don't, but I think this morning I'm going to look for him. Would you like that?"

"Oh yes, Momma. Tell him where I am so he can find me. He's so lost and needs me because he doesn't have any other friends."

"I see. Well, I'm going to look and see if I can find him, but for now, I think we should go back to sleep. You need your rest to get better."

"Okay, Momma. I feel better now. I think I can sleep. I love you, Momma. Night."

"I love you too, sweetheart. Get some sleep. Night." Marianne's eyes filled with tears. She would find a panda bear if it took all day.

God, help me find a bear he can believe is Floyd and give him something he can attach to and feel loved by. This boy has been through so very much. That's the very least this kid deserves. She shook her head, knowing what he'd been through, and it saddened her very soul.

Chapter 72

April 18, 1951
General Hospital

Arriving at the hospital this morning, Pastor Ryan had so many thoughts swirling around in his head that he felt like his brain had gone through the agitator of a washing machine. Trying to make sense of how to talk to Emily today and the delicate dance it might take left him a little unsettled.

Lord, I don't know how to do this. I feel so inadequate and untrained. I'm not a professional, but I know you will give me wisdom because I can't do this on my own. There are just three days until the wedding. We're running out of time, and I'm at a loss as to how to approach all this. Please, Lord Jesus, speak to me and through me. Give me wisdom and discernment and thank you for your promises of love, strength, wisdom, and grace. Amen.

"Approaching her bedside, he saw tears in her eyes. *Oh no. Something's wrong. This is not how I was hoping it would go today. She seemed to be better. One step forward and two steps back? Lord, I need you now.*

"Hello, Emily. How are you today?"

"I'm not sure."

"Can you explain that to me?"

"In my reading today, I learned that I've sinned and that Jesus died for sinners. And you and Becca have told me a lot about eternity and choices. I know I don't want to spend eternity in hell, and I do want to spend it in heaven, but I'm not sure how to get from here to there. I can't seem to connect the dots. Can you help me with that?"

"Of course. Believe you're a sinner and ask for forgiveness. Then believe that Jesus died for our sins because he loved us so much, he rose again, and ask him to come into your life. And you become a new creature. That's how simple it is."

"I think I want to do that. Can you help me, Pastor? I don't want to be scared anymore. I think God can help me with that, right?"

"God doesn't want us to be afraid. He's the one who gives us the strength and courage to face whatever is out there. You've already faced a lot of things, Emily, but there are more to come. With Jesus in your life, you have someone in you all the time who has conquered death and fear. He gives us what we need to get past it and be victorious like he was."

"There's real hope in that, isn't there?"

"There certainly is. You know what's so great about God? He is the God of second chances, third chances, fourth chances, and so on. He knows we are going to sin. We live in a sinful, fallen world with evil all around us. You already know that part, but every time we sin, Jesus stands before God on our behalf, so he sees us as sinless and perfect. He never sees our sin. Isn't that the best? That, my dear, is God's grace and mercy in a nutshell. Something we should never take for granted. Emily, God loves you so much that if you were the only one on this earth, he would have died just for you."

"Really? Oh, Pastor, help me ask Jesus into my life. What do I do?"

"Just talk to him like you talk to me."

"Jesus, I'm so sorry that I've sinned, and I thank you that you died for me. Will you come into my life and make me a new person, one who isn't afraid but has hope and joy? I've wanted that for a long time, and I know you're the only one who can give it to me. Forgive me for my sin and lead me forever wherever you want me to go. Amen."

"Did I do it? Is he in my life now?"

FROM SHADOWS TO DAYBREAK

"He certainly is. Emily, you are a new creation right this very minute and have become a member of the biggest family in all of creation—God's family. Congratulations and welcome to the family! How do you feel?"

"I feel excited—hopeful and joyful all at once. I know I'm going to be better, and with God's help, I can move on with my life and not be frightened of every little thing. I feel wonderful and light and—I don't know…different—different, good."

"You don't know how delighted I am to hear that. You have no idea how many people are praying for you and how God drew you unto himself so that you could be a member of his family—his child. That's very special. I'm so happy for you. You did make the right choice."

"Yes, I could see that maybe this was God's plan for me, but I didn't know how to get there. You helped me understand it."

"Emily, I need to ask you a very important question. What do you think about a visit with Heidi and Rosa? Are you ready to see them? I know they are missing you."

"I think I'm ready to see my best friends. I miss them too."

"Okay, this one's even harder. Raff and Maddie's wedding is in three days. I know you were supposed to be a candlelighter in their wedding. What do you want to do? Are you ready to be out knowing that people have likely heard everything about you? Are you ready to show the scars on your wrists? If you're not ready, it's perfectly okay. This is something that could be hard for you or the best thing that ever happened to you, but I can't make that decision for you. It's completely up to you."

"I don't want to miss the wedding. I have a dress and everything, but it won't cover my scars."

"No, it won't. You know, Jesus's scars never left either. When we see him in heaven, we will see his scars as a reminder of what he did for us. He's totally healed, but scars don't go away."

"People already know about me, right?"

"Some do, and some don't, but I can't guarantee that there won't be some who look at you and wonder. Most people are going to love you and be your friend. The rest of them can think what they want.

Do you think you could handle that? I know Raff and Maddie would love to see you there—Franklin and Kathleen too. Kathleen just got out of the hospital, so I think we'll have to make some allowance for her, but she'll be there as the matron of honor. What do you think?"

"I think I'd like to go and be a candlelighter with Becca. With Jesus in me, I think I can be strong and be with the friends I know I already have—even if they're the only ones."

"Emily, I'm so proud of you and the progress you've made. I'll tell Doc that you want to go. He'll be there too, of course, and me. So see, you have many friends already. I think you can do this. But *you* need to believe you can do this. The final decision is all yours. If something happens and you feel weak in any way, we're there—both Doc and I and all your friends. We'll lift you up. You're not alone anymore."

"I want to go."

"Okay then. I'll let Becca know, and she will make sure you get ready for church. If at any time you want to back out, you can. No one wants to push you into something you're not ready for, but personally, I think you got this."

"Me too, Pastor. With God, I think I can do anything."

"That's right in the Bible, Emily. Good job."

Chapter 73

April 18, 1951
General Hospital

Marianne walked into Lincoln's room with a surprise. She had a bag in her hand and when Lincoln saw her come into the room, his face lit up like an early morning sunrise.

"Momma, you're back!"

"I am. I can't stay away from you too long 'cuz I love you so much. I do have a little surprise for you, unless you're too tired."

"No, I love surprises. That's my fav'rite."

"Here, you check it out." Marianne, put the bag on Lincoln's lap and studied him, praying this would work.

"Momma, it's Floyd! He found me! He looks like he grew a little since he lost me, but he looks pretty much the same. He looks a little cleaner too like he maybe got a bath or somethin'." He hugged him tightly with a huge smile on his face.

"So he finally found you. He missed you, and it looks like you may have missed him too."

"Yeah, we've been friends since I was little, so he must have been very lonely."

"Well, I'm so glad you two friends are back together. I know what it's like when you lose a friend. It can be very lonely."

"Yeah, I think he's much happier now. He has all kinds of stories to tell me."

"I'm sure he does. Lincoln, I need to go to work this morning, but I'll be back this evening. Is that okay?"

"Sure, me and Floyd have to talk. Maybe we can eat together when you get back. It's been a long time since I had a real hamburger and french fries. Is that something we could do, Momma?"

"Of course, it is. If that's what you want, I think I can do that. I haven't had one for a while either. Would you like a milkshake too?"

"How did you know?"

"Just a hunch."

"What's that?"

"It means I had a good idea."

"Oh well, I do like milkshakes."

"What's your favorite?"

"Chocolate."

"I had a hunch."

Lincoln smiled. "What's your favorite Momma?"

"Mine is strawberry. So the order is two hamburgers, two fries, and two milkshakes—one chocolate and one strawberry, right?"

"Sounds good to me. I love you, Momma."

"I love you too. She walked over to him, kissed him on the forehead, and patted Floyd, saying, "Floyd, I'm so glad you found Lincoln. Now we can all be good friends."

"Floyd says that he's glad I have a new Momma, and he likes you. Maybe you could be his Momma too?"

"Well, of course, Floyd. Lincoln, I'll see you this evening, and we'll have a great dinner together. In the meantime, I think you and Floyd need to get some rest. He came a long way looking for you, and I'm sure he's very tired."

"Yeah, he says he walked a long way and needs to sleep awhile. So maybe we'll both take a nap before we have our long talk."

"I think that's a great idea. Bye, Lincoln. Be good to the doctors, okay?"

"You always say that."

"I know, and I'll always tell you that. So be good," she said, kissing his forehead.

Lincoln chuckled. "Yes, Momma, I will."

Marianne walked out the door, feeling like things were looking up, and Lincoln finally seemed content. What a burden had been lifted. Now she needed to figure out how she was going to work and take care of him—or maybe retire. She had enough years in, and staying home with Lincoln every day would be a joy. She needed to pray about this and let the Lord lead her, but she loved Lincoln, and the idea of being a mom at this age had been an enormous surprise, for which she was incredibly enthused.

Leaving the hospital, she smiled. "Thank you, Lord. You helped me make up my mind. It's time to retire, and I'm ready to begin a new life with Lincoln—and Floyd."

Chapter 74

April 20, 1951
Grace Community Church

The wedding rehearsal went as planned, except Kathleen stayed home to rest, hoping the wedding wouldn't be too much for her. Emily stayed in the hospital so she could build strength since it would be the first time she would be out as well. Both were fragile; therefore, people were concerned. All had been accounted for and wound up, and Raff and Maddie were beyond themselves with exhilaration and joy. Their lives as a married couple would begin the next day and a bright new future lay ahead.

Before the ceremony tomorrow, they would instruct Emily and Kathleen on how it would transpire. Franklin was going to receive quite the workout. First, he'd usher Hettie down the aisle, then Kathleen, and then the bride. Raff and Franklin would both usher the rest of the congregation.

They proceeded through the ceremony twice and then drove to Becca's Place for the rehearsal dinner—everyone's favorite café. The evening was entertaining, and everyone seemed to enjoy themselves.

When everyone left, Raff took Maddie home. They stood on the front porch and just gazed at each other for a long time. Then Raff took her in her arms and kissed her with so much love, Maddie's heart took flight.

"Maddie, tomorrow night, at this time, we will be married. We'll be at the hotel together and spend a whole week in each other's arms. I can't wait."

"I know, I'm thinking the same thing. I would ask you in, but I think I need to get some sleep and I think you do too."

"I couldn't stay anyway. I…a…need…to go. I love you, Maddie." He kissed her on the forehead and then her cheek. "Tomorrow afternoon, Maddie, I get to watch you walk down that aisle toward me in the most beautiful dress. If I don't faint, I'm sure I will never forget it."

They both laughed, and Raff turned and bounded down the steps toward the car. He waved goodbye as he slipped into the car, backed out, and headed home.

Chapter 75

April 21, 1951
Grace Community Church

With the church full once again, the wedding cheer and anticipation were in full swing. The church fairly dripping with romance. The large baskets up front were full of lilacs; yellow roses; yellow and white mums; daisy mums; yellow, purple and lavender tulips; daffodils; iris; some white filler flowers; and baby's breath. They were stunning! The candelabras on both sides held seven white candles each. Below the candles, of each candelabra, were swags of lilacs, yellow and white mums, daisy mums, iris, and baby's breath.

There were purple bows on each pew with baby's breath attached.

Raff had two yellow roses and a stephanotis, and Pastor Ryan, and Franklin each had a single yellow rose with a single stephanotis for their boutonnieres.

Emily and Becca had wristlets of three yellow roses with baby's breath.

Kathleen held a short cascade bouquet of yellow and lavender roses with baby's breath and trailing long ivy vines.

Maddie held a long cascading bouquet of purple and yellow roses, lilacs, stephanotis, and long, ivy trails that ran down her dress.

FROM SHADOWS TO DAYBREAK

It was a romantic and beautiful setting. When the organ started playing the wedding music, everyone hushed while the stragglers were ushered to their seats.

The candlelighters walked down to "Jesu, Joy of Man's Desiring." The candles were lit in unison, then they returned to sit in their respective pews. Emily sat next to Hettie so she could keep an eye on her, and Rebecca sat on the other side of the aisle. A soloist from the church choir sang "Because."

Pastor Ryan and Raff walked through the side door onto the stage, waiting for Hettie, Kathleen, and Maddie to be escorted down the aisle.

The hymn, "Amazing Grace," began playing on the organ, signaling the time for Franklin to walk Hettie down the aisle.

Franklin proudly ushered Hettie in her gorgeous, mid-length, peacock-colored dress with a satin collar and scattered rhinestones. The dress had three-quarter-length sleeves and a fitted waist, a relaxed skirt, paired with white short, heeled pumps and white gloves. On her wrist, she wore a corsage of yellow roses and purple alstroemeria, as the worthy, special guest. Placed perfectly on her head was a peacock-colored hat with a white feather and bow. She looked amazing and proud. The smile on her face was the biggest Franklin had ever seen her wear. Franklin gave her a tight, side hug and kissed her on the cheek before seating her. He loved her like one of his own family because she was that and more.

The music changed to "Precious Lord, Take My Hand." Franklin took Kathleen's arm firmly and ushered her slowly down the aisle, making certain she was going to stay seated on that stool and off her feet. He whispered in her ear to stay on the stool, and before he turned to walk back down the aisle, he raised a brow and gave her a warning look. She nodded in agreement after he kissed her on the cheek.

Then he walked back down the aisle. As soon as Franklin gave his arm to Maddie, "Pachelbel's Canon" began. Maddie took his arm, and he ushered her down the aisle.

Raff's eyes were transfixed on Maddie while she glided toward him, almost like her feet weren't even touching the ground. His jaw dropped, and his eyes danced. She was the most incredibly beautiful girl in the world, and she would be fully his tonight. He ruminated back to just a few weeks ago when he was confronted again by his life before he came to Christ, and the nightmares that filled him with doubts and fear he'd never be good enough for Maddie. It produced a momentary shiver to his heart.

Franklin kissed her on the cheek and whispered that she was lovely. Then taking her hand, he placed it in Raff's.

Maddie started to hand Kathleen her bouquet when it occurred to her, it may be too heavy for Kathleen. Since they were real flowers, both bouquets were heavy, but Maddie's was extremely so. No one had thought about this until now. Maddie walked over to Kathleen and told her that if they got too heavy, it was okay to lay them on the floor and not to worry about it. Everyone would understand, and even if they didn't, it was okay. Then she handed it to Kathleen. Kathleen nodded and whispered that she would. Partway through the wedding, Kathleen had to lay them down, but she hated doing it. She did listen to Franklin and stayed on the stool throughout the whole wedding.

A European princess had nothing on Maddie, and she did feel like she had just walked out of a fairy tale. Her hair was pinned up with flowers underneath and small curls on both sides of her face. She looked like an angel, so heavenly and pure.

Raff loved her so much. In just a few hours, they would finally be together. He couldn't believe she would be *his* wife. So beautiful not just on the outside but on the inside too. God had truly blessed him—after the kind of man he had been—to bring Maddie to him. Now to become husband and wife—the most incredible thing in the world. Gratitude filled his spirit as his heart filled with love. He'd never been happier. What an adventure they had in front of them!

Maddie was glad Raff didn't faint when he saw her, but it looked dicey for a few moments. He seemed a little dazed, then the smile which came over his face had been so big and filled with such love and devotion that Maddie could barely breathe. Handsome and so sweet, and in just a few hours, he would be hers forever. He would be her husband! Gratitude and joy washed over her like a soft spring

FROM SHADOWS TO DAYBREAK

rain. He fit the fairy tale for the role of Prince Charming remarkably well.

"Dearly beloved," Pastor Ryan began, "we are gathered here in the presence of God and those of you here to bring together in holy matrimony Raff Mayfield and Madeline Henderson—better known as Maddie—"

"Let us pray. Father, we thank you for these two people who love you and are about to begin a lifetime of adventure. We ask you to keep them bound to you and each other, no matter what may come. Give them your love to share which is far above their own. Help them to forgive each other and think of each other before and above themselves. Continue to lead and direct them in your paths, in the precious name of Jesus, Amen."

Raff and Maddie have chosen 1 Corinthians 13, for the scripture. It is called the love chapter for a reason.

> If I speak in the tongues of men or angels, but have not love, I am only a resounding gong or clanging cymbal... Love is patient, love is kind. It does not envy, it does not boast, it is not proud. It does not dishonor others, it is not self-seeking, it is not easily angered, it keeps no records of wrongs. It always protects, always trusts, always hopes, always perseveres. Love never fails. And now these three remain: Faith, hope and love. But the greatest of these is love. (Portions of 1 Corinthians 13).

"These verses tell us of a love we are incapable of having on our own. Raff and Maddie know as much as they love each other, they need the love of Jesus in action to come close to the kind of love that's in this passage. It's a higher call for a love that's spiritual. God will be the head of this home, but, Raff, you will lead Maddie and always support her. Love and respect her and she will admire and love you. It starts with us husbands. Love your wife with an exceptional love and always put yourself second.

Cheryl Fosnot Bingisser

"Maddie, your job is to allow your husband to lead, and to love and admire him for his leadership, for the way he is determined to love you, and to make a home and someday a family with you. He is your priority above any other human being, and God is the highest priority. Love him with your whole being. Always consider him before yourself.

"Put your whole selves into the marriage, and you will have a wonderful life. There will be joys, and there will be sorrows. You share the joys, and you share the sorrows. A marriage is between two people who become one. Come to each other and really communicate. If there's a problem, don't sweep it under the rug. Bring it out in the open and talk it through. If you need more help to fix it, that's what I'm for."

Everyone laughed at that line.

"Come in, and we'll untangle it together. That's what a healthy marriage looks like. You two have gone through my premarital counseling, and I do believe you are prepared for this. You also know your strengths and weaknesses. Remember to keep working on those weaknesses. There will be surprises, some good, and some not-so-good. You can weather them with the love of God working in each of you."

The vows were next, and Raff knew he would be too nervous to recite his own, so they decided to do the traditional ones that they would parrot after the Pastor.

"I, Raff, take thee, Maddie, to be my wedded wife, to have and to hold from this day forward, for better or worse, for richer or poorer, in sickness and in health, in joy and in sorrow, to love and to cherish till death do us part."

"Maddie, will you take Raff's hands and repeat after me?"

She repeated the vows.

"Do you have the rings?" They proceeded through the ring ceremony and slipped the rings on their fingers.

"And now, by the power vested in me under God and by the state of Colorado, I now pronounce you husband and wife. Raff you may kiss your bride."

FROM SHADOWS TO DAYBREAK

Raff took Maddie in his arms, dipped her, and then kissed her. He brought her back up, and the crowd laughed and clapped.

"Ladies and gentlemen, it is my pleasure and honor to introduce to you for the very first time anywhere, Mr. and Mrs. Raff and Maddie Mayfield!"

Everyone stood and clapped. Raff and Maddie scurried down the aisle and down the stairs. They kissed, and Raff remarked to Maddie, "Congratulations, Maddie Mayfield, my lovely and beautiful wife. He whispered, "What do you say we skip the rest and head right to the honeymoon?"

Maddie looked at him and whispered back, "I would love to, but we have a reception to attend. It won't take long, but we do have to act like we enjoy this part. They did all come to see us. Besides, we know these people. They will want to congratulate us and wish us well. We have to stay."

"Yeah, I know."

"Be happy and mill around. We only need to do this for an hour or so. Then I'll change, and we can go. Just remember, we bought all this stuff, so we might as well enjoy it."

"You're right. Sorry, Mrs. Mayfield. I'll be so charming and gracious you won't be able to stand me. That work for you?"

"Yep. Move, cowboy!"

"Maddie, look at all the gifts on those tables. It's going to take us a week to unwrap those."

"Yep. It'll be something wonderful to look forward to."

People were making their way downstairs, and the recessional was still playing. Poor Franklin was doing all the ushering out. He had quite the night. Kathleen, while waiting for him, had seated herself on the back pew. Once everyone was gone, Franklin sat beside her.

"You look really tired, Kathy."

"You don't look a whole lot better, but, yes, I am. Frankie, I wanted to go downstairs, but if I'm to be honest, I just don't think I can do it. I'm trying to do what Doc said, and I am really tired."

He took her in his arms and kissed her. "Okay, we could go home and get some sleep," he said with a flirtatious smile and a twinkle in his eyes. "Besides, I'm kind of tired too."

"Sleep, huh, Frank? What sort of sleeping? Why, Mr. Atwood, are you saying what I think you're saying?"

"That depends on what you think I'm saying."

"I think you're saying you want to leave and that you're tired." She grinned at him. "I know you, Mr. Atwood. You're up to no good. I do have to say I'm really tired, but not very sleepy."

"Mrs. Atwood, I love you." He kissed her on the cheek and laughed.

"Alright, c'mon. Hang on to me so I can get you to the truck. No falling allowed."

"I will. I have no desire to end up in the hospital again or lose little Bella."

"No, no, no. I thought we'd gone over this. It's not a girl. I have inside information, you know?"

"Oh, really?"

"Yep."

"From whom?"

"Can't tell. It's a secret."

"Of course, it is."

"Frank, I'm feeling weaker. Just hold me tighter."

"Okay. I've got you."

"I don't think I can walk anymore."

"Okay, I guess I'll do my Rhett Butler impression and carry you."

"Frank, I don't want people to see us."

"Oh, they'll just think I'm being romantic. So yes or no?"

"Okay, Rhett, carry me, as much as I hate it."

"I don't. I rather like being a handsome rogue. Ready, Scarlett?"

"Yeah, I'm ready, Rhett. You enjoy this a little too much."

"Yes, I do."

He picked her up and took her to the pickup. Those who watched it clapped, enjoying the romantic gesture. He made certain

FROM SHADOWS TO DAYBREAK

she was situated, then bowed, which made them clap even more, and then he limped around to the other side, and got in.

"You, okay?"

"Yes, I'm just tired."

"Okay, scoot over here. Put your head on my shoulder and get some rest. I promise I won't call you rude today."

Instantly, she fell asleep. He began to wonder if she had blacked out—unconscious. Her history frightened him. He jiggled her a little. "Kathy."

Nothing.

"Kathy!" he called louder. He started to panic.

"What, are we home already?"

"No, I'm sorry. I was just concerned that you had fainted again. Go back to sleep."

"Frank, you have to stop worrying about me so much."

"Kathy, it will never happen. I love you, and I want you to stay with me. I'll never stop worrying until you're strong and healthy, and even then, there will always be a question in my mind. So sorry. I can't follow your orders on that one. When we get home, you're going straight to bed—without me keeping you awake. You need to sleep."

"Sleep later," she said coyly.

"You know I would like that too, but you're too tired. Maybe after you've napped, but only if you're good."

"I love you, Frankie," she whispered.

"Oh no, you don't. I'm on to you."

But I told you I wasn't sleepy."

"Yeah, that's what you said right before you fell asleep on my shoulder."

"So I've already had a nap. I'm fine now."

Twenty minutes later, he announced, "We're home. Let's see how fine you are."

He opened her door and helped her to the ground. She took a couple of steps and then buckled. He picked her up, carried her into the house, and directly into the bedroom, laying her on the bed.

"Frankie, please kiss me."

"No. Please let me help you out of that dress."

"I would love that, Frankie." She pulled his head down and tried to kiss him.

"Please, Kathy, stop. You need to rest."

She tried to kiss him again.

"Stop! I'm serious. Stop it now!" Franklin got up, walked out the door, and slammed it. He didn't know what to do. He'd become so concerned about her and she'd not taken any of this seriously. He plopped into the rocker. *What am I supposed to do? I shouldn't have yelled at her or slammed the door. Lord, I'm so scared. I just want to protect her from herself. Sometimes she doesn't know what she can handle.* He shook his head and sighed. Then stood and limped back into the bedroom. He sat on the bed where she lay, crying.

"Kathy, I'm so sorry. Please forgive me for shouting at you. I'm scared, darling. Afraid of losing you. I love you so much, that I overreacted. I'm sorry." He took her in his arms and kissed her, then held her. "Please try to understand."

"I know, Frank, but you can't live my life for me. You can't hold on to me so tightly. I don't want anything to happen to me or the baby, but I think I know when I have enough energy to love you the way I want. Frank, I need to be able to do that. I love you."

His brow raised. "I understand. Will you always tell me the truth about this so I don't have to read between the lines?"

"I promise I will. There are a lot of things I can't do, but please let me do this when I tell you I can."

"I can trust you?"

"Franklin Atwood, now you listen to me. I told you I would never lie to you, and I won't. I let you carry me because I knew I couldn't walk. I'm sorry if I scared you, but please know I won't hurt myself. I won't jeopardize our baby's health or mine. I will do what Doc ordered. I don't like it, but I want this child as much as you do. And while we're talking about being so scared, don't you think you need to turn that over to the Lord? It's getting a little out of control. You have no control over another person's life. Only God does. Being a little scared, I understand, but, Frank, you seem to be beyond that. God doesn't want us to fear."

"Okay, I'm sorry. I need to let go of the reins a little, I guess. Forgive me please?"

"Always, my love. Now will you please help me out of this dress? I guess it's up to you whether you want to, well—"

"Kathy, come here." He kissed her long and with hunger. "Any more questions, Mrs. Atwood?"

"Whew! Not a one, Mr. Atwood! Frankie, you have to trust me, okay?"

"I get it. I promise I will try, but—"

"Yeah, I know, you'll take over if you think I'm getting too tired."

"Bingo!"

"Got it. Are we finally finished with this conversation because I'm tired of talking about it?"

"Yes, we're finished."

"Finally. Now what do I have to do to get you to kiss me?"

"Just quit talking."

"Well, it's about time. I could grow old waiting for you, Mr. Atwood."

Franklin laughed. "Wouldn't want that. We have a son to raise."

"Daughter."

"Whatever."

Chapter 76

April 21, 1951
Night

The sirens squealed through the country road on their way to the hospital. Still alive but hanging on by a thread. They didn't hold out much hope for him, even though his age favored him. They worked on him feverishly, keeping him alive until they could get him to emergency.

The police discovered the accident. A car was wrapped around a telephone pole and had to be flying way over the speed limit to do that kind of damage to the car and the pole. Still alive but barely breathing when the ambulance arrived, had been a miracle in itself.

Badly cut up, the only reason he hadn't died yet was the amount of alcohol he'd consumed, which relaxed his body, and he didn't even see the pole coming. He had blacked out before the hit. There were empty beer bottles in the car, and he reeked of alcohol. He didn't go through the windshield either, which was another miracle.

Before the ambulance pulled up to the hospital, they had received word they were two minutes out, so she called Doc to emergency. She gave him the information she'd been given and what could be awaiting them. It would take more personnel, so at least another doctor and another nurse would be necessary. More than likely, surgery would be required if he made it that far.

FROM SHADOWS TO DAYBREAK

The police recovered his wallet and ID among which was a card saying that he had been a student at Mountain View High School. There was no one else in the car, just the driver—just seventeen years old. Such a waste.

The doctors were ready when the teen was brought to emergency. They cut off his clothing and examined his body. He had been bleeding from everywhere and a couple of limbs were broken. They checked his neck, which was in a delicate position, so they put it into a cervical collar. He had stopped breathing twice on the way into the hospital.

They worked on him for hours, but his body had been too badly damaged to save him. His parents were in the waiting room, and Doc was elected to talk to them. He had done this so many times and never gotten used to it—especially when it involved a child. They were always the worst.

He walked over to the waiting room as the couple stood up in anticipation of the news Doc was about to impart.

"Hello, Mr. and Mrs. Matthews. Please sit down."

Mrs. Matthews spoke first. "Please, Doctor, tell us about Jeffrey. Is he going to be okay?"

"I'm so sorry, Mr. and Mrs. Matthews. He was in very bad shape, and there was nothing we could do. We did everything we possibly could, but he had stopped breathing twice on the way to the hospital. He was too far gone for us to help him. I'm so very sorry. Is there anyone I can call to be with you?"

"Can we see him?" his father asked, sadness filling his eyes.

"Just give us a few minutes to fix him up a bit, and you may see him and say goodbye. I'm sorry to intrude, but was Jeffrey a drinker?"

"No—well, not until after the incident at school, then he couldn't handle the way people looked at him and yelled at him. He was depressed and despondent."

"The incident?"

"I thought everyone knew about it. Do we have to do this?" demanded his father.

"No, you don't have to tell me anything. I was just trying to find out what happened to your child and why? It's such a waste of life."

Cheryl Fosnot Bingisser

"Look, he was one of the boys who attacked that girl at school. We're embarrassed enough as it is. We were thinking about moving out of the state because of all that's happened to us as a result. We've had rocks thrown at us, a brick thrown through our window, and people yelling at us to get away from them. It's been horrible. What Jeff did was awful. We know that, but what they're doing to the rest of the family isn't right either. The names were published at school, so everyone knew who was involved. Now this." He shook his head. "I don't think we can take anymore."

Tears sprang to his wife's eyes. He put his arm around her shoulder.

"I'm so sorry to hear that. There were so many consequences for their actions, they could never foresee. She attempted suicide afterward. I didn't know the things you're talking about, and if you're experiencing these, the other families probably are too."

Mr. Matthews spoke up. "They are. One of them has already moved. They couldn't handle it anymore. Another one kicked their son out of the house and told him they never wanted to see him again. The other family put bars on their windows, and they're afraid to leave their home."

Doc hung his head. "No one saw this coming. I guess we should have. I'm so sorry about all of this. None of this is right. Please accept my deepest sympathies and apologies for the way people have responded to you."

"Thank you. We appreciate that. Now when can we see our son?"

"They are working on him as we speak, but I'll go hurry them up. Please, again, accept my condolences." Doc left the waiting room and walked back into the room where Jeffrey's body had been readied for the morgue. He had to stop them so the parents could see him before he'd be sent down.

Doc told them to leave the body so the parents could identify it and say goodbye. They placed a sheet over the body and walked away. Doc walked back into the waiting room and told them they could come in, see the body, and identify their son, giving them some time to say goodbye to him.

Doc walked into his office at the hospital with his shoulders slumped and plopped in the chair behind his desk. Tears flooded his eyes. First Lincoln, then Emily, both the attacks and the suicide attempt, then Lincoln again, and now Jeffrey. These were just kids. The other boys and their families, unfortunately, had become victims as well. More evil and the consequences were being unleashed and so senseless. Did Jeffrey know the Lord? He had his doubts. Satan must be proud. Evil never stopped its quest. Something had to be done to save the boys and their families from this community gone crazy. It shouldn't have turned out like this. We all knew there would be fallout, but not like this.

Lord, we're in a terrible fix right now. Another child has been hurt; only this time it was fatal. Satan has finally claimed his first victim. Our first fatality from the sin of months ago. The families are being tortured by the community we hoped were caring for each other, and now the opposite has been happening. How can we fix this before further damage is done to these poor people? Help me know what to do. What's next, Lord? It seems there's so much going on, and now Satan has claimed his first death since this whole thing got started. It's not like he hadn't tried for more. Emily almost accomplished it. Then Lincoln was almost beaten to death. Aside from that, there were Kathleen and Miles, who had been suffering as well. Jeffrey didn't make it. Lord, help me deal with this in a way that will honor and glorify you. I need your wisdom and strength. Help me, please. Amen.

Chapter 77

April 21, 1951
Grace Community Church

Maddie changed into a dress she hoped would knock Raff's socks off. It hugged her curves down past the hips. A cap-sleeved dress of tan stretch cotton, with a subtle white floral print and illusion neckline, with a scoop neckline underneath. It displayed a midi-length hemline—a perfect going-away dress. Accessories included white gloves, white high-heeled shoes, and a cream large, brimmed hat, with white fur finished with a bow. She appeared to be the entire package—exceptionally beautiful and impressive.

Raff and Maddie moved spritely down the church steps toward the car. The goodbyes were filled with cheers, waves, and lots of rice. Everyone seemed filled with joy and good laughter. Raff guided Maddie to the car and opened the door, helping her into her seat. Once she slid in, he rounded the front of the door, opened his door, and slid in. He looked at her with a smile that was filled with excitement and adventure for what lay ahead. He started the car, and they both waved goodbye while Raff drove onto the road toward Denver.

"Mrs. Maddie Mayfield, will you slide over to me so I can finally put my arm around you and hug you close? Can you believe it? We are finally married."

FROM SHADOWS TO DAYBREAK

Maddie took off her hat, threw it in the back seat, then took his hand that was around her, wove her fingers through his, and kissed it. "I love you, Raff." Then she kissed his cheek.

"First, Maddie, that dress is a stunner. I've never seen you wear anything like this before. It's amazing, and yes, if you were out to impress, you certainly impressed me. Now more kisses on the cheek and let's get this honeymoon started. You ready for this, my sweet?"

"I'm way past ready. I was ready even before you proposed. We finally get to start our lives together as a married couple. It's taken forever to get here, and I'm going to love every minute of it. Raff, I love you so much."

"Maddie, I love you too, and I'm excited to start our adventure and journey. I'm going to remember this day for the rest of my life. Once we get our pictures back, we'll be able to pull all the memories right off those pages."

Just about an hour later they pulled into the parking lot.

"We have arrived at the place we're planning to stay for a whole week, just you and me together. No one else in the world matters anymore. It's all about us and just being able to hold each other and love each other. So what do you think of the hotel?"

"It's historic looking, really amazing, and I can't wait to get inside. I can see the lights of the lobby."

"Okay, let's grab the ten suitcases you brought and the two I brought. Can you handle the tux and the dresses? You brought a lot of stuff." He laughed. "Okay, so there are only four for you."

"Hey, a girl's gotta have choices, Mayfield."

"Yeah, I can see that. You've got enough choices here to last six weeks, not one."

"Quit complaining and let's get inside. I want to see what it looks like, then maybe get settled in our room." She gave him a flirty glance.

"Yeah, me too, especially the room part." He winked at her.

"They walked upstairs and the doorman opened it for them. The bellboy ran to get their luggage. Raff guided Maddie to the front desk to get their room number and key. She kept looking around stunned by how beautiful, yet old it was. The history of this place is amazing!" she exclaimed. "This is so great."

"It is—"

"Yes, sir, how may I help you?"

"We have reservations for Mr. and Mrs. Mayfield."

"Let me look here. Yes, here you are in room 324. It's right around the corner from the elevator. Here's the key for you, and if you need anything at all, just call the desk from your room, and we'll help you. I believe there's already champagne and glasses set up in your room along with the flowers you ordered. He whispered, "Enjoy your honeymoon, looks like you got yourself quite the lady."

"I do. She's terrific. Thank you for setting everything up for us."

After pushing the button for the third floor, the bellboy placed the luggage on the floor. They stepped off and walked around the corner. Room 324 was right in front of the doors. Raff unlocked it, told the bell boy where to take the luggage, and tipped him. Maddie moved inside and looked all around.

"Wow! This is astounding! I feel like I'm some kind of celebrity or something!" pronounced Maddie excitedly.

The suite was large and included a bedroom and a bathroom with a tub/shower combination. The living area was spacious and beautiful. The couches and chairs were lovely and comfortable. They had a view of the city, or at least a part of it, and the excitement for the week intensified.

"Sweetheart, let's sit on the couch and enjoy the champagne, okay?"

"Sure. I'd love cozying up on the couch with you and a glass of my very first champagne. Can I kiss you, my husband?"

"Oh yes, you most certainly can and will do a whole lot. Come here." He took her in his arms and kissed her so long and so passionately that it took her breath away. His lips claimed her for his own. Finally, completely his.

"Maddie, we don't have to hold back anymore. We can express our love for each other in a way we couldn't before. I, for one, can't wait."

FROM SHADOWS TO DAYBREAK

"Let's have a little champagne, hang up our clothes, and decide what to do next. How does that sound, Raff?"

"Sounds great." He poured the champagne, and they toasted to themselves and their new life together. They sipped it between kisses.

He took her glass from her and placed it on the table along with his, took her in his arms, kissed her long and hungrily, digging his fingers into her hair. "Maddie, I love you so much. I'm trying to be gentlemanly and gallant here, but if I'm to be honest, I...I...want... to go to bed with you. I'm so sorry if I'm pushing you. I don't want to. How do you feel?"

"I think since I need to get into my suitcase to pull out my nightgown, the sooner we get these suitcases unloaded and the clothes hung up, I can change, and we can go to bed. You're not the only one who's waited a long time. So have I, and I'm looking forward to it too. So c'mon, cowboy, and let's get this part done, so we can have the time together that we've dreamed about for some time now."

"Yes, ma'am." He jumped off the couch and moved over to unpack and hang up the clothes. In five minutes flat, everything was done.

"Amazing how fast you can move with a little motivation, cowboy," she said as she ran her hand across his chin and kissed his cheek.

Maddie stepped into the bedroom to change. She unpinned her hair, placed some jasmine cologne on her wrists, slipped out of her clothes, and shimmied into her nightgown. She stood in front of the full-length mirror and took a deep breath. Her heart had already begun to pound and hoped Raff couldn't hear it in the next room. She couldn't be certain it would stay inside her chest. She sat on the bed.

Fear clutched her heart like a vice, threatening to take the joy from her. So many what-ifs swirled around her. Hoping she would be adequate and he wouldn't be disappointed in her, her fears began to mount. *What if I do something wrong? He is so experienced, and I'm not. What if I make a mistake? What if he makes fun of me?* Uncertainty tried to take complete control of her, and she finally identified it for what it was—her insecurity—but she could be secure in Raff's love for her. He wouldn't do anything to hurt her in any way. She smiled, touching her fingers to her lips. That last, wonderful kiss they had together told her everything she needed to know. They washed all those doubts away and were instantly replaced by pure love. She straightened her spine and walked out of the room with renewed confidence and a smile that she hoped would melt Raff's heart.

Raff's jaw dropped and his eyes widened. "Oh, Maddie. You look…amazing, incredible, and so beautiful. I can't come up with the words. She was wearing a floor-length white satin nightgown covered with antique lace over the bodice and with wide straps leading to a sweetheart neckline.

"I take it you like it?" She giggled.

"Like it? I think you could say that." He could see the outline of her body through it and was so enamored, that he couldn't even move. "I just don't even have the words."

"Well, lucky for you, we don't need a whole lot of words where we're going."

He laughed. "Wow, my sweet, what scandalous speech."

"I'm not all talk."

"I guess not."

He took her hand and led her into the bedroom. He sat on the bed. She sat next to him. He gently laid her down and kissed her. Taking off his shirt, he threw it at the foot of the bed. He sat up, pulling her back up. She ran her hand over his chest, pulled his chin toward her, and kissed him. Then she dropped her head to his chest and sighed. "Never let me go. I want to stay like this forever."

"Wow, Maddie. I can hardly breathe. That was some kiss. I don't plan on ever letting you go anywhere without me. I love you, Maddie." He lowered his mouth to hers in a kiss, that was longer, sweeter, and more passionate than ever before.

She stood and stared at him. He stood in front of her. "Would you like me to help you with your nightgown, or do you want to do that yourself?" he whispered hoarsely.

"You can help me." She kissed him again. Taking in a deep breath, her heart racing and pounding like a hammer. She took his hand and placed it on her heart. "Do you feel that? That's what you do to me, cowboy."

FROM SHADOWS TO DAYBREAK

He took her hand in his and kissed it. "Maddie, you make my heart almost stop beating."

Raff folded down the blankets for her. Slowly, he slipped off her nightgown and placed it at the foot of the bed. He gazed at her and kissed her fervently and hungrily. He ran his fingers across her chin and touched her nose, her lips, and then kissed her again. "Maddie, you are so beautiful." Tenderly, he kissed her neck and her shoulder and ran his finger partway down her back inciting a quiver. Then he walked to the other side of the bed and undressed while she got under the blankets. They turned out the lamps on either side of the bed.

"Maddie," Raff whispered, "I love you so much." He took her in his arms and kissed her. The kisses increased in fervor and depth.

"Raff," she whispered, "I love you. Thank you for being considerate of my feelings."

"Of course, I love you."

He kissed her again. They expressed the love they had for one another that was so special and wonderful.

Later, they fell asleep in each other's arms. When Maddie awakened, she smiled, felt like it was everything she hoped it would be, and loved Raff even more. She uttered a quick prayer to God, thanking him for all that had happened on this incredible day that she would never forget. Then she fell back to sleep with a smile on her lips.

When the sun came up, Raff was already awake, lying there and staring at Maddie. Oh, how he loved her. Last night was perfect from the wedding on, and he was so happy it almost hurt. He watched her as she slept. How beautiful she was! How grateful he was to God for bringing them together, even after all the years of wanton living. He contemplated how Satan had tried to destroy his love for Maddie through the terrible nightmares he had just a few weeks ago. But all those fears and doubts were gone. He had everything he ever wanted, and he was happier than he'd ever been. God, in his mercy, had forgiven him and given him the gift of Maddie with whom he was privileged to spend a lifetime. Overwhelmed with joy, he took a deep breath. Maddie stirred and turned toward him.

"Well, good morning, Mrs. Mayfield. How are you feeling today?"

"Kind of tired."

"Well," he said flirtatiously, "we didn't get a lot of sleep last night, did we?"

"No, we didn't. I guess that means we might have to *rest* today."

"Sounds good to me. Feel like breakfast?"

"Nope. Kiss me, my husband."

"Okay, Mrs. Mayfield. I'll do anything to keep my bride happy." Again, they gave themselves to each other. Then simply lay there and talked.

"Maddie, I'm starving. It's noon. How about we order some breakfast and we can stay right here? We don't even have to get out of bed if we don't want to."

"I like the way you think, Raff. Sure, go ahead. I'm going to go brush my teeth and wash my face. I'll be back. You know what to order for me anyway."

Within a half hour, the food was brought in, Raff tipped him, then wheeled the makeshift table into the room. We could eat out in the living room if you want to. Whatever makes you more comfortable."

"That's fine."

"Okay." He pushed the cart out toward the couch.

They ate breakfast, celebrating their new life together—enjoying being together.

After pushing the cart out the door and closing it behind him, he suggested that it might be time to take another rest. Maddie said she felt tired, after all. He led her back into the bedroom.

Chapter 78

April 22, 1951
Becca's Place

    Being short two waitresses and Emily still out for a while, Rebecca had been waitressing—meaning, she had to be quick in getting orders back to the kitchen and transferring them out to the customers.

    The spring flu landed and swept through the town faster than a tornado. It left a lot of people hanging over the porcelain bowl, and the senior population and school-age children took the worst hit.

    She hated being shorthanded and hoped her girls recovered quickly. Glancing around, she noticed a man at one of her tables and hurried over to him. He looked agitated already, and she questioned if he'd been waiting a long time or if she'd missed him. She acknowledged that she'd been staring at him and was glad his watch had distracted him. He had the brightest blue eyes she'd ever seen. He was ruggedly handsome, with a strong jawline, and straight, thin lips. That his only flaw. He sported wavy blonde hair, perfectly coiffed, not one hair lay out of place. He could have been a model. Gorgeous didn't begin to describe him. She couldn't stop staring at him. Losing herself in his eyes, she quickly turned her head to break out of it.

    Wearing a three-piece charcoal-gray suit, and a paisley-red and-gray tie with a red handkerchief tucked in his breast pocket, he fancied himself a distinguished gentleman. Looks could be deceiv-

Cheryl Fosnot Bingisser

ing. Even though money didn't seem to be an issue, the virtue of patience did.

"What can I get you, sir?"

"Well, first, I'd very much like some water and coffee."

She handed him a menu. "Take a look at this, and I'll be right back with your drinks."

"Fine," he said, his tone flat and sounding anything but fine.

Rebecca ignored it, moved on to his drinks, and put them on the table.

"Have you decided, or do you need a few minutes?"

"Well, since you just handed me the menu, a few minutes might be nice. Thank you."

Again, a little rude. She already didn't like this guy and wondered why a burr had landed on his backside and why he decided to take it out on her, but again, she overlooked it.

"Okay then, I'll be back in a few minutes when you've had some time to peruse the menu." She left before he could respond to that. Clearing some tables and coming back to clean them, she glanced up in time to see him checking his watch again.

Of all the nerve. He was the one who needed the time. She determined to let him wait a little longer while she finished the tables and took the dishes out to the kitchen. Heading back to his table, she noticed him checking his watch again. She stopped for a minute and thought, *Do I make him wait longer, or do I do the right thing and take his order?* She wanted to make him wait, but her better, more mature self took over, and she decided to do the right thing. She walked over to the table.

"Well, sir, have I given you enough time to decide what you would like, or should I come back."

He replied sarcastically, "No, I'd say you'd given me enough time and then some."

"Good," she said, ignoring his comment. "Then what can I get for you?"

"I see you serve breakfast all day, so I'll have two eggs over easy, hash browns, and whole wheat toast, and I don't have much time, so can you hurry it up, please?"

336

FROM SHADOWS TO DAYBREAK

"I'll do what I can, sir. I don't cook the food. I merely deliver it." She turned on her heels and marched back to the kitchen, mimicking him. "I don't have much time, so can you hurry it up please?" *Pompous, arrogant, poor excuse for the male gender.*

She glanced toward the door and saw no new customers, so she relaxed for just a moment, pinned her hair back up from where it had fallen, and took a few deep breaths. There were still hours before she could close, and it had been a long day. The kitchen bell rang, meaning his order was up, so she stood, picked up the order, and walked over to his table. Just at that moment, someone at the next table dropped a glass. It fell and broke into a million pieces. The noise startled her. She dropped the plate directly on his lap "sunny side down," if you will, and the food spilled all over that very expensive suit. For an instant she just stood there.

Everyone in the restaurant turned and watched. Some even gasped. They waited for his reaction.

He looked up at her, not saying a word and not changing his expression.

Rebecca blushed. "Oh no, I'm so sorry, sir. I'll run back and get something to clean it off with. I'm so sorry."

He sat there, barely blinking. He picked up the plate and placed it on the table.

She scurried back to wipe up his suit, then realized that most of the food had landed south of the border, rendering her unable to help at all. She bit her lip. She handed him the cloth, and he started wiping off what he could. He threw the napkin on the table and stood.

"Well, I guess I'm not hungry anyway." Without flinching or changing his facial expression, he stood, walked out the door, and fled.

Rebecca walked back to the kitchen and took a dry towel to wipe up the mess from the broken glass of water and the food on his table. When that was under control, she picked up the napkin and headed for the kitchen where she immediately burst into laughter. It took her a while to gain control again and go back to the customers acting like nothing happened. Those in the restaurant who'd seen it, laughed as soon as he left Becca's Place.

She knew she had lost at least one customer at that point, but she really didn't care. She considered the whole thing extremely funny. The grouch had no sense of humor or sense of time and was totally unreasonable. Although she had to admit he didn't yell at her, and even though it had been an accident—she still thought he deserved it.

Chapter 79

April 26, 1951
Oxford Hotel, Denver

    The night of the ball had finally arrived, and Maddie was on pins and needles until she could get that new ball gown on for Raff. Confident that even after the other beautiful gowns she had worn—her wedding dress, her nightgown, and her going away dress—she knew this would wow him even more. Dressing up had always been one of her favorite things, and she loved it when Raff wore a tux. She'd never seen another man as attractive and handsome as he.

    Tonight, the two of them would kind of look like the plastic bridal couple they often placed on top of a wedding cake. That picture made her laugh. The only difference was this was real life; if only she could remember these days forever. She didn't think anything that came after this would ever be as exciting and wonderful as these days. But then again, a lifetime is a lot of years. God is very creative, so there would be a lot more to look forward to, but she also wanted to be able to look backward and remember these too.

    Maddie swept her hair to one side and added a rhinestone comb that held it in place. She left a few curls on that one side and pulled her hair down over her shoulder. Putting on the long diamond earrings she had borrowed from Kathleen, she inspected herself in the mirror. Everything looked good so far. Makeup on, hair done, jewelry on—it's time for the dress. Already lying on the bed, she unzipped the plastic bag in which it had been hanging and pulled it out. Stepping into it, she pulled it up, jostled her arms into the sleeves, and pulled it up over her shoulders. Raff had the last step. She needed him to pull the satin ribbon and tie it for her. Giving herself one last glance and extraordinarily pleased with the results, she twirled one last time.

Walking out of the bedroom, she gazed at Raff sitting on the couch in his tux, appearing so handsome she thought her heart would melt. She moved closer and stood in front of him. His jaw hit the floor, and his eyes grew as large as silver dollar pancakes. He couldn't even speak. He just perused her from head to toe. No words would escape his lips.

She wore a floor-length silver satin, ball gown with illusion fabric around the neck and a V-neck underneath, illusion long sleeves, and lace at the shoulder and the cuff. It was fitted to the waist, then flowed into a circle skirt. It had a bareback down to the waist and corset ties that tied into a bow, completing the formal look.

"Well, what do you think?"

"I think…I think…I can't speak. I don't know what to say."

"Well, say something. You're making me nervous."

"Maddie, I have never seen you look so incredible in my entire life. I can't find words to even describe what I'm feeling and seeing. Every man in this hotel won't be able to breathe once they get a good look at you. They'll all be jealous of me. Wow! You're indescribable. I think I need a larger vocabulary."

Maddie laughed. "Good, you like it then."

"Like it? Ah, I like it very much. You look stunning! I can't believe I get to take you by the arm parade you around the room, and make every single man down there wish they were me. But you're all mine. It doesn't get any better than that."

"I need you to help me with one little thing."

"What? Unzip you and help you into bed?"

"Not after all the money I've spent on this dress. Food and dancing first, then resting, cowboy."

He sighed. "Okay, if we must." He smiled. "Okay, what can I help you with?"

FROM SHADOWS TO DAYBREAK

"I need you to pull on the ties in the back and then tie it into a bow for me, please."

She turned around so Raff could tie it.

"Maddie, it's even beautiful in the back. This truly is one amazing dress, but you're even more amazing."

"No, I'm not taking this dress off yet, Mayfield."

He laughed. "Believe it or not that's not what I was thinking, at that moment anyway."

"Okay, sorry. Can you tie them for me?"

Well, I'll try. I don't want to make these too tight."

"I'll tell you when to stop pulling."

"Okay. Here goes." He started pulling.

"That's good. Now can you make a bow for me?"

"Like tying shoes, right?"

"Yes, but a little nicer, please."

"Got it. Do you want to look in the mirror?"

"No, I trust you. Let me get my heels and grab my bag, and we can go."

"I thought we could order champagne for dinner. Did you like it?"

"I don't know. I never really drank much of it. Raff, I've been thinking. Maybe having this regularly isn't a good idea. I mean, look where you've come from. Do you really want to jeopardize all that for a drink?"

"No, you do have a point. How about only on very special occasions? Does that work?"

"Yes, I think that would be fine. Let's stick with the nonalcoholic drinks. I really do think it's safer. The truth is, I don't want to lose you to anything, Raff. I want you healthy and crazy in love with me always."

"I don't think that's going to be hard to do. I'm flat-out crazy in love with you right now. Want me to show you how much?" he asked flirtatiously.

She elbowed him in the shoulder.

"I'll take that as a no." He laughed.

"Let's go, Raff. I want to eat and dance the night away."

Cheryl Fosnot Bingisser

"All of it?" His brow lifted.

She rolled her eyes at him.

He laughed. "Okay, let's go. I get it. Rest later."

"Finally. Man, you're thick headed."

"You just now discovering that?"

"No, I've always known that. I just forgot for a few minutes." She giggled.

They walked into the elevator and headed downstairs. Maddie got more excited with every floor.

They finally reached the main floor. They stepped out into the lobby and walked back into the restaurant. Raff's eyes darted around the room and noticed everyone turn their heads to observe them.

"Everyone is gawking at you, Maddie."

"No, they're gawking at us."

"No, you're the one turning their heads. There's a whole bunch of rubberneckers out here tonight." He laughed.

"It's fun to watch. Boy, do I feel important."

Walking into the restaurant, Raff spotted the headwaiter and told him they had reservations. He checked his book and took them to a table off to the side. Maddie knew Raff ordered extra candles, flowers of lilacs, yellow roses, purple iris, and baby's breath in a crystal vase, all on a white tablecloth. It was beautiful and terribly romantic.

Raff took her hand and kissed it. "Maddie, you look sensational tonight, and I love you so much. I can hardly keep my hands off you. Everyone is staring at you because you're so beautiful."

"Raff, this table is exquisite. You even ordered the wedding flowers so I can actually enjoy them. Can we take the flowers upstairs with us, and please stop embarrassing me?"

Raff laughed. "I'm sure we can take the flowers, and I'll stop teasing you for a little while, but it's hard to be good when I want to be with you so bad."

"I know, but get over it. You and I are dancing. Look on the bright side. I'll be close to you while we're dancing. Does that make it better?"

"Okay, I'll be good. Being close to you isn't a bad reward for being good. I can hang in there."

FROM SHADOWS TO DAYBREAK

"Good. Here comes the waiter. What drinks were you thinking about?"

"How about sparkling cider, will that work?"

"Yeah, sounds good."

They ordered drinks and dinner and had a marvelous time. They were so relaxed and relished being together.

Then Raff guided Maddie to the dance floor, where the band played so many romantic love songs. "Embraceable You" and "Be My Love" were Maddie's favorites. She laid her head on Raff's shoulder and they swayed to the music. They played waltzes, swing, and even a little jitterbug—most of the music from WW II and forward. When he spun her, her dress was like a Ginger Rogers dance costume. It was exquisite.

There were a lot of spectators who just watched the two of them and commented on what a beautiful couple they were. Most of them guessed they were newlyweds by the way they were dancing and the many times Raff kissed her. It was pretty obvious, but neither of them cared. Maddie had the time of her life and never wanted it to end. But everything ends at some point. And so did the evening. They announced the last song, and everyone came out on the dance floor for the final song. When it ended, everyone went back to their rooms or their cars.

"Raff, thank you for indulging me and for dancing. I know it's not your favorite, but I loved it. I loved being with you and just having you hold me. It was a very special evening."

"Hey, I enjoyed it too. Believe me. It's not a chore to hold you. I love that too, Maddie, I had a great time. Maybe someday we can come back and relive some of these memories. I'm sure they have dancing regularly, and it's not that far away."

"I would love to do that. Thanks, Raff. Maybe we can come back for our first anniversary."

"Sure, that sounds great."

They stepped off the elevator and walked to their room. Raff unlocked the door and guided Maddie through it.

Maddie looked at Raff. She placed the flowers on the coffee table. "I don't want to ever take off this dress. I feel pretty in it."

"Maddie, you're gorgeous in it, but you're gorgeous out of it too."

"Was that a hint, cowboy? Subtle."

"I'm sorry. I was teasing—sort of."

"No, it's okay. I'm ready to take it off and maybe get some rest." She raised her brow and grinned.

"Okay then. May I help you off with your dress, sweetheart?" He kissed her, and she melted into his chest.

"Yes, love. I need you to untie it so I can step out of it and hang it up. While he was untying it, she took out her comb and shook out her hair. It fell below her shoulders like a nutmeg-colored waterfall.

Raff raked his hands through it and kissed her neck and shoulders, as the dress dropped to the floor. She leaned back against his chest, sighing. A little groan escaped from deep in her throat.

She whispered, "I can hang it up later," and she got into bed.

Raff swooped her in his arms and pressed his lips to hers with a heart full of love for his new wife. They turned out the lights, came together again, and the joy in Maddie's heart almost burst through her chest. She loved him so much.

Raff and Maddie celebrated their love for each other. It was a gift from God and they were both grateful and tremendously happy.

Chapter 80

April 24, 1951
Two days ago

Becca's Place

While Rebecca was taking an order, she glanced over and noticed him sitting at the table nearby—the mystery man. She quickly turned back to her order pad and finished with the current customer. She glanced around, and he was the only table left in her station. She took a deep breath and walked over to the table and studied him. He looked up at her.

"Are you waiting this table?"

"I am."

He quietly got up without a word or expression and merely walked to another table and sat. She bit her lip to keep from laughing and walked straight back into the kitchen and let it out. The whole episode was ridiculously funny!

"This guy has quite the personality. I can't figure him out. Never saw him smile at all, but the fact that he didn't yell at me is one point in his favor. As far as I'm concerned, that's the only one. But he does intrigue me, and he does make me laugh, I'll give him that. Maybe under there somewhere is a sense of humor."

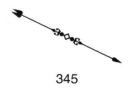

Chapter 81

April 26, 1951
Becca's Place

    Bussing tables, Rebecca scanned the door and noticed more people were standing in line. Rebecca hurried to take the plastic tub full of dirty plates into the kitchen and brought out a clean cloth to wipe off the tables. Then she made her way over to the door taking the family that was first in line. Guiding them to a table by the window, she seated them and glanced up to see that her mystery man stood there. Walking past him, her chin held high, she ignored him. She walked back into the kitchen and kept her eye on him to see if he moved. He didn't. He didn't glance at his watch every three seconds or seemed agitated at all. She stepped over to the family she had seated, as they were perusing their menus. After asking them what they wanted to drink, she took their orders while they continued reading.

    Rebecca brought back the drinks and set them down. She gave him an askance peek, and he still stood there. She hesitated to laugh, so she concentrated on the family in front of her. They each ordered and she took them back to the kitchen. She eyed the door—still there. Immensely enjoying everything about this, she took the order from another group that seated themselves. Continuing to neglect him, he finally seated himself. Unbelievable! He sat at her station! She didn't want to serve this dolt. Walking back to the family by

FROM SHADOWS TO DAYBREAK

the window, she chatted with them, asked about their children, but she glanced back every once in a while to see how he'd reacted. He was so handsome. Deciding she had overlooked his existence long enough, she walked over to his table and asked what he wanted to drink.

"I think just coffee and water would be fine. Thank you."

"I'll be right back." He sounded courteous this time around. Maybe he's not so bad after all. Holding both the coffee and water, she walked back and proceeded to put them down when the glass slipped out of her hand and landed on his lap.

Instantly he stood and ranted, "Lady, what did I ever do to you that you find it impossible to serve me without unloading on me whatever you happen to have in your hands? This is the second suit that I'll have to take to the cleaners, and I'm running out of suits."

Rebecca just stood there, gawking and trying to find her tongue. Suddenly, erupted in loud laughter, he sputtered a bit, then joined his laughter with hers. Everyone in the restaurant who witnessed it, laughed. They stared at each other for a few seconds, then he finally spoke.

"What is your name?"

"Becca."

He nodded. "Of course, hence the name 'Becca's Place' out front."

"How astute." She stifled another laugh, but he was making it difficult. He had a gift for stating the obvious.

"Well, I did graduate high school and even graduated from college, so I did learn how to read."

"Good to know. So that means you can read a menu, right?"

"I could, but I think I need to go home and change these wet clothes. If I have time, I might come back. Um…would you like to go out for coffee sometime?"

"Coffee?" She looked around and back at him, lifting her brow. "Look, whatever your name is—"

"Campbell. James Campbell."

"Right. James, if you want to go out with me, you're going to have to be a little more original than that. I have bucket-loads of coffee in the kitchen. If I'm not mistaken, I think there's a cup right in front of you."

He dropped his head and sighed. "All that education and I'm still stupid."

"I wouldn't say stupid…exactly, just…blissfully unaware."

"I'll humbly take that. How about bowling?"

"Well, that's original. I'll give you that."

"Fine, I'll go bowling with you, but only if you quit sitting at my table. There's a target right on the front of your suit. I've just been hitting it."

"He laughed. I like a girl with a sense of humor, and you certainly have one of those. How about tomorrow night after work?"

"Fine, pick me up here, at—what?"—she glanced at the clock— "seven thirty. Is that okay?"

"That will work fine."

"Alright, James. Just please wear something washable that doesn't have a target on it, okay? I never miss a bullseye. Never."

"Now that's a story I want to hear."

"Bye, James."

"Bye, Becca. See ya tomorrow night." He smiled and waved as he walked out the door."

"Hmm. He might be okay after all. Bowling." She commented, shaking her head, "So weird."

* * * * *

James was only standing long enough to know where her station was located because he wanted to sit at one of her tables. He found her interesting and amusing. She played games a little, and he'd never really met anyone quite like her. She was confident and walked with a straight spine and her chin up. He liked that. She seemed to be more than fluff. She demonstrated substance and had a sense of humor that he found entertaining and fascinating. He understood she had difficulty holding back a laugh the last time he saw her. He thought it very charming and entertaining. Not only that, but also she was incredibly beautiful, and those green eyes were like emeralds with a lot of wisdom and depth.

Chapter 82

April 28, 1951
Atwood Residence

    Watching *The Red Skelton Hour*, Hettie had her head back and her feet up and laughed at every laugh line in the script. She couldn't be happier with her surprise gift, even if she thought it was of the devil in the beginning. She changed her mind right after Ricky told Lucy he loved her. Yes, she loved that box in the corner, and it did keep her occupied at night.

    Kathleen had begun to teach her to read, but it became a slow process because she tired easily. At least the morning sickness had gone, but the weakness continued to cause problems. Franklin became better at keeping his distance, but he still observed her like a hawk. She lived in the chair during the day but had been able to get up and down on her own and even walk around the house. She was still too unstable to walk around outside. Even though most of the snow had melted, the ground remained so uneven that Franklin sort of put his foot down softly that she walked only in the house until the ground became more friendly.

    With Franklin out in the orchard more, watching the pruning, checking the trees, and rendering certain they were still healthy, he felt torn. Usually, being out in the orchard was something he looked forward to, but with Kathleen inside and still not 100 percent, he just wanted to be with her. Concerned she might resent the amount

FROM SHADOWS TO DAYBREAK

of time it took and be bored without him, but praying he might be wrong, he said nothing to her about it. He hoped teaching Hettie would take up more of her time. Hettie struggled to learn, making the process painfully slow and tedious for them both. Kathleen's weakness played an enormous part, so she taught in short spurts.

She had taken on the project of writing letters to Jessie with Hettie. That had become a real bright spot. Jessie wanted to know how the pregnancy had progressed and questions of all sorts for Hettie to answer in her next letter. Restoring their relationship had been a surprise for which Hettie was very grateful.

"Kathy, are you around here somewhere?" Franklin just came in from outside and didn't see her. He hung up his coat and took off his boots. He checked the bedroom. She wasn't in the chair, not in the bedroom either.

She is okay, he tried to reassure himself.

Kathleen walked into the room from the bathroom, and Franklin relaxed. Kathleen recognized the signs and didn't know whether to say anything or not, but she'd begun to feel that he'd worry himself to death.

Knowing this could cause an argument, she plowed ahead anyway. "Frank, we've talked about this before. You are worrying too much, and I'm becoming concerned about you worrying yourself to death. You worry about me. If you're gone, then what do I do?"

"I'm trying, Kathy, I really am. I'm still in my rocker, aren't I? I didn't go looking for you."

"Where in the world do you think I'm going to go? I spend all my time in three places. The bed, the chair, and the bathroom. Not exactly a world traveler."

Franklin laughed. "Point well taken. Come over here and sit with me."

"No, I'm mad at you."

"Why?"

"Because you still don't trust me. I don't know what else I can do to make you listen to me and believe me."

"I'm sorry. Come over here and sit on my lap. I said I was sorry. Let me make it up to you."

Cheryl Fosnot Bingisser

"No, because you're just going to try and kiss me and distract me so you don't ever have to change anything. I need you to take me at my word."

"Be reasonable. I'm trying."

"Yeah, but not hard enough. If I can't even go to the bath-room without you worrying, there's something wrong because the larger this baby gets, the more time I'm going to be spending in the bathroom."

"You're right. You're right. I'm sorry."

"I don't want you to be sorry! I want you to believe me. Frank, I can't do this. I'm sorry, but I can't. It's not working. Not for me. You are looking over your shoulder, checking every room to see where I am—I feel like a toddler. No, I'm not strong. I understand that, but I already told you that I have no desire to land in the hospital or hurt our baby. You don't listen to me. I'm sorry. I'm going to take a nap."

"Can I come too?"

"No. I need to think and rest. Leave me alone, Frank. I don't want to talk anymore. It never gets me anywhere anyway."

"Kathy, don't leave like this. Let's talk this out."

"Frank, I've talked about this till I'm blue in the face and you don't change. It's not like I'm doing anything to hurt myself, but you won't give me an inch. I might as well be on a leash." She walked slowly into the bedroom and shut the door. She flopped on the bed and a river of tears slid down her cheeks.

Franklin knew she was right, but he didn't know how to change. He sat there and prayed silently.

Lord, I know she's right. I just don't know how to change it. Well, honestly, yes, I do. I know I need to give my fear over to you. I know you will take care of her, so please help me give her what she needs and let her do those things she knows she can do without me driving her crazy or driving myself crazy. I love her, and I know you love her more. Please help me let go a little, help me trust her to take care of herself and our son. Thank you, Lord. Amen.

Pushing himself up from his chair, he walked into the bedroom and saw her crying. He sat down on the bed next to her and stroked her hair.

FROM SHADOWS TO DAYBREAK

"Kathy, I know I've been driving you crazy—myself too, I guess. You're right. I have been worrying more than I should. I'm backing off and will try to stay in the distance. I'm praying about it because I do worry, but I also know carrying around that kind of fear is contrary to God's word. I'm learning. Can you forgive me?"

"Frankie, I'm not sure I'm ready to talk to you yet. You're hurting me by not listening to me."

"Please, Kathy. I love you, and I was wrong. I admit it. Please forgive me."

"I love you. Of course, I forgive you. I'm going to trust that you and God will work on this together."

"Okay, can I take a nap with you?"

"That depends."

"On what?"

"Frank, are you sleepy or just tired?"

"I'm just tired, okay?"

"Well, it's about time," Kathleen declared. "We're finally on the same page!"

Chapter 83

April 28, 1951
Oxford Hotel, Denver

Packing up their things, leaving their hotel, was a bittersweet day. They had so much fun on their honeymoon, and so many memories, but now they were going home. They were going home to begin their real life that included dreams, disappointments, children, including broken arms, rashes, fevers, and all kinds of things that would no doubt come into their home—all kinds of memories—both good and bad.

"So, Maddie, do you think we made some memories that you'll remember forever?"

"Oh yes, it was so much fun. The hotel was fabulous, the service was amazing, and the ball was the highlight for me. Well, then there's you. You were kind of a highlight."

"Kind of?"

"Yeah, after a day or two you were kind of old hat, but I survived it. I have a lot of years to survive it, so I better get used to it." Maddie giggled.

"Wow. You don't hold back much, do you? So I'm old hat already. I wonder what I'll be like in fifty years."

"I don't know. I dread the thought of it."

FROM SHADOWS TO DAYBREAK

"Yeah, me too. Well, if you feel that way, I guess maybe I'll just sleep on the couch from now on. I'll just take my old hat and move downstairs."

Maddie scooted over to him in the car and kissed him on the cheek. "Mayfield, you may be an old hat, but you're my old hat, and I happen to like old hats. I have a few of my own."

"Really. So old hat isn't a bad thing then?"

"Oh no, it's just broken in. There's a lot of use yet to be had from an old hat."

"Okay then, if, you're sure."

Maddie laughed. "Okay, it was wonderful. Raff, you were wonderful. I never thought it could be such a great experience, and you are the best husband a woman could ever hope for. You made it easy for me. I'll never forget this week. I'll be talking about it when I'm eighty—if I can find my teeth."

Raff laughed. "Yeah, I think teeth would be the least of your problems. Maddie, you made everything perfect. Loving you is the biggest joy of my life, and there's a lot more joy to come."

"I'm counting on it, cowboy. After an hour, they turned into the driveway. Here we are, home sweet home. We're home, Raff. Boy, that sounds good, doesn't it?"

"It does indeed."

"Let's get everything in the house and start our new life in our new forever home."

"Okay, cowboy, lead the way. I'll even help with the luggage."

"You should. Most of it is yours."

"Choices, Mayfield."

"Yeah, I get it. C'mon, let's get everything up on the porch and into the house. There's a cold breeze out tonight. Might have to start a fire to warm things up."

"Who needs a fire when I have you?"

"Well said, my sweet. Well said." He chuckled.

They walked into the house and saw gifts all over the living room. There were some in the kitchen. They were stacked up against the wall. They were even on the couch. They were everywhere! They both stood there just trying to take it all in.

"Well, that'll give us something to do this week," Raff said, with a surprised look on his face.

"I guess so. Tomorrow seems like a good day to get started. I'm all for heading upstairs tonight. What do you think?"

"I think you're right. Maybe tomorrow morning we'll go to Becca's Place and get some breakfast and then come back and tackle this mountain of gifts. It should be fun to open them."

They managed to haul all the luggage upstairs to the bedroom and hang everything up. "Now what do we do? It is cold in here."

"Well, I was thinking of a good way to warm up and rest at the same time."

"And what might that be, cowboy?"

"Well, everything's unpacked, and we have this bed over here that's begging us to climb in. It's been pretty lonely, just eagerly waiting for someone to use it."

"Well, I suppose it's only the hospitable thing to do."

"Raff, will you help me off with my dress?"

"I'd be delighted, my sweet."

He unzipped her dress, and she stepped out of it. He kissed her neck. "Maddie, I love you so much. You are so beautiful."

She finished undressing and got into bed.

"Raff, I love you. You've made me the happiest wife on earth."

Raff climbed into bed. His lips met hers with a surge of passion and love. She kissed him back with the love of a wife for her husband. They were lost in the love each had for the other and wanted it to be that way forever.

"Old hat, huh?"

Maddie giggled.

Chapter 84

May 1951
Mayfield Residence

The next week, Raff and Maddie decided to have Franklin and Kathleen over for dinner to tell them about their honeymoon. The Atwoods hadn't seen the improvements that they had made to the house, so they were anxious to show them. They set the date for just two days away.

A knock on the door sent Raff to open it. Maddie came out of the kitchen to greet their guests.

"You are the first guests in our new home," Maddie announced proudly.

"We are honored to be your guests, Maddie. This is beautiful. You guys did a great job. No wonder you were excited about fixing this place up. It looks brand-new. You should be proud of what you've done here," Kathleen remarked.

"We are. It was a long haul, but it's done now, and we're loving it."

"Raff, why don't you take them on a tour while I check on dinner?"

"Okay. Kathleen, can you make it upstairs?"

Franklin just waited to see which way she'd jump.

"Well, I'm a little tired tonight, so maybe I shouldn't."

Cheryl Fosnot Bingisser

"Okay, Scarlett, let's go." Franklin picked her up and took her upstairs.

"Yes, Rhett. There are a lot of stairs."

Kathleen thought all the rooms were nicely done and so proud of Maddie for their color choices and the way they decided to paint each room.

"She has an artistic eye," commented Kathleen.

After the tour upstairs, Franklin took her back down. They looked in the kitchen and commented on the great job his crew had done on the countertop—quite a work of art.

Then Raff brought them back into the living room. Maddie said there would be a few more minutes until dinner was ready, so she sat with them.

"Frank, look at that chest. Isn't it beautiful? I'm so glad you're enjoying it."

"Yes, it was Maddie's idea to bring it down from the attic. Kind of classes up the joint, don't you think?"

"It should. That chest is worth a lot of money. It was my dad's. Incidentally, are you enjoying the books?"

Raff and Maddie sent a puzzled look at each other. "How do you know about the books?"

"Because I gave them to your father in that chest after he saved me from drowning."

Raff and Maddie looked at each other. "Well, mystery solved."

"We've been driving ourselves crazy trying to figure out how his father had these and couldn't find any logical reason for any of it. Here it was, from you. Wow! Raff, there's your box and bow you wanted."

"Yes, it is. Boy, am I glad we had you over. I didn't think we would ever find the answer to those questions. Thank you for telling us."

"Glad we could be of help. The chest looks great in here, but why haven't you put the books out here too? They would look wonderful in here, and it would be easier to think about reading them if they were handy."

358

FROM SHADOWS TO DAYBREAK

"She's right. I don't know why we didn't think of it before. Besides, they should be shown off rather than gathering dust in the office," Maddie stated.

"Good point. Let's move it out tomorrow, then we can put that other bookcase in the office instead."

"Okay, people, dinner's ready."

They had a lovely dinner together. Kathleen seemed tired, but Maddie didn't say anything. She hoped the two of them could get together soon to chat—girl talk. "Kathleen, can I come visit you at the cabin? I'd like to chat with you without the men around. You know, girl stuff."

"You have no idea how much I would love that. Then maybe another day, all you girls could come so we could have a nice talk together. We haven't had a chance to chat for a while now. I would like to see everyone again. Besides, I want details of the honeymoon. You know, things you can't talk about in mixed company," she disclosed conspiratorially.

"Sounds great. Let's do it. I'll talk to Becca and get back to you."

Kathleen turned toward Franklin. "Frank, I'm getting tired. Would you mind taking me home, now? Thank you for such a lovely evening. It's wonderful to see you two doing so well, and I love your house and wish you many happy memories here—ones that last a lifetime."

They hugged each other and said goodbye.

Maddie stepped into the kitchen and cleaned up. Everything was spic and span again and ready for the morning. She walked into the living room.

"Raff, I'm tired, I think I need some rest. Are you coming up with me?"

"Of course, I could use some rest too."

When they were in bed, Maddie commented on the mystery that had finally been solved. "Wasn't that something? They knew all along, and we never talked to them about it."

"Yeah, it's kind of funny."

"Yes, but you got what you wanted—everything all boxed up with a bow and a note."

"Everything but the prescription. That may take a while with Miles still out."

"It's pretty great to have it all done, though."

"Maddie, come here, sweetheart. Did I ever tell you how much I love you?"

"I think so, once or twice."

"You and I in this home are going to make so many wonderful memories. This is just the beginning of a life we will share right here for many years. I couldn't be happier that God gave me you and that we have a love for each other that is so deep and strong. It's incredible. I love you, Maddie, with all my heart and soul."

"I love you too. You are the perfect husband for me, and I've never been happier to share a life with you in this home."

He took her in his arms and kissed her as they shared their love for each other. Both were thankful that God had blessed them so much by bringing them together with a love that only he could have given them.

With Maddie still in his arms, Raff began to pray aloud, "Father, thank you for bringing us together with a love for each other that's strong and led by you. Please keep us seeking your will and doing whatever it is you have for us. Bind us together and keep us together no matter how hard things may become. Thank you, Father, for your love that is one we can never truly understand, but we believe in, because we see how it changes lives all around us. In the name of Jesus, we pray. Amen."

They kissed each other good night and fell asleep with Raff's arm around her.

Behold, what manner of love the Father hath bestowed upon us, that we should be called the children of God. (1 John 3:1 KJV)

Acknowledgments

Saying thank you to many people isn't difficult. I want all of them to know just how much I appreciate their help in finishing this book.

To my family, to whom I go for constant encouragement—especially to my son, Steve, and my daughter, Charisse. They provided a "go, Mom" cheer when they could see my enthusiasm for the project waning. They kept my spirits up. Jen, my daughter-in-law, continued to impress upon me the need to have my first book published while I continued to argue with her. Needless to say, she won.

To one of my best friends, who has been a sounding board for storylines and a fair reading critic, I am so very grateful. Kathleen (and no, I did not name my character after her, although she believes with all her heart that I did) has been a godsend and a companion on our research-gathering trip to Denver this year. We go on all our vacations together. Thank you for always being there for me and for listening to chapters over the phone when I was stuck or couldn't wait until you visited.

To another dear friend, who was my writing partner for over forty years, Robbie, I will always be grateful for all the projects we did together, expanding my ability to write, although a book was something I thought was impossible for me. I believe I even turned you down when you suggested we write one together, just months before I started writing one. Ironic, to say the least.

To the editors, Samantha Confer and Laura Jones, my publication specialists, the artists who did the covers, at Christian Faith

Publishing, who guided me through the process to see this book finally published, I thank you all.

Most of all, to Jesus Christ, my Savior, who asked me to take pen to paper (or use my laptop) and write *The Gift of Christmas* and this follow-up book, along with two others. I thank you for the privilege. It has been a joy, and even though I argued with you as well, you knew best and helped me get through it all. I will never cease thanking you for whatever talent you gave me and with which you entrusted me.

About the Author

Cheryl lives in Western Washington and is a firm believer in Jesus Christ. Her life mostly revolves around her family of two grown children, eight grandchildren, and nine great-grandchildren—ten by the time this book is released. (And yes, she is that old.) She loves shopping for Christmas gifts at the Cracker Barrell gift shop, so it's a very good thing that there isn't one there locally. She likes to travel with a best friend—short road trips and short trips by air. (Getting old is not for sissies.) Sharing her home with a mini-Shih Tzu named Cocoa, who is blind and an unabashed drama queen, provides all kinds of entertainment with a little added frustration.

She loves writing and has been doing so for forty years, with all kinds of projects—none involving a book until just last year.

www.ingramcontent.com/pod-product-compliance
Lightning Source LLC
LaVergne TN
LVHW040932131224
799041LV00012B/86